Henri and the Angels

by

Ellen-St. James

ISBN Number 0-9655913-0-1

Published by I.S.E.
Negaunee, Michigan 49866

Manufactured in the United States of America
99 98 97   10 9 8 7 6 5 4 3 2 1

A letter from the author

Dear friends,

I always believed I had a guardian angel and as a child, the Guardian Angel Prayer was my favorite. Perhaps because of the many prayers I learned as a youngster, this one was the easiest? Knowing myself so well, this is definitely possible. I do know that I always felt safe knowing God gave me this "special friend" to watch over me.

In later years, the "prayer" was said less often. For some reason, we change. As I reflect on the past, I recall the time in my life when the doubts began slipping in about the "truths" I'd been taught as a child. I always believed in God, but at this particular time I felt alienated from Him. My path in life was becoming increasingly turbulent and because of this, I found that I was being forced to make some serious decisions. Decisions that weren't allowed because of my previous training. At this time, I felt unworthy of God's Love.

Those feelings didn't last long because this was when my guardian angel made his presence known to me. I remember thinking at the time that he came to save my soul.

After thoroughly convincing me that he truly was my guardian angel, he answered many of my questions. Most of my first questions were of Heaven; a place that earlier I was sure I would never see. The answers came back swiftly and so very simple. At one point I asked if he was giving all this information in a simple way, because I'm basically a simple person. He smiled and told me the answers are all very simple and that people make everything so difficult. "People teach fear," he said, "God is love."

The angels are often quoted as saying, "fear not." Trust them, they mean it. Everything he revealed felt right to me. I began to feel wonderful about this newfound information. Most importantly, I learned I wasn't such an awful person.

Earlier teachings taught me fear and that's what caused me to feel unworthy. All fears were lifted. My doubts vanished too. Much of what I had been taught in my younger years was the truth, minus that dreadful fear.

I kept my wonderful new feelings private. Maybe you've heard from others that have experienced encounters with their angels, how some people tend to think they've gone off the deep end. I thought at first maybe I had. My angel understood and proceeded to gently convince me otherwise with words of God's love and many little miracles. Perhaps someday I will tell that story; it needs to be told.

I believe all of the answers my angel gave me and my life has changed dramatically as a result. Instead of feeling unworthy and fearful, I love myself now and can share that love with everyone around me. I'm not afraid of anything. Most importantly, I feel the strong surge of love flowing from God to all of us that want it. I consider "Him" my Heavenly Father in every sense of the word. I will be forever grateful that He sent my angel to help me and have to admit, I felt extremely special and favored.

Now I will tell you what happened after I changed into this new person. I soon learned that, no, just because an angel came to me did not make me any more special than anyone else on this earth. As a matter of fact, I considered the fun part of this new experience over when he suggested what I should do with my answers so that others could also benefit. His wish was for me to put the answers into a story. He actually called it a "tale".

You need to know that this suggestion came as a shock. I'm sure I would have done just about anything else for this wonderful new friend, but I stood before him with absolutely no writing skills. I explained that the most I had ever written were a few letters here and there to friends and family, when I absolutely had to. I had no idea how to use a typewriter. Before raising seven children, I worked as a beautician. (But of course, he already knew all of this.) This was the first time I ever argued with an angel. He smiled and waited for me to come around. And I did.

My brain began working overtime. I came up with a great idea. I could find a professional writer to do this for me. I would help, of course. He shook his head 'no.' This was to be my job. After giving the entire situation much thought, I knew I really wanted to do it. I wanted to share my answers, but how?

I began to pencil a few ideas on paper. Actually, the ideas for this tale came easy. He said he would help. I was soon to learn however, that his writing skills were no better than mine. Or was it a skill I was to learn?

On a lazy October afternoon, I found myself browsing through a used book store. I was about to leave when an old green book fell on the floor in front of me. "Learn How to Type," it read. I picked it up. Penciled at the top was $.25. I bought it, even though there wasn't a typewriter in my house. When I returned home the book was tucked away with a promise that some day I would learn.

I sat with my notebook and pencil on occasion, moving further into the story. Knowing I could never learn to type, I figured once the story was handwritten, someone could type and edit it for me. I had this project under control and took time off for the upcoming holiday season.

Christmas Day arrived. I could hardly wait to open the large, beautifully wrapped package waiting for me under the tree from my husband. He always gives great surprises. After carefully unwrapping the mystery package, I couldn't believe my eyes. It was a typewriter. Only now, when he reads this, will he truly know how I felt. I absolutely did not ask for one, nor did I want one. I had taken care of that problem in my mind. I acted happy and thankful to my wonderful, thoughtful husband, knowing with dread I now had to open the "Learn How to Type" book that got tucked away forever. The lessons began. This chore did not come easy and to this day I can only type a few words a minute.

My venture into writing this "tale" has been eight years long, part-time of course. I will not burden you with all of the details, but I'm here to tell you, I have definitely had angelic intervention prodding me along the way. If I were truly a skilled writer, that entire eight years would be another story.

I considered the "tale" finished so many times. My angel patiently shook his head "no". The rewrites are too numerous to mention. After one of my "just finished" declarations, I remember how happy and relieved I was that "my part" was over. My plan was to send it off to a publisher and after they accepted, as I was sure would happen, the experts would "fix" it for me. I learned very soon that wasn't "the plan." I had another chore to do.

My husband came up with an idea that he was thrilled with. According to him, all problems were solved when he presented me with a new computer. I loved him dearly for his thoughtfulness and told him so, but inside, I nearly died. Now I needed to learn how to run this thing. I was exhausted from my efforts to learn. After attending writer's groups, classes, seminars, reading writer's books and magazines, I had more to do.

That job turned out okay. The story eventually made its way into my beautiful new computer. Another accomplishment that pleased me immensely. Until this computer told me that most of my sentences needed re-structuring and pointed out many errors. I re-wrote again. And many more times. It's still telling me to re-write some sentences. I do believe, that at this point, if I don't stop now, you'll never read about Henri and the Angels.

With all of my efforts, I may never reach perfection in my writing skills but my angel appears to be satisfied with my efforts. Lately, I definitely get the feeling he's reluctant to tell me there's another "tale" to be told. I learned early on, "you don't argue with angels."

Before I leave you for now, I wanted to say that throughout this writing venture, a thought drifted in and out of my mind. Were the answers really given to me in this light and airy way, so that we could better understand?

At my guardian angel's request, I must remain anonymous. Hence, the pen name--

Ellen-St. James

The Guardian Angel Prayer

Angel of God, my guardian dear,

To whom God's love commits me here,

Ever this day be at my side,

To light, to guard, to rule and guide.

Amen.

Henri and the Angels

Chapter 1

*O*pening the large mahogany door to His office, God quietly entered. Walking softly across the room, He paused briefly to look out the large bay window where animals grazed freely in the fields below. While observing this peaceful scene, He recalled the previous Saturday's guardian angel meeting.

He remembered watching from behind the curtain as the angels filed in and took their designated seats. It amazed Him to see how many more angels were added each week. The long tables seating them now seemed endless and the faces of those situated at the far ends could barely be seen.

In the early days, He and his first group of angels sat around a large oval table discussing the events of the week gone by. Those original angels were still with Him. His heart filled with gratitude for these special helpers and all of the others that had since been added.

The angels enjoyed the Saturday visits and God felt it gave them a much needed break from their daily assignments; part-time guardian angels covered for them while they attended. The few hours spent in the meeting hall seemed to renew their spirits, sending them back to work with a new zest.

Angels carried a much heavier workload these days. God overheard a few of the senior angels talking about "the olden days," when things were a lot less hectic. Back then, more leisure time could be found. Thinking about these modern days made Him sigh, how times have changed. He turned from the window and walked over to his desk. The Palace was quiet on Sunday. It felt strange to be in the office on this usual day of rest, but today He could not avoid it.

God had a meeting with James, one of His guardian angels that held an extremely busy schedule. He was the guardian angel to an eight-year-old boy named Henri, and acted as senior angel in Henri's household. James also helped to keep a close watch over the small town where Henri lived. The town, called Pleasant Valley, was in big trouble and God knew the people living there would need plenty of extra help.

Settling into His chair, a glance at the clock told Him there was time to spare before His meeting with James. God reached for the files on Henri and his family. Opening Henri's file, He looked to the most recent chart. A smile crossed His face when it showed that nothing had changed. Henri's chart displayed many gold stars. Instructing the angels to place the stars next to the good deeds was one of His better ideas, He always looked to them first.

God thought about how drastic Henri's life would be changing. During a life on earth, the original plan occasionally needed altering. God never felt happy making such changes, but as always, anticipated the glorious day when these people received the gift of Heaven. On that special day, all of life's secrets would be revealed. Yes, every person living on earth would find out what their purpose was.

The next file read Lucille O'Reilly, Henri's grandmother. Better known as "Gramma" to her family. This small, feisty lady, read her Bible daily and spread the good word to anyone that would listen. Better than that, she practiced what she preached. It reflected on her charts, as she too, had many gold stars. She taught her family about God and His angels. The lessons would be invaluable as the family moved further into their lives. God noted how each day she thanked her guardian angel for the little miracles done to make her life easier and wished more would believe they had these silent helpers.

The bottom of the chart showed that she still tried to save her husband's soul. Helping others reach the ultimate goal concerned her greatly. God liked that because He intended Heaven to be for everyone, including Henri's grandfather.

His birth name, Charles O'Reilly, headed the next file. A stubborn old man, he refused to let her change his way of thinking. Being a non-believer, he never entered a church. Charles didn't interfere with her beliefs and never interrupted her sermons to others. He sat quietly and listened, sometimes slipping out to the back yard for a puff on his pipe. Especially when she started talking about the angels, he knew those lectures tended to run long.

Nevertheless, Grampa was a good man. Reflecting on his charts were the many acts of kindness he showed others. God checked the last entry anxiously and felt disappointed to see that Charles still held onto his major flaw. He was still prejudiced, but God knew that Isaac, Grampa's guardian angel, would continue to help him overcome this imperfection.

Mary's file lay open before Him. She was Lucille and Charles daughter, and Henri's mother. He thoughtfully looked the pages over, reflecting on her many good qualities. Her most important jobs were performed well; a good wife and companion to her husband John, and a wonderful mother to

Henri. She wasn't quite as strong as she would soon have to be, but God knew she absorbed the lessons her mother taught. Mary would gather strength from that knowledge in the future.

Mary embraced life and all it had to offer. Anything of a serious nature was not for her. She allowed her husband John, to do any worrying that needed to be done. God knew she would be perfect for John when He instructed the angels to arrange the meeting that brought the two of them together. Matchmaking was one of His favorite tasks, and with these two, everything went according to plan. Both Mary and John obeyed the gentle, silent urging of their guardian angels and fell in love at first sight.

God wanted someone extra special for John. His life had not been the greatest before meeting Mary. His parents passed away in an automobile accident when he was three years old. Forced to live in an orphanage, the child never laughed again. God knew something had to be done and recalled the day when He asked Jake, John's guardian angel, to appear to the little guy as his imaginary friend.

Jake, more than eager to give his charge comfort in person, played joyously with the lad daily. John loved his new friend and wore a smile whenever he appeared. He eventually figured out who this companion really was, and still talks privately to his guardian angel daily.

God scanned a few more charts pertaining to other folks residing in Pleasant Valley. Because of various problems, they had extra angels in their households. When finished, He reclined in His chair, letting His thoughts drift back to the day when all the troubles began.

James discovered the polluted water. He had accompanied Henri and his mother to the nearby lake where they went for a swim. While lounging on the beach with his friends, James became aware of Henri coughing and choking in the water. He flew to his side and with much relief, found that his mother had everything under control. Henri had

4

tripped on a log and toppled over for a few seconds, swallowing a small amount of water.

Just after the ordeal, James, still in the water, noticed a most peculiar odor and beckoned his angel friends over to confirm what he suspected. Their faces contorted as they sniffed the water; something was definitely wrong.

Not that long ago, God instructed all angels working on Earth to report any such findings immediately. He was disappointed by the unsightly pollution and the disastrous problems resulting from it. James promptly reported the findings to God, and He rushed a group of environmental angels to investigate the problem.

The water reeked with poison and in no time at all they found the cause. That was the easy part. Now the local residents needed to be alerted as soon as possible. The angels went to work immediately, mapping out the discovery in the finest of details.

God adjusted His chair to sit upright. With disgust, He recalled what the environmental angels had found. The problem began when a man named Mr. Johnson came into town and bought up a large parcel of land. He built a huge factory on the property. The townspeople were elated because it created much-needed jobs and they began to look at him as if he were a king. Little did they know that his factory dumped deadly waste into the lake, polluting their only water supply and Mr. Johnson was fully aware of the situation. Thinking of what the truth would do to the residents of Pleasant Valley unsettled God. Good people resided in that town and until now, they led simple lives. Soon their daily routines would be miserably disrupted.

Chapter 2

*T*he clock read nine-thirty and James knocked at the door. Shaking His thoughts away, God answered, "Come in James, please, come right in."

James walked in looking a bit nervous. His blonde hair was combed straight back and he wore a dark pin-striped suit. God stood to shake his hand, and then quickly scanned His own attire, realizing He should have changed out of His blue jeans. "I was out with the horses earlier and didn't take the time to change. Have a seat James. It's been quite some time since you and I have had a private meeting."

James stiffly took a seat in the chair nearest God's desk.

God sensed his nervousness and searched for words that might put him at ease. "I thought about you earlier when I was out in the fields trying to get the attention of a few horses that ignore me. Animal behavior still seems to be one of your specialties and I could really use a few pointers from an expert. Everyone continues to talk about you and the famous Noah's Ark mission. They will forever be amazed at how you persuaded the animals to climb aboard after the efforts of others failed. Poor Noah exhausted himself trying. You accomplished that task in the nick of time. The rains began only minutes later. Your work amazes me, James."

"Thank-you Sir."

God's eyes twinkled as He reminisced, "What a surprise for Noah when he learned that he alone did not accomplish the task. Everyone reacts the same when they hear of the many helpers that were sent their way. I told him the story of how you came in and saved the day."

James relaxed and rearranged himself in the chair. Crossing his legs, he then spoke confidently, "It wasn't really all that difficult. By the time I arrived, the animals were exhausted. After being hassled for so many hours by the other angels, I merely told them what to do and they did it." He folded his hands in his lap. "I had a great time on that assignment. We all did."

God, pleased to see him at ease, said, "I see from many of your latest works that you have the same talent with birds. Your abilities are outstanding James, that's why I chose you for this assignment. I must say, you're doing a wonderful job, as I knew you would."

"Thank-you." James appreciated the compliment, but still wondered what this meeting was about.

God read his thoughts and His expression turned grave. "We'll be working closely on this Pleasant Valley project, James. We both know this mess is about to break wide open."

"Yes it is," James replied.

"I feel we should meet regularly. You won't mind slipping away once in a while? It would be extremely helpful."

"I wouldn't mind at all, Sir." James, hardly able to contain his excitement, continued, "It would be most helpful." Coming to The Palace regularly to meet with God, was indeed an honor. "I had no idea why you summoned me and I must admit that I felt a bit nervous."

"Everyone enters my office shaking like a leaf. Have you ever heard of my behaving like a tyrant?"

"Oh no. Absolutely not. It's not that we're afraid or anything like that. It's because you are God."

"I know," God sighed, understanding fully. After a brief smile, His face turned solemn. "This mission is a tough one, James. The people will need strong guidance. I feel their angels are well prepared and your reports show that you agree."

"Yes, I do." He paused, "A few of them know they'll need the help of more powerful angels for their charges but, yes, they are ready and able."

"Your household?   You feel secure with your coworkers?"

"Absolutely. We've talked about this extensively and they're ready." Pausing briefly, he added, "About Buffy, Mary's guardian angel . . . I realize this is her first earthly assignment. We've all agreed to keep an eye on her because she is new. So far she's been wonderful."

James' face reflected amusement. "We get the biggest kick out of her. She's quite a character. There's never a dull moment in our household."

"You're right about that," said God. His eyes revealed a loving tenderness at the mere thought of Buffy's unique characteristics. "She's a handful."

He paused briefly, "There will be much sadness, James. We both know how trying the job of a guardian angel can become. If any one of them should need a break, the substitutes are a call away. Please remind them often. We have a few very stubborn angels, I've seen some refuse to leave their charge even for a moment. A brief 'time out' refreshes all of us."

"I'll remind them."

"T.J. will remain available, James. He'll continue to keep an eye on Henri when you have to be away."

God paused, and as an afterthought said, "He needs to keep busy right now."

James could tell that something was amiss where T.J. was concerned. T.J. hadn't mentioned anything to him and he didn't want to pry. "T.J. gets along well with the other angels in the house. He's a whiz at card playing and gets a big kick out of beating the others. I appreciate having him around. He's wonderful with Henri."

God picked up the files that He previously reviewed. The two of them discussed the residents of Pleasant Valley that would get extra help. When finished, one file remained in His hand and He tapped it lightly on His desk. James saw that the name at the top read, "Bob Green."

"I'm not certain about what is going to happen with this one," said God. "I don't think he'll be open to the help we send his way. His family caters to him and they love him dearly but, unfortunately, he cares only for himself. Let's hope he doesn't hurt them."

Laying the file on top of the others, He asked James to swing his chair around so he could see the big screen TV. Reaching into the top drawer of His desk, God pulled out the remote control and pushed a button. The screen flickered to life.

"As you know, we have three pastors in Pleasant Valley. I have instructed their guardian angels to inspire them with a special message. I want each congregation to hear what I have to say."

He brought the town in clearly on the big screen. "I'm anxious to see if they could accomplish this task. We'll check out each of the three churches."

The picture they viewed could have come out of a story book. It appeared to be a perfect little town on a beautiful spring morning. Unlike the larger cities, the downtown area of Pleasant Valley remained the main business section. Homes with tidy yards lined the streets leading into this shopping area. The three churches sat on the outskirts of the city, each looking the same with their fresh coat of white paint and traditional tall steeple. The only difference was in the denominations.

God brought the first church into view which sat off by itself on the north side of town. They could hear birds chirping as people headed inside to attend services. Some walked in alone, others with their families or friends. The scene pleased God. James felt a lump in his throat as he watched. Both knew these folks to be good, honest, hard working people and found it upsetting to know their lives were about to be miserably disrupted. They watched in silence as others emerged from their cars and filed in. The birds singing in the background were also blissfully unaware of the events about to unfold.

God broke the silence when He spotted the man who would be the major player in those events. The man strolled briskly into church. "Isn't that H.G.? I hardly recognized him. He's lost a lot of weight! That physical fitness program has done wonders for him."

"This just amazes me," said God beaming. "H.G. used to be more than chubby. Now he looks as though he could run a marathon. I would definitely say he is ready to take that jog you have planned for him. I honestly did not think he would be the person for the job."

James said, "Motivating H.G. wasn't easy, but we needed him to complete the plan. His own angel deserves the credit for moving him off the couch and we all took turns keeping him inspired after that. It was a tough job at first, but now he's addicted to his daily workouts. He runs every day, and obviously feels great about himself."

"It shows," God said, "He is a changed man! One thing still puzzles me though. How will you get him to run the trail leading to the pipe that's dumping waste into the lake? It's hardly accessible."

James felt a twinge of pride. "We really wanted to save that part as a surprise."

He saw how anxious God was to hear the plan and was eager to tell. Reluctantly (but not really), he said, "I suppose everyone will be mad at me for telling, they wanted you to watch it on the big screen. You'll have to feign surprise when you see it."

God nodded yes, eager for James to continue.

"It'll be so easy," James said with excitement. "H.G. is crazy about deer. We needed him for this job because of his obsession. When I send one running out in front of him, I know he will follow it. As the deer turns down that trail, he'll be right behind. There's no question in my mind, H.G. will pull this off."

The plan intrigued God. "He does love deer, no doubt about that. Who will see that the animal obeys? Or need I ask?"

James didn't answer, but his face told the story. "We do have one small problem," he said modestly, "but I think we have it figured out. Hopefully, he'll see the pipe before he trips over it and falls. He may be too absorbed in watching the deer. The angels plan to pile plenty of leaves around for a cushion, just in case. I'm sure he'll be fine."

James added with confidence, "He will have a few choice words if he trips. Knowing H.G., it'll be because the deer got away, not because he fell." As an afterthought, he said, "I'm afraid more words will fly when he makes that dreadful discovery."

The subject dropped as the services began inside the church. They watched in silence. Bob Green rushed in late and his family scooted over to make room in the pew. God started to whisper to James about the man and caught himself. "For a moment I felt like I was sitting inside the church."

James understood because he felt the same when the services began. It touched him to know that God would whisper.

God continued, "Bob Green isn't such a bad guy. Even though he goes overboard with his demanding ways, he does a good job as mayor of Pleasant Valley. Maybe he'll surprise me, the way H.G. did."

11

James did not reply. He personally had a hard time tolerating Bob's selfish behavior. Everyone always had to do what Bob Green wanted, just to keep peace. James knew what a difficult time Bob's angel usually had with him. Encouraging this man to get along with others was becoming an increasingly frustrating job because of his high ego. He played the role of mayor to it's fullest and then some.

The pastor started the sermon. Both James and God watched the big screen intently. "Blessed are those that believe when they cannot see," the pastor began.

God's face showed great relief. "That's it, James. The congregation is receiving my message. Now let's hope the other pastors follow their instructions."

Looking as curious as a child, He flicked His remote control, anxiously awaiting the next show. Church number two was also in the middle of services. That pastor was equally inspired and word for word related the sermon exactly the way God intended.

The third church held many people and the sermon had not quite started. They spotted Henri's family, minus Grampa, seated in the very front pew. God brought the picture in closer.

"You know, James. It bothers me that Henri hates the color of his hair. I think it suits him well. He's a fine looking lad."

"I agree. He wouldn't be Henri without red hair, but he hates it because some kids at school started calling him 'carrot top.' It's the same group of boys that are always getting into trouble. Henri really gets upset when they tease him and they get immense pleasure from their actions."

"I know. They're three bullies who are easily influenced by the opposing angels." God shook His head. "The battle never ends."

The sermon started. "Blessed are those that believe when they cannot see."

The faces of those present confirmed they were listening closely. God smiled with satisfaction and flicked the remote control, bringing them to the homes of those not attending services.

They found Old Man Jenkins rocking in his chair. Nothing seemed to bring him out of the deep depression he suffered following the recent death of his wife. With the impending upheaval, God wondered if he too, would accept the help sent his way.

Close to the downtown area sat the home of Henri's grandparents. Their house resembled a small cottage with squares on each window. Shutters stood on each side, and window boxes held bunches of newly planted annuals. The buds on the plants looked as though they would pop open at any moment in the early morning sunshine. Rose bushes bordered the immaculately groomed front yard.

Moving into the kitchen, they found Henri's grampa. Singing along with the music on the radio, he poured his heart into the preparation of a special dinner. He did this every Sunday while his family attended church and today's surprise would be fried chicken with all the trimmings.

The neon colored apron he wore caused both God and James to chuckle. They knew Isaac, Grampa's guardian angel, persuaded him to pick out such an atrocity.

James said, "Isaac does that on purpose, because of how prejudiced Grampa is."

"I know, I've watched what happens when Isaac takes him shopping. Wait 'til Grampa finds out his own guardian angel was black. Not to mention his reaction when he sees that Heaven is real. He's in for quite a shock all right."

After touring other homes, God pressed the mute button. They discussed the danger that planet Earth was in with pollution taking its toll. God talked about the environmental angels and how they helped more people take action to fight the growing problem.

"Groups of concerned citizens from many cities are crusading for a cleaner environment. Of course, it's too late for Pleasant Valley. There's no hope for a town with poisoned water. When this tragedy hits the media, more people will join in and hopefully get the planet cleaned up. The pollution must stop." God stood up and stretched.

James took this as a cue that the meeting was over. They shook hands and James was told that a messenger would notify him of the next meeting. Glancing again at the pin striped suit, God told him to feel free to dress more comfortably.

James left the office elated. Feeling important to think he would be coming back to The Palace regularly, he floated swiftly down the hallways. He couldn't wait to get back to tell his coworkers, knowing they were waiting for a full report.

Back in his office, God resumed viewing the big screen. With the chicken dinner ready, Grampa proudly set the table, making sure everything was perfect. When finished, his guardian angel whispered something in his ear and Grampa promptly retrieved the blue napkins, replacing them with white ones covered with yellow flowers. Isaac smiled at Grampa's obedience and patted him on the shoulder. God figured the angels had a plan of some sort.

Turning off the big screen, God quietly left His office, closing the large mahogany door behind Him.

****

James arrived back at the household while the family returned from church. The other guardian angels waited anxiously at the door, wanting to know every detail of his meeting with God.

"Just calm down," said James. "We'll talk in the living room while the family has dinner."

Moving swiftly to the next room, the angels took a seat on the couch. James followed. Observing their eager faces, he looked tenderly at each one of them. Isaac was first in line. His huge brown eyes pleaded with James to get started. Anna, Gramma's guardian, sat next to him. Being a patient angel, she used the spare moments to review her notes for Gramma's lecture to the family.

Jake, John's angel, sat next to her. He and T.J. were conversing. Buffy, Mary's guardian, could wait no longer. "You always do this to us James. Every time there's news, you stand and stare at us. It's so aggravating. I think you love making us wait."

James calmly said. "I was merely collecting my thoughts and did not mean to stall."

Sitting with her arms folded, Buffy stared at the ceiling, waiting for him to continue. The others hid their amusement. She dearly loved news from Heaven and they knew how impatient she could be.

James summarized his meeting with God. When finished, he reminded them again that God had available subs if anyone needed a break. "This job promises to be difficult. These people will need our constant guidance. Card playing will have to cease for a while, as well as chatting on the phone with friends in Heaven."

It was evident that the lecturing annoyed his coworkers. In the past few months they had heard it repeatedly. Anna stated emphatically, "I will not be taking any breaks. I've been by Gramma's side for all these years, why would God even think I would leave her at a time like this? I'm the one who has her teaching the others about Him and the angels. I guess I just do not understand." Pouting, she looked to the floor.

Knowing how easily she became offended, James said, "You're taking this the wrong way, Anna. God knows you are more than able to do the job. He merely wants us to remember that help is always available. What's wrong with a break now and then? We take them when times are good."

James then added, "Anna, God wanted me to tell you how much He appreciates the work you have done. He said that knowing about Him and the angels will help the family immensely through this dreadful ordeal."

Anna's eyes softened, but Buffy felt left out and quickly interrupted the conversation. "Well I happen to think she makes Gramma preach too much!"

James intervened. "That's not true and it's not a fair thing to say, Buf. There is news for you, too. God also said that you were doing a great job."

"He said that? He said that about me? God Himself?" Buffy's eyelids fluttered as she basked in the compliment.

"I don't lie Buffy. Never have, never will. God also commented on how pretty Mary looks with the blue ribbons in her hair. He knows that you persuade her to wear that color and thinks it looks great with her dark hair."

Buffy was extremely pleased to have that personal message from God Himself. So were the others when James relayed God's words to them. In better moods now, each angel agreed that if they ever needed a break, they would take it.

Buffy, ashamed of her behavior, apologized to Anna. "I just wanted to know if God said anything about me. That's the only reason I said you preached too much. Honest Anna. I am really sorry." Her eyes begged for forgiveness.

The angels always forgave Buffy. They disregarded her flare-ups because they understood her and found her to be amusing. Buffy was Buffy and they loved her dearly. James watched on as she and Anna chatted about how important their jobs were. Buffy, as usual, treated Anna extra kind so that Anna would think well of her again. He had to chuckle. This angel was entertaining.

James recalled a major issue concerning her that had recently gotten settled, much to his embarrassment. All of the angels listened to WGOD daily on the radio. It was the angels' frequency that played soothing music. The station also brought news from Heaven and announced various activities of interest to the angels. The only problem encountered was on Tuesdays when the station played rock music for three hours straight, with no intermission. Buffy loved the rock, and kept the radio at the loudest setting as she bounced around to the tunes. The others did not share her enthusiasm for the music and plenty of arguments resulted. When he could stand it no longer, James put in a call to God for help.

Help he received. God sent a pair of earphones, thus solving the problem. Thinking about it embarrassed James again, such a simple solution and one he should have thought of. As busy as He was, God didn't need another problem. He just laughed about the situation and said everyone should enjoy the music they listen to.

James joined the others in light conversation. Anna excused herself when she saw that Gramma would be starting to lecture the family at any moment. Standing by her side with notes in hand, she was ready to help when the lecture began.

****

Chapter 3

*H*enri eagerly took his place at the dinner table with his parents and Gramma. With church over, his mood was great because the rest of the day promised to be great fun. Grampa began serving the dinner he had prepared for them.

"I like your apron, Grampa. It has brighter colors than the one you wore last Sunday." Reaching for the potatoes, he spooned a large helping onto his plate. "Are you coming to the ice cream social with us this afternoon, Grampa? And . . . "

Gramma interrupted. "The aprons he wears are ridiculous. The colors are so bright they hurt my eyes. We will be going to the ice cream social, but no, we are not going to the carnival afterwards. Everyone knows how I feel about those rip off artists passing through this town. The rides cost too much and I have never heard of anyone winning at those silly games they have."

She looked at Grampa and told him to take off the silly apron and sit. He took his seat, saying, "Lucille, you've forgotten about the teddy bear I won for you years ago."

He then agreed about the rides getting more expensive, but in the same breath assured her that children still loved to go.

"Well," she said, "I guess I'm just getting too old to be walking around the carnival grounds. You can have more fun without me tagging along."

Henri put his arm on hers. "Don't say that Gramma. You're not old."

She quickly blinked her eyes to prevent any tears from falling. Everyone at the table remained silent. They were aware of how much more irritated and tired she was becoming with each passing day. They'd given up on asking her to see a doctor, as she always refused, claiming it was just "old age."

Gramma led the prayer before their meal, lecturing afterward about the morning's church sermon. As always, she stopped briefly to tell Grampa if he spent half as much time in church as he did fishing, his road to Heaven would be paved. The lectures, she claimed, were to teach him some religion.

"Blessed are those that believe when they cannot see," she began. She then preached without pause for several minutes.

The family ate as they listened to her explain what the words meant. When finished, she told them again that God and his angels are always by their side.

Grampa was pleased when Gramma finally stopped talking and began to eat. Until she picked up her napkin and saw the yellow flowers printed all over it. Her face brightened and he knew she was about to start again.

She began, "These flowers remind me of a very special day I had just last week. I felt so tired that morning and the weather outside was dark and gloomy. When I looked out the window, I could not believe my eyes! They had covered the lawn with the prettiest yellow flowers I'd ever seen!"

Henri's eyes widened. "Who did?"

"The angels of course!" Gramma exclaimed. "They knew how awful I felt, and wanted to brighten my day."

Her smiling face held a peaceful expression. "They wanted to let me know they were with me. Angels do many things for us to make their presence known, we only have to open our eyes and notice."

Henri loved her angel stories and wanted her to continue. "Like the special birds they send?"

"That's right. I've told you about them before."

Gramma was tired and didn't want to talk any longer, until she remembered what Grampa had said about the yellow flowers. Looking at him scornfully, she told the family how mad he got because the flowers ruined his lawn. To please her, he apologized and said she was right, the angels had indeed put them there. He promised not to dig them up.

The family ate in silence. After picking at a small amount of food, Gramma stood and excused herself. She complimented Grampa on the meal he prepared and expressed her desire to rest for a while. Leaving the room, she turned back once to say she would be ready for the ice cream social at three o'clock. Grampa, feeling disturbed about her behavior, excused himself and stepped out the back door where he lit up his pipe.

John watched as his wife made circles on her plate with a fork. He knew how worried she was about her mother.

"Your hair looks pretty today, hon. I like it when you wear blue ribbons. You'll be the prettiest lady at the ice cream social."

Mary tried to smile. "I know you don't like to see me sad, but Mom has me worried."

Henri said, "How'd she know we were going to the carnival?"

"She knows everything, Henri. I could never figure it out when I was young. She just knows. Now finish your carrots and peas. We'll get this mess cleaned up, maybe it'll make her feel better."

Between each bite of food, Henri's questions continued. "Remember when she told us that her mother saw an angel? Her mother was your Gramma, right? And her name was Henrietta." He rolled his eyes. "That's why my name has to be Henri, with an 'I'."

"Yes, she would be your great-grandmother and was a grand lady. You should be proud of your name.

"I know. Now tell me the story again."

"Henrietta was a young girl at the time, probably about your age. She was trying to cross a wide creek on a log that served as a bridge. The log was slippery and halfway across, she became afraid and couldn't go any further. That's when the angel appeared and helped her the rest of the way."

"Tell me again what my great-grandmother said the angel looked like."

"She wore a beautiful white dress and had huge sparkling wings. A white light surrounded her and after leading Henrietta to safety, she disappeared into that light."

"I wish I could see one," said Henri, "then I could believe as good as Gramma does. Do you think I ever will? Sometimes I pray to see an angel but nothing ever happens."

"God decides, Henri. If He wants you to see one, you will. I've heard of people hearing their angel's voice, and one lady said she heard choirs of angels singing when she was sick.

I suppose God allows certain people to hear or see them so they'll tell others that angels are real."

"They are real," said his dad.

Mary looked at him. "Sometimes I wonder why you never talk about them. I know you believe they're around."

"Of course we have guardian angels and right now I wish they would clean up this mess."

Dad began picking up dirty dishes and the others joined in.

****

Anna was pleased about her plan working out so perfectly and thanked Isaac for persuading Grampa to set out the napkins with yellow flowers. "I wanted the family to hear her story."

"My pleasure, Anna," said Isaac. "That was quite a day for all of us. We saw more yellow flowers on that day than they will ever see in a lifetime."

Buffy started laughing. "It was so funny. Remember how the wind kicked up just as we threw the seeds with the magic growing dust?"

Her voice grew shrill as the laughing increased, she could barely speak. "Seeds blew all over the neighborhood in a wild frenzy. The neighbors had complete fits of anger as they watched the dandelions sprouting up before their very eyes. It was just awful!" She covered her face, giggling even harder.

"At least we accomplished our mission," said Anna seriously. "Gramma loved them."

Buffy still could not stop laughing and soon tears rolled down her face.

James said, "Come on, Buf. It was funny, but not that funny."

"I can't help it. I never saw magic growing dust work before and the flowers popped up so rapidly! I just couldn't believe it."

"That's because it was magic, Buf." Anna wanted the silliness stop.

The others ceased laughing. Buffy, noticing them watching her, wiped away the tears and made an effort to act normal. Her voice was still shaky when she asked James if he thought God would ever allow Henri to see an angel.

"I don't know, but I keep my costume pressed and ready just in case."

"Have you ever been allowed to appear as an angel?" Buffy wanted James to tell them about some of his adventures. The others loved hearing, too.

James didn't mind sharing his experiences. "I haven't appeared often with wings, and when I did, my appearance's were brief because I never had to deliver any messages in angel attire. The missions went quite smoothly. I'll never forget my first experience."

As if transfixed by the memories, he added, "How grand I felt! Encircling my angelic presence was the usual brilliant, bright light. My glittery wings, so perfectly shaped, sparkled beneath the illumination. It was awesome. Total admiration shone in the young boy's eyes . . . I'll never forget it."

Buffy closed her eyes and envisioned herself in costume. "Do tell us the whole story, James. I'll need to know these things if I ever have to appear to Mary."

Eager to tell, he began, "Years ago, the people on earth believed all angels had wings, so that's how we appeared to them."

Anna interrupted. "Some people still cannot picture an angel without wings."

Buffy showed her impatience. "That's why we keep our costumes ready, Anna."

"Anyway folks," James continued, *"My situation was much like the one I am in today, with my charge being a little boy like Henri. His greatest wish was to see an angel and he prayed constantly to have that wish granted. God finally decided the time was right and gave me the honorable task because I was his guardian angel. Like I said, the appearance lasted only a few minutes, but I'm telling you one thing, that boy spent his entire lifetime telling everyone he ever knew, about me, the angel that appeared to him. He lived to be 102 years old."*

Buffy didn't want his storytelling to end. "Did you ever appear without your wings?"

"Many times, but I'll only tell one more story today. I have a busy schedule. Let me think of a good one."

James floated upward to his favorite position, lying in mid air on his back. With arms folded behind his head, he began his story. "It was a new assignment. I was to be guardian to a newborn. You know how God wants us to arrive at the household a good month before the due date?"

The angels nodded their heads yes.

"As it turned out, the mother went into labor early with some major problems. This was a serious emergency and the entire household went into a panic. I say 'entire' because I am including their angels, who were just as distraught as the parents. To make matters worse, when the husband finally got his wife out to one of the most worn out cars I had ever seen, it would not start."

Buffy, totally enthralled with the story, asked, "Whatever did you do, James?"

"Well, I got myself under the hood with the husband to get the thing started. Invisibly of course. It was not an easy task at all and I remember how hopeless the situation looked when I first saw that decrepit old engine."

The same questions were asked by the others, "Did you have to use magic? Why didn't the other angels help?"

"Yes, I used magic. Plenty of it. Their own angels had absolutely no mechanical knowledge and even if they did, they probably couldn't have used it. Not while they were so hysterical."

"What would they have ever done without you, James?" Buffy believed James was always the hero.

"Special angels with mechanical knowledge would have been called in. They were lucky to have me there because, I do know how to fix a few things."

James looked down and grinned at finding them so captivated with his story. He continued on, a bit more dramatically. "The vehicle slowly began sputtering down the highway. With many miles to go, would you believe, the back tire blew out? We weren't even halfway there. Not a car could be seen on the road and there was not a house in sight. The angels looked to me once again for help, so I moved to the rear of the car where I spotted a spare tire in the trunk, and then proceeded to quickly make myself visible. The distraught husband came back to check out the situation and was deeply relieved to find me there. As a matter of fact, he almost kissed me."

"That's because you were his hero, James. This is such a good story. What happened next?"

"Settle down, Buf." James, his face a shade of red, continued, "I asked the expectant father if he had a jack and fortunately, he did. With the tire changed, they were on the road again. I quickly switched back to my invisible self and caught up to them."

The story intrigued Buffy. "You are sure he didn't see you change into a person in the beginning and just didn't say anything?"

"He didn't see me. I'm positive about that, but, later it did occur to him that I appeared out of nowhere. His wife said there was no question about it, an angel had helped

them. The baby was a girl and she named her Angela. After me, the angel."

"That is so cool," said Buf. "I want Mary to be able to see me."

"Maybe God will permit it some day. I'm positive that somewhere in your angel career you'll be making a personal appearance."

With story time over, James disappeared to a quieter place to do his paperwork.

Buffy was left dreaming about the day she would appear to Mary. The other angels shared a few of their own stories.

Isaac noticed Anna looking his way. He knew something was on her mind, and had a good idea of what it might be. "Okay Anna, what is it?"

"Gramma won't be well enough to attend the ice cream social today, and Grampa will have to stay home with her. Do you think you could watch over both of them so that I can go? They'll be resting anyway and you can read your books. Everyone knows how much you love to read."

Isaac had planned to go. "You're the one that just had a fit because you didn't want to take a break. Every Sunday you meet with your friends at church. I never go anywhere because Grampa stays home. I was about to ask you to stay so I could go to the carnival, my friends would like to see me, too."

"I know. I'm sorry. Go ahead and enjoy yourself. I guess I just panicked a little, thinking of how busy we're going to be. I really don't want to leave Gramma."

He felt sorry for her and mumbled, "No, you go ahead. I'll stay home."

T.J. saved the day. "You can both go. I'm really not in the mood to be sociable and I think I would enjoy the peace and quiet immensely. I'll be the sitter today and that's final."

Knowing he meant it, they said no more. An air of excitement filled the room as they anticipated the fun they would have.

Jake, after sitting quiet all morning said, "I get to be first in line for the roller coaster!"

Everyone agreed that he would be.

****

Chapter 4

*H*enri and his parents finished the kitchen work and joined Grampa as he tended his garden in the back yard. Seeming to be in better spirits, he proudly pointed to the few plants that were breaking through the ground and showed them the section he just spaded where tomatoes would be planted soon.

Henri fell to his knees, putting his nose to the freshly turned earth. "I love the smell of this dirt! Do you suppose the last frost has been here yet?"

"We have to wait a little longer son; it's not quite time to plant yet. All danger of frost must be gone. You'll know when 'cause I'll need your help then."

His mother ordered him to get up off the ground. "You're going to ruin your Sunday pants, Henri! You know better than that."

Henri leaped to his feet and brushed the dirt off his knees. "I'm sorry Mom, I forgot. Can I pick some lilacs for Gramma?" He ran to the bush that held the first few blossoms. "She probably doesn't even know they're out yet!"

"Pull the branch down to get them, here, let me help." His dad lowered the limb while Henri eagerly picked the precious signs of spring.

Grampa said, "We'll bring them to her after she's finished her nap."

His family saw the worry cross his face again. None of them wanted to talk about whatever could be wrong with

Gramma, so they sat around the picnic table chatting about unimportant things.

Henri watched them while they visited. Holding the flowers to his nose, he thought about how much his Gramma loved the fragrance and couldn't wait to give them to her. She said she knew for sure it was spring when the lilacs came into bloom.

Grampa sensed Henri's impatience and said, "I think we should get those flowers into the house before there's no smell left to them."

Holding the flowers protectively, Henri headed for the house with him.

"Put them in her favorite crystal vase." He pointed to the cupboard where it could be found. "I'll see if she's awake."

Henri busied himself with the task and arranged the flowers perfectly. Grampa returned in seconds with his head hanging. "I'll bring the lilacs to her. She doesn't feel like going to the social."

Henri handed the bouquet to his grampa and noticed how his shoulders slumped as he left the room. He called out to him, hoping to cheer him up. "When she smells the flowers, she'll feel a lot better!"

Grampa didn't answer, nor did he say anything when he returned from Gramma's room and the two of them headed back outside. Grampa's face looked stern when he stood before Mary and John and made his announcement. "I will not put up with her foolishness any longer. She will be going to the doctor tomorrow, and that's final."

He picked up his hoe and began chopping away at the earth. Mary and John breathed a sigh of relief with the strong action Grampa decided to take. They also knew by his behavior that it was time to leave and said goodbye as he continued to take his frustration out on the dirt.

Henri and his parents headed for the ice cream social. Because of the beautiful spring day, the parking lot overflowed with cars. After finding one of the few remaining spaces to park, they headed straight for their friends who were gathered at a table under an enormous oak tree. Henri ran off with his friend, Corey.

The topic of the day seemed to be the barn dance which would be held the next Saturday night at Mayor Bob Green's farm. The dance was always in his barn, and as usual, the people complained about the location. They were irritated because everything had to be Bob Green's way. No one ever challenged him because they cared about his wife, Connie. She had more than enough problems to deal with just living with him. They weren't about to cause more. His entire family behaved similarly, keeping their mouths shut and agreeing with him. This was the only way to ensure peace in their family.

Another topic stirred the air. It seemed Mr. Johnson, the man who owned the factory, had accepted the invitation they sent him to be at the barn dance. The people acted like God Himself would be there. He was definitely their hero, after all, if it wasn't for his factory, they would not have such good jobs. Delighted to be invited, Mr. Johnson said he wouldn't miss it for the world. Everyone hoped they would be able to speak to him personally.

The ladies chatted about what they would wear to the big event. Soon the men became impatient, they wanted the ice cream they came for. Excusing themselves, they made their way to the long line of people with the same idea. The ladies were not far behind.

Everyone attending the event ate ice cream until they could barely move. Corey and Henri finished their third helping and were off again to play with their friends. But not for long. Racing back to their parents, they announced that everyone else was leaving for the carnival and began pestering

30

their parents to leave. The adults told them to sit and be quiet at least twenty times, but the boys finally got their way. Other parents were equally annoyed and they too, agreed to leave.

The Ferris wheel could be seen high above the trees as Henri and his family neared the fairgrounds. Henri loved carnivals and could feel his stomach flutter when they pulled into the parking lot. His hand held the door handle, ready for a quick exit when his dad pulled into a spot next to where their friends had just parked. The families then walked to the ticket booth together.

Chattering excitedly, everyone got caught up with the squeals of laughter in the air and the carnival music playing loudly in the background. Not one of them felt like running to the long aisles of food booths because the smells of exotic dishes nauseated them. They were still too full of ice cream and decided to check those out much later.

With large rolls of tickets in hand and smiles on all their faces, each family headed for the action. Parents handed each child their allotted number of tickets. Children old enough to be on their own ran to their favorite ride. Excitement of the carnival flowed through their veins as they explored every event.

The children's faces were crimson as they ran excitedly from one ride to another. Surprisingly, not much time passed before their appetites returned and many could be found lined up at the various food displays. Hot dogs, sausages, french fries with vinegar poured on them, and onion rings so greasy it was a sin. You name it, they ate it. But slowly, as exhaustion set in, each found a place to sit down.

The sun could be seen settling beneath the clouds as the long lines of people waiting for food began to diminish. After waving goodbye to friends, Henri's family began the search for their car. That took a while because they couldn't remember where they were parked. Finally, after they swore

31

their legs wouldn't hold them up any longer, they found their vehicle and crawled wearily in. They left the grounds.

Chapter 5

*E*xhausted from their day of fun, the family returned
to the quiet of their home. John switched on the lights and
Mary headed straight for the phone. When Gramma answered,
she told Mary she was sick and tired of everyone worrying
about her and that she had decided to go to the doctor. "This is
going to be settled once and for all," she said, "you just wait
and see, he'll hand me a bottle of tonic and send me home. I'll
be feeling better in no time, and it'll be so good to have all this
nonsense over."

Gramma said nothing about Grampa forcing her to go,
but Mary didn't care and prayed her mother's words would
prove to be true. She wanted her mom to feel good enough to
be at the barn dance on Saturday night. The woman could
dance circles around anyone, and everyone enjoyed her
company. Mary hung up the phone feeling much better, at
least her mother would finally see the doctor.

John waited in the living room. Sitting with his wife
in the evenings, mulling over the events of the day, delighted
him. His eyes lit up as she entered the room and sat beside
him, tonight they would talk about their exciting day.
"Everyone seems thrilled about Mr. Johnson coming to the
barn dance. I think it's really nice that he accepted the
invitation. He seems to be an 'okay' guy."

Mary reluctantly agreed. "I'd like to meet him, but
doesn't it bother you to know how mother feels about him?"

"About him having shifty eyes?"

"She's usually right, you know. When she says that, something's wrong."

"I can't imagine what it could be, Mary. He seems all right to me."

She scooted closer to him on the sofa, knowing he'd put his arm around her. He did just that as Henri bounced into the room and found them cuddling. A grin crossed his face as his dad pulled him down to the sofa with them.

"What did you like best about the carnival, son?"

"I loved all the rides except one. Corey wanted me to go on the roller coaster but I wouldn't do it. I hate that ride. He even wanted to go in the tent to see the fat lady. Is she really the fattest lady in the world? I didn't like that either. I told him we shouldn't stand and laugh at her with the other people. Why would she want to be in the carnival?"

"Maybe she has no other way to make money." John gently stroked his son's head. "I don't know if she's the fattest lady in the world, but I'm sure it doesn't bother her. She's probably used to everyone staring at her."

"It has to bother her," said Mary. "Maybe she can't get a different job because she's so big she can't fit anywhere. This is silly to talk about, let's go to bed. It's been a long day and there's school in the morning. Aren't you lucky Henri? School will soon be over for the year."

"I hate school. If those kids keep calling me 'carrot top,' I'm going to quit."

His dad told him that quitting was out of the question, and he should try to ignore them. Changing the subject, he said, "I have the whole week off from work and I plan to get some chores done around here."

"Chores had better be on your mind, my dear," said Mary, "the neighbors are going to start complaining if we don't spruce this place up a bit. Starting with the fence, it needs a paint job desperately."

34

"That is first on my list. There's also plenty of work you can help me with, Henri."

Mary could not stop yawning. "Come on guys, bedtime. Nothing will ever get done if we don't get some rest."

Together they climbed the stairs. John tucked Henri in after listening to his prayers. Joining his wife, he said, "What can we say to him? God can't change the color of his hair. It's pitiful how he prays each night for the same thing."

"I know. Hopefully, the kids will stop teasing him. Let's get some sleep." Leaning over, she kissed him goodnight.

Mary hustled to get breakfast prepared the next morning. Henri's bus was due to arrive at any second and her husband just learned he would be starting the chores alone that day.

"You knew about my exercise class this morning, John! I wouldn't dare miss it. It'll take forever to work off the junk food I ate yesterday." She pinched the fat around her middle. "Just look at this!"

"Hey, you listen to me. I'd love you no matter how fat you got. Now wouldn't you rather paint the fence with me? You'd burn plenty of calories."

Grabbing his lunch from the table, Henri said, "I'll help you after school, Dad. Unless you want me to stay home, then I could help you all day!" He set his lunch back down.

John picked it up and put it back in his hand. "See you after school, son. I love you."

Disgruntled somewhat, Henri kissed his parents goodbye and ran off to catch the bus.

"I almost let him stay home, Mary. Children shouldn't hate to go to school."

"You're an old softy. He's okay. Life can't always be a bed of roses. He'll learn how to handle the situation."

John was frustrated at not being able to help.

Looking at the clock, Mary let out a shriek and made a mad dash for her room to change. Returning, she planted a kiss on John's cheek, telling him she would not be gone long. "Sit back and rest while I am gone. Turn on channel ten; there's a gossipy talk show on right now. We'll start the fence together later. See ya!"

She was out the door. Wearing her shiny blue leotards with her hair pulled back the way he liked it, melted John's heart. Leaving the yard, ribbons bounced with her hair as she blew more kisses from the car.

John waved, his eyes moistened as he thought about the happiness she brought to him. Always bubbly and full of fun, Mary made each day delightful for everyone around her. She insisted on many family outings, and they almost always included her parents. Both were fun loving like her, until lately, that is. They didn't smile anymore, and seldom left their home. Henri and his grampa used to fish often, that also ceased. John could not wait until everything returned to normal. He counted on a good report from Lucille's doctor so that they would soon all laugh together again. Mary's parents were very special to John, replacing the parents that he lost a long time ago.

John never did turn on the talk show, finding the quiet of the house to be more relaxing. He figured that Mary would enjoy helping him paint the fence because it would keep her out of the kitchen. Later, he planned to take his family to eat at Porky's barbecue, one of her favorite places.

John reclined in his chair and gazed out the window. H.G., their neighbor from up the block, ran by. He started his physical fitness program a while back and John heard that he became obsessed, running twice a day. His neighbors also saw him jumping around in his backyard doing calisthenics. He looked a lot better; John had to agree with the others about that. Looking down to his own growing belly, he realized that some day he would have to start a program himself. H.G. made all the neighbors feel guilty.

Startled to see Mary drive up so soon, John checked his watch. Time had passed so quickly. As she bounded through the door, he said, "I can't believe you are home already. It seems like you just left."

"You probably fell asleep. I'm going to shower and change. I'll be right back."

He turned on the TV. People screamed and hollered as a game show played. Bids were being taken for something. Turning it off, he decided he'd better get the paint stirred.

Mary joined him in the garage a few minutes later. Grabbing her pail of the prepared white paint, she followed him outside. "I suppose our fussy neighbors will be ecstatic when they see us painting. This fence is so chipped, it looks speckled."

"Be quiet, they can usually hear everything we say." He lifted the lid and dipped his brush in. "They constantly groom their yard. We have to admit that it does look good."

"All they ever do is work, John. I'd die if I were that woman. He makes her do chores continuously."

Mary started painting, working on the opposite side of the fence from John. It was evident that she didn't love the task. "I just hope they appreciate our freshly painted picket fence."

He replied, "They've thrown enough hints our way. I suppose we'll have to paint the house before the summer's over. I'm not looking forward to that."

Mary's hair already had streaks of paint in it and the job was clearly getting on her nerves. "You don't have to look forward to it because we're not doing this year! I have many activities planned for this summer and none of them include work."

She lowered her voice. "They'll have to be satisfied with the fence. Maybe we'll plant some flowers around to make the yard look good, but we won't be doing anymore. I can promise you that!"

John didn't have time to answer because their neighbor, H.G., limped pathetically into their yard and literally threw himself at their feet, groaning. "Help me, please help me. Oh God, how could you let this to happen?"

Holding his head, H.G. began rolling around on the grass appearing to be in a great deal of pain.

"What happened to you?" Both were shocked to see him in such a state and because he held his head, Mary asked if he hurt both his head and his leg.

The pain seemed to torment him as he turned over and lay flat on his back with his arms and legs sticking straight out. "My ankle is wrecked and who knows, probably my entire leg! I tripped on the curb. It happened so quick . . . It's pretty bad . . . I need help!"

He then rolled to his stomach and pounded his fists on the grass. "Oh, God! Why? Doesn't anyone realize what this will do to my program? I can finally run eight miles, and now this!"

John and Mary could not believe how he carried on. John checked H.G.'s ankle and found it to be swollen.

Mary asked, "Shouldn't we take him to the hospital?"

"That's exactly what I have planned."

They helped H.G. get up off the ground. He hung on their shoulders as they struggled to get him to the car and his eyes were filled with tears as John drove to the hospital in silence. Neither he nor Mary knew of any words that could comfort him.

Pulling into the hospital emergency entrance, John leaped out of the vehicle and headed straight inside to get help. He returned with a male nurse pushing a wheelchair. The nurse took over from there, helping the tormented man inside.

****

   *James arrived as the nurse began pushing H.G.
inside. The angels had contacted him immediately following
the accident. He could see that his first job was to quiet the
others because they were clearly upset. H.G. had a brief wait
before seeing the doctor and sat silently with John and Mary.*
   *Buffy was wild, overreacting as usual. "The plans
are ruined, James! How will you ever tell God?"*
   *With hands on her hips, she turned to Zephyr, H.G.'s
guardian angel. "I don't know how you could have let this
happen! You were supposed to guard and protect him!
Don't you understand the plan?"*
   Zephyr wearily sat himself down next to his charge.
   *"That's enough, Buf." James, ruffled now, tried
hard to remain calm with her. "This was an accident and we
have informed God."*
   *He looked to Zephyr who was now slumping over
with his hands covering his face. "Look what you've done to
him, Buf."*
   *James moved to Zephyr's side. "It happened so fast,
James. When I saw H.G. starting to fall, I used every power
I knew of to get him upright. It just wasn't possible. I feel
like such a failure."*
   *"Accidents happen, Zeph. Angels aren't '100
percent' perfect. You tried your best and God understands.
He doesn't like the plans disrupted either, but He knows you
didn't let it happen on purpose."*
   *The nurse came out to bring H.G. to the next room
where the emergency physician, Dr. Adams was ready to
examine him. John accompanied them.*
   *James used his eyes to warn Buffy not to follow. He
and Zephyr passed through the wall to the examination room
where the injury was tended to.*

After checking his foot thoroughly, Dr. Adams told H.G. it wasn't broken. "You have a severe sprain and you must stay off it for a while. We'll give you some pain pills to ease the discomfort."

H.G. clearly panicked, "How long is a while? I run eight miles every day!" He then told the doctor the history of his physical fitness program, as if it would change the diagnosis.

Realizing that nothing would change, he resigned himself to the inevitable and hopelessly said, "It's all over for me now."

The doctor told him it would be a few weeks before he could stand on the foot with all of his weight, and longer before he would run again. He told H.G. he was really sorry.

Zephyr said, "I wish H.G. could see how I feel. Little does he know how hard I tried to save him. At least his foot isn't broken. When I couldn't break the fall, I held his ankle as straight as I could. It must have helped."

James patted his shoulder. "Forget about it now. The plans will be delayed slightly, but have no fear, H.G. will pull it off. He'll be discouraged for a while, but we'll all work with him to keep his program going. God said we could use a little magic. Just a small amount, to speed the healing. He'll be on his feet in no time at all."

"We can use magic?" A spark of hope crossed Zephyr's face. "What exactly did God say?"

"He said 'no instant miracles, just speed the healing process a little'."

They left the room with H.G. after the hospital attendants outfitted him with crutches. Zephyr hovered much closer to him than usual; the angel still displayed frayed nerves.

James understood. Similar things happened to him throughout his career as a guardian angel. "You remind me of an overly protective mother, Zeph. Relax. You did your best. God doesn't expect any more than that."

Buffy joined them as they came through the lobby, and as usual, felt sorry about her outburst. Waiting for them gave her time to think about how rude she'd been. With remorseful eyes she asked Zephyr, "How's H.G.'s poor leg?"

James gave the quick report, deciding he wouldn't make this easy for her. Somehow Buffy had to learn to think before she spoke. This problem occasionally occurred with angels freshly out of school. Working on their first assignment, they usually had the idea that they would be the perfect angel; much better than the others.

"Zeph," she said, not able to look at him. "I didn't mean what I said, not at all. Just ask James. Sometimes I say things without thinking. I'm really sorry and I'd like to make it up to you." She bit nervously at her lip.

Looking up, Buffy could see he wasn't listening. Zephyr stayed close to H.G. and would not look at her. James could tell that she felt horrible and could have sworn she had tears in her eyes. As uncomfortable as he felt for her, he still wasn't going to smooth things over. She had to learn and knowing Zeph, it would probably be a few days before he would be friendly with her again. James doubted she would ever hurt the feelings of another angel. They left the hospital.

****

H.G. remained quiet as he clumsily made his way into the car. Mary and John tried to be helpful but he grew more irritable with each word of kindness.

"I'm all washed up," he said, slamming the crutches to the car floor. "It'll be close to a month before I can even stand on this foot. I'll have to start all over and I'll never do it. Do you have any idea how much time and effort went into this program?"

"It'll heal fast," said Mary. "You'll be up and around in no time at all. Quitting your training is a dumb idea. Look how much better you feel when you run." She knew instantly that she just said the wrong thing.

"Of course I feel better when I run! Don't you understand what I've been talking about? It's over. Sitting around waiting for this ankle to heal is not only going to ruin the endurance I've built, just watch the fat pile back on my body. I've lost thirty pounds you know, and it was hard work."

Mary wanted to help him. "Perhaps you should think of an alternative plan, I know you're upset, but your program doesn't have to be over. Television offers daily workouts. Maybe you could work with them temporarily, it'll help keep your body toned. You can do the strengthening exercises without hurting your foot, just don't jump around when they do aerobics. You have a stationary bike, don't you?"

"I have one, but a lot of good that'll do. I need two feet to make the thing go."

"You can do it with one foot H.G. I've done it before when my bunion was acting up. Just keep moving the best you can to keep your heart rate up. That'll keep you somewhat fit until you can run again." She rolled her eyes impatiently. "It's just an idea."

"I know you're trying to help. Thanks. Maybe I'll give it a try."

Mary wished she could help him, but realized he first needed time to get over the shock of the accident.

John changed the topic of conversation to one that interested H.G.. "Do you have any deer coming to your yard yet this spring?"

He brightened at the mention of deer and answered, "Two are back. The others must still be in their winter yards, but it won't be long before they all return. They'll be hanging around eating the food I put out until the neighborhood gardens start producing."

"It's too bad the deer just don't stay at your place to eat, H.G.. The neighbors get angry when their gardens are raided. I can hardly believe they travel so close to the downtown area."

"They'll go anywhere for fresh vegetables, that's for sure. I wish they would stay in my yard. I love watching them. Deer fascinate me. They're beautiful and very interesting animals."

H.G. told them all he knew about the habits of deer. Mary smiled, pleased that John diverted his mind temporarily. His spirits were somewhat better when they helped him out of the car and into his house.

The afternoon sun made painting a little more difficult when John and Mary returned to their project. The heat slowed them down and both agreed that the mood just wasn't there anymore. H.G. stayed on their minds.

Mary dipped her brush into the paint and after pulling it out, watched as large drops of white plopped back into the can. "You know John, I'd be pretty upset if I were him. I can't ever remember having anything that bad happen to me. It's frightening to think of how fast things can go wrong. Poor H.G.."

"Why does it frighten you? I'd never let any harm come your way."

Mary lifted the brush from the can to the fence and shrieked as paint dripped all over her pants. "Oh no! Look what I've done! I thought the brush finished dripping!"

"It happened so fast." She grabbed a rag and began wiping the spots furiously. When the paint smeared all over, she threw the rag in the air. "John! Look at this mess! My pants are ruined!"

"Mary, calm down. They're old pants and it doesn't matter. Come over here, what is really wrong with you?"

She wiped her eyes, leaving traces of paint on her face. "I'm being a fool, I know. I guess it made me think of how quickly things can happen. Like H.G.'s life. Now that he's hurt, everything will change for him. What if something awful happens in my life?"

He stood to look in her eyes. "You don't have to worry about anything, ever. I'm here to take care of you. You got that?"

She shook her head "yes."

John wiped the paint off her face as Henri's bus drove up. "Here's our boy. Looks like we'll get this job done before nightfall yet."

Happy to see them outside working, Henri yelled, "I'll be right out to help, after I get my old clothes on!"

He ran into the house returning just as quickly. "Gramma's on the phone and wants to talk to you, mom. Should I tell her to call you back?"

"I'm coming, Henri. I need to talk to her."

Anxious to hear about her mother's appointment, Mary grabbed the phone and eagerly put the receiver to her ear. "Hi mom, I want a complete report. What did the doctor say?"

Her mother answered smartly, "It's like I told you and the others; I'm a bit run down. He gave me a bottle of tonic and said I'd be out dancing again in no time at all. Now I hope everyone will stop bugging me."

"We're only concerned because we love you and the bugging will stop once we see you're feeling better."

"Well, you can stop now. What did you and John do today? Did any painting get done?"

"A little." Mary told her mother all about H.G.. After the conversation she felt better about her mother's health, but frowned when she noticed the phone had paint on it. Grabbing a sponge, she wiped away the smudge, vowing she would never paint anything again.

Henri and his Dad painted faster after Mary reported the good news about her mother. Mary picked up her brush and looked on with dread at all the work.

John noticing her expression said, "It'll go fast, Mary. We don't have that much more to do. I thought you and Henri might like to eat at Porky's later. How about that?"

A smile crossed her face. "That would be nice. I guess with so many interruptions today, I got out of the painting mood. I'll be all right."

Her husband complimented her. "You look wonderful with the white freckles on your face, sweetheart."

She pretended to come at him with her brush. "When I get done with you, there'll be more than freckles on your face! You'd better behave if you want to keep your help."

They began to paint with great haste. It was early evening when they neared the end of the task.

Henri announced, "We're almost done and I'm starving!"

The last few panels of fencing received their coat of paint as Old Man Jenkins walked up to them eager to chat. He'd heard about H.G.'s accident and wanted to know the details. John explained what happened as he pounded the lids on the empty paint cans. They were anxious to get cleaned up and leave, but the neighbor wanted to hang around and visit.

Impatiently, Henri blurted out, "We'll talk to you, tomorrow, Mr. Jenkins. My mom hasn't eaten a thing all day, and we have to go to the barbecue joint. We'll see you later."

Mr. Jenkins promptly left.

"That was so rude, Henri. I can't believe you said that to him."

"I didn't mean to be rude, Mom. I'm starving."

"But you were Henri, and you need to realize that sometimes elderly people have no one to talk to all day. He's been especially lonely since his wife died, and why did you call Porky's a joint? His friend owns that restaurant. What you said embarrassed me."

"Mr. Jenkins always calls Porky's a joint. He knows we're hungry, I'll go see him tomorrow after school. It'll be all right."

"Try to be a little more patient with older folks, Henri." Mary hoped they did not offend the old man. "C'mon, let's get cleaned up. You did tell the truth when you said I hadn't had a thing to eat all day. Let's go eat."

After scrubbing up, they left for Porky's Barbecue.

Chapter 6

*J*ohn's week off from work proved to be productive. Together he and Mary cleaned the attic, put the basement in order, and spruced up their yard until it looked as perfect as the neighbors, especially with the painted picket fence. On Saturday morning they planted petunias in the front flower bed. Several neighbors walked by, stopping to compliment them on how nice the yard looked. They chatted with Mary and John about the barn dance that evening, everyone looked forward to it.

After putting the final touches on their front yard, the couple decided to take a short nap. They wanted to be well rested for an evening of fun. Henri would be spending the night with his friend, Corey. Because of a shortage of baby-sitters in Pleasant Valley that evening, the parents decided to share what few they had. Almost everyone in town would be attending, except for Mary's parents. The tonic hadn't provided results for her mother yet. Only a week had passed since she started taking it and the family wasn't too concerned, except for the fact she wouldn't be going to the dance.

Corey's family picked up Henri in the late afternoon, while his parents busied themselves, preparing for the big event. Mary didn't allow John to see her until she was completely ready.

When she finally appeared before him, he had to catch his breath. She looked like a little doll, wearing a blue and white checkered square dancing outfit. Her hair was pulled back with a matching bow.

John whistled, "You're beautiful, Mary." Gathering her in his arms, he twirled her around in circles. Her full skirt blew in the air with petticoats showing.

"You'll be the belle of the ball, as usual."

"You look pretty darned handsome yourself, John. Every woman at the dance will have their eyes on you. You'd better be careful." After a look of warning, she giggled.

Standing before the mirror, she said. "I knew we'd look more together if your shirt matched my dress."

"All I can see is a man and a woman who are perfect for each other." Giving her a hug and kissing her quickly, he said, "Let's get out of here before we change our minds and stay home."

"Not a chance. I've worked too hard getting ready. Let's go." Grabbing his arm, she led him out the door.

The drive into Bob Green's yard overwhelmed their senses as loud music blasted and chattering mixed with laughter filled the air. Mary was so eager to have fun that John had to hold her from running to the barn.

"We'll get there soon enough, hon. Slow down or you'll fall. You won't look nearly as beautiful covered in mud."

The evening turned out to be all they'd anticipated. Almost everyone from the town of Pleasant Valley attended and each appeared to be having a great time. Even H.G. showed up and loved the attention he received because of his crutches. He bragged to everyone about how fast he could go on his stationary bike using one leg, and said one little fall wasn't going to wreck his life. Mary was pleased.

The tables overflowed with food. Everyone brought their favorite dish to pass, and a roasted pig was nothing but bones by the end of the evening. The people ate until they were stuffed.

Music played through the evening, but few people danced after the huge meal. Those still able to move had a great time on the floor, whirling and twirling to the commands of the square-dance caller. Their faces, red and smiling, reflected the fun they were having. Mary and John continued dancing until the wee hours of the morning. Finally, they admitted to exhaustion and after saying their good-byes, left the barn, hand in hand. Riding home in silence, they sat close to one another, each remembering all the fun they had.

"How will we ever get up for church tomorrow, John? Or should I say today? Aren't we just awful, carrying on all night? I had so much fun."

"So did I. We'll make it to church, sweetheart. A couple hours of sleep will make us as good as new. We'll pick Henri up at nine-thirty and then get your mom, no problem."

A few hours of sleep was all they did get. They made it through the service and leaving the church, both were happy that neither one had fallen asleep.

After the services, Mary's mother started with her questions, wanting to know every detail of what went on at the dance. Mary talked nonstop the entire way to her mother's house, filling her in on everything that had happened. She still hadn't stopped talking when they sat down for the dinner Grampa had prepared.

When she figured Mary had told her everything, Gramma asked about Mr. Johnson. "You haven't said one thing about him, Mary. I suppose everyone hung on him all evening?"

"Oh my gosh!" Mary's hands flew to her mouth, "I almost forgot about him! He made his grand entrance a couple of hours after the dance started and then suddenly tripped and went flying through the air. No one saw how it happened but he fell flat on his face in front of everyone! I noticed it when some people near him let out a scream. Everyone crowded around to help him. He looked so embarrassed and his clothes were covered with straw! I felt really sorry for him."

"He was covered with straw?" Asked her mother, amused.

"He fell near some bundles of straw and it stuck to him. People standing near tried to help brush it off. Crowds clung to him all night, everyone waited for a chance to talk to him personally. I spoke with him briefly. You know, mom? You're right about his eyes. They are shifty."

"You're darn right they're shifty, he gives me the creeps. You mark my words, we're going to find out he isn't what everyone thinks he is. Something about that man doesn't set well with me."

A chill crept up Mary's spine.

"Stop talking like that," said Grampa. "You don't even know the man. We should all be grateful for what he's done for this community. I think you two better stop gabbing and eat before everything's cold."

The family ate in silence. Only the sound of silverware clinking could be heard.

"What was the sermon about today?" Grampa spoke first.

All faces turned to him in surprise. Sermons were never on his list of things to talk about.

Gramma took advantage of the situation and answered. "Do unto others as you would have them do unto you."

"All the more reason you shouldn't say unkind things about Mr. Johnson," Grampa quipped.

Gramma didn't reply, not knowing what to say and the others looked uneasy. Finally Henri spoke. "She didn't mean it Grampa, not like you think. She just has a feeling about him and didn't say anything bad."

Gramma responded timidly, "What I said about the man, it really wasn't okay and I'm sorry. Let's finish our dinner now, I didn't mean to be unkind."

Mary glared at her dad, but knew she should keep quiet. His behavior was most unusual.

Gramma soon excused herself from the table, saying she had to rest for a while.

"Me and my big mouth," said Grampa, regretting what he said. "Worrying about her is driving me nuts! I feel like a mean old goat. That stuff she's taking isn't doing a damn bit of good!"

Standing, he reached for the pipe tucked in his back pocket. "I'm sorry for being so ornery."

He bolted out the back door, leaving it slightly ajar. In seconds, a trickle of pipe smoke found its way to the dining room. The familiar smell told the remaining family members he needed time alone.

****

The angels were gathered in the living room and James was nearly finished with the account of his brief meeting with God.

Buffy interrupted. "He's smoking again, Anna," she said, sniffing the air.

James impatiently asked, "Who is smoking again? What are you talking about now?"

"Grampa. After promising his wife he would quit, he's out there smoking."

"Buffy. I have important things to talk about. What's wrong with you?"

Isaac butted in, "It really isn't any of her business, but if you must know, Grampa told his wife this week he would quit smoking the pipe. He said it to pacify her and he can't quit now, not while he's so worried about her. Honestly, Buf, I think you're just trying to keep everyone's mind off what you did."

Isaac turned to Anna and said, *"Does it bother you Anna? That he's smoking?"*

"He did promise he'd quit, Isaac."

"What is this?" Asked James, "We're having a meeting and it isn't over yet. Can I please finish?"

Shaking their heads yes, each one looked accusingly toward Buffy.

James continued, *"With the little bit of magic, H.G.'s leg will be healed in no time at all. The plans are only delayed for about two weeks."*

He paused while glancing Buffy's way. *"Why are you so nervous, Buf? Your eyes are bouncing all over the place and you haven't stood still since our meeting started. What's wrong?"*

It only took a second for James to understand. He had put the issue aside, deciding to talk to her privately, after the meeting.

Buffy realized that James knew and looked at him defiantly, *"I've already apologized to God about it, James. I sent Him a telegram this morning."*

The other angels watched her, hiding their amusement. James said, *"What you did took a lot of nerve, Buffy. Did God actually see you trip Mr. Johnson?"*

Her voice rose to a high pitch, *"I don't know what came over me!"*

James tried to handle the situation calmly, not wanting to embarrass her further. *"That type of behavior is totally against the rules, Buffy. I just don't understand you sometimes."*

"I'm really sorry, James. Yes, God saw me do it. I didn't know He was at the dance." She blinked her eyes hard and gasped. Burying her head in her hands, she said, *"He stood right behind me when I tripped Mr. Johnson. I felt Him tap my shoulder and when I turned around I couldn't*

believe my eyes! Oh James! It was just awful. That's why I sent Him a telegram apologizing again."

She started to cry hysterically, trying to speak at the same time. "I don't want you to be mad at me either, James, I'll never, ever do anything like that again."

James softened, but this new display of behavior really threw him. He'd seen angels weep before, but this was ridiculous. "Now calm down, Buf. My plans were to speak with you about this alone, after the meeting."

He searched for words to use in this most difficult situation. "We have all made a few mistakes ourselves. What did He say after you did it?"

Still crying, she replied, "He told me He was going to pretend He didn't see it this one time."

Calming down, she continued, "I'm not a good angel, James. I couldn't control myself when I saw Mr. Johnson come in the room, I hate what he's doing to the people in this town! I thought about how disrupted my poor Mary's life would become because of him. That's what made me do it!!"

Bending over, she covered her face with her hands and began bawling again. "I feel just awful!"

James felt his nerves beginning to fray. God said to be patient with her but he was finding that it wasn't easy. The excessive crying was not normal and he'd never seen anything like it before.

He put his arm around her. "You're not a bad angel, Buf. Now tell me about the telegram you sent God, and please stop crying."

Her eyes found the ceiling and she blinked her eyelashes rapidly. It seemed to help. "I wrote that I was eternally sorry for my actions and said that if He wanted me to resign, I would."

God hadn't mentioned any of this to James. "Did He answer?"

She shook her head yes. "He sent a singing angel with the answer. He tried to cheer me up, saying in a song that I was a good angel."

"Then why are you acting this way?"

Wiping her eyes, she looked at the other angels in the room. "Because everyone thinks I'm a misfit. God probably hasn't heard about what I did to poor Zephyr." She sniffed, "I made him feel rotten about H.G. hurting his foot. I love being a guardian angel, but I keep doing everything wrong."

James said with compassion, "Buffy, Buffy, Buffy. Someday, you're going to look back and laugh at your little mistakes. We've all made them. But most important; we must learn from them. What we are taught in school seems easy, but actually working as guardian angels is another story."

All angels present nodded in agreement, eagerly waiting for him to continue. They wanted her to feel better and knew his 'words of wisdom' would help.

"We're thrown all kinds of curves. We must always remember that everything's not going to go as smoothly as we would like. I guess we could all use a refresher course at times: To remind us that our jobs are to help our charges through this most difficult role, living their life on earth as God intended. Each and every person will have some degree of hardship to endure."

Stopping briefly, he gave Buf a smile, "We can't be beating up every person who disrupts their lives. We have to be strong."

He wondered if this would be a good time to talk about the crying. Handling it delicately, of course. He had to deal with the problem because he didn't want it to happen again.

"Buffy?"

"Yes James?"

He could tell she felt better. *"Without offending you, I have to know if you cry like this often? I mean, I've never seen you cry before."*

Anna came to her rescue. *"Some of us shed a few tears now and then over sad things."*

Anna also found the crying a bit extreme, but didn't see a problem with it. The other angels defended her too. Buffy, pleased with their protectiveness, bathed in the love that flowed from all of them.

She told James sweetly and calmly, *"I had a problem with crying when I lived on earth as a human. I remember getting on everyone's nerves."*

Privately, she recalled how irritated her dad would get when she carried on like she did today. James reminded her of her father in that respect.

"Just because I cry doesn't mean that I'm not strong, James. I realize I have much to learn. My work has been easy up until now and I'm sorry I allowed myself to lose control. I'll never cause harm to the enemy again, I promise."

She sheepishly grinned, *"I'll try not to cry anymore either, you won't tell God I cry, will you?"*

"Well, I would think He probably knows about it," James wanted to discuss the matter with Him. He knew it wouldn't be good if she fell apart like that when the trouble really started. Which reminded him about what they were here to discuss.

"We should really return to what we were talking about," James ordered. *"About H.G.. The plans are set for late August now, which is only two weeks later than originally planned. By the way, Buf, H.G. is keeping fit by riding the stationary bike. It would have been a disaster if he quit. He's also working out with the ladies on TV, when no one is watching."*

55

Buffy beamed with satisfaction, because it was her suggestion that Mary coax H.G. to keep working out. She vowed to try much harder to be a perfect angel.

The meeting ended and they discussed their recent weekend of fun. Each one that attended the ice cream social enjoyed the event, but all agreed the carnival was tops, with the roller coaster taking first place as the most fun. Hanging onto the back of the seats as they flew behind, gave them great pleasure.

Henri and his parents were ready to go home, meaning the social hour was over for the angels.

Anna asked one last question about the barn dance, wishing she could have attended. Especially after hearing that God showed up.

"Did He dance at all?" she asked the others.

"Just once," answered Jake.

"It sure wasn't with me," said Buffy. "Not after what I did."

"He danced with Becca," said James.

Anna wanted to hear more, "How do you know James? You weren't there, were you? Isn't Becca the angel that works at the dime store?"

"Becca's charge works at the dime store. I have to go."

Almost out the door, he said to Anna. "I danced once with Becca too." He flashed a smile. "See you later!"

Isaac told her that T.J. and James took turns watching Henri that night, so each could attend the barn dance.

Anna went in to check on Gramma and found her lying on the bed still awake. She felt unhappy about what Grampa said to her, but also knew he was right. Gramma still found it difficult to be kind where Mr. Johnson was concerned. She sensed something was very wrong with him and the nagging feelings would not leave her.

Anna helped her forget, inspiring her with happier thoughts having nothing to do with Mr. Johnson. Gramma soon drifted off into a deep sleep.

****

Chapter   7

*H*enri and his parents sat in the car ready to leave for home.   Grampa walked slowly away from them after saying goodbye.

"I think I should stay here with him," said Henri. "You'll both be sleeping all day anyway. He looks so sad."

His mother preferred he didn't stay. "I think Gramma will get more rest if you aren't around. She'll hear you and Grampa talking and want to get up."

Henri's dad thought differently, "I think you should consider your dad's feelings, Mary. It'll be good for him to have Henri around. He needs other things to think about, couldn't you see he practically begged you to let him stay?"

"John . . ." She wanted to argue but felt too tired. "Go ahead and stay, but please be sure that your gramma gets some rest."

Henri eagerly jumped out of the car before she changed her mind. "I promise. See you both later."

Running off to join his grampa in the garden, he yelled, "I'm back!"

"Then get over here and get to work. I need all the help I can get with these weeds. They grow faster than the plants, I wish it were the other way around."

Henri knelt down beside his grampa and helped with the weeding. When finished with that chore, they hoed the area around each little plant. Henri loved working in the garden and especially liked it when his grampa stopped in the middle of whatever he was doing and pulled out his pipe, always looking to the window to make sure Gramma wasn't watching. With the coast clear, he'd light up, inhale deeply, and let out a sigh. He would then tell Henri the importance of watching the plants carefully.

"Just like little babies," he'd say. "Give them enough water and food, and don't let the weeds choke them to death. Never forget to hoe around each plant; it gives them more air to breathe."

Henri wondered if Grampa would do it today. He barely said a word while they worked. Only once did he talk, when he said he wanted to put the tomato plants in the ground after the sun set in the evening. The weatherman had predicted there would be no more frost this spring.

"Why do we always put the tomato plants in when the sun starts to go down?" Henri asked.

Grampa explained how shocking it was for the plants to go in the ground after living safely in their pots in the warm house. "It gives them more time to adjust before the sun comes up the next morning. The plants will still wilt a little for a few days, especially when the sun beats down on them."

Henri finished hoeing. He hoped his mother would let him stay long enough to help with the planting.

"Well, I guess we're about done, Henri," Grampa set his hoe down as he pulled the pipe out of his back pocket. Gazing toward the window and seeing the coast clear, he quickly lit it and inhaled deeply. He then talked about the importance of watching the plants closely.

Henri sat on the ground looking up at him. Holding his hoe upright, he listened as Grampa told about the plants once again. But this time he only watched Grampa's lips move, barely hearing the words he said.

His thoughts drifted to his gramma, and he wondered why she wasn't getting better. Henri didn't want her to die like poor Mr. Trombly, his old bus driver. No one knew what ailed him either.

Grampa tapped the ashes from his pipe and tucked it in his back pocket. "Are you getting hungry? Hey, where's your mind today, boy?"

"I was thinking about the little plants. I'm getting hungry, but we shouldn't wake Gramma."

Just as Grampa was about to say something, Gramma stuck her head out the door and asked if they wanted lunch. Henri felt relieved to see her alive. They found poor Mr. Trombly dead in his bed.

The two of them headed toward the house, both were pleased to hear the cheerfulness in her voice. After washing their hands at the outdoor faucet, they headed for the kitchen, noticing immediately that Gramma had put lipstick on and combed her hair pretty, just like she used to do.

"I've warmed up the leftovers for you two. How's the garden coming along?"

Henri eagerly replied, "We pulled all the weeds and hoed around each plant. Grampa said we could put in the tomatoes tonight." He spotted a plate piled high with leftover ribs. "Oh good, we're having ribs again. I'll have a bunch."

He held his plate as Gramma filled it. Lifting the plate to his nose, he smelled the steaming pile, "Porky's can't make ribs that smell this good. Grampa makes the best sauce."

Henri ate like a hungry bear. Sauce ran down his chin as he asked if Grampa would ever give out his secret recipe.

Handing him two napkins, Gramma said, "Wipe your face dear. He'll never give up his most prized recipe, not even to me."

She ate heartily, which surprised both of them. This was just like old times. After supper, Grampa said he had a few more things to do outside before the tomatoes got planted. He told Henri to visit with his gramma for a while, knowing it would please her.

She brought out chocolate chip cookies, Henri's favorite.

Eagerly grabbing one, he picked a couple of chips out of the cookie and popped them in his mouth. "Do you think Mr. Trombly went to Heaven?"

The question took Gramma by surprise. She sat in the chair next to him. "Why would you ask that?"

"I miss him. He was the best bus driver."

She could tell something else bothered him. "Why else?"

Henri picked another chip out of the cookie, watching as crumbs fell to the table. "I feel scared about people dying. He never went to church. Can people still go to Heaven if they didn't go to church?"

"I believe they can, Henri. Mr. Trombly was a special man, and I can't imagine God not letting him in. He set a good example of how God wants us all to live."

"How's that?" Henri looked up.

"We must be kind to people and never hurt anyone."

"So it's okay if he didn't go to church? He must be in Heaven now?"

"God decides who goes to Heaven, Henri. You know how I feel about the importance of going to church. We learn about God and how He wants us to live. Personally, I like to hear that He's always by our side. Life can be full of burdens at times and I think those choosing not to attend services have a more difficult time coping when hardships are sent their way. Life is easier when we have faith in God. Trust me on that one."

"Does everyone have a guardian angel? Even if they don't go to church?" He nervously nibbled at the remainder of his cookie.

"I can't picture it any other way dear, but something's troubling you. Are you thinking about quitting church?"

She feared this would happen some day, and hoped it wasn't so.

61

"I like church, Gramma. Some kids at school said if someone doesn't go to church, they'll burn forever in hell. It scares me to think about it and I worry that Grampa doesn't go."

She could see he was frightened. It reminded her of her younger days, when the thought of death sent shivers up her spine. "Remember what I said about Mr. Trombly?"

"That he went to Heaven because he was good?"

"I'll never believe God turns away good people because they didn't go to church. It doesn't make sense. Some people live in areas where there are no churches, and they never heard about God. If they're good people, He wouldn't turn them away."

"Mom said that God isn't mean."

"I agree with her, and don't you worry another minute about your grampa. He's a wonderful man and I know some day we'll be together in Heaven."

"But I don't want either of you to die. I feel scared about people dying, don't you?"

"When I was young like you, I did. I didn't think I would ever be good enough to go to Heaven. They talked a lot about burning in Hell back then too, and it frightened me."

"How'd you stop thinking about it?"

She recalled the very day it happened for her. "I visited often with an old woman that lived next door to us. One day I told her of my fears and she very simply told me to stop thinking about Hell and get on with my life. She said I should spend more time thinking about God and His angels and how much they love me. And by doing so, I'd automatically live the way He wanted me to and have nothing to worry about. From that day on, that's exactly what I did, and it works."

"But there really is a place called Hell? And a devil?"

"That's what the Bible says, and I believe it. The devil can influence people in a bad way, just as the angels can influence them to be good. I would imagine there's a constant battle going on between the two. But like I said, I prefer to think only of God and His angels. If you do the same, you'll have no fear."

"Tell me some more about the angels. Did the old woman like them too?"

"She talked about them constantly and taught me a lot about them. So did my own mother. I told you about her seeing an angel."

"Yes, you did. Do girls have girl angels and boys have boy angels?"

"I don't know the answer to that. It's probably another one of God's big secrets. He has many."

"Mom says one of His biggest secrets is why we are all on earth and not living with Him in Heaven having a bunch of fun. Do you think it would really be fun there? It sounds pretty boring to me. Everyone sitting around on golden thrones playing harps."

She laughed, remembering how she used to think almost the same way. Grampa came in and asked what was so funny. It made him happy to see her laughing.

Henri said, "We were talking about Heaven and the angels. I'm still wondering how they get us to do things. I wanted to ask you that, Gramma."

"I told you before. They fill your head with good thoughts and ideas. It's very easy to listen to them."

"How do I know a bad angel isn't telling me what to do?"

"Remember, we're only going to think about God and the angels. That keeps the bad guys away. We know the difference between good ideas and bad ideas, right? And we know which actions would hurt us or someone else. It's simple."

Grampa didn't want to hear any more about Heaven and the angels. That's all she talked of lately and it was making him uncomfortable. She sounded as though they were coming to haul her away. Not being able to stand the thought of her absence, he wished again that she'd get over whatever was ailing her.

"Time to plant tomatoes," he said abruptly. "The sun is low enough now."

Henri stood, "I'll help carry them out. You believe Heaven is real, don't you Grampa? Do you think it'll be fun?"

Gathering pots of tomato plants in his arms and appearing to be somewhat irritated, he answered, "As long as they put a fishing pole in my hand when I get there, I know I'll have fun. Now let's get to work. Did you ask your parents if you could stay?"

"I'll call Mary," said Gramma, "I'm sure it'll be okay." Lowering her voice, she asked him if he would please be a little more patient with Henri's questions and then told him to never say anything that would dissuade him from going to church.

Grampa rolled his eyes impatiently and left the house. He and Henri began setting the plants into the small holes he had dug. They worked fast so the shock wouldn't be too great for the little seedlings. The task neared completion when Henri asked if Grampa thought the angels were helping them.

"Can we talk about something else, Henri?" Seeing the crushed look on his grandson's face, he quickly said, "You have to understand that sometimes I get grumpy when I work intently."

Grampa pointed to the newly planted seedlings. "Look, the plants haven't even begun to wilt. I'll bet the angels are holding them up."

Henri looked down the two rows of plants. They hadn't wilted at all. "Or maybe they're watering them when we aren't looking?"

"Could be, son, could be."

They worked quietly; each lost in their own thoughts. Grampa broke the silence and surprised Henri with what he said. "Come to think of it, Henri, I did hear an angel story once. It happened years ago."

He stopped his work, searching his memory for the story he had almost forgotten.

"Old man Jenkins told me the story. It happened to him when he was young. We called him Frank back then."

He pulled the pipe from his back pocket. Henri waited calmly and watched while he packed tobacco into the bowl. Grampa took his usual look around before striking the match to light up. After inhaling deeply, the smoke rolled out of his mouth forming perfect circles. When the ring of smoke disappeared, Grampa continued his story.

"We were sitting in the local bar drinking beer, the night he told me about the angel that saved his life."

"Did he see the angel?"

"Just listen to the story. On a cold winter day, Frank decided to get out of the house and do some ice fishing. Arriving at the lake, he cut a hole in the ice and fished for a short period of time. Nothing bit his hook so he pulled the line out and started walking to another spot. He hadn't gone more than a few feet when it happened." He stopped to re-light his pipe.

"What happened?" Henri wanted to know right away.

"Hang on, son." The wind had kicked up and kept blowing the matches out. When finally lit, he continued. "Frank figured the hole he fell through had been covered over by a thin layer of ice and snow. When his leg broke through, the rest of his body followed and he sank to the bottom of the lake."

Grampa inhaled the smoke and after a few seconds, let it pour out of his mouth as he continued, "He said he couldn't see a thing down there 'cause it was so dark. His clothes were heavy from being wet and weighted him down. Frank couldn't swim at all and knew he was a goner."

He paused again.

"And?"

"Frank felt arms encircling him and remembered feeling as though he was being propelled upward. And then nothing. He doesn't remember a thing except laying on the ice nearly freezing to death."

"How'd he get home?" Henri was spellbound.

"After laying on the ice for a short time, someone came along and found him."

"Who? I'll bet it was another angel. Or maybe the same one."

"Could be. He swears an angel hauled him out of the water even if he didn't actually see who it was. A stranger found him laying on the ice and took him to the hospital. Frank never saw the guy again after he dropped him off. You know . . . as I think about it now . . ."

He paused once again, tapping the pipe against his foot to dispose of the ashes. "Strangers have never hung around this town, especially in the dead of winter."

Henri's eyes were huge. "Angels helped him! It had to be! Gramma said if it's not your time to die the angels will save your life. That's part of their job."

"That's what she always says."

He tucked the pipe into his back pocket and announced it was time to get back to work. "Two plants are left; we'll each take one."

Patting the soil firmly around each one, the job was finished on time. The sun had buried itself behind the earth, leaving the sky painted a brilliant red-gold.

Grampa stood, putting out a hand to help Henri to his feet. "Let's go, son, we're finished. Just look at that sky. It's telling us that tomorrow will be a beautiful day."

Walking hand in hand to the house, Henri looked back once. Since the tomato plants still hadn't wilted, he smiled, knowing the angels were holding them up.

Chapter 8

Spring moved gradually into summer and the children of Pleasant Valley were kept busy with various activities while on vacation from school. Some attended craft classes at the city park and for the more active, games helped to pass the time away.

Henri and Corey played together daily. If not attending the classes or playing games, they traveled around town on their bikes.

Henri's dad worked overtime at the factory leaving Mary with little to do. Out of loneliness, she began helping with the children at the park. Finding it to be great fun, she volunteered to help chaperone groups of youngsters hiking the nature trails up near the lake. Henri was proud of her. All of his friends liked his mother.

The busy days helped keep Mary's mind from the growing problem with her mother. She wasn't getting any better and refused to go back to the doctor. The past few Sundays she didn't even get up to go to church. Most of her time was spent sleeping. Her dad was no longer himself at all. He spent every minute worrying about his wife. And that was how the summer slipped by.

Soon the days grew shorter, typical for the month of August. The afternoon sun became intensely hot. Grampa welcomed the change, knowing the remaining tomatoes would ripen more quickly under the heat.

He busied himself picking the other vegetables that also ripened faster now. Finding he had an abundance, again enabled him to share his bounty with the neighbors.

One Friday evening, early in September, Grampa called Henri asking if he could come over the next day to help pick tomatoes. They were ready to harvest and the fear of an early frost was getting greater.

Henri, eager to help, arrived later the next morning after shopping for school clothes with his mother. Seeing his grampa already working in the garden, he shouted out to him as he parked his bike next to the house. "I'll bet you didn't think I could get up this early!"

Happy to see him, Grampa answered, "I sure didn't. Grab that basket by the door; we have a ton of tomatoes to pick. Seeing them all ruined by the frost would be pretty sad."

Henri was ready to work, and with a basket in hand, stood eagerly at his side.

"Your gramma said she was going to start canning today. She's getting the jars ready right now."

Henri started picking. "She's feeling better?"

"Seems to have more energy. I found her up with the birds this morning." He didn't seem too enthusiastic.

"Maybe, if she's feeling better, we can do some fishing later?" Henri asked hopefully. "If we hurry with this work there might be time left."

"I don't think so, son, she'll need help with the canning. I have to help her; it's a big job."

He regretted not being able to fish with his grandson anymore, but he couldn't leave her. She talked crazy lately. Telling him silly things, like where she kept important stuff and how much soap to put in the wash. She even wrote down recipes for some of his favorite meals, recipes that she knew by heart. It frightened him to know her thoughts were about dying.

"We'll go again, Henri. As soon as she's on her feet."

Henri knew that meant when she felt better. "Okay."

They finished picking before noon and when they returned to the house, Gramma was back in bed and only six jars were clean and ready. After finishing that task, Grampa and his grandson canned twenty-four jars of tomatoes that afternoon.

Exhausted after their work, both collapsed onto the couch. Grampa ruffled Henri's hair and said, "I appreciate your help, my friend. I couldn't have done all this without you. I sure don't have to worry about Gramma not having enough tomatoes for her oxtail soup this winter."

After the words came out, he realized oxtail soup was one of the recipes she'd written down. Pushing that thought from his mind, he stood and walked to the window. Shoving his hands into his back pockets, he gazed around the neighborhood. Henri sensed his sadness and joined him, putting his arm protectively around Grampa's waist.

A few silent minutes passed by before Henri pointed to the figure of a man running up the sidewalk, "Hey, look! Here comes H.G., and he's not limping anymore!"

A smile brightened Grampa's face, "Well I'll be. He did it. When he first started running again, it was a pretty sad sight, dragging that leg behind him. I didn't think he'd keep it up."

"Neither did anyone else, but whenever he went by, they cheered him on. People ran out of their stores and clapped for him when he hobbled passed. Corey and I helped too. We followed him on our bikes and told him to keep going. He told us to get lost, but we knew we were helping him."

"You did well, son. Look at the smile on his face. His running means a lot to him. I'm glad he didn't give up. C'mon, let's check out the 'fridge'. I need a snack."

70

Henri helped Grampa nearly every day with his garden until summer was declared officially over, and the dreaded day arrived. He soon found himself standing in line outside the school with his friend Corey.

The children chattered loudly up until the bell rang. Excitement always ran high on the first day back to school. Most of the students were happy to be standing in a different line this year, knowing it brought them into a higher grade. Not for one boy, though. His name was Buck, and he had to go back to the same grade.

"Buck's a flunker, Buck's a flunker," chanted the usual group of bullies. "You must be a real idiot, Buck," said one of them. "Flunker!" He stuck his tongue out at the embarrassed boy.

Henri told them to stop and they turned on him. "Shut up, carrot top." They were happy to have another kid to pick on. Henri pretended it didn't bother him and motioned for Buck to follow him and Corey. They ran around the corner of the school building. Looking back, they saw the same boys hassling someone else.

"Last year," said Henri, pointing to a strip of bricks on the building, "these bricks came up to my chin." Standing next to them, he said, "Now look, they're almost to my shoulder."

"You really grew, Henri!" Buck anxiously measured himself, "But I'm taller than you!"

Corey tried next and as he did, his sister Jamie came running over. Finding herself the same height as Buck, and in the same grade now, they became quick friends. The two of them ran off to the playground. Buck obviously forgot about the bullies.

Corey was mad, "I see they're still calling you 'carrot top'. "We should have punched them good."

"It wouldn't make them stop. I'm gonna find a way to change the color of my hair. I hate it. I'm the only kid in school with red hair."

The bell rang. Mass confusion took over as the children searched for the correct line to stand in. The teachers came out with a list of who went where. When Henri and Corey saw they had the same teacher, they laughed as they dodged for the correct line to get in.

Kindergartners lined up next to them. Some of the children hung on their mothers, crying hysterically. They didn't want to be left alone at school.

Corey asked Henri, "Did your mother bring you on your first day of school?"

"Yep."

"Did you cry?"

"Of course not, silly." But Henri remembered that he had.

They reached the third grade room. Walking in, Henri noticed an odor that reminded him of the stuff his mother cleaned the house with. He reckoned they scrubbed the rooms before school started. Corey motioned to him to move fast as everyone scrambled to find a desk at which to sit, each trying to make sure they'd be sitting next to their friend.

Miss Nelson, the third grade teacher, watched with her hands on her hips. She stood at the front of the classroom, clearing her throat loudly to stop the noise. She wasn't smiling. Instant silence pervaded the room. You could have heard a pin drop. Miss Nelson requested that everyone come back to the front of the room and line up. Slowly, each child shuffled forward, where she proceeded to seat them alphabetically.

They knew that this teacher spelled trouble. Word was out about her being mean, but they didn't think she'd be this bad. When she passed out books that would be used for the year, a soft mumbling of complaints blanketed the room.

Children from last year's third grade had complained about how hard the class was and now these students had the books to prove it.

The tall skinny teacher told them to open the math books. The new group of third graders quickly scanned through the pages. Sneaking looks at each other, they had the same thought in mind. The math problems sitting before them looked completely foreign and impossible to learn.

That first day went painfully slow. Everyone rejoiced when the dismissal bell rang and they dashed for the door. Miss Nelson promptly ordered them back to their seats. "We will always leave this classroom in an orderly fashion."

She pointed to the first row. "Those of you with your last name beginning with 'A,' may stand." They stood and she said, "You may leave now, in single file of course."

Expressionless, they marched passed her. Not until they felt the freedom of the outside did they utter their disapproval.

"She's a troll! Third grade is awful!"

Loud complaints poured from their mouths. Corey and Henri were no exception. Grumbling as they each carried an armful of books to the bus, both vowed they hated school. All of their homework had to be done by tomorrow.

Bursting through the door to his home, Henri complained nonstop to his mother about the awful first day of school. She patiently listened as he ranted and raved. When he finally finished, she explained how important it was for the teacher to have control of the children in her classroom. She said that sometimes teachers seemed mean in order to achieve order, and assured him that Miss Nelson would get nicer.

His mother's words proved to ring true. Henri still groaned about the homework but he began to like his teacher. Only a week after school started, she took the class on a field trip to the local newspaper. When the students heard about it, they jumped for joy and professed they had the best teacher in the world. After the outing, Henri leaped off the bus in a great mood. Seeing his grandparent's car sitting in his driveway elevated his excitement. This was the best day of his life!

His Grampa stood by the door grinning when he bounced up the steps. He held his fishing pole in the air for his grandson to see. Henri's mouth dropped open and he ran to the garage to get his pole. Now he knew for sure this was the happiest day of his life. The fishing trip also meant his gramma must be well again.

When Henri returned, Grampa told him to give Corey a call to see if he wanted to go. He was so excited that his hands shook as he tried to dial the number. Corey was allowed and Henri said they would pick him up in a few minutes.

He ran to his gramma and gave her a big hug. She felt different and skinny. Like a bunch of bones. Too happy to dwell on it, he figured it was because she had been so sick. He knew she'd probably eat more now that she felt better.

Chattering about the minnows they'd have to pick up, Henri and his grampa headed out the door for the long awaited adventure. Gramma smiled as she watched the two of them off together again. Seeing them happy-made hiding the pain worthwhile.

Corey, holding his fishing pole and tackle, waited anxiously at the end of his driveway. Grampa and Henri loaded him and his equipment into the car and headed for the bait shop.

Parking out front, they raced into the store. The boys ran straight for the minnow tank, rolling up their sleeves on the way. Into the cool water went their arms. The small fish slipped through their hands, tickling their fingers. This experience was always a highlight of their fishing trips. Grampa snickered as Corey excused himself to the bathroom. Feeling the cool water always made him go.

Henri's fingers remained dangling in the water as he hung over the tank. He became mesmerized watching the faces of the little minnows while they nipped at his fingers. Loud voices coming from the check out area startled him back to reality. The sudden outburst nearly sent him falling to the floor. Sensing the seriousness of the situation, he instinctively pulled his hands from the water and quickly dried them on his pants. Hustling down the aisles of fishing gear, he soon stood safely at his grampa's side.

Henri's heart pounded fiercely as he listened to him shouting at the bait shop man. "I'll have to see this with my own eyes! This is bull crap, that's what it is!" Grampa took Henri's hand. "C'mon son, let's get out of here."

Henri sounded weak and shaky, "I'll get Corey."

He ran to get his friend. His grampa looked madder than he'd ever seen him and he didn't dare ask why. He and Corey met him at the door. Grampa rushed them out to the car and once inside, squealed out of the driveway leaving stones and dust flying in the air. They headed down the road leading to the lake. Henri and Corey rode in silence, oblivious to the roadside sights. Not only were they frightened out of their wits, but Grampa drove so fast the scenery looked like one big blur.

Corey whispered to Henri. "Where's the minnows? What's wrong with your grampa?" He too, had never seen Grampa this mad. His face looked almost purple.

Henri shrugged his shoulders and made motions to keep quiet.

.   Grampa spun his tires as he pulled into the parking lot at the lake. Before getting out of the truck, he barked, "I heard they condemned the lake! I'll be right back!"

Neither one of the boys new what "condemned" meant. Their eyes followed Grampa as he rushed over to where two men were tossing tools into the back of their pick up truck. They saw Grampa's mouth yelling. Corey rolled the window down so they could hear better.

"It's not some kind of joke!" shouted one of the men at Grampa. "The lake is condemned and you don't have to be screaming at me! I heard the factory's been dumping its waste into the water. We don't know much more than that right now. Watch the evening news, that's all I can tell ya. Now if you don't mind Charlie, we have to finish putting these signs around the lake."

Grampa stood helplessly as the truck pulled away. Turning, he motioned to the boys to join him. Corey and Henri got out of the car and together they walked to the beach where one of the signs was displayed.

It read: "No Swimming. No Fishing. This Lake Condemned."

Henri timidly asked, "What does condemn mean, Grampa?"

"The lake is poisoned. The factory dumped its garbage in the water and ruined it. I don't know what will happen now, our drinking water comes from this lake. The whole town could be in big trouble."

Panic grabbed Henri, "Someone can probably fix it. Can't someone fix it?"

"I have no idea what can be done, Henri." Grampa wearily sighed, "Let's sit down."

They sat on the big old log they always used for fishing. Grampa pulled the pipe out of his pocket and solemnly lit it. The three of them sat watching the water, which looked as though nothing was wrong with it.

Grampa puffed hard on his pipe. He couldn't understand how something like this could happen without anyone noticing. A horrible thought crossed his mind. His heart fell as he thought about his wife. She devoured the fish he caught from the lake and she drank at least a half gallon of water a day, saying it washed impurities from the body. With each thought his heart beat faster. He knew if he didn't get away from there, he would be sick. Rising to his feet, he said, "Let's go. Let's get out of here."

The boys trailed behind as he stomped to the car. Climbing into the driver's seat, her words came back to him. "You just mark my words; that man is up to no good. I can feel it in my bones."

How did she always know what was happening? Stronger pangs of fright shot through him. She knew she was dying.

They didn't have to wait for the evening news to get a full report. Special reports flashed across the television screen all afternoon. When Henri and Grampa entered the house, the newsman relayed the story of how H.G. was out jogging and accidentally tripped over a pipe that he discovered was dumping waste into the lake. After testing the water, the Health Department shut the factory down until further notice. The owner, Mr. Johnson, could not be found.

****

Hovering over the family, each angel stood at attention. They were ready to assist their charge in any way they could. Buffy, dry eyed and confident, sat with her arms around Mary, sending her calm and reassuring thoughts.

"How sad it is," said Anna, "The way one man can mess up so many lives. In his pursuit for money and power, Mr. Johnson has destroyed an entire town."

Solemnly, they watched the newscasts as more of the details unfolded. They experienced the same horror as the family they were caring for. Not able to shield them from the terrible deed done, each angel felt hopeful that with their God-given powers, they could help get them through the imminent danger.

When becoming a guardian angel, they were told of the many changes that would occur throughout a person's life on earth. After rigorous schooling and on-the-job training, an angel knew he would have to be dedicated.

God trusted them completely to give their personal charge all the love and guidance needed. Every angel vowed their devotion on the day they graduated from Guardian Angel School. On that very special day, each angel received their golden angel-wings pin.

Sacrifice was necessary to serve as one of God's special helpers. Their lives in Heaven could have been that of pure joy and free of any responsibility. But they didn't choose that, preferring instead to be of service to others. The rewards for the job were extremely satisfying with the ultimate satisfaction being when their charge reached that final goal. Heaven.

****

Chapter 9

*T*wo days later, the residents of Pleasant Valley felt a greater panic. The newspaper and local television channel reported that there would be no new water supply. Drilling a well would be impossible because there wasn't any good water to be found. Out of town experts were called in, but that didn't help.

Not one person living in the town needed to be told what their fate would be. They knew. One by one, the families left the area, searching for jobs in the bigger cities. Sadness prevailed as longtime friendships ripped apart.

John began his search for work in the big city. He spent entire weeks looking and returned on the weekends to be with his family. It saddened him to be away during this time when they needed his presence at home. He was proud of Mary. She displayed a newfound strength through this most trying time. Especially as her mother grew sicker with each passing day. The tragic news of her beloved town was truly taking its toll on her.

Mary persuaded her mother to return to the doctor. She and Grampa went along for the appointment. The doctor advised them to take her to the big city where she could see a specialist. Grampa decided to make all of the arrangements. He wanted to have her examined as soon as possible, but it wasn't to be. His wife collapsed that very evening. Grampa called for an ambulance. He accompanied her on the way to Pleasant Valley Hospital, and after phoning his daughter, found the bed where his wife lay unconscious.

Sitting beside her, he begged her to wake up. It didn't happen. His entire being felt helpless at the sight of her frail body lying so still. He thought about all of the things she would be saying if she could. Grampa knew she wasn't afraid and wished he had the faith she possessed. Without her, he had nothing. Holding her tiny, pale hand, he laid his head next to hers. That was the way his daughter and grandson found them as they rushed into the room.

"What happened?" Mary called to her mother, but received no answer.

Her dad lifted his head as he continued to look at his wife. He told Mary that the doctor checked her briefly and was waiting for results on a few tests. He couldn't talk any more. Mary left to find someone that could give her more information.

Henri stood by his gramma's side and stared at her. The way she looked frightened him. His hand rested on his grampa's bent over back. They stayed that way until Mary returned with the doctor. He wanted to re-examine Gramma, so the three of them left the room. The doctor returned shortly to tell them what he thought. Henri didn't stay to listen, returning instead to Gramma's side. As he watched her, he thought about the angels. She said they would help when needed. "All we have to do is ask."

Kneeling beside the bed, he folded his hands. "Please angels, she told me to ask for help when I needed it and I really need it now. Tell God to wake my gramma up. He can't let her die. I don't know if He knows it or not, but our water is bad, so we have to move. We can't leave her here. She has to be well so she can move with us."

He then looked up to the ceiling as if he would find God there. "God, if you can't come. . . ."

Covering his mouth with his hands, large sobs shook his small body. His thoughts finished the plea. "If you can't come, could you please tell your angels to help us? My gramma has to wake up." He sobbed silently, not wanting his gramma to be sad if she woke up and found him crying.

****

Just about the time James could take no more, his beeper sounded. He anxiously responded to God's call and they discussed the situation at hand. Following the conversation, James sent T.J. out to get Buffy and Isaac with explicit instructions to get Grampa and Mary back into the room immediately.

****

Henri remained on his knees with his hands covering his face. Small sounds came from Gramma's mouth. Thinking he heard her calling his name, he stood. Her eyes were barely open as she tried to smile. He whispered anxiously, "Gramma it's true! You were right! God really hears us!"

Henri then spoke louder, "I asked Him to wake you up and make you better and He did it! The angels helped Him! You're going to be all right now!"

Grampa and Mary came into the room and were astounded to see her awake after just being told that her chances of ever coming out of the coma were slim. Gramma spoke in a small, weak voice. "God always answers our prayers, Henri."

Barely breathing, she continued, "It may not always be exactly how we want Him to, but He does answer us."

Her eyes closed briefly and they could see that breathing was difficult for her. "Let Him . . . decide . . . what's best."

Gramma gazed around the room, trying to figure out where she was. Henri moved aside as Grampa took her hand

and told her what happened. Relief flooded over him to know she would be okay.

A small smile crossed her face as she looked from one to the other. "Who was shaking me so hard? . . . Was it you, Henri, . . . trying to wake me?"

They told her not to talk. Henri figured the angels shook her to get her to wake up.

Gramma said, "I love you all very much. Don't be afraid." She closed her eyes, still smiling. Little did her family know that the words she spoke were the last words she would speak in this life.

Mary and Henri had just gotten home from the hospital. It was early evening and they were exhausted after spending so many hours with Gramma. Mary had tried relentlessly to find John. It surprised her when he walked through the door only minutes after they did. She fell into his arms and cried uncontrollably. Between sobs, she tried to explain everything that happened since the day her mother collapsed. She didn't like making such a scene in front of her son, but could no longer control her emotions.

John helped her to the couch and after she laid down, put a cool wet washcloth to her head. Henri sat in a chair next to his mother watching sadly, as his father spoke soothing words to her.

Mary slowly regained her composure and urged John to go to the hospital to be with her dad. Feeling that she and Henri would be okay, he left.

Henri took a seat on the floor so he could be closer to his mother. He was relieved that his dad was back. "He'll make everything better, mom. You'll see."

But she knew differently. Stroking Henri's curly head, she said, "You know Henri, maybe everything won't be okay. Gramma might not make it."

"You mean you think she'll die? Well, she won't! I talked to God and asked Him to fix her. I told him about us, that we had to move and she needed to come with us. She's going to be okay because He already did part of what I asked Him to do."

"What do you mean?"

Remember the first day at the hospital? When you and Grampa were out in the hall talking to the doctor?"

"Yes."

"That's when I did it. I asked God to wake her up and He did."

"I didn't know that, Henri." She had no idea what to say to him. He felt positive that everything was fine. She needed to prepare him. Things didn't look good at all.

"Henri, you know how much Gramma has always wanted to see Heaven? This could be her chance. She's very sick. Don't you think she would love to see her angels?"

He wouldn't listen. "Can I go to bed now? I'm tired and if I get lots of sleep, we can go to the hospital earlier tomorrow."

"Henri, we need to talk about this. Maybe God thinks it would be best for your gramma to be with Him, it could happen."

He ran to his room. Following him, she said they would talk again the next day. After kissing him good night, she trudged wearily back to the living room and dropped herself onto the sofa. Faint beams of evening light filtered through the window as she fell soundly asleep.

Henri was not so lucky. He fought sleep, determined to wait until his dad came home, knowing it would make him feel safe. A few hours passed. Henri heard the front door open and his dad's voice spoke softly. He couldn't make out the words, but heard perfectly when his mother let out a small cry, "No, no, no!".

83

Leaping out of his bed, he tiptoed to the door and listened. She was crying. A crack in the door allowed him to peek through and he saw his dad holding his mother in his arms. Grampa sat alone in a chair with his head hanging to his chest. Henri knew. His gramma was dead!

He dove for his bed and covered his head with the blankets. Feeling betrayed by God, he vowed to stay in bed forever. He curled up into a ball under the covers, hating the word "dead."

****

This was a difficult time for the angels. The family members, so consumed with the shock of Gramma's death, were unable to receive the calming thoughts being sent their way. God permitted the angels to use a special magic to help ease their pain and they went right to work administering the fine spray that would sedate their charges enough to allow words of comfort to seep into their sub-conscience. Beams of soothing energy radiated from the loving hands of each angel to their charge. They were confident that very shortly the effects would be noticed.

****

Henri heard the small creak his door made when it opened wider. His mother spoke to him.

"Henri, I know you're awake." She knew that he'd already heard the news when she saw his small curled form hiding under the covers.

She sat on the bed. "Please come out. We have to talk."

The bed shook as Henri sobbed, "I hate God so much! I'll never come out. I asked Him to help and He didn't. I hate Him and I want my Gramma."

John came into the room when he heard the outburst. His wife held her head in her hands, unable to cope. He sat on the opposite side of the bed and told Henri to come out from under the covers.

"I know how you feel Henri, but you must not say you hate God. Your gramma would not like to hear that. Come out now and we'll talk."

"She can't even hear what I said, Dad. She's . . . dead!"

He cried harder, trying to speak between sobs. "I asked God to help us. She said He always answered . . . I guess she . . . lied or maybe she didn't really . . . know."

The last word spilled out almost silent. He stopped crying and appeared to be somewhat calmer. All three of them did.

Mary pulled herself up and with a now steady voice said, "It's okay to be angry, Henri. We are too, and we're very sad. God had to decide what was best for your gramma. She was so terribly sick."

She paused, blinking back tears. "He did wake her so she could say goodbye. I think God answered your prayers in a way that would be good for all of us. Thanks to your prayers, we were able to talk to her one last time."

His voice still muffled by the covers, Henri said, "I wish He would just have made her better."

"I know, Henri. I do too. But we also have to remember how much she wanted to see Heaven and the angels. It's very hard for us not to have her with us, but I know she's happier now because she's not sick anymore."

"I have to check on Grampa," said his dad, "he's also sad and said he doesn't want to live without her. Henri, we have to help him be strong. He lived with Gramma a lot longer than we did and he's going to be very lonely."

Henri peeked out as his father was leaving. His eyes were red and puffy, and his nose was running. Sniffing he said, "I really didn't mean that I hated God. I'm just so sad. I know people have to die. But I didn't want it to happen to anyone in our family."

Mary laid down beside him and stroked his forehead. It surprised her when he drifted off to sleep so quickly. She wiped away the remaining tears from his unhappy little face. Thinking about the horrors that had consumed their lives in such a short period of time, she wondered how much more could possibly happen.

Growing up, Mary had never really understood her mother when she talked of how cruel life could be at times. Her life had been such fun, and mostly free of pain. She now wondered how long the pain would last.

The next few days were the most difficult for the family to get through. Gramma was laid to rest under the branches of a large oak tree in the Pleasant Valley Cemetery. It was where she would have wanted to be, in her beloved town of Pleasant Valley.

Chapter 10

****

*G*od anxiously awaited the arrival of James. At nine-thirty, the soft knock on the door came. "Come in."

God admired how proud he held himself as he walked through the door. It spoke of great confidence. "It's looking good, James. You and your troops are doing a fine job. Henri's family is doing as well as can be expected at this time, and again I have my fine group of dedicated angels to thank."

After a brief pause, He continued. "Gramma is ecstatically happy here. She didn't have to adjust at all. She knew she was in Heaven the second she arrived. Her family and friends are with her now. They're showing her the sights and have a huge party planned to celebrate her arrival."

"When she came for her appointment with me, she walked through the door and her first words were, 'I've been waiting for this day forever!'" God mused, "I wish it were that easy for everyone."

James needed that happy news and recalled his first venture into Heaven. It hadn't been so easy for him. Back then, there were no churches or any place to learn of the hereafter.

Reading his thoughts, God said, "People are luckier in these modern days, but many still don't believe."

Picking up the remote control, He then tuned into the town of Pleasant Valley. The first stop, Mayor Bob Green's household, was a pathetic sight. God dismally said, "He did it early this morning, James. Bob committed suicide. The poisoned water problem was too much for him to bear."

This news didn't surprise James, but he felt saddened as he viewed the aftermath of the man's actions. The unnecessary grief and suffering he caused his family would take a long time to heal.

"To see the results of his actions is not a pretty sight, James. Each member of his family thinks it's their fault. Guilt. He dropped that on them along with grief."

"I know."

"His future held promise. With three extra angels, he would have gotten through this troublesome time. He surrendered to self pity." God shook his head sadly. "He never got the message of hope the angels sent his way."

James knew of the great plans God had for Bob Green's family. A solution was just around the corner.

Viewing the man's grief-stricken wife, God said, "I'm keeping the extra angels in the household until I can figure out how to fix this mess."

Bob Green had ruined all of the plans that God had arranged for his family.

Henri's household flashed across the screen. Henri sat beside Grampa. He held a picture album in his hands and together they looked at memories. The family appeared sorrowful, but they were at peace, accepting the help that was so silently sent their way.

"Buffy's proving to be a strong angel," said James. He didn't know if he should bring up the crying episode yet. God already had plenty to worry about.

God said knowingly, "I see she hasn't shed a tear."

"I should have figured you know about her." James said.

"Buffy's fine. It's not that unusual for an angel to cry. No need to worry. She adds a little fun to our sometimes overworked days."

"I'll agree with that. That angel is full of surprises." James chuckled, "She's promised not to take revenge on the bad people anymore."

God's face showed a loving tenderness. "She learned an important lesson that night."

"Not to trip anyone when you're around?"

They laughed and God said, "She'll never do anything like it again."

"I know." James noticed a twinkle in God's eye. He figured they were both thinking the same thing. Neither of them felt sorry for Mr. Johnson when he fell flat on his face in front of the entire town. The fall at the dance had a new meaning to the townspeople now that they knew what Mr. Johnson had done to the water.

Still watching Henri's family, James talked about how much the magic helped their grief. "Soon after the spray was administered, they were able to accept the calming thoughts we sent their way."

God answered, "It takes a little edge off the pain and gives them needed strength to get through those first few days. They were exceptionally receptive to it, having the faith usually helps."

He pressed a button on the remote and quickly scanned through the few remaining households. God told James that a small number of angels had problems moving their charges in the right direction.

"Some of the people are still in a denial stage. That'll change when the store holding the large supply of bottled water closes. When they have to start traveling to the big city to get food and water, they will know what has to be done."

James saw that it hurt God to watch His people enduring such hardships. Both knew it couldn't be any other way.

Old Man Jenkins rocked in his chair. God told James that He would allow the man to remain in Pleasant Valley.

"The plans were for him to live with his daughter out West. He refuses to go. I can't blame him, he wanted to celebrate his 100th birthday in Pleasant Valley and would have. But those plans have all changed too. He's also sick from the water. Mr. Jenkins will be here soon."

James watched as the old man rocked in his chair, and wondered what the plans would be for Mr. Johnson.

God knowingly answered, "He'll pay for the destruction he caused. His day will come."

They discussed in detail, the move Henri's family would be making to the city. "It's been a while since you've worked in the big city, James. You've probably heard how much it's changed. I will continue to work closely with you and the other angels, until the lives of those involved are running smooth once again."

James nodded in agreement and waited while God seemed to be contemplating His next words.

"What lies ahead for you and your coworkers will be difficult also. Residing in Pleasant Valley has kept you from having much contact with the real world. What I'm trying to say is that it's a jungle out there."

James interrupted, wanting God to know his understanding of what the future held for them. "I'm aware of the rapidly growing corruption, we hear the news reports. We also heard a great deal when we attended the angels' meetings."

God, reminded of something important to say, broke in. "I wanted to tell you that as soon as the family settles down a little, we can send the substitute angels on Saturdays. All of you can then attend the guardian angels' meetings again."

"James, Pleasant Valley is a mess, but it's nothing compared with what else plagues the earth. The drug problem is out of control, and the crime would boggle your mind. I'm thinking seriously about taking stronger measures."

God talked at great length about the problems. The discussion reminded James of a similar situation that occurred many years ago. Not as many people inhabited Earth then, but a large percentage of them were out of control. God sent His Son to straighten things out.

James recalled vividly Jesus' purpose for visiting Earth. He taught the people what God expected of them; to love Him and one another with all their hearts.

"Not many people believe I'm still around," He said to James. "I do many things to prove My presence, but a great number have lost faith. It's making our jobs that much tougher."

"I know. From what I understand, our enemies are working overtime."

"They're out in full force, that's for sure." God stood and walked over to the window where His animals grazed below.

"Come look, James. Such a peaceful sight it is."

Joining God, he agreed. They watched as several different species of animals munched grass together in harmony.

"My people could be living peacefully if they had continued to live as my Son instructed them. My wishes were simple. Refusing to follow them has caused nothing but grief for everyone involved."

Slightly amused, He added, "But of course, with all the different personalities running around, there's bound to be a few disagreements down there. We can live with a few arguments."

More solemnly He said, "Some people have harder roads to travel than others. My Son told everyone I walk with them always. To those with faith, this eases their load."

"That is true, but it means nothing to non-believers. Some wonder why their lives are a mess and use that problem as an excuse to justify their wrong doings. It's easy for the evil angels to manipulate those poor souls. Everyone is born with a conscience, and they do know right from wrong." It angered James to think about the enemy.

"That's our biggest problem right now. I give my people all the help they need to get out of the messes they create, but many still refuse."

"I know." Said James, feeling sorry for those who find it too difficult to shake the enemy loose. "They have such miserable lives because of it."

"Many ask for help but when given the answer they find it too difficult to make the necessary changes. They need stronger faith. Not only in Me, but in themselves."

James agreed, but said, "The good people, whether they have faith or not, live in fear now. They're scared to go outside their home and when they are home they fear that someone will break in and rob them of their goods, or worse, kill them. I know how dreadful the big city will be."

"It's going to be a tough job. Pleasant Valley was one of the few remaining small towns that hard-core evil had not yet touched. But it happened and their lives must go on."

God walked back to his desk and sat down, the weight of the world planted firmly on His shoulders. "The good people, James, I'll never disappoint them."

"I know. Gramma is a perfect example of that."

****

Chapter 11

*R*eturning to the household, James found the family still congregated in the living room. Henri, seated at his grampa's side spoke softly to him, "You have to come live with us, we can have lots of fun together. We'll go to your house to get more clothes and you'll need some of your stuff."

"Not yet, Henri. I can't go back there yet. I don't want to make any decisions right now. Please talk about something else."

Henri looked at his grampa's face. He didn't look the same. He hoped he wasn't going to get sick and die like Gramma. His dad told him Grampa looked that way because he was so sad, and said the same thing when he wouldn't eat.

"I'll be okay, Henri," said Grampa, noticing Henri staring at him again. He could never tell his grandson how lonesome he felt, or that he wanted to die, too.

Mary sat quietly thinking about better times. At intervals she'd talk softly about some of the things her mother used to say and do. Everyone found a level of comfort from her words.

As much as Henri missed his gramma, he began to accept her death. But he was afraid to pray that Grampa would stop being so unhappy. He wasn't sure how God would answer, and wasn't about to take a chance.

John remained gentle and strong for all of them. After enduring much sadness in his own life, he could easily bring solace and strength to the others. Many worries presently occupied his mind, but he put his job searching efforts on hold until he felt secure his family was okay. Concern about finding work weighed heavily on him, he hadn't received any offers yet and had left his resume at dozens of places.

He would take any job at this point. Their savings were dwindling and he needed money, they had to make that inevitable move soon. John missed Gramma. Oh, how she loved her angels. He shared those feelings and knew he was fortunate to know his own guardian angel, "Jake." John smiled as he recalled the time in his life when Jake acted as his imaginary playmate. He never discussed these memories with anyone.

John visualized what Jake might be doing right now. Probably scurrying around, trying to persuade someone to hire him. Together, they managed to handle the problems that came along.

Realizing he'd been deep in thought, John looked his family over. Finding them content, he raised his feet to the foot stool. His thoughts drifted back to a long time ago when he lived in an orphanage. He remembered when he first discovered the existence of his own guardian angel. The orphanage had been run by nuns, and they thought he was mentally ill because they found him talking to himself on several occasions. John didn't realize that he was the only person that could see Jake.

The nuns had taught the children about guardian angels and somewhere along the line John figured out that Jake must be his, especially since no one else could see him. He began conversing silently to him and never told anyone about his friend because it wasn't fun being called a mental case. He encouraged his family to ask the angels when they needed help, but mostly, he left the angel talk to Gramma. John recalled the many times in his life when Jake helped him. He didn't believe in coincidences; he knew better.

Jake told him a secret one day when they were sitting on the floor in his room at the orphanage. John remembered they were making tall buildings out of blocks when Jake told him that he could do magic for him.

"Don't worry about anything and have no fears," Jake said. "Believe that I will help you with any troubles you may have, and trust me always. In one way or another, John, the magic will be done."

Jake also told John he would always be his friend, but the day would come when John would no longer be able to see him. Not long after that, Jake stopped coming to his room. John was too young to understand the true meaning of Jake's words, but as he grew into adulthood, he figured it out and knew that Jake had indeed, helped him through many tough spots. It helped him immensely to know Jake was by his side, but John knew he still had to do the footwork. He dreaded leaving his family once again to continue his search for a job.

****

The angels could relax a little with the family feeling a bit better. The healing had begun; with time and a touch more of magic, the hurt would dwindle.

"They are accepting Gramma's death so well because of the good things she taught them," said James, "I call it planting seeds. That's what she did when she "preached" to them. She planted the seeds, and now they are sprouting in their minds. Gramma couldn't have left them a better gift. Looking down from Heaven, she'll see that all of her lectures paid off."

Buffy began to get emotional. "Oh James. You are so wise. I hope someday I can be as good an angel as you. I'm going to be the best for my charge. You are so right about Gramma's lectures. I keep reminding my Mary about the best parts; she smiles at the thoughts I send her."

Gazing off into space, she added, "We must thank Gramma's angel, too. She spent a lot of time helping her with the lectures. I miss Anna. Do you think she'll stop by to see us?"

"She's getting some rest and relaxation right now, but I'm sure she will. God wants her to take a vacation before she begins another assignment."

"Did He say anything about Gramma?" Asked Isaac. "We all miss her."

James gave a full account of everything that happened when she first arrived. The others were delighted to hear the news. It reminded them of the happiness they felt on their own arrival.

"It's so wonderful," said Buffy, starry eyed. "I know all of you remember when you first got to Heaven."

She became very dramatic and continued, "Words can never describe the true beauty of Heaven and the love felt on the moment of arrival. Could any of you ever describe it?"

Their heads shook "no" in unison.

James interrupted, knowing she was in one of her theatrical moods, which meant she'd talk all day if they let her. "Excuse me for the interruption, Buffy. Didn't you want to hear what God had to say?"

Not the least bit annoyed at the intrusion, she responded calmly, but seriously, "You did it again, James. Why didn't you tell us right away?"

"You never gave me a chance. He said all of you are doing a splendid job and soon we'll be able to attend the guardian angels' meetings again. Our full time attention to the Pleasant Valley problems must continue for the time being. Once we settle in the big city, providing things are running smoothly, the substitutes will return."

That news brought smiles to their faces. Each angel missed the weekly meetings.

James continued, "He also said a big surprise awaited us at the next meeting we attend, because we've done so well."

Buffy's mouth fell open. "Good Lord in Heaven! Do you think He'll announce our names over the loud speaker?"

She twirled around on one foot and like a ballerina, her hands held a pose above her head. "That would be so grand! My friends will tell everyone that they know me personally."

She looked to the others who watched her in amazement. "Don't you all agree? We'll be well known throughout all of Heaven. Won't this be great? Oh, do tell us when it will all happen, James."

"I've already explained, Buffy. A definite date cannot be set. You can be sure that God will not forget. I think you are overreacting to what I said. We will not be famous."

He had to stop and chuckle. "But if you think so, I guess that's okay."

"Oh, I do, James. Everyone will hear about us. I feel so important."

He knew he'd probably never understand her, but he could see the humor had a wonderful influence on the others. A lot of tension left the room as they all laughed with her.

Later, James could see Jake motioning to him. "Yes, Jake?"

"I hate to change this great mood but, we all heard about Bob Green. I can imagine how upsetting it was to God."

"You got that right," said James.

Jake continued, "Poor John has dealt with many more problems than anyone in this town. He'd never think of committing suicide. He's getting his phone call today, by the way."

Jake briskly rubbed his hands together. He looked as excited as a little kid. "He'll know it's good ol' Jake, coming to the rescue." His face beamed. He couldn't wait for John to receive the good news.

"How'd you get John to know your name?" Asked Buffy.

"I got my ways," said Jake smiling broadly, "we can't give away our trade secrets."

She pleaded with James, "make him tell, James."

"Jake has to tell you. I'd be doing a dishonorable thing if I told. Watch this Buf." He turned to the window and made a motion with his hands. Within seconds a small yellow bird landed on the windowsill.

"How do you do that?! If you can't tell Jake's secret, then tell us how you make birds obey you. Now that Gramma isn't here, they should be landing for Mary to see."

Her eyes drifted toward the window. "Gramma always knew we were around when she saw the yellow bird land on her windowsill. Please, James, please teach me how to do it. You must have shown Anna."

"Buffy, I love you but our specialties are our own. I will not give away my secret. I put the birds there for Anna. Her specialty was lectures. I'll tell you what though, while we're working together, I'll help you find one of your own. How about that?"

"Could you do it soon, James? It'll be so wonderful to have my own specialty. I can just see it when Mary knows for sure I am here for her."

Gazing off, her eyelashes fluttered as visions of the occasion came to mind. "She'll talk to me constantly and I'll become her hero . . . Oh James, if I could do the bird trick, I'd bring flocks in."

"I believe you would do just that, Buffy. Please be patient, I said I'd find you a specialty."

Isaac said, "It'll be easy to find one for you, Buf. The hardest part will be making Mary aware that it's you who's doing it. Grampa still doesn't know it's me picking out those wildly colored aprons. Have you noticed they always match my shirts?"

Isaac laughed, "He doesn't recognize anything I do. But it doesn't bother me."

"That's because Grampa doesn't believe in angels. Mary does and she'll know instantly it's me when I do something special." Buffy had visions of Mary thanking her for the cute little tricks, exactly like Gramma used to do with Anna.

James said, "I'm sure you will succeed in bringing her attention to what you do. I'll start to think about a specialty for you later. Right now I have to get back to work. That bird isn't going to stand at attention much longer."

James turned his attention to Jake, "Don't forget your plan for John today. It's his turn to talk about angels."

"I know, he will." Jake could always count on John to do as he told him.

Buffy felt sorry for Isaac. "Some day Grampa will know how much you help him. You'll see."

"I'm really anxious for that day, my friend. But most of all, I can't wait to see the look on his face when he sees I'm black. I'll get plenty of satisfaction then." Isaac smiled broadly. His pearly white teeth sparkled next to his dark skin.

"Are you mad at him for being so prejudiced?"

"Not at all, Buffy. I love him with every ounce of my being. It's just going to be funny. As far as his prejudiced behavior," he winked at her, "I'm still working on changing that. I think I have a plan that'll work and it's not too far off in the future."

James announced that everyone should pay attention.

Henri and his grampa played intently at their game of checkers. It was Henri's move and instead of taking it, he felt an uncontrollable urge to look toward the window and stared momentarily without saying a word.

Finding his voice, he exclaimed, "That's Gramma's bird! The same one she showed me one day! It sat on her windowsill to remind her about the angels. She told me a long time ago that when she died, her angel would send a bird to let us know she's happy in Heaven. Do you think her angel sent it? She said the birds bring us comfort from God."

They all watched the yellow bird sitting so patiently on the sill. Tears streamed down Grampa's face, and Mary's too. Everyone knew that it was most unusual for a goldfinch to be in this part of the country. No one said a word.

John spoke, "It's true, everything Gramma ever said about the angels is true. I know it for a fact because mine has helped me through every day of my life."

He finally shared his story about Jake. All of them listened closely as he revealed some of his most hidden secrets concerning him and Jake. A few of the stories brought sadness and tears flowed in the room. The bird remained on the sill as he talked. Time seemed to stand still.

John finished by telling them always to thank the angels for their help. Silence pervaded the room when he finished. The ringing of the phone startled them.

John answered and after hanging up, he related the news to his family. It was a job! He would be starting in two days, on the second shift and it was at the one place he really wanted to work. The factory looked clean and the pay would be good.

"If I leave in the morning," he looked hopefully to his wife, "I can start looking for a place for us to live. Do you think you'll be okay, Mary?"

He glanced to Henri and then to Grampa whose head was hanging. "The timing is bad, I know." He didn't want them to feel he was abandoning them.

"We'll all be fine, John." Mary was relieved to know John had a job, but still found it hard to smile.

Lifting his head Grampa said, "John, you have to leave, we understand that. You have a family to take care of. I'll help Mary. Don't be worrying about us."

John, grateful for his words, said with enthusiasm, "I'll look for a house with three bedrooms, and a place outside for Mary's clothesline. And of course, Grampa will need a space to put his garden."

Grampa quickly replied, "Hold on John, don't be making plans for me. I'll stay with Mary and Henri until you return, but I can't make any promises about leaving town. I'm not up to it."

They weren't about to pressure him now, but knew he'd leave with them when the time came. They wouldn't have it any other way.

"I can't wait for us to be together again," said Henri. "I'll miss you, Dad."

John took Henri in his arms. "I'll miss you too, son. I won't be gone long."

"I know. I'm going to ask Jake to help you find a house. You'll find one fast."

"You can ask your angel too, Henri."

"Mine can't leave me. Jake will have to do it alone."

"You're right about that, I would prefer he stay here with you. And don't forget, you're going back to school tomorrow. You've had enough time off. No more pretending that you're sick."

Henri wondered how people older than him always knew 'stuff.' "I hate school now. Nothing's the same. So many of my friends are gone and I'll never see Corey again now that his dad found a job across the country. Why should I even bother going back? Some of the teachers are gone and we'll be leaving anyway."

"Henri, please just do as I say. I know how painful it will be with your best friend gone, but you'll see. Things will get better. We have a big adventure ahead of us."

"I know dad. I'm sorry I'm so much trouble sometimes." He looked to his dad for pity but didn't get any, just a hug from his mom.

Grampa decided he should give them some private time and stepped out the back door. Reaching into his back pocket, he pulled out his pipe, packed it with tobacco and lit it. Looking around wasn't necessary anymore, but he thought about his wife as he inhaled. Hating his life without her, he wondered if the horrible pain would ever go away. He watched as the smoke drifted off with the wind and wished he could float away with it. The endless stream of tears fell from his eyes once again. Pulling a crumpled hankie from his pocket, he wiped them away.

The thought of moving depressed him further. Silently he murmured, "What's the difference where I live now? I'll never be the same no matter where I am."

Thoughts of his wife's lecturing popped into his mind. "Selfish thoughts," she called them, "put others first. You'll find little time left to feel sorry for yourself." The voice in his head seemed so real, as if she were with him. Knowing this to be impossible he still promised to try harder. He just wished his family would stop acting so concerned about him. He hated it.

Grampa thought about how Henri stared at him constantly. "Scared to death I might die too," he said aloud. Drawing in deeply on his pipe, he decided he'd try not to wish himself dead again. To crawl in a hole somewhere and never come out sounded like the perfect solution sometimes. He knew what his wife's feelings would be about that too, and it wasn't good.

Faking a small smile, he returned to the house. That smile did wonders for the family. Grampa watched as the yellow bird left the window sill and wondered if the ache would ever leave too.

****

The last light in the household dimmed as the family retired for the evening. The angels lounged around, conversing softly. James floated up to his favorite position, lying above the others, in midair, with hands behind his head. His face reflected total satisfaction as he stated, "This was one of those rare, perfect days, everything fell into place according to our plans. What a great day!"

T.J. agreed. "It sure was. All family members drifted off to sleep much easier tonight."

"It was a good day," Buffy added. "Mary's happy about John's job. She still feels afraid to be left alone, but

she understands that it's temporary. I personally think she's getting much stronger. Do you?"

Seeing the others agree with her, she wondered what James thought, but could only see his back side as he floated above them.

"What do you think, James? I can't see your face, you know."

"She's doing exceptionally well, Buf." He continued to stare off contentedly.

Buffy, pleased with his comment said, "I've been trying really hard with her. It isn't easy you know. Our life was so much fun before all of this misery started."

She recalled a few of the exciting things they used to do and then said, "I can't remember one single day that we worried about anything. Finding something interesting to entertain us was about all we had to think about. I gave her such good ideas."

She sighed, "We had so much fun. I miss all of my angel friends that moved away too. Maybe I'll look them up when we can go to meetings again. We had so many good times together."

"You knew it wouldn't stay that way Buf," said Jake. "I can't think of one person on earth that has a totally enjoyable life."

"I know Jake. I only said it was such fun back then. I'll help Mary laugh again, when we get to the big city. There has to be a few activities that we'll enjoy together. I'll help her find a busy exercise club with lots of people running around. She'd love that, she hasn't exercised in a long time. It'll help her mind drift away from her troubles, and we'll meet so many new friends."

Buffy gazed wistfully off into space, visualizing the great time she would have in the big city, when all the problems were over.

James turned over, looking down at her. "I hate to ruin your happy thoughts, but I think we should spend more time thinking of how we can better protect these people. It's going to be mighty rough in the big city, Buf. We've talked about that. You can't have her running around freely like she did here. It's going to be dangerous. You do understand that?"

"I do."

Her dreams dissolved. She remembered his earlier words of warning and said, "I'll think of something we can do at home. I don't know what it'll be, though. Mary hates needlepoint or anything that relates to sitting still. For that matter, so do I."

"T.J.," said James, "tell Buffy what you know about the big city."

T.J. rolled his eyes. It was the same big city he'd worked on during his last assignment. "Buffy, you had better forget about venturing out to exercise clubs. None of you will believe it when you see it. It's rough. Go with your guard up and prepare yourself for the worst. The enemy is out in full force and because of the widespread use of illegal drugs, they are succeeding with their bad works. People are turning to evil left and right."

He paused. They saw his emotions rising. "My last mission started there. I would prefer not to talk about it today. I failed miserably and it still bothers me."

Not one of the angels dared to ask him about it. Something awful must have happened to leave him in such a state. They asked more about the drug scene. Horror struck them further when they learned that young children now indulged in this deplorable past-time. At the end of the conversation, T.J. had them convinced that trouble lurked ahead.

****

Chapter 12

*T*he fourth day of December showed no mercy. Strong winds blew snow around the moving van, making it nearly impossible for the movers to do their job. Mary stood at the window watching them struggle. Every time they tried to load a box, a gust of wind pushed them in the opposite direction. An odd feeling clung to her, like maybe something was trying to stop them from doing the job.

The kitchen door whipped open and the wind pushed the workers through. Mary offered the half-frozen men a cup of coffee. They accepted gratefully, eager for a break before venturing back outside.

"I almost feel that this bad weather is an omen," said Mary nervously. "Like something's trying to tell us we shouldn't be moving."

Henri entered the kitchen and couldn't take his eyes off one of the frozen men. Ice coated the strands of hair extending beyond his stocking cap and his lips were swollen to twice their normal size from the cold. He could barely move them as he said to Mary, "This is typical winter weather, Ma'am. Just a brief storm. Trust me. This isn't an omen. After everything I've heard about this town, you're lucky to be gitten' out alive. Won't be long b'fore everyone left here'll be droppin' dead from the water. It's good you're leaving."

The man then slurped loudly from his coffee cup and wiped the swollen lips on his jacket sleeve. Noticing Henri staring at his mouth, he said, "My lips swell in cold weather, sonny. It grosses me out too."

"Henri, don't stare!" Mary hated it when he stared at people. But this guy did look funny.

The man said, "It's okay." He then told them, "You'll love the big city. There's lots' of action, if you know what I mean. Well heck, just the other night...."

John entered the room and interrupted him. He wasn't sure where the conversation would go, and didn't want to take the chance of the man frightening his family. "Look out the window, guys. Looks like the weather's cleared a little."

They did just that and saw the wind had died down and the snow stopped falling. The workers ended their break and walked out the door with the sofa. They finished their job easily in the calmer weather and were soon on their way. The family stood in the empty living room watching as the van pulled out of the driveway.

Staring at the bare walls, not one of them wanted to say, "let's go." Grampa spoke, "It's time to leave the misery behind and get on with our lives." He started for the door; the others followed.

Henri and his family took one last look at the vacant house as they drove away. Not one of them talked as the car made its way down the street that they had lived on. No tears were shed as each person sat with their own private thoughts.

They passed Old Man Jenkins shuffling toward his mailbox. With his head bent down, his arms held his coat shut to protect himself from the cold. The family heard of his refusal to leave Pleasant Valley and their hearts went out to him. His coat fell open when he waved goodbye. He quickly covered himself and looked away.

Henri turned to glance out the back window and watched as the figure of the old man faded from view. He wiped hot tears from his eyes and swallowed hard. Old man Jenkins looked pathetic. Henri knew he would die back there all alone. The car made a left hand turn, bringing them onto the road that would take them away from Pleasant Valley and into the big city.

The family rode in silence for the first few miles. Grampa sat with his eyes closed, pretending to be asleep. His stomach churned as he mournfully recalled the wretched loneliness that consumed him when he returned briefly to his own empty house. It took only seconds to gather the few belongings he wished to take with him. The house was dark and so miserably silent as he wandered through each room. Memories flooded back to him in giant waves. To end the torment, he quickly gathered a few of his belongings and left them in a pile on the floor. John picked up his possessions later that day.

Grampa repositioned himself in the car in an effort to shake the thoughts away. Trying hard to think about nothing proved to be impossible. He felt miserable about having to live with his children and even though he loved them dearly, he believed that young families shouldn't have to take care of their parents. They didn't need an old man hanging around. But he had no choice, they would not allow him to stay back there. If they could have sold their houses, there would have been money to find either a larger house, or two separate homes. But no one would buy a home in Pleasant Valley. Again he tried to push all thoughts aside. This time it worked and he fell asleep.

John drove in silence; trying to find the right words to tell his family once again of the dangers in the city. Not wanting to terrify them, he knew that strong warnings were necessary. He began the conversation by telling Mary he wanted to discuss the importance of being cautious.

"It's a big change, moving from a small town to a big city. The neighborhood where we'll be living is not the safest, but it's better than others. Hopefully, we won't have to stay there long."

Mary tried to make light of the situation, "Oh, John, stop worrying so much. You've already talked about this and sometimes I think you are totally ignorant of what we do know. Don't forget, we did have a TV and we even watched a few crime stories. People steal and get murdered. We promised you we wouldn't go out after dark."

More seriously, she said, "What about you? Isn't it dangerous walking out to your car after work? It's dark at midnight. Do you lock your doors? I heard criminals hide in the back seat waiting to attack when the owner comes back to his car."

"I lock the doors. Someone was mugged in our parking lot and the employees usually walk out together now. We watch out for each other."

"Stop worrying John, we'll learn how to be safe. Don't forget, we have guardian angels to help us."

Henri's ears perked up at the mention of angels. "I'll bet they'll be just like that super-hero on TV. The one that saves everyone. Our angel will probably come swooping down just like him if anyone tries to get us!"

His dad said, "I'll bet they're a lot like him, Henri. I know they try their hardest to keep us safe. But we still have to keep our eyes open, to help them with their jobs."

"I'll keep mine open," Henri began to fantasize. "I'll bet I do have a super angel. He's probably the strongest one around."

He imagined how his own angel might be and envisioned him flying through the air holding a sword, daring anyone to harm the boy he was watching over. The picture of what his angel might look like comforted him.

John talked more about the house he rented. There were only two bedrooms and no place for Grampa to have a garden or Mary to have her clothesline. He hadn't signed a lease because he was sure this would only be temporary.

109

Mary knew John wanted things to be better for them. The worry of the neighborhood weighed heavily on his mind despite everything she tried to say to make him feel better.

Rubbing his arm, she said, "With the super angels on our side, we'll be just fine. I'm happy we're together again and you're right. This will be an adventure."

Pointing toward the landscape, she made an effort to divert his attention. "Just look at how lovely the hills look. The freshly fallen snow makes everything look so fresh and clean."

The countryside did look beautiful. They enjoyed seeing the different neighborhoods and the expanse of land in between. This was a new experience for them. They had never done any extensive traveling together. Pleasant Valley had provided everything they needed to keep busy.

Hours down the highway brought them closer to the outskirts of the big city.

Henri said, "These streets are getting wider. Why do they have to be so big?"

His father explained about the expressways, and how the pavement had to be extra wide to handle all the cars. "Sometimes they are called freeways and this one will turn into six lanes as we approach the city. The traffic isn't too heavy right now, but it gets much worse at five o'clock when everyone gets out of work and heads for home."

He looked at his watch. "It won't be long now. Hopefully we won't get caught up in the rush hour."

The traffic increased as they entered the depths of the big city. Henri's eyes grew large as he watched the cars speeding past them. Weaving in and out of traffic, it looked as though they were racing each other. His mother hung onto the door handle. She eventually closed her eyes. Grampa, still asleep in the back seat, had no idea of the terror that began to grip them.

"I guess everyone's getting out of work." John watched the highway intently. No one saw his hands shake as he held them firmly on the steering wheel.

"John! Please. Slow down!" Mary became almost hysterical.

John reduced his speed and the results were even more frightening. Horns began blasting away at them. People driving the fast-moving cars gave them angry stares as they shook their fists and made odd gestures with their hands. John found himself becoming unnerved. Quickly finding an exit, he turned off, having no idea where it would take him. Fortunately, he spotted a mall, drove to it, and pulled into the parking lot. He and the others stared straight ahead in a daze, following the abrupt halt.

Finally able to speak, John said, "That was an adventure right there. My first time deep in the city, traveling with the five o'clock traffic. Let this be your first lesson, Mary. Do all of your driving before everyone leaves work."

Visibly upset, she said, "It's going to be a miracle if I ever drive again!"

Grampa woke up. "Are we here?"

"No," said John. "We decided to stretch our legs. We're going to walk around this mall for a while and find ourselves a bite to eat."

"A mall?" Henri anxiously opened the car door. "I've heard about malls, but I've never seen one."

His dad was anxious to show them because there were no malls in Pleasant Valley. "Well then, let's go in and have a look around. You'll like it."

Piling out of the car, they headed for the door that led them inside. Trying to see everything at once, Henri said, "What a great place to shop when it rains! This is like being downtown in a big building."

The change of scenery relaxed them and they strolled leisurely from store to store. Mary became excited to know she could spend a day getting all of her shopping done in one spectacular place like this. She spotted a grocery store and hoped there would be a mall in her own new neighborhood. But of course, it would have to be far away from that dreadful expressway.

Henri glanced up at the tall ceiling one more time and when he did he bumped into someone accidentally.

"Hey, watch where you're going, kid! Do you think you own this place or something?" The strange looking guy he ran into looked furious and continued to glare at Henri as he walked over to join his friends.

Mary protectively took Henri's hand and motioned to Grampa and John to sit on a vacant bench nearby. She pointed to a waterfall not far from them, hoping to draw their attention away from the peculiar looking group.

Henri stared at the strange looking person he ran into. He now stood with his friends next to a soda fountain and they all looked odd. One had purple hair, and another green. Each one of them had a weird hair-do and wore what looked like earrings all over their faces. He couldn't even tell if they were boys or girls. The voice of the guy he bumped into sounded deep, so he knew he was a boy. Two of the kids had no hair at all.

Henri pointed in their direction. "What's wrong with them? That one has hair sticking out all over. He must use hair spray. Or is it a she?"

Whispering, his mother said, "Stop staring, Henri! They might be 'punk rockers.' I saw some on a TV talk show. Or they could be kids that belong to gangs. Don't look at them, they could be dangerous."

Henri softly said, "Do I have to fix up like that while I live here? I'd shave my head, then no one would call me 'carrot top' ever again."

"Don't even think about it! You don't have to be like them. I'm sure there are only certain groups of kids looking like that."

"I thought we were going to eat," said Grampa.

"Let's get out of here." John led them to a restaurant nearby. The menu hung on the outside wall and when they attempted to check it over, they realized it was written in a foreign language.

"I think we'd better look elsewhere," John said.

They found a place that served hamburgers and after their meal, were back on the road again. John checked out his map before leaving the parking lot and feeling secure about his directions, drove comfortably down the expressway. The traffic had thinned out and all passengers were able to relax. Grampa closed his eyes again, while Mary and Henri watched as John pointed out places of interest.

Tall buildings stood out against the evening skyline. John named a few, explaining that they were called high-rises. Henri tried to see the tops and wondered where they ended.

Driving further downtown, they saw groups of people standing around on the street corners. Henri and his mother found it strange to see many people out after dark. In Pleasant Valley, almost everyone watched television after dinner. Especially in the winter, they stayed inside to keep warm.

"What are these people doing, Dad? Why are they standing out in the cold? It doesn't look like they're going into the buildings to shop. I think the stores are closed."

"They just sort of hang out here. Some don't have homes, and the rest of them hang around visiting with their friends."

"They have no homes? Where do they sleep?"

"Just a few are homeless. They sleep wherever they can find a place. Park benches, old boxes, and some sleep on sidewalks."

Mary was appalled. "I saw this type of thing on the news, but it seemed so far away, not in the same city where we'll be living! We'll have to try to help."

Henri thought about the problem. "Why can't the people owning the stores let them sleep inside at night? Or what about that church over there? Our church back home would let them sleep on the benches. They always give clothes and food to the needy."

John said, "I think a few of the churches open their doors for sleeping when the temperature drops way down. There are also shelters where they can sleep."

Mary was grateful that her family had a home waiting for them. She had no idea what it looked like, but knew there would be warmth. It broke her heart to think of homeless people, but to see them was even worse.

Henri pointed to buildings with bars on the windows. "Hey Dad, look! There are jails everywhere!"

His dad explained that the buildings were just ordinary stores. The bars were to keep the thieves from breaking in. He hated telling Henri about this; it was depressing.

"The thieves are supposed to be in jails, Dad, not the good people. That doesn't seem fair."

"It isn't." John didn't tell him that some homes had bars on their windows too. With crime at an all time high, people were scared just living in their homes.

"Let's talk about something else, John." Goose bumps ran up and down Mary's arms. The tales of the big city were fast becoming a fact.

Henri sat back and closed his eyes. He visualized his mighty super-angel again. A smile crossed his face as he watched him swoop down with his large sword. The angel fought off a group of bad people that were trying to get him. Henri imagined him saying, "I'll save you always, Henri. Never fear, I am here!"

He felt safe. The angel became similar to his dad's imaginary friend. Henri believed the hero in his mind was indeed his very own guardian angel. He thought it would be neat if his super angel would open all the church doors. Then the poor people could go inside to keep warm anytime they wanted. He fell asleep knowing his angel would help.

Henri hadn't slept long when his mother called out to wake him and his grampa. They were sitting in the driveway of their new home. John opened the car doors for them to get out. It was dark and hard to see, but Henri saw well enough to know the house looked okay. Looking to the houses next door worried him though, because they were much too close to each other. He knew he could never walk between them and worse than that, if one caught on fire, all of them would burn.

"Come on, Henri, hurry." His dad opened the front door and flipped the light switch on.

Mary liked the house. "This is nice, John. You said it was shabby." She explored each room, telling them where each piece of furniture would be placed.

Satisfied that the home would be adequate, the family left for the closest motel. Their plan was to stay for one night. They would meet the movers in the morning and put their belongings in order as soon as possible. The next day promised to be a busy day.

The motel they chose appeared to be quiet and cozy. Henri went into the office with his dad to see if they had two rooms. While his dad registered and paid, Henri looked around in the lobby. The large room had lots of plants and a long desk. He'd never seen a motel lobby before and felt proud to be there with his dad. His dad let him carry the keys. They returned to the car to get his mom and Grampa, then hauled their suitcases out of the trunk.

Henri opened the door to room 53 and was first to see the large bedroom with a television. John told him to open another door to find the room where he and Grampa would sleep. Henri did, but it was a bathroom.

"The other door, Henri." His dad set the luggage down. Henri tried the door but it was locked. They had to go out in the hallway to unlock the door to the next room.

Upon entering, Henri saw two big beds, "Look dad, me and Grampa have our own beds!" He jumped on the first bed, announcing that Grampa could have the other one. His dad opened the adjoining door and everyone made themselves comfortable as they settled in for the evening.

It didn't take long for the family to fall asleep that night. The excitement and long ride had exhausted them. Even Grampa, after his many naps, slept soundly once again.

Minutes later, they woke to the shrill screaming of many sirens. The noise pierced their ears and frightened them out of their wits. John ordered his wife to stay in bed as he rushed to the window to look. "There are police cars everywhere!"

Mary panicked when she saw all the flashing lights and hopped out of bed. She nearly flew to check on Henri and her dad.

Her dad stood frantically at the window, "What on earth is going on?"

"I have no idea. Henri . . ." She looked to his bed and saw a lump under the covers.

Her body shook as she went over to him; she tried to stay calm. "Don't be frightened Henri. Your dad's finding out what happened. We'll be okay. Dad, come sit with Henri. I'll go see if John found out anything."

Mary returned to John's side and listened as he talked on the phone. Whomever he spoke with, told him that the desk clerk had been shot by someone trying to rob him. The ambulance rushed the injured man to the hospital. No one knew anything more. Hanging up the receiver, he related the details to Mary and the two of them went to tell the others.

Mary crawled into bed with Henri and held onto him for dear life. John squeezed into the same bed and they worried themselves to sleep. They woke the next morning to find out that the nice desk clerk had died.

Arriving at their new home, they were tired and distraught. The movers pulled in behind them. Smiling broadly, the man with long hair asked how their first night in the big city turned out.

"Some guy at the motel got murdered!" Henri anxiously announced. "It was awful. There were police cars all over the place and the murderer got away!"

His dad changed the subject by asking if they knew of a restaurant close by serving breakfast. The mover directed them to a small cafe a few blocks up the street.

"Look for the drugstore called Abe's. You'll find the restaurant next to it. They got good chow."

The mover was glad to send them on their way, because he feared he would say something to upset them further. These people reminded him of a show he used to watch on television about a family of hillbillies that shared the same experience of moving to the big city from a small town. His heart went out to these seemingly innocent people that were forced to change their lifestyles so drastically, but in the same breath he was happy to know they wouldn't die from poisoned water. He and his buddy began unloading the family's personal possessions from the truck.

Henri and his family had no problem finding the restaurant. They were eager to be seated in the friendly little place.

John said, "We have to forget what happened last night and get on with what we must do. Today is going to be a busy day for all of us."

"You're right about that." Mary picked up the menu. "I'm starved." She hungrily looked it over and decided to have a large helping of pancakes. The others ordered the same. A friendly waitress came over and poured their coffee. Henri watched as she rapidly chewed her gum. It looked to him like it would come flying out of her mouth any moment and she never stopped chewing when she asked for their order. His mother's expression warned him to stop staring.

Stirring the cream into his coffee, John told Henri that as soon as they put the house in order, they would find out where he'd be going to school.

"We can't wait too long. You've already missed a lot of school. Can't have you repeating third grade."

Henri was afraid to start a new school. He couldn't even imagine what it would be like. "First I have to get used to living in a big city."

"You'll get used to both at the same time, Henri. It won't be easy going to a strange school, but you'll be fine. I was nervous when I first started my new job, but I found plenty of nice people working there. The same thing will happen for you, just wait and see." He stirred his coffee once again and took a sip.

"If anyone calls me carrot top, I'm going to leave," he said firmly.

The waitress appeared above them smiling broadly and still chomping on her gum. Carrying a large tray loaded down with their breakfast, she swiftly passed each person their plate.

Mary complimented her on the quick service and began putting generous portions of butter and syrup on the stack of pancakes sitting before her. Feeling satisfied after the first bite, she began telling Henri how the kids at school used to make fun of her shoes, calling them 'big brown boats.'

"Your Gramma bought my shoes a size larger than I really took. She said I'd wear them longer because my feet grew so fast. They were clumsy, brown, Girl Scout shoes and I hated them. The kids laughed and pointed at my feet."

"I didn't know kids were mean in the olden days," said Henri. "Why did you have to wear Girl Scout shoes? Were you a Girl Scout?"

"No. Mother told me the shoes gave me good arch support. I wasn't supposed to care what the kids said. She said I should learn from their behavior, and never make fun of anyone. I learned, but it was still awful having them laugh at me."

Mary's eyes narrowed as she glanced toward her dad. She remembered how he agreed with her mom. She begged him to buy her black shiny shoes like the other girls wore, but he wouldn't do it.

Grampa saw her scowling expression and definitely recalled the incident. "At least you have good decent feet to walk on now. Be thankful she made you wear them." He continued eating.

"They aren't healthy at all, Dad. I have corns and bunions. When I was old enough to buy my own shoes, I bought cute ones that were smaller than my size because I hated how big my feet looked. I ruined my feet. Walking through that mall today, I would have given anything to have those old brown shoes again. My feet were killing me."

Grampa displayed his all-knowing look.

When they were nearly finished with their meal, a bald headed man came to their table. "My name is Abe and I own the drugstore next to this restaurant. I saw this young fella's red hair and had to come over."

He rubbed his bald head. "Believe it or not, I had that same color hair at one time and it was just as curly. I lost all of it when I was twenty-one and it never grew back."

His eyes twinkled as he spoke to Henri, remembering when he was young and how much he too, hated his hair.

Henri liked the nice man. Nevertheless, he still wanted another color and wondered if the kids had teased him too. He didn't ask. Nor did he ask how the man lost his hair. Instead he gave him a forced smile.

John introduced his family to Abe, telling him they'd be living just a few blocks up the street. Abe then spoke mainly to Grampa and told him to come over to the store and "shoot the breeze" with him sometime. Grampa's face brightened and he said he would be delighted to stop by. He liked Abe, and was happy to have a new friend.

Leaving the restaurant, John told Henri he'd find many nice people like Abe at school. "Not quite as old, but nice."

Henri still didn't want to go to the new school.

****

The angels looked on as the family members put their house in order.

"Pretty rough night," said T.J. knowingly. "It's too bad they were terrorized on their first night in the big city. I told you it would be like this. You all still look shook up. Quite a shock, right James?"

"That's for sure. What a difference from the last time I lived here. 'High rises' weren't even heard of back then. It's wild out there now. Almost unbelievable. That's one big battle going on."

Isaac's eyes grew huge when they mentioned the previous night. Only the whites of his eyes showed against his black skin as he exclaimed in horror, "It's a war zone! Our fellow angels are engaged in down right combat with the other side! I can see how they have their hands full trying to save their people from the clutches of evil. I realize this type of war has been going on for ages. I've seen a few battles myself, but never of this size!"

Buffy appeared calm considering all that had happened. She wasn't going to let any of them know the sheer terror she felt. "I heard all about this stuff from a friend of mine who lives in a big city with her charge."

She spoke softly as she filed her nails. "My friend said that she had 'warrior' angels helping her. We'll probably have to get some too. I'll send a telegram to God soon. He'll want to know how bad it is here."

"As if He doesn't know!" She was getting on Isaac's nerves. "Don't you recall James saying that God has had just about enough?"

Now her eyes showed the fright she was trying to conceal. "Isaac, don't be so upset! I just want Him to know we need help! My friend said the warrior angels are much stronger and are specially trained for conflicts such as these. We need them now!"

James felt their panic, but he also knew that this neighborhood was fairly safe. "Settle down, you two. Are you forgetting that we're angels? God said we could ask for help, but I hardly think we need it at this moment."

Buffy said, "Our fear is for our charges, not ourselves!"

James answered, "You're a strong angel, Buf. We'll all be fine. It's not as bad in this area, but I think you had better forget about any exercise classes in the heart of the big city."

Jake wanted to help calm her. "God knows about the big city. If you find yourself in a dangerous situation, He's only a beep away. A "warrior" can be here in a split second. Try to keep Mary on safe ground. You shouldn't have to be worried."

Buffy looked hopeful. "Maybe I can get Mary interested in needlepoint! Or perhaps sewing. We won't mind staying home."

The other angels found it hard to believe she really meant what she said. But she did and at that moment silently promised herself that she'd never let Mary out of the house, much less out of her sight.

James said, "There will be plenty of safe places to go. You'll see. Mary isn't going to go running back to the area that frightened her." Buffy took a deep breath and squinted her eyes. Her lips tightened as she said, "If she does, I'll send for those stronger angels immediately. They aren't going to get her!"

James suggested they take out their manuals if they had them. "The chapter on Winning the Battle should be helpful. It won't hurt to brush up on our skills. I can send for extra copies if any of you are without yours. When the pick-up angel stops for the charts, we can have her drop the books off."

Isaac said he was already reviewing his. The others needed one.

"I wish I had become a 'Warrior' angel," said Buffy, "I'll bet they are mighty and never get scared. We'll probably get to see some up close."

James hid a grin. He wouldn't tell her that being afraid was normal for an angel sometimes. Especially being new at the job, she had much to learn.

He remembered well. "I would reckon we'll see plenty of the warrior angels. Study your manual, Buffy. You'll have a copy in your hands at the end of the day tomorrow. There are many good tips in the book. Forgetting safety guidelines when we lived in Pleasant Valley came easy."

"Those were the good old days," said Buffy, rolling her eyes.

"You'll be okay. Like I said, you are a strong angel. You wouldn't be here if God thought you couldn't handle the job."

Her mood changed to that of sophistication. "I'm just teasing, James. Honestly. I'm ready, but I'll glance over the book again, anyway."

The others wanted to laugh but held it back.

Isaac held his manual and began questioning his coworkers. They made a game out of the quiz, pretending to be back in training.

Speaking as a teacher would, Isaac reminded them, "And no visible actions." He looked directly at Buffy. "That means, like when you tripped Mr. Johnson."

Buffy said smartly, "Certain things are allowed." She was not going to allow him to embarrass her.

Her eyes quickly darted to the others and she said defiantly, "We can move things if no one's watching. I saw

Anna move Gramma's glasses once when she couldn't find them. And maybe I did it once or twice for Mary. No one in the family saw me do it and neither did any of you."

Jake said, "I know about one incident. When Mary took off her ring to clean vegetables, she accidentally threw it out with the scraps. You pulled it out of the garbage for her."

"You weren't even there!"

"Anna told me. She saw you take the ring out of the garbage and put it on the floor near the stove. You knew Mary would find it and think she dropped it on the floor."

Buffy's hands went to her hips, "Well, she was so upset when she couldn't find the ring! She prayed hard for help! I had to do something!"

Isaac said, "There's nothing wrong with that, Buf. Don't get so uptight. You did it well and no one saw you. A 'smooth move,' I'd call it. Anna said your efforts to mentally tell Mary failed."

"That's true. She was so upset she couldn't receive my message."

James told her he'd have done the same thing. He asked Isaac to tell them about his friend they met at the restaurant.

"Old Abe's guardian angel. What a surprise it was to see him!" Isaac told of the days when they worked together. "He's a good friend. When he saw Henri's red hair, it reminded him of Abe when he was young. He asked me if Henri hated his too. When I said he did, he prompted Abe over."

James felt grateful for what Isaac's friend did. "It also helped Grampa, a new friend will help him adjust to his new life and will help to ease some of his pain."

James realized each member of the family needed new friends. Finding them would be the next major project for the angels.

124

"How did Abe lose all his hair?" Buffy asked Isaac.
"Stress. His parents and only brother died in a house
fire. Abe was away at the time. He suffered such shock
when he heard, his hair fell out and never grew back."
"That's just awful." Buffy asked Isaac if he could
tell some stories about when he and his friend used to work
together. Isaac was more than pleased to tell a few tales
from days gone by.

****

Chapter 13

*T*he day arrived when Henri had to return to school. In the early morning he stood with his parents before the principal of the largest school they'd ever seen. Mary and John answered all of the necessary questions and presented records from the last school he attended. When finished, the principal called a girl from the outer office to escort him to his new classroom. Leaving the principal's office with her, Henri turned back to give his parents another pleading look.

"It'll be okay," said his mother reassuringly. That was all Mary could say to him as she held back tears. She watched as Henri held onto the girl's hand and walked down the long corridor.

She and John were leaving the building when she couldn't go any further. "I hate this, John. The poor little thing. I can just imagine how he must feel."

Mary held her mouth to keep herself from crying. "I feel as frightened as he does."

Taking John's hand, she pulled him out of the building, toward the car. Then she abruptly stopped. Not able to hold back this time, she began sobbing hysterically.

"He'll be fine, Mary. This experience will help Henri. It's just one of the many hard things he'll have to do in his lifetime."

Mary shouted, "I happen to think he's had enough learning experiences for a while! We all have! Enough is enough!"

Tears welled from her eyes. John had no soothing words for her. He too felt the same burdens, and knew the same pain.

Quieting down somewhat, she softly said, "All I can see is that skinny little red-haired kid walking down that big corridor scared to death. He's too young to have had so many bad experiences. He's just a child." She started crying again.

They stood in the parking lot with her sobbing and John holding her. A man walked by and asked if he could do anything to help. John solemnly shook his head no and the man walked away, looking back once.

John knew she needed a good cry and didn't care what anyone thought. He was proud of how strong she'd become, and knew she held her grief inside to protect the others. When she quieted down, they walked hand in hand to the car.

Mary said, "I finally found out what 'hard times' means. I really never understood when Mother talked about them. My life was so easy. As I look back, it seems like a thousand years ago. Is this what everyone calls growing up? Is that what's happening to me?"

"Maybe so." He helped her into the car.

"Well, I hate it. This is definitely not fun."

"I know." He started the engine. "It has to get better, Mary. It just has to. You'll see." He didn't sound too hopeful.

They stopped once on their way home. John found a flower shop and dodged inside. He returned carrying three red roses. Mary smiled fondly, her first impulse was to put them to her nose. "It's been a long time since I've smelled roses."

As they drove away, she talked about how much the fragrance of roses reminded her of the old life. The aroma of the beautiful flowers had filled her parent's home every summer. "Mom had to have rose bushes all over the yard and Dad picked them fresh for her daily. I miss her so much!"

Smiling wistfully, Mary inhaled the fragrance again, "This brings back such comforting memories, John. Thank-you." Hot tears warmed her cheeks once again.

Back at school, Henri met his teacher, Mr. Addison, and this was the first time he had ever seen a black person up close. He gave Henri a broad smile as he welcomed him to his third grade class. After introducing him to the other students, the nice teacher escorted Henri to his desk that sat at the end of the first row.

Henri watched as the other children craned their necks to stare at him. He just knew it was because of his red hair and hung his head.

In an effort to make Henri comfortable, the teacher continued with the lessons for the day. It worked because the children turned back around and watched him. Henri raised his head and looked down the long rows of kids. He noticed they represented many different nationalities.

A few looked tan. Some had white skin. There were many different shades of black and he could see two that looked like they were either Japanese or Chinese. He remembered seeing the same kind of people in his books at the other school.

Mr. Addison told everyone to open their math books to page 120. Henri opened his and felt bewildered.

"Henri," said Mr. Addison.

Everyone turned around to stare again.

"We'll have to discuss the chapter you were at in the book at your other school. I'm sure it won't be the same page or perhaps this is a different book. If you'll come to my desk when the lunch bell rings, we'll look over them together."

The teacher then continued with the lessons. The heads turned back around. Soon the lunch bell rang and he nearly fell off his chair. It rang much louder than the bell at his other school. He remained seated while the others left the room and then ventured down to Mr. Addison's desk.

The two of them found that Henri was further ahead in his studies than the others. Mr. Addison closed the books and set them aside. "At least you won't have to work extra hard to catch up. Come on, I'll show you where the lunch hall is."

Mr. Addison placed his arm around Henri's shoulder as they left the classroom. Henri felt good inside. The smell of pizza filled their nostrils as they headed down the hall to the lunch room.

Walking through the lunch line with Henri, the teacher showed him where to pick up his tray and utensils. The smiling lady serving lunch gave him two large slices of pizza and offered him green beans but, he shook his head 'no'. After choosing a beverage, Mr. Addison took him to a table where several children from his class sat.

Mr. Addison told Henri where to sit and visited briefly with everyone at the table. When the teacher saw that they included Henri in their conversation, he slipped away. Three of the girls were also new at the school. They'd been there only a month. Their names were Amanda, Alicia and Carrie.

Eager to befriend Henri, they told him how much they liked this school compared to their old one. The other children at the table were equally eager to talk with him. Randy and Joey asked if he liked to play baseball. When Henri said yes, they wanted him to sign up right away.

Henri was sure that a boy named Bobby would be his best friend. They lived on the same street and he said he'd show Henri which bus they rode. Henri explained that his mother planned to pick him up after school because of this being his first day. They planned to meet for the bus pick up in the morning and promised each other they'd ride together every day.

Near dismissal time, Henri's mother anxiously waited in the car outside of school, dreading to hear about his miserable day. When the school door bolted open, children burst through, spreading every which way in search of their ride home. It took a while before Mary spotted Henri. He came out of the building laughing with other children by his side. She got out got out of the car and headed toward him. Henri saw his mother and after saying a few words to the others, ran to meet her.

Mary saw his happy face and nearly started crying again as relief flooded over her. They walked back to the car together while he talked nonstop about the good day he had with all of his new friends. He couldn't say enough about his wonderful new teacher.

"He's the best, Mom! His name is Mr. Addison and he could tell how scared I was."

Henri told her everything the teacher had done to make him feel welcome. His mother listened intently, so grateful to the man who had been kind to her son. He was a changed little boy from the one she'd left in the morning.

"Guess what else?" Henri said. "He's black. And so is my new best friend."

He didn't feel afraid to tell her about him, but then said hesitantly, "Do you think we should tell Grampa? He hates black people. What if he won't let Bobby be my friend?"

"Your grampa doesn't hate black people, Henri. He doesn't even know any. The racial fighting on television upsets Grampa. That's when he says everyone should have stayed in their own country."

Henri said, "Grampa said that when the world was made, each kind of person had their own place to live. He showed me on the globe how large bodies of water separate the countries."

"I know the story," said Mary, well versed on the subject. "If they wouldn't have invented boats and planes, everyone would have stayed where they belonged, within their own boundaries."

She laughed aloud. "I think it's funny. Gramma used to get so mad when he talked about the boundaries."

"I'm happy boats and planes were invented. I like all the different people at my school. We even have oriental kids in our class. I'm not sure what they are but they all talked nice to me."

She patted his leg with her hand, "And I'm pleased about that. Don't you worry one bit about what Grampa might say about your friends. I'll take care of him."

When they walked into the house, Henri began telling Grampa about his great day. Mary caught her dad's reaction instantly. When Henri mentioned the black teacher and black friend, he looked at her with his eyebrow raised. That was always his concerned expression.

She threw her purse on the table and told him his attitude had to change. "People of every race live around here and they aren't going to move away because you have arrived! Henri is free to bring home anyone he wants; I trust his judgment. His friends, be they black, yellow, white, or red will always be welcome in our home. Hide in your room if you can't handle it!"

Her dad backed off when he saw her temper elevating. "You sound more like your mother every day, Mary."

Looking to Henri, he said, "Your little friend up the road, what's his name?"

"Bobby," came the small voice. "He's very nice. I know if you just talk to him you'll like him too."

"Don't you worry about it, Henri. I'll like him."

Mary could tell that was hard for her dad to say, but also knew she had to handle him sternly, just like her mother used to do. She whispered as he went out the back door for a smoke. "Thanks Dad, he was pretty scared to tell you about the black people."

Her dad didn't say anything. The door shut quietly behind him.

Returning moments later, he said that since he still had his coat on, he would run up to see Abe. Almost every day Grampa walked over to see his friend, always picking up a fresh gallon of drinking water from Abe's store after forbidding the family to drink water out of the tap.

Bobby came over the next day after school. Once introduced to Grampa, he chatted with him as if he'd known him all his life. Grampa was quite taken with the boy and didn't mind when Bobby followed him around asking questions.

"Does Henri have a dad? I forgot to ask him."

"Yes, he does. You'll have to meet him on the week-end though. His dad works the second shift."

Henri watched happily as his grampa and Bobby became friends. One day, Bobby asked Grampa and Mary if he could bring his parents over to meet them. With permission granted, he brought them over after dinner that same evening. Grampa acted a little nervous, but along with Mary and Henri, greeted them gracefully.

Bobby introduced his mother as Opal, and his father, Tyrone. They appeared to be pleasant and both families agreed that they should know each other if the boys were going to be friends.

Mary served coffee. She and Opal became fast friends, as did Grampa and Tyrone. He and Tyrone discussed everything from politics to what their favorite foods were. When Tyrone began a conversation about their neighborhood, Grampa became uncomfortable.

"This is not one of the safest neighborhoods, but it's better than most. God only knows how hard I've been trying to find a safe place for my family to live. People of our color are not welcome in many nicer areas, you know. Despite the laws against discrimination, there are still those that try their best to keep us out. But I'm still looking." Tyrone looked hopeful.

Grampa felt bad. He liked Tyrone and could tell how concerned he was about moving his family to a safer area. Because of this man, he silently vowed he'd be less judgmental in the future. He was glad Tyrone didn't know about some of his previous statements. But as his friend talked on, he feared his former feelings could be read all over his face. Grampa wished the conversation with Tyrone would change to something else.

Tyrone warned, "We just have to remember always to keep the doors locked. Anything could happen. Only a half mile from here, they are vandalizing homes now. Crime is spreading rapidly. There's no doubt about it."

Looking directly into Grampa's eyes, he continued, "And I must add, the police caught a few of the vandals. It seems they are both black and white."

Grampa squirmed in his seat. He didn't know how to take what Tyrone said. His body perspired heavily and he couldn't stop his face from turning red. Relief washed over him when he saw that Mary wasn't looking his way.

Tyrone sensed his uneasiness, but didn't appear bothered. He asked, "Do you play cribbage?"

Grateful for the diversion, Grampa eagerly replied, "Sure do. I'll get the board. We can play in the kitchen."

Rushing off to get the game, he almost tripped on a scatter rug. Grampa became furious with himself when he realized how he really reacted to Tyrone's question. When asked whether he played cribbage, it astounded Grampa that a black man knew how to play. He wanted to kick himself for thinking it. A nervous wreck now, when he opened the end of the board to get the stored pegs, they spilled to the floor. His hands shook as he attempted to gather the black and white pegs.

Tyrone entered the room and his voice startled him further. "Let me help you with those."

133

He knelt beside Grampa and began picking up the pegs for him.

"Many black people where you used to live?" Tyrone asked, a bit amused.

"Actually, no." Grampa cleared his throat. He knew the man could see right through him.

They stood now and Tyrone held out the hand that held the pegs. With a grin on his face, he asked, "Black or white?"

Grampa turned shades of red again. Choosing the black pegs, the game started. He found Tyrone to be an excellent cribbage player.

Tyrone enjoyed Grampa's company thoroughly. Mary liked Opal. She felt at ease with her strong yet gentle nature and found herself pouring her heart out to her. All the horrors of her recent past came flooding out in words.

Opal listened with compassion, hardly able to believe the extent of it. "I've had a lot of heartache in my day girl, but nothing compared with what you've been through."

Mary's new friend shook her head with sympathy. "I'll tell you what, I'm gonna keep you so busy you'll forget all of this. You just let Opal take care of you, child."

Her arms encircled Mary, her big heart beating with compassion. Mary knew she had made a friend for life and looked forward to spending more time with her.

The evening passed quickly. They couldn't believe the hour when they checked the clock. It was almost midnight. When Tyrone and Opal said they had to leave, Mary begged them to stay longer so they could meet John. "He'll be here in just fifteen minutes. Please stay."

They agreed. Grampa and Tyrone started another cribbage game.

John arrived shortly afterward and at first he thought his eyes were deceiving him. Not only did he find it most unusual for the household to be so lively at that time of the night, but the entire scene floored him. Grampa playing cribbage with a black man? Laughing and talking with him?

Not giving him a minute to digest the scene, Mary quickly and proudly introduced him to their new friends. John happily shook hands with them and from that point, the visit lasted another hour. Because it was now Saturday morning, they could all sleep in.

A lot of good things happened that Friday evening. After their new friends left, John could see a changed man in his father in-law. His wife seemed much more like her old self, giving him hope that the Christmas season, which was coming up fast, might just be a little happier for all of them.

Chapter 14

*H*olding true to her promise, Opal called Mary around noon the next day. She had all kinds of plans for the two of them, and started the day by showing Mary all of her favorite places to shop. They began their Christmas shopping that afternoon.

The two of them also found they were of the same religion. One day, while out shopping, Opal had to stop by her church to do a small chore. She introduced Mary to the pastor and left them alone while she went about her business.

Mary liked this church. She hadn't even started her search for one that her family could attend and felt a little guilty about waiting so long. Especially when the pastor talked about how badly the attendance had dropped over the years.

"Years ago we had four services every Sunday morning." His chubby round face smiled fondly at the memories. "Back then, the people packed in here like sardines in a can. Sometimes we had standing room only."

He shook his head sadly. "Now we hold two services on The Sabbath and people straggle in, half filling the church."

Mary registered her family. The pastor wanted to know if she would like to get involved with the same women's group that Opal belonged to. He told her of all the good works they did. Mary said she'd consider it after the holidays were over.

Opal returned a short time later with a box filled with Christmas decorations. She held a list of addresses and asked

Mary if she would mind making a few stops with her. The people she would see were shut-ins and she had an ornament for each of them; to hopefully brighten their day.

"Each member of our group will visit ten of the people on the list. They're either very sick or too old to attend services on Sunday. Mary, they love having visitors. You don't mind, do you? I think we have enough time for two stops before the boys get home from school."

"It sounds like fun to me. Who are they? Dumb question, I don't know anyone around here."

After saying goodbye to the pastor, they left the church. Opal told Mary about the first man they would see. His name was Mr. Olson, and he was ninety-seven years old. "It's only been a few months since he hasn't been able to drive. His family had to lay the law down after he had a minor accident. He's lucky to be alive. The man is almost totally blind and stubborn as a mule. They finally convinced him to stop driving before he hurt himself or someone else. You'll love him, Mary. He's so nice, and really funny too. The other person is in the hospital and what I understand, she's on her way out of this world. She's quite sick."

Mary quickly shook her head no. "I can't go into a hospital yet, Opal. It's too soon since mothers' death. . . . I couldn't stand it. I shake just thinking about a hospital. I'd probably start crying or do something stupid. I'd upset the sick woman."

Opal understood. "We don't have to go today, Mary. I know how you must feel, but sooner or later you may have to visit someone in the hospital. You really should walk around inside one, just to know you can."

"Not today."

They got into the car and buckled their seat belts. Mary was glad she wasn't driving; she still hadn't attempted driving in the city traffic.

137

Visiting with the old man turned out to be a delight. His eyes sparkled when Opal handed him the tiny Christmas tree. Totally thrilled with the ornament, he placed it on the coffee table and after seating the two women, hustled around in the kitchen, preparing tea for them. The racket he made sounded like he was making tea for an army. Pots and pans banged together and when they could hear he finally had the water on to boil, dishes began rattling. Visualizing the scene caused them both to giggle.

He finally appeared, carrying a tray filled with cups and saucers. His hands shook so badly the dishes rattled. They helped him set the dishes in place on the table and while waiting for the tea pot to whistle, he told them funny stories. The brief visit was enchanting and when it was time to leave, he made both girls promise they would visit again soon.

They had one more stop to make: The nursing home. The woman they were visiting was Gloria Dalton and she had just recently been released from a hospital.

"She has a little more recovering to do," Opal said as she opened the door to the nursing home, "and then she can go back home."

Opal whispered to Mary as they approached the information desk, "I've heard this isn't the greatest place. I'm glad she doesn't have to stay long."

She asked the nurse for Gloria's room number. The woman acted agitated, but gave it to her as she pointed in the direction they were to go.

Finding the room, Opal saw her friend and called her name. Gloria did not respond. Her eyes were open, but she only stared at the ceiling. Opal looked to see if she was breathing. Satisfied to find her alive, she looked at the lady in the other bed who slept soundly.

"Gloria, it's me, Opal." Gloria looked at her and faintly smiled. She immediately closed her eyes and went to sleep.

"I'm leaving this little ornament with you, Gloria. I'll come back to visit when you're feeling better."

Mary and Opal looked for a nurse on their way out, hoping she could tell them if something was wrong. Finding no one nearby, they left.

Opal was furious. "I've heard rumors about this place and others like it. They drug some of the people in there unnecessarily! Poor Gloria doesn't even know what's happening!"

She told Mary that some nursing homes in the area had been shut down after being investigated. They proved abuse of the elderly patients, along with the excessive drugging.

"Can't Gloria's family see what's going on?" Mary found this situation difficult to comprehend.

"As far as I know, the few relatives that Gloria has, live far from here. She was childless and her husband has been dead for years. I can't understand why they have not investigated this place. I'll find out who her doctor is and hopefully he can look into it."

Mary agreed it was a good idea. She did not like that nursing home and felt uneasy being there.

They arrived home before the youngsters were out of school. Mary found a love letter on the table from John. Smiling as she read the words, the letter helped divert her mind from the terrible place she had just visited.

****

Buffy waited impatiently for James to get home from school with Henri and nearly attacked him when he came through the door.

"You're never going to believe what I have to tell you! We went to a nursing home and the people were all drugged up! It was just awful!"

"Now slow down and tell me exactly what happened."

139

She told the whole story. When finished, he asked her if they stayed long enough to talk to the other angels.

"We sure did. They said there was an investigation and the owners of the home didn't get caught because a friend of theirs worked in the investigator's office. She informed them of the inspection day and they reduced the patient's medication a few days before the scheduled day. Those creeps passed the test with flying colors!"

Buffy took a deep breath and continued. "The angels hate the way their charges are drugged excessively. Can you imagine how bored they are with these people staring straight ahead like zombies? They said that God is furious and has the detective angels working on it. The girl in that investigator's office is going to get caught and so are the owners of that dreadful place. But they feel like it's taking forever."

"You can be sure they'll get caught," said James. "It probably seems to them like it's taking forever. Meanwhile, all they can do is sit around and wait."

"That's right, and they feel terrible about it. But they did have something else to tell me."

Buffy's eyes brightened as she was about to reveal her treasured bit of news. "What I have to tell you is exciting . . . and comes straight from Heaven. But I'm not supposed to tell anyone. Not all of it, anyway."

Knowing he more than likely already heard, he played along anyway. Just watching her made it worthwhile.

"Please, Buf? Let's hear it. I could use some exciting news, especially if it's from Heaven."

"Well okay, but I'll only tell part of it. Where's Isaac and T.J.?" She gazed around wide eyed and nervous.

"Visiting Abe, with Grampa."

"We can tell them this part later. Remember when Grampa was reading in the paper about the night all those different colored lights showed up in the sky? And how

140

everyone thought they might have been UFO's? Then they decided it was the Northern Lights?"

His head got tired of bouncing up and down as he nodded yes. He'd heard the story.

"Well, it was neither of them. It was God. He had just plugged in his outside Christmas lights and decided the display was so beautiful he'd give the whole world a glimpse of the spectacular colors. Isn't that neat? If the people on earth only knew what those lights really were!"

"That is special. Now what else?"

"Well," she said looking around to make sure no one else heard. "Promise you won't breathe a word of this to anyone else? You can't ruin the surprise for them." She gave him a look of warning.

"I promise."

Her face grew serious as she whispered, "Okay. God is going to start the Christmas celebration in Heaven earlier this year. He feels it'll be necessary because he wants every angel to be able to attend at least one full day. That includes us. They told me He would provide a sub for everyone. Even those that haven't left their post for ages. That's us, James. You, me, Isaac, Jake and T.J.." She finished her announcement and felt good that she was the bearer of good news.

"That's wonderful," he said.   "When will we be told?"

"It's going to be very soon.   It's a pre-Christmas surprise. I would assume you'll be the one to get the message and then you'll have to tell us. Just remember, act surprised. This is supposed to be a secret. Don't breathe a word of this to the other angels. If you do, you'll wreck their surprise."

"You can count on me to keep my mouth shut. Now, if you'll excuse me, I have things to do. Thanks for sharing with me, Buffy." He winked at her and left the room.

Later, he overheard Buffy calling to Isaac and T.J. when they came through the door. James could barely hear as she whispered to them, but he did understand the words, "big secret." Sneaking a look, he saw her gesturing wildly as she whispered to them. When finished he could hear her making them promise they wouldn't tell Jake.

James chuckled and shook his head side to side. "Buffy, Buffy, Buffy," he silently said.

****

Chapter 15

*W*ith Christmas one week away, Henri looked forward to his holiday vacation from school. He and Bobby had many plans made and were looking forward to the shopping they were going to do that evening. Their mothers promised they could go along with them to the mall.

Tyrone and Grampa joined them. The boys paired off with the men so they could pick out presents for their mothers. Later they went off with their moms so presents could be selected for their dads and Grampa. It took a long time to make their purchases and when they left the mall, each boy could hardly keep the secret of what they'd bought for the others.

After the shopping trip, Tyrone drove them through the surrounding neighborhoods to view the Christmas light displays. With the snow softly falling, the many different colored lights brought a peaceful feeling to the entire area. Caroling played on the car radio and as everyone sang along with the tunes, the spirit of Christmas took over their souls. The boys begged to pick out their tree that evening.

"Don't forget what the plans are, boys," said Tyrone. "In the morning we pick out the Christmas trees, and string lights on our houses. If we picked them out tonight, Henri's dad would be left out and that wouldn't be fair." John and Tyrone both had Saturday off from work. Tyrone and Opal were going to do everything possible to help make Christmas special for this family.

Early Saturday morning the men and boys left to search for their trees. The two women went to work baking batches of Christmas cookies. Mary's kitchen filled with festive aromas as they pulled trays of assorted goodies from the oven. They decorated them the minute they cooled, talking nonstop as they put the final touches on each one. When the boys returned, they walked into a kitchen filled with scrumptious goodies.

After allowing their loved ones to sample a few of their creations, the two mothers sent them out to put up the lights, providing instructions about where each set would hang.

By mid-afternoon, with the chores completed, each family sat in the middle of their own living room, sorting through boxes of ornaments just pulled out of storage. The Christmas trees would soon come to life with lights and their treasured pieces.

Henri was in charge of the music at his house. He chose his favorite tape to play first and the first song to fill their home was "Oh Christmas Tree." His dad finished stringing lights on the evergreen. Plugging them in, he announced that the decorating could begin. Grampa was first. He took out a small box that he had taken from his home and carefully lifted out the contents, he said, "This was very special to Gramma. She said it looked exactly like her own guardian angel." He placed the prized possession at the very top of the now glowing tree.

Henri asked, "Do you think she really knew what her angel looked like?"

"She does now," replied his mother fondly. "She does now."

Their home smelled of fresh pine from the newly cut tree. The family members hung each precious memory with care. After placing an ornament on the tree, a step back to look, made sure it hung in the perfect spot.

This festive occasion came laced with sadness. Each person knew the Christmas season had been Gramma's favorite time of the year and they missed her very much.

****

The angels enjoyed the day, too. Buffy made each of them notice the special angel cookie she inspired Mary to decorate. The angel's dress was painted with colored frosting that matched the blue outfit Buffy wore.

Their pre-Christmas surprise arrived as Henri's family put the finishing touches on their tree. Noel, the singing messenger, delivered the announcements. Adorned in his angel costume, he bellowed out the invitation to the tune of "Hark the Herald Angels Sing."

Noel was hilarious, but the singing message got the point across. God invited each angel to spend a full twenty-four hours at the Christmas celebration in Heaven. The lyrics in the song told them that God would provide a substitute angel to watch over each charge while they attended. Now the big decision would be which day they wanted to attend.

This comical angel was truly entertaining. He also blew on a trumpet, and burst out laughing with them when he completed his message. "It was hard to keep from laughing while I sang. Did you like it? I made the whole skit up myself."

He handed them a special engraved invitation containing all the information he just sang.

Buffy quickly looked to the others to make sure they acted surprised. Clapping her hands together loudly, she said, "It was a wonderful skit and I can't believe we are allowed to come to the celebration! This is such a surprise!"

Seeing all the excitement in the room, assured her that all went well. She said to the messenger, "Do you sing

145

all of your message's Noel? I loved the singing message you brought me back in Pleasant Valley. You can't imagine how it cheered me up when I was so distraught."

Feeling important because she already knew him personally, Buffy then said to the others, "Remember I told you about the message I got from God? This is the same angel that delivered it."

Noel didn't hesitate to share a bit of his history with them. "I sing all of the messages. It's my specialty and I do it to get a laugh. I was a comedian on earth. When I got here, I had a difficult time trying to decide whether I wanted to work at a comedy club in Heaven, or be a special delivery angel. My biggest desire was to be an angel of some sort. When I passed all of the tests that qualified me to be one, I had a conference with God. Together we decided that this would be a good job for me. I can be an angel, and still make everyone laugh."

They loved Noel and wanted him to hang around for a while. Buffy gave him a big hug and asked if he had any other news from Heaven that he wanted to share. "How about the activities during the celebration, are they the same as last year? Has the Christmas caroling started yet? Oh, do tell us everything!"

"Haven't you been listening to WGOD? The carols started a few days ago. God asked the angels to start singing just after he showed the world His light display. You did hear about that spectacular event, didn't you? The channel is also providing a list of the various activities taking place each day and the invitation includes a schedule. Take a look inside."

Buffy asked if the Christmas celebration had started earlier this year.

Noel answered, "God first thought it would be necessary, but after checking the availability of subs, He found that the usual week of celebrating would be sufficient.

Every angel can attend this year. The music started earlier though. You know how He gets at this time of year. Listening to the choirs of angels singing carols is his favorite past-time. He keeps His window to the courtyard open so He can even listen while they practice!"

Everyone knew how much God loved Christmas because it was the one time of year when most of the people on earth had love in their hearts. Watching them choose a special gift for their loved ones gave him great joy. He spoke on this subject yearly at the guardian angels' meetings.

His message to the guardian angels repeated itself each year. "Encourage your charge to keep the presents simple, or better yet, encourage them to give a gift of love or kindness. We must never allow them to lose the spirit of Christmas because of money." All of the angels applauded His words.

Noel was ready to leave. "I have to get on with my deliveries. It would be best if you'd let me know today when you want to attend."

"That's easy for me," said James, "I always go on Christmas Eve. I'd like to start at eleven o'clock P.M.."

Buffy's hair flew as her head swung to look at him. She wondered why he chose that day and assumed she'd miss something important if she didn't do the same. "Why Christmas Eve, James? Do you think that day is better than the others, or what?"

T.J. answered. "Everyone knows that Christmas Eve and Christmas Day are the best."

"Every day of the week is fun!" Buffy blurted, "I'm never going to be able to decide which twenty-four hours I want."

Noel impatiently looked from one to the other as they argued about which day would be best. He relaxed when he realized that because of their situation, it would be a difficult decision to make. They had not left their post in days.

Isaac said, "I will take the same days that James chose. That's when they serve the best food and the celebrations are at their peaks."

Buffy wanted to go with them. "Can we all go at the same time? That's when I want to go, too. I know Christmas morning is the best! I almost forgot how much I love hearing the Christmas music being played all over Heaven on the loud speakers." Her eyes looked dreamy as she anticipated the upcoming celebration.

Each angel signed up for the same twenty-four hours. Noel was happy to have the decision making process over. He picked up his shiny gold trumpet and played along with the tune that came across Henri's tape player. "Silent Night" was an angel favorite, and they watched with their hearts filled with love as the family sang along quietly with the music.

When Noel finished playing, he said, "I like that kid with the red hair, what's his name?"

"Henri."

"He's working hard at cheering everyone up. There must have been some sadness in this family?"

They told him about Gramma's death.

"I'd say that boy would make a good angel. He has what it takes."

Noel gathered his things. "I'll see you guys around. I've got work to do."

"Thank you," they said in unison.

Noel used his wings to make an exit. He left singing 'Joy to The World'.

"Maybe I should have started earlier on Christmas Eve," Buffy said, feeling uneasy about her decision. "I probably should have consulted with my friends in Heaven first. I'll want to see them too. What do you think James?"

He told her she probably should take more time to think about it. "You may still have time to change your mind, but if I know you, you'll be doing it every few minutes. I don't know if God will appreciate your pestering Him that much."

"I wouldn't pester Him." Buffy changed her mind again. "I'm okay with my decision, really. It's just so hard because I've always spent the whole week celebrating. There are so many parties to attend, and of course I want to tour the Palace. The decorations are different every year. I

forgot to ask if there would be tours on Christmas Eve. I know they don't have them on Christmas Day."

Jake knew the tours lasted until noon. "You'd better get yourself in line as soon as you get there if you want to be a part of the last one."

"For sure I will; I have to take the tour. The fudge is the best part of it all." She ran her tongue over her lips. "I love it!"

"What fudge?" Asked Isaac. "I've been taking the tours every year and I have never heard about any fudge."

"Well," said Buffy, "then you probably never stayed to hear the choir of angels sing after the tour."

"I knew they sang, but I always had to leave." He grinned, "Because of the parties."

"Too bad for you. They serve the fudge after the angels sing. And there are tables of it. It's the most delicious fudge you will ever taste."

Seeing she had a captivated audience, she went on, "It is the chewiest, nuttiest, and tastiest chocolate fudge that you will ever find anywhere and guess what else?"

"What?"

"It's God's own recipe. A person whose name I can't mention said God watches over every batch that they make to be positive they follow His recipe to the very letter."

The others decided they'd stay for the singing after the tour. They had never heard about the fudge and were anxious to sample it.

"Since we're taking the tour together," said T.J., "why don't we hang around with each other the whole time? I think it'd be fun." He looked to the others.

They agreed, but Buffy was a bit reluctant. "It sounds like fun, but I was planning to phone a couple of friends to see if they'll meet me. Can they come with us? You'll all like them and I haven't seen them in ages. They'll be so happy to see me."

James broke in. *"They can come, but you know the rules for the phone while the crisis is on, Buffy. I will make an exception for tonight. If you can be brief with your calls. How many do you have to make?"*

She started to count on her fingers. *"Well, there's Jessica, Jennifer, JoAnna, and I can't forget C.J. Oh, I can't forget to call Brian and Jason. There's two more for sure, Daniel, and Alex. They're new in Heaven and they count on me to show them around when I'm not busy. "*

"Just a minute here," James interjected, seeing it was getting out of hand. *"Why don't you call the first person on your list and have her notify the rest of them?"*

He then added: *"Just remember to tell them I'm first in line for the tour."*

Agreeing, she rushed to the portable phone. Her hands shook so much from the excitement that she could barely dial the number. James and the others watched with humor as she talked rapidly, trying to include everything in her one phone call.

James told the others they could make a call if Buffy ever got off the phone. They didn't care to. Each one, happy enough to have the twenty-four hour break.

Henri's family retired for the evening. The angels tuned their radio to WGOD. Choirs of angels came across the airwaves and, as usual, the caroling was superb. Listening to the sheer beauty of the music made their emotions run high.

"This is turning out to be a wonderful Christmas," said Isaac, *"My heart is near bursting. I am so proud of Grampa. He gave me the best Christmas present I have ever received. Watching his smiling face when he plays cribbage with his new friend just makes my heart swell. Do you guys have any idea how hard and long I've tried to get him to change his ugly way of thinking?"*

"We know."

151

James commented, "You have every right to feel on top of the world. What a job it must've been to persuade him to soften to the family. God wanted the two families to become friends and Grampa could have blown it for everyone."

"Well, he didn't," said Isaac. "I know all of his weird ideas about each race staying in their own country is now over. He's suffering from guilt now, but it'll pass."

James added, "Wouldn't it be great if the rest of the prejudiced people in the world turned over a new leaf? A lot of problems would be solved."

"I'm just happy about Grampa right now." Isaac felt at peace for his charge, he'd worked for years on that one flaw. "And I must say that Tyrone's angel helped a great deal."

"He really had Gramps going that night," said T.J. "The best part of that scene was when Tyrone held out the cribbage pegs and asked him if he wanted black or white. I loved it. Ol' Gramps nearly flipped. He learned that night all right and it couldn't have been a nicer family that helped him."

Buffy finished her one phone call much later and announced part of her news. "Jessica is going to call everyone to let them know I'll be there at eleven o'clock on Christmas Eve. I'm not sure how many will be going with us, but she thought it was a wonderful idea for all of us to go together. It'll be such fun. And James, she can't wait to meet you. I told her how mighty you are."

Excitement had her bouncing all over the place. "Thanks so much for letting me use the phone. I enjoy talking to my friends."

"No problem, Buf, but you do understand, we're still on alert? When things are more settled, you can resume your normal everyday phone calls."

He looked to the others knowing they thought it was much more peaceful in the household without her daily chattering on the phone. He decided to find a solution to the problem: perhaps a phone booth.

"We were talking about how nice Tyrone's family has been." James said.

Buffy eagerly responded. "They're wonderful! I love their angels. They really keep us busy and we're finally having fun again. I'll bet they loved Noel too! Isn't he something?"

All of them agreed and the room became silent as they listened to the Christmas caroling. Buffy interrupted when she remembered a piece of news she had just received. "I almost forgot to tell you! Jessica said her friend took the first tour of The Palace today. She stayed to listen to the choir of angels afterward, and guess who sang with them in the front row?"

The angels looked to her for the answer even though they were positive about who it would be.

"It was Gramma," she said with a gentle smile.

****

Chapter 16

*W*ith the magic of Christmas behind them, Henri and his family fell back into their normal routines. A month had passed since the holidays and they were feeling somewhat secure that the New Year might just be bringing in more pleasant days. There had been no upsetting incidents and the neighborhood remained quiet.

John began to work overtime at the shop and it pleased him to be able to put some money into savings. He still had hopes of moving his family to a safer area. His friends at work were keeping their ears and eyes open for any house that might become available in the areas where they lived in the suburbs. John knew something would be found, and didn't feel especially pressured.

Those feelings changed drastically on a Friday night, the first week in February. John had gotten out of work earlier than usual and was anxious to surprise his family. He whistled along with the music on the car radio as he drove home. The whistling stopped when he turned down the street that he lived on. Blue and red flashing lights lit up the neighborhood and he could see two police cars and an ambulance blocking the road further up. Not knowing whether it was his house or the neighbor sent his heart racing. As he moved in closer, his body relaxed somewhat when he saw that whatever happened appeared to be a few houses up from his.

Parking his car in the drive, John could see his wife and Henri watching from the window and ran in to make sure they were okay. Neither one knew what happened, but said

Grampa went to find out. John left, and after making his way through crowds of people, found him.

Because of the excitement, Grampa spoke rapidly, "Two people have been shot, John. I talked to their neighbor and he said he heard their car drive up and it wasn't two minutes after they got in their house that he heard the gunshots and called the police. When they arrived, Mr. and Mrs. Hansen were lying on the floor bleeding."

As they stood talking, the ambulance pulled away. The red lights flashed bright in the dark and the sirens urgently wailed. John and Grampa walked back to their home. Both carried a sick feeling with them.

John relayed the story to Mary and Henri. Not until the morning news, did they know for a fact, that their neighbors were dead. The television reporter said that Mr. and Mrs. Hansen were carrying bags of groceries into their home when they interrupted a burglar at work. He apparently shot them as they walked through the door. Henri went back to his room after hearing the sad news and Grampa put on his coat and hat, saying he was going to visit Abe.

Arriving at the drugstore, Grampa found the pharmacist with some friends. They were watching as workers put bars on the windows of Abe's drugstore. The man that lived next door to the Hansens said, "They never had a chance, just walked in the house and got blasted away. I saw them drive up. It wasn't seconds later I heard the gunshots and called the police."

"I suppose they don't know who did it," said Grampa. "Now we're going to have to worry about who gets it next."

Abe asked them to go inside for coffee. They sat around the old soda fountain discussing the situation, each hoping the other would know what action to take. Many ideas were hashed over and each man agreed that it was time to take the law into their own hands, but none of them would have the guts to do it. A few of them decided to buy a gun to keep in their house for protection. They still felt helpless.

Grampa returned to the household feeling worse than when he left. John sat alone in the living room when Grampa's rage exploded. "This is one time in my life that I can honestly say I'm glad my wife isn't here! She could never have lived like this!"

He regretted the words as soon as they left his mouth.

"I'll get you all out of here when I can," said John. "We wouldn't have this problem if we could have sold our houses. At least we would have a better choice of where to live. The guys at work are looking in their neighborhoods for a house that might come up for rent. I should have enough money for a deposit now, and the first month's rent." Nevertheless, this present situation sickened him.

"I didn't quite mean what I said, John, I'm sorry. It's just hard to believe what's happening. Everyone in the neighborhood is afraid. People shouldn't have to live this way." He shook his head in disgust.

Entering the room, Mary could feel the weight of depression hanging over the two of them. She didn't feel much better, but knew some attitudes had to change. To be afraid was one thing, but living the rest of your life scared, frightened her even more. She suggested they invite their friends over for cards.

"We can't let this ruin our lives. Everyone's acting like the world is ending!"

Henri came out of his room. "What I would like to know is why didn't their angels help them? I guess maybe there aren't any super-hero angels!"

His dad said, "That's not a fair thing to say, son."

Henri's lips trembled. His visions of mighty angels shattered. "Then why did they have to get murdered? They were nice old people. Other people get saved."

Mary stood with her hands on her hips, ready to pounce. "What happened last night was terrible and I'm sure their angels tried to help!"

She threw her arms in the air and her voice grew louder. "Who knows? Maybe Mr. and Mrs. Hansen would have been left crippled from their wounds had they lived. Maybe God didn't want them to suffer! I wish I had some answers myself. Some people are saved, and some aren't. That's just the way it is!"

She sighed, knowing her mother would have had the right answer.

John was frustrated too; sometimes there were no answers. "It's true Henri, many times people are miraculously saved from such tragedies. We don't know why, but they are. I read an article a while back where a man lost control of his car and dropped off a cliff and lived through the ordeal. He said he was barely conscious when the car hit bottom and swears that someone pulled him out just seconds before the car burst into flames."

Henri interrupted, "Maybe he just didn't remember getting out by himself."

"That could be. No one was there to see. Yet he swore someone not only pulled him away from the burning car, but stayed with him until the ambulance arrived. He said the stranger held a bandage to the wound on his leg and disappeared into thin air when the medics arrived."

Henri asked, "Was the bandage left behind?"

"I don't know the answer to that." John continued with his story, "The medics were astounded that the accident didn't end his life. Even more incredible; he severed a main artery on his leg and hadn't lost a significant amount of blood. No one understood why. The injured man swears an angel helped him, and said that God must not have wanted him yet."

The story helped Henri somewhat. "I guess it could be true. Now I remember Gramma said the same thing about the angels saving you if it's not your time to die. I hate it when anyone dies."

"Everyone has to die, Henri," said his mother. "That's just the way it is. I don't know of anyone that has been on earth forever and death is scary to all of us. Maybe we're frightened because we don't know for sure what happens when we die. I'm glad I believe there is a Heaven. When Gramma died it was the only comfort I had. Knowing she was there, and not sick anymore."

Henri stood with his shoulders slightly stooped. "Me too, but I still hated it. I hate the word dead. I feel sorry for dead people."

"Gramma said the person who dies is lucky because he finally gets to be with God. We should feel sorry for the people left behind because they won't see their loved one until they die."

Henri thought about what she said for a moment, "That could be true. Gramma's probably not sad like we are. She's probably having fun, and maybe the Hansens are too. It was so terrible for them to get killed, but maybe they're happy right now. They can probably eat all the ice cream they want."

"You must be hungry, Henri," said his mother.

"No, but Gramma said you could have anything you wanted in Heaven and I think I'd take all the ice cream they'd give me."

Mary pushed the ice cream issue, feeling hopeful the family would lighten up. She hated the gloom in her home and knew of no other way to get rid of it. "I'll get you some. Sounds good to me, too. Anyone else?"

Not waiting for an answer she quickly exited the room. Minutes later she called them in for their treat. Henri felt better imagining that the Hansens were eating ice cream in Heaven, but it reminded him of an awful story he recently heard at school. He stopped eating and stared at his bowl.

"You're not finished already," said his mother. "What's wrong?"

"I was thinking about something else."

He stirred his ice cream around in the bowl. "I just remembered what my friends said happened to a little girl last year. It's awful, but she's probably having ice cream in Heaven, too. I hope so."

"What are you talking about, Henri?" His dad didn't recall hearing that story.

"Someone grabbed her when she was walking home from school and they found her dead a month later. The kids tell me lots of terrible stories. They said the girl was tortured and told me what the word meant."

His parents had no idea what to say. Grampa surprisingly, came to their rescue. "That reminds me of a time when Gramma and I watched a news story that sounds similar to what you're telling us, Henri. A small lad was missing and massive searches were conducted. Everyone looked for him and he was finally found dead. He too, had been tortured. The whole town mourned for him. I remember what your gramma said about it."

Pausing briefly, Grampa shifted in his chair while folding his hands behind his head. "She believed the little boy never felt a thing and said that when the angels find themselves powerless over a situation, God allows them to block the victim's mind from knowing what is happening. It prevents them from feeling any physical or mental suffering and death comes peacefully. I believe that."

Henri thoughtfully said, "It could be true. I remember when my friend Corey and his dad were in a car accident. Corey got a really bad cut on his arm. He said it was weird because he never felt it happening and it surprised him to see the blood. His arm hurt later at the hospital, though. Probably the angels blocked his mind when it happened so he wouldn't be scared."

159

Grampa said, "I'm sure they did. Gramma believed that was one of the ways the angels helped. I'm beginning to believe plenty of things she said."

The phone rang. Opal and Tyrone wanted them to come over for a visit. Deciding it was a good idea, they walked up the street to their friend's house.

Henri and Bobby scooted off to Bobby's room. The others sat around discussing the murder. "It's those drugs," said Tyrone. "They are destroying the world. The addicts steal to keep their habits going and they don't care who they kill in the process. I don't know when this is going to end."

Opal was sick of hearing about it and told him so. "Let's play a game or something. I personally don't want to think about this anymore."

The others agreed, but Tyrone had more he wanted to say on the subject. He asked Mary and John if they had visited the city park yet. They hadn't and wondered what there was to know about it. He explained. "It's quite an education and I told Bobby I'm taking him there. I want him to see what goes on just in case he ever gets it in his head to try drugs. Many addicts hang out at the park, and from what I understand, they get their 'fix' there. You've never seen anything so horrible. I'd do anything to keep my son from the temptation to try drugs and I'm positive this scene will leave a lasting impression."

"You're scaring them, Tyrone. Can't we please talk about something else? I don't want to hear any more of this!" Opal clearly did not want her boy at that park viewing anything.

John disagreed with her. "It couldn't hurt Henri to see either. I'd like to go myself."

Mary said nothing. She'd speak with John later.

"Next weekend," said Tyrone. "We'll go next weekend."

Opal pulled a favorite game out of the cabinet and slammed it on the table. She wasn't pleased because she knew when Tyrone said he was going to do something, he did it.

She passed around the paper and pencils. The object of the game was for one person to pick a card with a specific word on it. The person then had to draw a picture of the word, and their partner had to guess what they were drawing.

All discussions of drugs and evil stopped. Playing the game magically diverted their attention to having fun.

****

The angels joined in, playing the game they loved most. They each worked with their charge, whispering in his ear which picture to draw that would best describe the secret word.

Playing the game had everyone laughing. Not only did the afternoon pass quickly, but it erased the events of the past twenty-four hours from the minds of all the players. At least for the time being.

Henri and Bobby had joined the others when they heard the laughter. They drew better pictures and won several rounds.

"This is the one game I excel in," said James. "Henri draws every picture exactly as I instruct him to."

His bragging made the others try even harder, but he kept winning.

Buffy wanted to quit because she hadn't won at all. "You're winning because you're so much older than us, James. We were doing well until you came in."

"I don't call twenty, old, Buf. And you can't quit as long as Mary's playing." James didn't want her dropping out because he liked beating all of them.

"She can think without me. Mary does have a mind of her own, you know."

161

Buffy helped Mary with a few more pictures. They weren't good enough and John couldn't guess the secret word. Flustered, Buffy quit and stubbornly sat with her arms folded. "You might think you're only twenty," she said, "but I'll bet you're really a million years old."

"I'm still twenty though, come on don't be a poor sport." It was too late. Mary then decided she didn't want to play anymore. The game came to a halt when Opal gave up too. She had snacks prepared and left for the kitchen to fetch them.

T.J. sat alone and quiet. He didn't have anyone to help with the game. James asked him if he was bored. "Not at all, James. I've had a lot on my mind."

James could see it was more than that. "It's not fun living in these parts, I know, but we have to keep going, buddy."

T.J. decided to tell James what occupied his mind. "The park that Tyrone talked about. That's where my ex-charge is."

"What do you mean, your ex-charge?" James wondered if he would talk about his last mission. He had no idea what happened, but knew the experience devastated T.J..

"I call him my ex-charge now, because that's what he is. His name is Billy and he was always a sweet and gentle boy. I'd been his guardian from the day of his birth. All the horrors started when he turned fifteen. Even though he tried hard to find one, Billy never had a close friend. I spent a lot of time rounding up acquaintances for him, but it never seemed to work. He was a quiet child and played alone. As he grew older, he turned into a 'bookworm'."

T.J. smiled at the word and the thought of how nice Billy had been. "His brain resembled a computer, soaking up every detail of everything he read or learned like a sponge. I called him a walking dictionary. The kid had high grades in school and was very bright, but so lonely."

T.J. paused sadly before he went on. "I guess the loneliness got to him. A few kids began hanging around him at school, to get help with their school work. They were not a good influence and poor Billy just felt happy to have someone to talk to. One was a female, and she really irritated me. Billy let her copy his homework and became totally taken with her. She used him, pretending to be interested in him as a boyfriend, but I saw how she and her real boyfriend laughed at him."

James could see how the situation sickened T.J. and told him he didn't have to talk about it.

"I have to, James. I'm finding that it helps to talk about it. I would still be waiting at the park if God hadn't sent me away."

"Why did He send you away?"

"Let me finish about how it started."

"Okay."

"Billy was thrilled with his new friends, especially the girl. Just having someone to eat lunch with sent him to school a happier person. She began pressuring him to try drugs. He was eager, but frightened. Billy would have done anything for that girl and wanted her to think he was 'cool'. She also sold drugs."

"James, I tried to stop him. He heard me and knew he was doing wrong. Billy suffered a lot of guilt, but he wanted his friends more."

James helped T.J. with words, "He felt guilty because you were putting such strong anti-thoughts in his head. I know what you mean." James understood, the guilt sometimes brought the person back to normal.

"I really tried James, and God sent two stronger angels to help."

Sadly, James shook his head. "Because of his close relationship with the girl, the opposing angels could easily manipulate Billy, especially when he took drugs."

"Without a doubt!"   T.J. shook his head in agreement, "The more drugs Billy took, the further he pushed me away. When he took his first drug, the evil forces moved right in, pressuring him to do more.   It's hard to believe the strong hold they can get on these vulnerable kids."

T.J. sighed, and continued with his story, "With the extra help given to me, Billy was doubly guilt ridden. But he turned the other way, taking more drugs to get rid of the guilt feelings. He's hopelessly hooked now and totally controlled by the wrong angels. I hung around in the background for a long time but, God finally told me I'd be more appreciated elsewhere."

T.J. once again looked close to tears. "Leaving Billy out there in so much trouble was the hardest thing I ever had to do.   It was as though he changed into some kind of monster, James. He doesn't even look the same."

James said with compassion, "God will let you know if Billy wants help.   The warrior angels are working overtime, I hear. They'll know if Billy calls out for help."

"That's what I wait for. He just has to ask and have the desire to quit. I'm ready to give all the help needed. He's pretty far gone though, and the road back won't be easy." T.J. shook his head, "It just doesn't look good."

The angels of both families visited on the opposite side of the room, glancing occasionally to where James and T.J. stood conversing. They could tell a private and serious discussion was in progress and didn't want to interrupt.

"T.J., it's important that you don't see this situation as your fault." James assured him.   "I heard you calling yourself a failure, and you are wrong about that. Billy is the weakling here, not you. People are born with a conscience. They know right from wrong. We provide more than enough pressure to sway them the right way. Everyone has a free will. He used his free will to go the opposite way."

"I know, but I love him and it hurts. I'll wait for his call forever. I spent sixteen of his seventeen years with him. The last year was a living hell."

T.J. didn't wish to discuss the situation anymore and halted the conversation by calling out to Isaac.

"Hey, Isaac ol' boy, I see you not only cured Grampa of his major flaw, but now have him talking about angels! What's with you? Where do your extra powers come from? How about sharing your secrets with us?"

The others laughed at his playful sarcasm.

Isaac shared his expertise with them. "It's really quite simple, my friends. Once you get over the largest hurdle, everything else just kind of slips into place."

Taking a deep bow, the others applauded him.

"On the serious side," said James, "we were lucky Grampa came through for us."

James explained to the angels of Bobby's family about the situation that took place earlier that day in Henri's house. "The last thing we need right now is for them to lose faith. I'm sure that will never happen, but wouldn't it be easy for them?"

The angels sat in a circle on the floor talking about the big question in the minds of most people. "How can God let things like this happen?" Or, "Is there really a God?"

They took comfort in knowing the day would come when their charges would know all of the answers. Most importantly, they would understand thoroughly, why God's reason for secrecy was important to the purpose of life on earth. They also talked about the magic they used in their work and how true the story was that Grampa told about the little boy that didn't feel a thing. It was indeed, the magic the angels used.

Buffy stood and clapped her hands loudly, wanting everyone's attention. James rolled his eyes, wondering what *she was about to do now. He had no idea what to expect this time.*

She looked at each one and asked a simple question. "If you could tell your charge one of God's secrets, which would it be?"

They answered together, "Guardian angels are real!"

****

Chapter 17

*H*enri and his family returned to their home after an afternoon of fun with their friends. Henri complained of being tired and went to his room. While changing into his pajamas, he thought about Mr. and Mrs. Hansen, still feeling upset about their death.

The clock on his dresser told him it was early evening but, Henri didn't care as he climbed into bed. He laid still, staring at the small glass angel holding a violin that his mother gave him for Christmas. Closing his eyes, he envisioned his own angel and knew he never wanted to stop believing. His angel looked mighty and as he ventured closer, he took Henri by the hand. Together they headed for the stars. Henri fell into a deep sleep.

The following week was uneventful, until Friday. Henri and Bobby were having lunch together and a boy that sometimes ate with them came over to their table. He acted strangely, pointing at them and using foul language. This was the first time anyone had even mentioned Henri's hair at his new school.

"Hey red, where'd ya get the weird looking shirt? You look like a girl with that red curly hair." He started laughing as he pointed at Henri.

"What's wrong with you, Jack?" Asked Bobby. "Leave Henri alone."

He couldn't figure it out. Jack was always nice and this behavior frightened them.

"Nothing's wrong with me, black boy. Why don't you hang around with your own kind. You two look like a couple of weirdoes."

"Or queers," said two others joining in the laughter. "Jack said you both were starting to get on his nerves. We don't like that. As a matter of fact, we'll meet you after school tonight." He held his fists up and punched at the air.

Henri and Bobby were terrified of the older boys and were both scared to death to move from their seats.

"We didn't do anything," whispered Henri to Bobby, his voice shaking.

Bobby stood up and grabbed Henri's arm. "Let's get out of here!" They raced out of the lunch room.

"We'll see you two after school," the boys called out after them.

Henri and Bobby ran breathlessly into their classroom where they found Mr. Addison eating lunch. The teacher couldn't imagine what was wrong with them. Henri's face was a scarlet red and Bobby trembled all over.

"What on earth happened to you two?" He asked.

They poured out their story. Mr. Addison sadly shook his head, "Jack was in my class two years ago. He was always so timid."

"Well, he's really mean now," said Bobby half crying. "He ate lunch with us last week and he was nice. What happened to him? They're going to beat us up after school, and we didn't do anything!"

"Come sit over here." Mr. Addison pointed to the chairs next to him. He offered them some potato chips. They said no.

"You're seeing first-hand what drugs can do, boys." Mr. Addison was not happy at all.

"I've had my eye on Jack and I can tell you who he hangs with now. They've been after him for some time to join their gang. It looks as though they finally succeeded."

The teacher shook his head. "That's how they all get. Drugs change kids overnight, as you could see."

He briefly lectured them on the evils of taking drugs and told them he'd give them a ride home after school. "Wait in your seats when the bell rings. I have a few things to do before we leave, but it won't take long. I can give you boys a ride for the next few days. This will blow over soon."

Mr. Addison didn't want to tell Henri and Bobby that if he made any trouble for these kids, it would be harder on them for telling. He planned to watch the group of bullies closely. With the help of the other teachers, they'd get them for something. They were always in trouble and it was only a matter of time before they would be expelled from school. It made him sick how they terrorized the other students, making their lives miserable.

Still shaken, Henri and Bobby thanked him. They were allowed to stay in the classroom for the remainder of the lunch hour.

True to his promise, Mr. Addison gave them a ride home. Riding in silence most of the way, each one regretted the situation.

"Mr. Addison?" Asked Henri.

"Yes?"

"Do you believe in angels?"

"Angels?" He hadn't thought about angels in a long time and scratched his head. "Real angels, Henri? Like guardian angels?"

Henri shook his head "yes". The teacher recalled his mother talking about guardian angels a very long time ago. She was no longer living, but he smiled at her memory.

"My mother used to talk about them. She said everyone had their own special angel to watch over them, and they helped us get to Heaven."

"How do they help you get to Heaven?" Bobby asked. "Do they carry you up there?"

169

"She said they helped us to behave, because we have to be good in order to go to Heaven."

Mr. Addison remembered believing what she told him and his brothers, such a long time ago.

Bobby said again, "Do they carry us to Heaven after we die? If we were good?"

Henri told him he was pretty sure the angels carried people to Heaven, adding. "I know they do lots of things for us."

Both Bobby and the teacher were intrigued with the conversation, especially Mr. Addison.

"Henri, what made you think about the angels?"

"My gramma's dead now, but she loved angels and taught me lots' of stuff about them. She said when we believe, they make us feel safe. You reminded me of one. I feel safe riding home with you."

Mr. Addison blushed and didn't know what to say. Looking through his rear view mirror, he saw the little red-haired boy looking out the window. His heart ached for him. He'd learned a little about Henri's background and heard of the small town he came from.

He knew how bewildered this family must feel. A move to the big city in this day and age, was like being thrown to the wolves. The teacher wished he could tell the boy everything would be okay, but somehow the words couldn't pass his lips. His heart went out to Henri and his family.

Mr. Addison dropped Henri off last and watched as the small figure of a boy walked up the drive. He found it hard to shake the feelings he held inside; feelings of helplessness where the boy was concerned.

His thoughts returned to his mother and the angels as he pulled out of the driveway. He wondered when he had stopped thinking about his own guardian angel.

Mary's rage could hardly be contained as she listened to Henri tell about his day at school. She tried to stay calm as his story unfolded, but found it to be extremely difficult as rage tore through her.

She was grateful to Mr. Addison for giving the boys a ride home, but equally happy to see Henri go to his room to study so that her anger could be unleashed. Feeling unable to cope anymore, she yanked the bag of potatoes out of the cupboard and threw them on the table. Going to the drawer holding pots and pans, she banged them around until she found the one she wanted, exaggerating each move. The more she could slam around, the better she felt.

Grabbing a chair to sit on, Mary began savagely peeling a potato. She cut her finger and didn't even notice the blood pouring forth as she continued to peel. Her dad heard the noise earlier and stood by the door watching. He ran for some paper toweling and while wrapping her finger, demanded she settle down. He'd heard the entire conversation between her and Henri and told her it didn't sound all that bad.

"Didn't you hear what he said?! Those drug headed kids are going to beat him up. I can't take anymore! We're not safe here and I hate it!"

Mary opened the toweling and looked at her finger. The tears came. She laid her head on the table and bawled.

Her dad didn't know what to say to her. Henri came out wondering about the commotion and thought his mother was crying about her finger.

Protecting Henri, she stopped crying in his presence and started laughing almost hysterically. Grampa, concerned about her sanity, said he would fix supper, and instructed her to go read a book. Relieved to see his mother looking happy and laughing, Henri went back to his room.

Mary became quiet after bandaging her finger and said to her dad halfheartedly, "I guess what I have to do is get really tough like some of those women I see on television. I especially liked the kind that belong to motorcycle gangs. Some are strong enough to handle anyone. Nobody shoves them around."

She stopped talking and sniffed the air. "Where are the roses? I smell roses."

Looking oddly at her dad, she said, "Can't you smell them? I suppose I'm losing my mind now!"

"My nose doesn't work as well as it used to," he stated, "but I don't see any flowers, just that plastic rose on the counter."

"I think I'll take your advice and take a break. It looks like I need one."

Her dad watched wearily as she left the room. He worried about her.

Mary read a book and two hours passed quickly. When her dad announced that supper was ready, she realized the reading had helped her forget for a while. "I'll get Henri, we'll be right there."

Henri was sleeping soundly. "Hey, sleepy head, supper's ready."

Not getting a response, Mary moved closer to him and felt her heart drop. "Henri, are you okay?"

Panic spread quickly through her until he slowly rolled onto his back and opened his eyes. "I have to sleep a little more, Mom, I'm very tired."

Her body relaxed and she was able to say, "Grampa fixed a good meal for us. He's waiting, come on."

She put her hand to his cheek. It didn't feel any warmer than usual. He fell back into a deep sleep. It was most unusual for Henri to sleep right after school, but Mary considered all he'd been through that day and decided to let him rest some more. Quietly, she left the room.

Joining her dad in the kitchen, her eyes went directly to the place he had set for her. She felt a lump in her throat as she looked at the small plastic rose he'd placed in a glass. It sat next to her plate and the flower looked pathetic, kind of beaten up, similar to what she was feeling. But she smiled, his thoughtfulness touched her heart.

"How pretty, Dad, thank you. Your meat loaf looks wonderful too."

They both sat at the table. Mary told him Henri was still resting and how she figured he needed it after the horrible day he had. She didn't tell him that she had thought for a moment that Henri was dead. Her mind was beginning to play tricks on her.

Grampa shook his head slowly. "It won't be much longer, Mary. We'll find a safer place to live, and a better school for Henri. I can help a little with the money. We'll get something. Now let's eat and not think about anything unpleasant."

They ate in silence.

Henri appeared as they were cleaning up the dishes. Rubbing his sleepy eyes, he said he was starved and devoured every bit of food on his plate. Any worries his mother had, left as she watched him eat.

They retired to the living room after dinner and turned the television on for the evening news. Henri wasn't interested, saying he had a ton of homework to do. When leaving the room, the news flashed on. Hearing the name Pleasant Valley, stopped him in his tracks. The broadcast was about the environmentalists being very concerned about what had happened to the town.

173

The reporter spoke rapidly, "And they found the water to be badly contaminated. Now the concern is mainly about some unexplained deaths that occurred in the past. We understand that new health problems are emerging and a thorough investigation is underway at this time."

Clearly, the reporter was upset as he continued in a strong voice, "We urge anyone that lived in the town to seek help if they have experienced any flu-like symptoms, extreme fatigue, vomiting, or dizziness. See your doctor if you have these or any other unusual symptoms."

The newsman showed footage of the now, almost deserted town. Seeing the place looking so desolate was pathetic. They interviewed Mr. Jenkins who looked much older and so sad as he told them of his refusal to leave. "I'll join my wife soon," he softly said, "she's been gone a few years now. There's nowhere else I wish to be. We loved this town." He rocked slowly in his chair.

The news reporter said that because of the death of this little town; major changes were taking place across the country. Factories were the main targets of the environmentalists and the inspectors in charge were looking for anything that could be contributing to the growing pollution problem in the country.

"It is truly sad," he said as the pictures of the lifeless downtown area crossed the screen, "that an entire town had to die before any major action took place around the country."

After the newscast the family said nothing. Again, they were sickened.

"I'll finish my homework now," said Henri. Before leaving the room, he looked to his mother. "Don't be afraid, Mom."

John worked overtime that evening. Mary told him what happened to Henri at school when he returned home, she didn't mention what they'd heard on the news that evening.

John insisted on getting up early to drive Henri and Bobby to school in the morning, telling his wife that it was the only way he could feel they would be safe. She decided not to wake him up because she worried he wouldn't get enough sleep for his job the next day.

Her plan didn't work. John awakened early and dressed. He had breakfast with Henri and told Mary again that he wanted to make sure the boys arrived into the school building safely.

She argued, saying she could do it and had a mind to take care of those drug heads herself. "I told Dad yesterday that I'm going to get tough. I've had it, John. I'll no longer live in fear of the creeps that are making our lives miserable!"

"I can understand that, my love, but I'll not allow you to put your life or the boys in danger. You have no idea what a person on drugs is capable of."

He stood and wiped his mouth with a napkin. "Come on, Henri, let's go."

After delivering the children safely to school, he talked to their teacher about the incident and was assured they would be safe. Mr. Addison told him he'd drive them home daily until he thought it would be all right to ride the bus again. John thanked him many times before he left.

The weekend arrived and Tyrone had John on the phone early Saturday morning. He was taking Bobby to see the park and wanted John and Henri to join them. John believed the experience wouldn't hurt Henri and might reinforce the dangers of taking drugs. Mary didn't agree.

"It'll frighten him even more, John. He already knows about the evils of using drugs. He's being forced to grow up too fast and I hate it. All he wants to do any more is sleep. His bed is the only place he feels safe."

"Mary, I feel strongly about this. It won't hurt him at all."

175

She could feel herself giving in, but didn't want to. "John, can't you see what is happening to him? He's gone from a fun loving little kid to a serious, constantly worried little man. And he's only going to be nine years old."

Henri joined them. John told him what Tyrone wanted to do that day, and why.

"I'll go, Dad." He saw how worried his mother looked and said, "I won't be scared Mom, honest. Maybe we can help some of the people. We'll tell them not to use drugs."

She looked at her son with a concerned expression. "You can go, honey, but you won't be getting out of the car. These people can't be helped until they help themselves."

Worried about Henri, she said to her husband, "I'm going with you."

They left for the park shortly after that with Opal, Tyrone, and Bobby. Finding a troublesome sight, Mary instantly wished she had gone with her first instinct, to keep herself and her son at home.

They sat in the car and watched. There were people of all ages. Some were hanging onto each other as if it were the only way to keep from falling. A few were lying on the cold ground. The park benches were full of strange acting people.

One older boy stood alone, laughing and talking to no one. Tyrone pointed to a small group that stood off in the bushes and said they were probably purchasing more drugs. "I've seen that man in the blue hat before. I'm sure he sells to these people. See him handing something to that girl?"

They did, and watched as she went running off holding a small package. Tyrone pointed to the building she disappeared behind. "That's probably where she's 'shooting' up."

Bobby asked, "What do you mean, Dad? What is shooting up?"

"Sometimes they use needles to get the drugs into their bodies. Like when you get a shot at the doctor. They do it themselves with dangerous drugs."

"I didn't know that. I thought they took pills and smoked funny stuff. Are they having fun?" He looked inquisitively to his dad. "Isn't that why they do it?"

"Does it look like fun, Bobby? Look at them!" He pointed to a girl vomiting. The boys watched with wide eyes.

Henri's voice sounded shaky when he said, "I don't know why they're doing this. It doesn't look fun at all."

Tyrone very carefully tried to explain. "I talked to someone once who had been hooked on drugs. He said it started out being fun. You see, when a person first takes them, they feel wonderful, until they realize they can't live without them. That's called addiction, which means, the body craves the drugs. A drug addict shakes and gets violently sick until he can get more. Then it's no longer fun. The drugs are expensive, and money has to be found to keep the habit going. It's horrible, as you can see."

Both boys watched the scene intently, each one understanding more of what was going on. Bobby said, "If they hang around here, they must not have jobs. How do they get money for the drugs?"

Henri answered. "Some of them steal, Bobby. And they don't care if they have to kill a person to get the money."

Shivers went up Mary's arms. It made her sick to watch these poor wretched people. But she said nothing. Opal also sat in silence.

"Is that guy on the ground sleeping?" Asked Bobby. "He must be so cold."

"I'm sure he doesn't feel a thing," said his dad. "More than likely he's gotten too much of a drug in his bloodstream."

They watched as an ambulance pulled up. "Sure enough," he said, "I'll bet he overdosed."

The medics came running with a stretcher and started to examine him.

"That's enough," said Mary, "let's get out of here right now!"

Tyrone started the engine and they left the park. The boys wanted to know what overdosing meant. He explained it to them, telling them more about the evils of using drugs and sternly warned them to "always say no."

"Will those people ever be okay?" Asked Henri. "Can't the policemen help them?"

"The police have tried hard to stop what's going on at the park, many have been shot while trying. Rehabilitation centers can help the addicts get off drugs. It's difficult to quit and they need all the help they can get. Some are able to kick the habit with the wonderful help they receive."

"I don't know why all those people don't go there," said Henri.

Opal answered. "Many of the centers are overcrowded. From what I understand, it's not easy for the addicts to get in. It's sad, especially when they want the help and can't get it."

She wondered if the boys were really ready for this experience. It was evident that both of them were deeply affected.

They stopped for lunch at the restaurant next to Abe's. Henri and Bobby ate in silence, trying to absorb everything they'd seen.

Eventually the mothers agreed that no harm was done. Especially after hearing each child vow they would never take drugs. Tyrone and John believed the trip served its purpose.

Chapter 18

*T*hat evening Henri asked his dad if they could have a private talk. When his dad joined him in the bedroom, Henri was sitting on his bed holding the little glass angel his mother gave him for Christmas. The angel held a violin.

"I love this angel," he said to his dad.

His fingers traced the outline of the angel as he gazed at it. "I've decided if you and Mom think it's okay, I'd like to play the violin."

His eyes found his dad, "We have a string orchestra at school, and I know other kids in my class that go to it."

John knew his mind was too busy for such a small question. "Is that what you wanted to know Henri? If you could learn to play the violin?"

"I want you to tell me about the devil. Gramma said there was a devil but she didn't like to talk about him. Does he have helpers, just like God does?"

John didn't expect that question at all. After a brief thinking period, he answered, "I'll tell you what little I do know about the devil."

He scratched his head. "To be perfectly honest, I never think about him. I believe there is one. And, from what I understand, he does have helpers. The nuns at the orphanage told us about them. I remember it was Sister Helen that told the story."

He lay back on the bed and Henri did the same. John's eyes went to the ceiling as he began his story.

"She said there had been a big disagreement between God and one of His angels. If I remember correctly, the angel's name was Lucifer. God had to be away for an important meeting and left Lucifer in charge of His office. When He returned, He found him sitting in His chair, with his feet on the desk. Lucifer informed God that he didn't wish to be one of His helpers anymore because he wanted his own kingdom. I guess he loved being in command. Now, remember Henri, this is what the nun told me."

Henri nodded 'yes'. He wanted to hear the rest of the story.

His dad continued, "Lucifer told God that a few of the other angels, some friends of his, wanted to join him. God felt betrayed and told Lucifer to gather these friends together and come to His office."

"Lucifer did as he was told and returned with the others. They were the very angels that God had been having problems with and He promptly threw all of them out of Heaven."

Henri didn't understand. "I didn't think anyone was bad in Heaven. I don't know if I believe this story."

"I know, but listen. Sister Helen said that in the beginning, before God was completely organized, there were adjustments that had to be made in Heaven. The biggest adjustment was ousting those few troublemakers. Heaven then became the peaceful place that God had intended it to be."

"Where did they go?"

"She said the place is called Hell. I don't know where it is. She said Lucifer took his few followers with him and started a kingdom of his own."

"Well, at least we know he only has a few bad angels." Henri felt better about that. Just a few couldn't do many evil things.

"That was in the beginning of time, Henri. She said they needed more members in their kingdom and each one went to work on earth, searching for as many weak people as they could find to join them."

"Weak people?" Henri swallowed hard. "What do you mean, weak people?"

John realized he was getting in a bit too deep. He wanted Henri to understand, but didn't want him scared. After searching his mind for the right words, he continued. "Weak people, are people that are easily swayed. They don't have a lot of confidence in themselves, so they look to others to tell them what to do."

"Are they like the people in the park? Letting someone tell them to take drugs when they probably knew it was wrong?"

"That's a good example, son."

"I do understand, dad. It's like that kid at school. Jack. He used to be nice until the bad angels got him to take drugs. He was weak."

Henri thought about all of the awful things that were happening, and sadly said, "There must be a lot of Lucifer's helpers in the world."

John sat up and looked down at his son. "There are a lot of good helpers too, son. We have to listen to what they tell us."

"I learned about that from Gramma. And in church."

He held the little angel up and looked at it. "She said not to think about the bad guys. If we think about God and the angels every day, the others won't even bother coming around us."

"Gramma taught you many good things, Henri."

"I know. When we talked about the devil one day, I was scared because the kids at school said if you weren't good and didn't go to church, he would get you and you'd burn in hell."

"Maybe no one ever told them about how God forgives? He knows how hard it is to be perfect all the time.

181

If we are sincerely sorry, He forgives us. Everyone can go to Heaven."

"Even the people in the park?" Asked Henri.

"Even the people in the park," said his dad.

Henri got off the bed and put the little angel back on his dresser. "I'll always believe that I have my own good angel, Dad. You're lucky you know who yours is. I'll bet you never stop to think that maybe the angels are just a fairy tale."

"I am lucky to know mine, Henri. And you are right, I never stop to think that maybe it's just a fairy tale. You shouldn't either. As a matter of fact, my boy, I'll just bet yours could be trying to tell you who he is. Maybe he plays the violin."

"Maybe he does, but I'll bet he is very mighty and a super-angel!"

His dad smiled down at him. "Goodnight, son. Those are good thoughts you have. You can't go wrong when you have a super-angel for a friend."

Chapter 19

*I*t was early Saturday morning when the phone rang at the household. The caller had good news. One of John's friends from the factory found a house for rent in his neighborhood. John wrote down all of the details and after hanging up the phone, let out a holler.

His family came running, thinking he was either hurt or had gone crazy.

"What's wrong with you, John?" His wife asked. "You woke everyone up."

"My friend found a house! We're going to look at it this afternoon. It sounds perfect; it's in a peaceful neighborhood."

They all shared his enthusiasm and couldn't stand to wait until the afternoon to go look at the house. Mary put a pot of coffee on and grabbed a bag of sweet rolls. She was too excited to be cooking a regular breakfast and after placing the goodies on a plate, announced the breakfast served. She begged John to call the man right away and find out if they could look at the house earlier.

Of course, he did what she wanted. They were soon in the car and on their way to 553 Oak Street. Finding the beautiful little subdivision posed no problems. The quiet neighborhood was a picture of peace and tranquillity. When they pulled into the driveway, and saw the pretty little home, each person in the car knew they were going to love it.

The man that John had talked to on the phone came out of the house to greet them. He was the landlord and introduced himself as Bob. He invited them in to look around. "We just put the 'For Rent' sign out. The former tenants moved out a few days ago and this home is ready for another family."

Bob anxiously showed them each room. He could tell they loved the house and told them they could move in right away if they wanted to. John talked with him about the surety and rent, and they discussed the lease. When finished, John said he would like to talk privately with his family before making a decision. Bob understood and went next door to visit his former neighbor.

The family loved the house. Mary did not want to leave without knowing she could have it. She found a place for her clothesline in the backyard and Grampa had plenty of space for his garden. But better yet, the rent was affordable. John was happy that his family shared his enthusiasm about the place.

Earlier, the landlord told John to make a speedy decision because he had other families coming in the afternoon. He said the house would rent fast.

John looked at smiling faces when he said, "Well, I guess this is it, then. I'll sign the six-month lease and write him a check."

When the landlord returned, he found the family talking about who would get which bedroom and he couldn't have looked more pleased. "Looks like you've made up your mind," he said. "You're going to love this place. I lived here with my family for quite a few years. All three of our children grew up in this house. After they left, we needed something smaller."

He and John took care of the business matters and when finished, Bob told them they could move in any day. John said they would start hauling a few boxes over on Monday and continue through the week. "We'll finish on Saturday, that's my day off."

John shook hands with the man who told him he was pleased he'd found a nice family to rent the house to. "You have to be careful who you rent to," he said.

The family left and drove through the neighborhood, each feeling good about the decision made, until Henri began thinking about his friend Bobby. He hated leaving his best friend, and knew how sad it would make him. Not wanting to say anything to the others because of their happiness about moving, he wondered how he would tell Bobby.

Henri saw his friend later that day and told him all about the new house. Tears threatened to spill from Bobby's eyes. "What if I never see you again, Henri, and what about our parents? They love being together."

Henri had planned everything he was going to say. His face brightened as he told Bobby. "We'll still be visiting all the time, my mother told me that. She said she would look for a house for you and your family in our new neighborhood!"

Henri's words helped. Bobby's face held a smile when he said with excitement, "We can talk on the phone until she finds our house! We can live next door to each other for the rest of our lives!" The conversation ended with a promise to always be best friends.

Chapter 20

*G*od smiled when James entered His office and handed him a piece of paper with a few lines written on it. After telling James to take a seat, He said, "You met Noel at Christmas time. The angel with the singing message?"

"We loved him! I'd never forget Noel. We laughed until our sides ached."

"Noel's one of the great comedians. He sends jokes on my fax machine. I found these when I arrived this morning and I've been chuckling ever since. Go ahead and read them."

James read the jokes over and had a good chuckle. God handed him a full page of them. Together they howled until tears formed in their eyes and their bellies shook.

Wiping his eyes, James asked, "Does he do this often? These are great jokes. This guy is talented! I suppose he makes them up himself?"

"That he does. They pour out of him like water. I've heard a few before, but they still amuse me. I'm telling you, there's nothing like a good laugh."

"That's for sure. A bit of amusement melts problems away. Temporarily, anyway."

God smiled broadly, "I agree completely. Noel worked as a comedian during his earth life. I'll never forget when I first met him in this office. As usual, he stood at the door shaking like a leaf, I'll never get used to that."

"It's because you're God, The Supreme Being. This will never change. We love coming to your office and feeling nervous is part of the ordeal. We talk about how we tremble for days afterward. You can't take that away from us," James grinned.

"I understand that, but I also enjoy feeling 'regular' sometimes."

"We know. You make each of us feel like your very special friend."

"Which you are. Now getting back to Noel. I wanted to tell you about his first time here."

"Please do."

"I told Noel how much I appreciated the work he did for me on earth. You know, James, he had no idea what I was talking about. I remember him saying, "You must have me mixed up with someone else. I was just a comedian." God paused, looking at James to catch his reaction.

James respected humble people and smiled fondly.

"Can you believe that? How little he thought of himself? Just a comedian. I reminded him that it was I who gave him the talent to be one and he used that talent as I intended it to be used. To entertain my people and bring necessary smiles to their faces. He made them laugh and I told him how important that was to me."

James handed the jokes back to God. "These were great. He had us in stitches when he came to our household singing the Christmas invitation. We certainly appreciated the diversion, that was during some very trying times."

"That's exactly what I mean. Everyone needs a good laugh, including myself. Noel finally understood what I was talking about. Can you believe he never figured he would go to Heaven while he lived his life on earth?"

"Why? Did he think he was a great sinner, or what?"

"He said it was because he made so much money and his mother always talked about money being the 'root of all evil.'"

James crossed his legs. His expression grew serious as he thought of his present situation. "Which it can be, as we both know only too well."

"That's exactly what I told Noel. But I reminded him that he earned every penny of his money honestly. He worked hard and enlightened my people along the way. He liked what I said."

"And so he's been sending you jokes ever since?"

"He sure has, and I never want him to stop."

God glanced over the jokes before setting them aside. "These are so great. I have many good comedians on earth, but many of them should clean their act up a bit. I don't like how they offend some people. I find that I can be amused without the jokes being nasty. It pleases me that they use their talents, but a different direction is needed." He paused. "Of course they have angels trying to help. I hope they get the message."

"I agree."

"Speaking of talent," said God, "I see you are working on Henri's. Playing the violin will be good for him. Music does wonders for the soul and all of his family will enjoy it. I suppose his idea sparked from the little glass angel you sent his way?"

"Buffy gets credit for that one. She persuaded Mary to give it to him for Christmas."

"I've watched all of you closely. Moving to the big city wasn't easy for anyone." God looked solemn. "The move to this other neighborhood will help some."

James agreed. "We feel safer having the warrior angels close by. After the double murder we all knew it was necessary. Actually, we've learned a lot from them and of course, Buffy badgers them with questions."

With fondness He replied, "My warrior angels. They'll stay with you until you're moved. One will stay posted outside the house in the new neighborhood. The family will be protected well. They don't need any further grief at this time. Their load is heavy enough to carry right now."

James agreed completely. God remained silent for a short time. His manner appeared serious as He began, "Do you realize the entire world knows about Pleasant Valley now? The media's done a decent job with the coverage, thanks to the environmental angels. They haven't stopped pestering them. You'll see, James, it's going to get better. More people are aware now and that alone makes the angel's job much easier. We're on our way to a cleaner earth. I don't need all of these premature deaths."

"That's for sure." James understood how important each life on earth was. He also knew when God set out to do a job, it got done.

"I hope you don't mind if we return to that notable park you recently visited."

Not waiting for an answer, He picked up the remote control and tuned in. "It's sad, James. This is going on all over the world now. Drugs are ruining so many lives. We do get a few of the people back each day, but the battle is ferocious."

"T.J. told me what happened to Billy. He's really upset about the situation. We couldn't get near him at the park. The place is infested with the enemy."

"I saw you trying to get close to Billy. That wasn't a good idea, James. I only allow the warriors to go in there. I understand your wanting to help, but it takes a much stronger angel when they are at that stage of dependency. The angels out there work hard trying to convince addicts to make the decision to quit and get on with their lives. T.J. will be notified immediately if Billy wants help and is willing to accept it. It's not easy to crawl out of that hole. Not many are brave enough to try."

It disgusted God to see these people so far gone on drugs. "There's no way they can carry on with their purpose in life in such a state." He watched the big screen for a few more minutes before turning it off.

Laying the remote control down, God said to James, "Let's go outside and play with the horses for a while. I have a secret I was going to share with you, but I've decided to wait until our next meeting."

He stood and fastened a beeper to His belt. A playful smile crossed His face. He knew how much James hated secrets.

James remained in his chair. "I'm not going anywhere until you tell me the secret."

God held the door open. "Come on, I'm leaving."

James stood and walked out; God behind him. He said no more. He hated secrets.

They began their stroll down the long hallway. James said, "If you tell me today, I'll show you how to get your horses to do anything you want them to."

God said, "I know something Buffy's done that you don't know about." He looked to see James' reaction.

James abruptly stopped. His face dropped. "Now what's she done?" Being in charge, he felt responsible for the actions of the angels in his household. He didn't think he missed anything.

"Don't be so serious, James," said God amused. "She'll always be a maverick. I find her behavior a source of pleasant humor. Buffy's a bit whimsical, but she's a good angel."

"What did she do?" He would not walk any further until he was told.

"Come on, keep moving. I'm going to tell you."

They walked further down the hall. James asked, "Is this the secret?" His voice sounded loud in the empty hallway.

God must have noticed too, because he talked softly when he started to tell about Buffy.

"No, this isn't the secret. I've already told you I'm not going to reveal that yet. This is about the trip Mary and Opal took to that dreadful nursing home."

"You knew about that?" Asked James, and then, "But of course you did."

"Just because I must be everywhere at once doesn't mean I miss anything. I'm working hard on getting that place shut down."

"I know. But what happened?"

They reached the doors to the outside. God drank in a breath of air. "The air is freshest here in Heaven, isn't it wonderful?"

"Yes it is. Now, what happened?"

"Let's sit over here on this bench; it's one of my favorite places to think. Come on."

Noticing James' impatience, He decided to stop teasing. They sat down and He began, "When Buffy met the angels that worked at the home, she was particularly impressed with the actions of Joelle. Joelle's been around for a long time and she's a real sweetheart. She's in charge of an old man that stays at the nursing home. He's one of the victims there. His mind was sharp before he arrived."

"He was treated at a hospital for a broken hip. The old man had a wonderful sense of humor-always making everyone laugh. Nurses, doctors, patients, it was a delight to watch him. Until he went to that awful place to recover further. He's in a drugged state now and never smiles, except when Joelle does her magic."

James had a good idea what was coming. He knew Buffy was still looking for a specialty and was afraid to ask. "What magic did she use?"

191

"Now listen. It upset Joelle when she saw the staff at the nursing home drug the man. They do this sometimes to make their work easier, you know."

"I know. It's disgusting."

"Well, Joelle never saw the man smile again and of course it bothered her. She asked me if she could try the rose spray. The man loved roses and when he was well, he spent entire summers working on his rose plants. His flowers were beautiful and he passed them out to anyone walking by. He brought smiles to a lot of people."

"I can imagine." James was anxious to hear the rest of the story.

God leaned back on the bench. "I told her she could use the rose spray."

"You mean the bottled spray?"

"Yes."

James recalled using the same spray once. He used the scent of oranges and it came in really handy when a charge of his lost his spouse. The woman had loved the smell of oranges. Because the man believed in the afterlife, when James sprayed it, he knew his wife was near and the fragrance brought him great comfort.

God continued with the story, "Even if the old man had no idea what was going on around him, when Joelle sprayed the scent of roses near his bed, the man smiled. Buffy was enchanted when she saw the effect of the spray."

James' heart skipped a beat, "She didn't get a hold of a bottle, I hope." All he could imagine was the house constantly full of rose scent. Knowing Mary loved roses, he quickly added, "Buffy's not ready for it. I know her. She will abuse the privilege and we'll all get sick of the smell."

He then remembered smelling roses the other day. She had already used the spray! Mary wondered where the smell came from and Grampa thought she might be going crazy.

God watched as James realized what was going on. "Settle down, James. Buffy means well. I personally don't believe she will abuse it. She only has one bottle and to get more she has to come to me."

"She never asked for permission?"

"It's okay. Buffy conned Joelle out of a bottle. She'll be rationing it. You'll see."

God chuckled as He recalled watching Buffy sneak the bottle into her pocket after Joelle gave it to her. It pleased Him to see that she used it properly, spraying the scent lightly at just the right time for Mary. "You have no need to worry. She loves to comfort Mary, which is good. James?"

"Yes?"

God smiled, "Cool it."

They both laughed. God stood and putting his tongue between his teeth, let out a shrilling whistle. A beautiful black stallion came running wildly toward him. He petted the huge animal and said to James, "Out of all the horses around here, Champ is the only one that minds me."

James laughed when he said, "Let's just try to do something about that."

****

Chapter 21

*B*y Saturday afternoon Henri's family had moved all of their belongings to their new home. They had another reason to celebrate. Today was Henri's ninth birthday. With many things to do, his mother still had a cake baked and decorated. She also bought his favorite ice cream. Bobby and his parents were invited to come over, but they declined, saying they made previous plans that were impossible to break.

After blowing out his candles, Henri ate the ice cream and cake quickly. He couldn't take his eyes off the red package shaped like a violin. Finally being granted permission to open the gift, he lovingly held the musical instrument in his arms, envisioning himself playing beautiful music.

The violin had a special place to sit in his new room. He went there often to pick it up and place it under his chin, holding it just like the little glass angel held his.

On Monday, Henri started his new school and wasn't afraid this time. Everyone stared at him, but he knew it wouldn't last long. His teacher seemed nice, but she wasn't anything like Mr. Addison, who would always be his favorite.

Henri sat in his new classroom missing Bobby. He looked at the new kids around him; they were okay, but he didn't think he would make another best friend here. It hurt too much to leave them and he never knew when he would have to move again.

He never heard from Corey again, and had no idea where he was. Henri was disappointed that Bobby couldn't come over for his birthday. The thought occurred to him that maybe he'd never see him again, either. But that couldn't be so, because Bobby promised they would be best friends always.

Henri learned that he would be having music class twice a week. His music teacher, Mr. Long, looked kind of funny with tightly curled hair that stuck out all over. The man seemed nice enough, but Henri had to wonder if maybe he was one of those punk rockers. He cast the thought from his mind when he figured this man was too old to be hanging around with those funny looking kids. He tried hard not to stare at him.

Mr. Long told Henri he would have an older student work with him privately to help him learn faster. The teacher also said he'd have to practice hard to catch up with the other students, but he expected Henri to be playing along with the others soon.

Henri stayed in the music room and listened to other children practicing a song they were preparing for a small concert. He still could not take his eyes off the teacher. As the students played their songs, Mr. Long waved a stick in the air. His eyes were closed and he wore a huge grin on his face as he swayed to the music. Henri thought he looked much like a clown with his hair sticking out so far. His mother would have scolded him for staring.

An older boy came up to Henri and introduced himself as the violin coach. His name was Steve and he told Henri he would meet with him twice a week until he could play music well enough to be with the others.

That first week of school moved smoothly for Henri. He signed up to play baseball in the spring. A couple of boys, wanting to befriend him, asked if he wanted to join their team. Much to his relief, no one said a word about his red hair.

The family settled comfortably into their new home. Some of the neighbors stopped by and introduced themselves. Mary knew she would be having fun. She began having coffee in the mornings with a few of the other ladies and once again, found herself looking forward to each new day.

Days passed by peacefully. John still insisted they keep the doors locked, but all of them slept much better in the new neighborhood. They totally enjoyed the absence of screaming sirens off in the distance.

Signs of spring began popping up all over as snow piles melted and the days grew longer. Henri saw the first robin and watched as it pulled a worm from a bare piece of ground where the snow had melted. The worm looked long and rubbery. He waited for it to snap in two, but it didn't. The bird flew off with the long worm hanging from his beak.

Henri loved his violin lessons and practiced every time he had a spare moment. He was proud to be learning so fast now because, in the beginning he couldn't get the hang of it. Everyone in the house kept shutting his bedroom door when he practiced, but very soon he could play "Twinkle, Twinkle Little Star" perfectly and his family wanted him to play it for them often. His mother said he would soon be another Mozart.

He played small songs beautifully, soon catching up to the others in his class. Henri got used to the teacher's wild hair and realized that Mr. Long really loved his job; teaching children how to appreciate the beauty and power of music.

Absorbing everything he was taught; Henri learned quickly. He developed a strong attraction to the works of Mozart, who was the teacher's favorite composer.

Henri saw Bobby every Sunday when the two families had brunch together after church. He wondered why Bobby's family never wanted to come over to see their new home. They always had an excuse when invited. Mary and Opal continued to run some errands together. Not as often as before, but they were still best friends. Mary continued to refuse the hospital visits, but did accompany Opal to a few of the nicer nursing homes.

Every Wednesday of each week they visited shut-ins, people who couldn't leave their homes. Mary considered many of the older folks her friends, and looked forward to seeing them each week.

Opal informed Mary one day that the awful nursing home had finally been shut down. She said that Gloria recovered quickly once she moved to another home and was taken off the strong dose of drugs. Gloria's doctor forced another investigation, thanks to Opal alerting him.

The stories the old folks told, entertained Mary and she could listen to them for hours. It reminded her of when she listened to her mother telling tales of days gone by. She repeated many of her mother's stories to these people and even found herself talking about angels to them. Talking about the angels brought a sparkle to their eyes. Some said they hadn't thought about theirs for a long time, not since they were children and learned about them in Sunday School or church. A few patients had close relationships with their angels and shared their angel experiences with the others. Opal appreciated what she was seeing. Mary brought a renewed joy to these people by talking to them about God's special helpers. It surprised Mary when she realized she sounded more like her mother every day.

Angel talk continued at the nursing home each week during their visits. Opal and Mary enjoyed listening to the old folks tell about the special things their guardian angels did to help them each day. A woman named Kathleen had a great story to share that happened only since the angel discussions started. She admitted to being somewhat skeptical at first, but wanted to believe and told of how she asked her angel for a special favor. For three nights, she prayed that her daughter Junie would come to see her. It had been almost a year since their last visit. Kathleen said that Junie had a hard time watching her mother grow old.

"I never expected it to work. I guess I was testing my angel," she told the others excitedly. "But it did. After the third night of my asking for help, I'll be darned if Junie didn't walk into this very room the next day. I still can't believe it. I'll thank my angel every day for the rest of my life."

One of the other ladies said, "I've always believed an angel was at my side, but she sure isn't as speedy as yours. It takes forever for mine to get anything done!" They all laughed.

Kathleen continued with her story. "Let me tell you what my daughter said to me."

"First of all, she timidly walked through the door, probably thinking I'd throw her out! When she saw I was happy to see her, she sat on my bed and held my hand. Junie told me that in the past three days, each time she looked in the mirror, she discovered more wrinkles on her face. The thought of herself getting older consumed her and she felt awful for the way she'd behaved toward me. The poor girl apologized over and over, and has been here almost every day since." She threw her hands in the air. "She's driving me crazy with attention!"

Mary and Opal could see how positively happy she was. The woman continued. "I truly didn't realize the angels were so powerful. From now on I'm going to be careful about what I ask for."

Kathleen smiled sweetly and dried her eyes. "I hope you all know it was in jest when I said she was driving me crazy. I'll be eternally grateful for her new attitude. Thank you, Mary, for introducing me to the angels." She reached for Mary, giving her a big hug.

Mary left feeling heavy hearted. Her mother had spent hours teaching her about the angels and she knew she should be feeling fortunate to know about them. Instead she felt sorry for letting the days slip by without even noticing their presence.

Her eyes searched the sky and she said, "Thank-you." In her thoughts, she apologized to her angel for not paying enough attention. She then watched as Opal walked toward her sniffing the air.

"I smell roses," said Opal.

"You must be wearing a rose perfume?"

"I didn't put any perfume on this morning." Mary opened the door. "I smelled this same fragrance once before. Where is it coming from?" She sniffed the air again.

Opal grinned. "I'll bet it's your guardian angel."

She wasn't teasing, "You really have those people tuned into angels. That's all they talk about. It's wonderful what you've done for them and I love you dearly for it."

Mary halfheartedly said, "While I waited for you, I had a case of the 'guilt's'. My mother taught me so much about the angels. I don't know why I always forget about them being around."

"I know how you feel," said Opal, looking off in the distance. "You've opened my eyes more to these Heavenly beings, and I feel the same way. I've always believed in them. I've seen many unexplained incidents that could only have come from a higher power. But I forget too. And it does make me feel ashamed of myself."

"Maybe it's just because we're human," replied Mary. Opal said that was a big possibility.

Grampa raked several piles of leaves, and was stuffing them in bags when Mary arrived home. She figured he must have been working in the yard for hours. His face glowed from the fresh air and the grass looked well groomed.

"Spring has sprung!" He shouted as she pulled into the driveway. "John's been pacing the floor. He didn't think you'd get back in time for him to leave for work. It's good to see you out driving again."

"I find it a little frightening, but I know I have to do it. The yard looks wonderful!" She glanced at her watch and dashed into the house.

After a quick kiss, John left for work. They waved to each other as the car pulled out of the driveway. Her eyes drifted to where her dad was bent over, pulling leaves out of the flower beds. It pleased her to see him active in the yard; he appeared to be doing much better now. She reflected on how time does heal, but momentarily realized she still missed her mother terribly.

Mary tidied up the kitchen. Looking around, she saw that the men had tried, but they never seemed to do it exactly right. Wiping off the counters and table, she vowed she'd never allow them to know that she cleaned after they did. Men always thought they could do everything so perfectly.

With the house so quiet, she sat in the recliner and put her feet up. She had a fulfilling day and a beautiful one at that. Spring had sprung.

Smiling contentedly, she recalled the pastor saying that spring meant a 'new beginning.' She knew that rang true for her family. They had a safe home now, and new friends. Henri left for his new school each morning happy. Grampa had a new place to put his garden. Everything felt better to her now. Her eyes grew heavy as she thanked her angels once more.

Voices in the yard woke Mary. After realizing she had fallen asleep, she bounced out of her chair. Looking out the window, she saw that Henri had returned from school and watched as Grampa pointed to the plot of ground chosen for his garden. Mary stepped out to the back porch where her dad showed Henri a small group of newly sprouted greens in the flower bed.

"I can tell you right now, Henri. These little fella's here are going to grow up to be daffodils."

"You know everything, Grampa." Spotting some light green shoots near the fence, he ran over to them. "Come see these. I'll bet they'll be tulips!"

Grampa strolled over, shaking his head no. "Just weeds, Henri, but look in the back. That budding bush will bring us lilacs this year."

Henri spotted his mother standing by the door. "Hi Mom, come see all the plants we're finding."

She waved, saying "hi" back to him. Tranquility washed over Mary. The warm balmy wind blew through her hair as she watched her loved ones coming back to life. A new beginning.

Henri ran in circles around his grampa. He loved springtime. Mostly because he could set his heavy boots aside and run free in his tennis shoes. He practically flew through the air without the extra weight of those boots and his heavy winter coat.

Two ladies from up the street strolled over. They stopped to chat with Mary, then asked her to walk with them. She willingly accepted, pleased to be included.

Chapter 22

*H*enri's baseball team began practicing every day after school. He became fond of his new friends. The entire family felt comfortable in their new surroundings and enjoyed each day thoroughly. Grampa had many people stopping by to visit as he worked in the yard. They always asked about his garden. He began promising his new friends a supply of fresh vegetables as they ripened on the vine. Sometimes he stayed outside and pretended to be working, so that his friends would stop by to chat.

Saturday morning brought promise of a sunny, beautiful day. Henri and Bobby talked on the phone early and decided to go to a movie that many of their schoolmates had seen. Mary agreed to take them. Opal didn't want to go because she hadn't been feeling well.

The movie theater overflowed with children and their parents. Loud chattering and popcorn fights didn't seem to annoy any of them as they laughed throughout the funny movie. Parents brave enough to accompany their children, enjoyed watching them have a good time. This type of venture did require patience and Mary had it. She had as much fun as the kids, and found the movie funny, but the chaos entertained her more.

They left the theater in a great mood. Mary asked Bobby if he wanted to come over and see the new house. When she told him she baked a batch of brownies early that morning, he didn't refuse. Bobby would walk miles for anything chocolate.

Bobby thought their new home was wonderful and explored each room. After eating a few brownies, he wanted to call his mother to let her know where he was. Mary found it odd that he argued with her on the phone. It sounded as though she didn't want him at their house. Bobby hung up the phone and said he could only stay for a little while.

He and Henri quickly left and headed for the park. Henri wanted to show Bobby where he played baseball. He never dreamed it would turn into one of the biggest nightmares of his life.

A few of his friends were there. When they saw Henri with Bobby, they started calling both the boys nasty names. Soon other kids joined in and rocks began to fly in their direction. Henri had no idea what was going on, but Bobby knew. He grabbed Henri's arm and started running.

Bobby shouted to Henri, "They hate me because I'm black. Run faster or they'll kill us!"

Henri's legs felt like rubber as he and Bobby ran for their lives. They practically fell through the kitchen door. Henri's parents thought the kids might have a heart attack as they gasped for air and pointed outside. Both boys, frightened out of their wits, tried to talk at the same time.

John and Mary could barely make out what they tried to tell them. Grampa came in from outside to find out what the problem was. He figured most of it out by the looks on everyone's faces.

Bobby was heartbroken because he thought it was his fault. The youngster clearly wanted to go home. Grampa encircled the boy in his arms. No words could ever help this dejected little boy feel better.

Henri sat with his elbows on the table. His hands covered his face. He couldn't believe what happened and felt like his life was over. His friends; he could not understand why they did that.

Bobby couldn't be soothed and begged frantically to be taken home. They could only grant his wish.

Nobody waved to them as they drove through the neighborhood. Nasty glares replaced the friendly faces of what had been their friends. The family's good feelings shattered when they realized they were instantly hated.

But worse than that, their hearts went out to Bobby. He felt ashamed. The attempt to help him feel differently didn't work. Bobby thought it was all his fault that Henri's friends would hate him now and had visions of his best friend being stoned or killed when he went to school.

John and Mary now understood why their friends never came over. They were trying to protect them. Mary's arm remained around Bobby as she spoke softly to him. John became uncomfortable as he approached Bobby's house. Earlier, he remembered the conversation he'd had with his friend at work about the house they were now living in. The man's words had no meaning to him at the time.

"You'll have to get over there right away," his friend said. "This guy certainly doesn't want any undesirables living in that house, if you know what I mean." So anxious was John to move his family, the comment passed over his head.

The friend also said, "He doesn't dare put an ad in the newspaper. You know what kind of person might come around. We'll have none of that in our neighborhood."

John felt stupid now. Tyrone told him many times how difficult it was for him to rent in a safe neighborhood. He and his family weren't allowed in because of their color.

Opal and Tyrone met them at the door when they arrived and knew instantly that something was terribly wrong. They remained calm as John relayed the story, feeling embarrassed as he spoke. His friends tried to put him at ease.

Opal said, "It's our fault, not yours. We should have told you about that neighborhood. They hate blacks. We didn't want to spoil your happiness."

Mary was enraged about the whole ugly situation. "You should have told us, Opal. We never would have moved there!"

Tyrone spoke. "That's why we didn't say anything. We would have prevented you from living in a safer place."

Bobby had gone to his room but Henri stayed on the couch listening while their parents argued about who was right. His stomach churned.

John argued with Tyrone. Opal and Mary began raising their voices at each other and soon each of them began to display anger. But it stopped suddenly and all was quiet as they simultaneously began sniffing the air.

"It's that smell again," said Opal. She sniffed deeper.

Mary giggled. "This is nuts."

The men had no idea why the girls started laughing and wanted to know where the strong rose scent came from.

"It's Mary's angel," said Opal smiling. "She does it all the time. Maybe she hated the arguing."

The two women began laughing and their husbands had no idea what was going on. Henri held his nose as the scent became stronger. He was glad they stopped arguing, but also wondered about the fragrance.

The air in the home definitely changed and it wasn't just the smell. Their moods lightened. Henri ran off to Bobby's room, holding his nose.

Mary suddenly realized the silliness of the situation. "They're not going to make me miserable. Here we are arguing because of those lousy neighbors. I won't let them

205

tear our friendship apart. They can't stop us from being friends and you <u>will</u> be coming to our house. This is just plain ridiculous."

Tyrone spoke, "It really isn't silly, Mary. We can always be friends, but we won't be coming to your house. You have no idea what grief your neighbors can cause and we won't let that happen to you."

"They can't make me any more miserable than they already have! What could be worse?"

He told them to expect hate letters in the mail, for starters. "And we mustn't forget the rocks that could come flying through your windows."

Mary looked around for Henri and then remembered he ran off holding his nose. She didn't want him to be frightened further.

Opal told Tyrone to stop with the warnings. "You're scaring them and I don't like it!"

"At least they won't be shocked like they were today." Tyrone wanted them to be aware so they could protect themselves.

Mary and John felt okay about being warned. They joked about it later, saying at least they would be able to board up their windows before the rocks started flying. The conversation changed to pleasant topics and the issue didn't come up again. They agreed they would always be friends, no matter what.

When Henri returned with Bobby, they too, appeared to have removed the incident from their minds.

After many hugs, the friends said goodbye, for now. Henri and his family drove most of the way home in silence, each wondering what the future would bring.

Henri finally said, "I'm so glad that Grampa doesn't hate black people anymore."

Both his parents wished that Henri would never have known about Grampa's former feelings. They had to deal with it though, and explained as best they could how people can change. Mary told him how terrible Grampa feels now for having had such foolish thoughts.

She added, "He feels worse than we do right now, because he knows that his behavior was much like the neighbors."

John defended Grampa, "He was never that bad, Mary. Your dad never hurt anyone and never would. He became prejudiced because of what he watched on TV. He deplored the racial fighting, but never said he hated black people."

Henri understood. "What happened to me and Bobby must have been racial fighting. They even threw rocks at us."

His mother said, "It was. But I don't believe your friends have any idea why they did it. They watch the behavior of their parents and think they have to do the same."

As an afterthought, she said, "You know what all of this reminds me of? Dogs. They bark at any other dog that comes near their territory. Animals. That's what these people remind me of."

John chuckled. Henri visualized how scared all of the kids were of a neighbor's dog back in Pleasant Valley. It was a bulldog and had the meanest face that Henri had ever seen. He remembered when he and his friends had to pass the yard where the dog lived. They stopped at the house next door and waited for enough nerve to run past. One of the kids shouted, "run," and they ran frantically past the area where the dog barked viciously. Big, ugly, pointed teeth snarled at them as they visualized the chain breaking at any moment. They were sure the animal would eat them alive. Goose bumps covered Henri's arms as he recalled the event. He'd felt the same fear that morning as he and Bobby ran for their lives.

"I know what you mean, Mom. The neighbors act just like that mean bulldog we used to live by. I'm really glad Grampa isn't like they are."

His mother replied, "Try to forget about how Grampa was, Henri. He's a kind man and never meant to hurt anyone. Let's not mention his behavior again. Okay?"

"Okay. I think he just made a mistake."

"He did."

Driving through their neighborhood, John thought about how sad the situation really was. They weren't guilty of anything bad, just loving their friends who happened to be a different color. John was back to where he was before . . . frightened for his family.

Hate letters came in the mail. They threatened Henri's family, telling them to get out of the neighborhood. None of the letters had a signature. Rocks didn't fly through the windows and no physical violence occurred, but the family suffered rejection. Some of the children at school called Henri names. He quit the baseball team.

"I don't care," he said. "At least I have more time to play my violin."

His attitude helped. They all preferred to not have any friends in the neighborhood rather than associate with these people.

On a Sunday morning as they left for church, Henri noticed other people in the neighborhood getting into their cars all dressed up. "I guess they're going to church, too."

After thinking briefly, he said, "They must go to a different church than us."

His mother said, "I've never seen any of them at the church we go to."

Henri was confused, "They must not be learning what we learn. We're supposed to love one another and not cause other people any hurt. Maybe God has different rules for different churches . . ."

208

Chapter 23

*S*ummer arrived. The family lived in their own private world. They left their 'safe' neighborhood to visit with Bobby's family on occasion. Mary looked forward to the visits with her older friends every Wednesday when she and Opal made their nursing home rounds.

Grampa's garden flourished and as always, he swore it was because he didn't use chemicals. Only organic fertilizers were allowed around his plants. When the garden began to produce, he wondered what he would do with all of the extra vegetables. This garden was much larger because he had planned to share with his new friends. Mary assured him she'd bring much of it to the church. They knew of folks who would appreciate the extra food.

Mary began to worry about her dad again. He seemed to be forgetting simple things. One morning he went out to pull weeds in his garden and returned moments later, wondering why there were no weeds to pull. She reminded him that he'd pulled all of them out the previous evening. He then revealed to Mary the growing concern he had about his absent-mindedness. After talking about it, both agreed that old age does that to people. His daughter put the subject on hold.

On a late summer evening, the family sat in the living room munching on large bowls of popcorn. They watched intently as a suspense movie played on the television. A loud knock at the door startled them. They never had visitors and couldn't imagine who it could be. John motioned to the others to stay where they were and reluctantly went to find out who was knocking.

Opening the door halfway, he peered through and found a large, gruff looking man with straggly blond hair, standing on his porch. The man held a scruffy hat in his hands as he smiled broadly.

John just looked at him; he didn't say hello.

The man spoke in a rough voice. "My name is Burky. I mean my real name is Wilfred O'Reilly, but my friends call me Burky. I live up the street and I've been meaning to stop by, but I work so late every day. I heard what happened to you and your family, and I'm mighty sorry. Thought you might like to know that there is one friendly person around."

John, surprised at what he said, put his hand out to shake Burky's. He introduced himself and feeling secure with this large, bear of a man, invited him in to meet the family.

Mary, her dad, and Henri stiffened when he first came into the room. But soon they were completely at ease with him and appreciated his coming over, wanting to be their friend. They visited well into the evening and learned that he too, was an outcast.

"You can't let them bother you for a moment," he told them. "Go ahead and have any kind of *#!*#+!# friends that you want. I do. I have friends of every color and they visit me at my house whenever they *#!*#!*#! want to. I continually get hate mail and plenty of *#!*#!*#! nasty looks, but I'm still alive!" He slapped his leg as he roared with laughter.

Henri liked him. He watched Burky's belly shake when he laughed and wondered what his parents thought about the swear words coming out of his mouth. Maybe they wouldn't notice.

****

The angels had a new friend named Orville and he was Burky's guardian angel.

"Oh, wasn't he wonderful," said Buffy, after Burky and Orville left. "Burky's so big and strong. And isn't he the kindest man you've ever met? I just love him." She gazed off into space, fluttering her eyelids. Lately she'd been acting like a movie star.

The other angels saw she was in one of her moods as she spoke in a very dramatic manner. James called it her theatrical mode. "Which one did you love most Buffy, Burky or Orville?"

"Both of them, of course. I thought they looked and acted the same. I think Orville did such a wonderful thing. Bringing that big, adorable Burky over here to meet the family. They needed a friend so badly."

She stopped briefly to cross her legs, in an elegant way of course. Lately, Buffy was using a fan. She smoothed her skirt and then gazed at the others, fanning her face rapidly as she continued to speak with an air of sophistication.

"You know, my friends. Sometimes I feel as though we are all in a theater, each having our own part to play. It's just so exciting when a new actor comes on the set. Burky reminded me of a knight in shining armor. He's rescued the family from the isolation that this dreadful neighborhood has inflicted upon them. They are thrilled to have a new friend. I will be forever grateful to God for sending one to them. Don't you all feel the same way as I do? That God is the director and we are the actors?"

They tried to hide their amusement. James said, "Buffy, are you sure you're all right? I hear that you and Mary are watching a lot of those soap operas these days."

"Well, maybe we are." She looked away smugly. "We haven't got much to do these days! I never see the neighborhood angels anymore, and if I do, it's only briefly. They're so busy trying to get those rude charges of theirs to soften up and be nice."

The thought of the situation disgusted her. "They've all but ruined our lives with their behavior. You're at school with Henri all day. You don't know what it's like to be rejected."

James was aware of how drastically she and Mary's lifestyle had been altered. All of their lifestyles, for that matter. He remembered how positively thrilled Buffy was when all the fun started up again. She fluttered around visiting with any of the neighboring angels that had time to visit. He felt sorry for her and her ruined social life. However, she did have to get used to how quickly circumstances could change. They were able to count on the family's predictability, but the people surrounding them threw all the curves.

"It's true, Buf," said James. "We are very much like actors, all having a part to play. I'm equally as happy that the new player arrived."

He found it amusing to think of the situation as she did, and said, "Orville played his part with no problem. He admitted that because of Burky's work schedule, the meeting had to be delayed, but Burky followed Orville's silent urges with no problem. I agree. He's much like a knight in shining armor, coming to their rescue." A subtle grin crossed his face.

Knowing that James shared her outlook, made Buffy happy. The others observed as the two of them discussed the issue. They also loved the entertainment.

Buffy's eyes moistened and she dabbed at them with a hankie. "They needed a friend so very much. How could those neighbors be so cruel? I didn't expect anything like

212

that to happen. I really believed we'd be safe and secure here. Especially with the warrior angel guarding us, he should have warned us. I was terrified when I saw those kids throwing the rocks."

"We've talked about that already, Buf," said T.J. "We did keep them from getting hurt. And don't talk so loud, the warrior is just outside."

Buffy whispered, "I didn't mean it, I was just so scared when I saw the boys running frantically down the street. The enemy followed so close. I know that mighty Mike helped to save them, thank God he and James could use magic on their legs. They practically flew to make their escape."

"Mighty Mike has been a big help," said James. "We can't expect him to always predict the actions of others. Situations can occur so quickly. His stronger powers do aid us in keeping our charges from harm. Being powerful, Buffy, is mighty Mike's specialty."

Isaac found a perfect opportunity to tease her. "Shall we talk about your new specialty? The one you found all by yourself? I wasn't there, but I heard all about it."

"I wasn't trying to sneak, Isaac. Ask James." Buffy looked to James, waiting for him to explain. He only grinned as he recalled the incident.

"Leave her alone," said Jake. "She couldn't help it if the sprayer on the bottle got stuck and flooded the room with rose scent. You all have to admit that her little magic trick helped everyone out of an uncomfortable situation."

Isaac admitted that he shouldn't have brought it up again, but added, "I wish I could've been there. It sounds like all of you had a good chuckle."

Buffy didn't like them talking about it. Her biggest problem now was that only a small amount of the scent remained in her hidden bottle. She was afraid to ask for

213

more because she hadn't asked for permission to use it in the first place.

James didn't have time to be upset when it happened. He was too busy trying to fix the sprayer. She was grateful for his help, but fretted over the loss of the precious rose scented liquid.

Buffy decided the topic of discussion needed to change. She asked, "Is there any reason why Burky doesn't have a wife?"

Jake looked at her oddly as he stated, " I saw you looking directly into Orville's face when he talked about that very subject, Buf. Were your ears blocked?"

"I know I was looking at him when he talked," she said. "But I was listening to Mary as she chatted with Burky. We were both so happy he came to visit. I pretended to be listening because I wanted Orville to know that I was friendly and interested in what he had to say."

James shook his head, "You don't make any sense. How can you be interested when you aren't listening?"

Hiding his amusement, Jake said, "Just let it be, James. She sometimes has a hard time explaining herself. Tell her what Orville said."

"Orville said that he's asked God several times if He would consider sending a woman Burky's way - a special woman. Burky's had many girlfriends, but so far, there haven't been any sparks." He winked, "If you know what I mean."

Buffy did. James continued, "Orville also said that God has been hinting about some plans He has for Burky, but isn't ready to reveal them yet. You know how He is about matchmaking."

"I do," said Buffy. "He loves to make all of the arrangements. Orville will just have to get Burky to the right place at the right time."

She folded her hands and looked romantically into the air as she remembered how it had been with Mary and John. Love at first sight.

"It will be wonderful to watch Burky falling in love," she said gazing off in the distance.

Buffy's eyes resembled stars as she reminisced. "I remember all of the instructions I had to follow when Mary was to meet John. I played the most important part."

Somewhat ruffled, Jake replied, "If it wasn't for me, Buf, they never would have met! You almost ruined everything when you urged her over to the wrong guy at the dance!"

Buffy, startled out of her enchantment, looked pleadingly to James. "Make him stop, James, I did no such thing. I had her all fixed up for the occasion. She looked so beautiful, I couldn't help it if the wrong guy flirted with her."

Glancing at Jake through squinted eyes, she said, "I followed every one of my instructions very carefully. You're the one that had no control over John."

James intervened, "What's most important, is that they found each other that night. It may have been a little frustrating when every detail didn't go according to plan, but the mission was accomplished, thanks to the two of you. And because of your success, here we are, sitting here tonight, enjoying each other's wonderful company!"

A soft rumble of laughter broke out. Jake told Buffy he was sorry for saying she almost ruined everything.

She apologized for trying to take all of the credit. "It did take both of us to make the wonderful plan work. Mary and John have been happy together. They've helped each other through some really tough times, I know that takes a special kind of love. God knew how much they needed each other. When He does the matchmaking, it's always so perfect."

"Our director does everything perfect," said James.

Chapter 24

*A*nother summer slipped by with signs of autumn filling the air. Trees began turning brilliant shades of red and gold as the mornings grew cool. Circumstances remained the same in the neighborhood. Some things didn't change with the season. Henri's family continued to be ignored by the nearby residents. The nasty glares remained, but the hate mail stopped.

Henri spent his extra time playing the violin and on occasion, played with Bobby, at his house, of course. Burky became a cherished friend and visited with the family frequently. They loved him dearly. Dearly enough to overlook his major flaw, the swearing.

Early one Saturday morning, Henri and his family were up early having breakfast. It was to be an important day. The church needed a new roof and they would be helping to put one on. Burky was going too. His plans were to be at their house at eight o'clock.

He insisted on taking Saturday off from work to help, saying he was the best roofer around for miles. The family learned early on that Burky's heart overflowed with kindness for everyone. They were thrilled that he wanted to help, especially since he wasn't even a member of the church. He wasn't a member of any church, for that matter.

The topic of Burky's profanity had never been thoroughly discussed in the household. They so valued his friendship that to talk about it made them feel disloyal to him.

That particular morning Henri wanted to ask his dad a question on the subject, but hated to bring it up. His dad could tell that something occupied his mind, because he only picked at his food.

"Henri, what is it?" He asked. "You've barely eaten a thing and we have to leave soon."

"Dad," it pained him to ask. "Do you think Burky will swear at church? I'm so worried that if he does the pastor will throw him out in front of everyone and the people will think he's bad. I love Burky."

"I love him too, son."

His dad thought it over. He wondered himself about the swearing earlier, but cast it from his mind. "Burky doesn't realize he's swearing. I've seen a few other people with the same problem. Every other word they utter is a swear word and it just appears to be the vocabulary they grew up with. They don't curse anyone, they just swear. I can't say whether he'll use that language at church, or not."

John chuckled to himself at the thought. There would probably be some pretty surprised faces, especially from the do-gooders.

He added, "If he does, he does. He's still our friend. We all have imperfections, Henri. If anybody gets mad at Burky, I don't care. I've yet to meet a person that doesn't have a flaw. If we refused to be friends with people because they aren't perfect, we wouldn't have any friends. He's a wonderful man and an excellent friend. The goodness in his heart makes him about the finest human being I've ever met. I'll just bet that God thinks so, too."

"I'll bet he does, too," said Henri. "I don't let myself hear the words."

"That's one of the reasons we don't want you to use that type of language, son. It sounds bad. There are probably some people that aren't friends with him because they are offended by his swearing. They won't allow themselves to

217

know him because they think he's bad. We must always try to overlook the flaws and find the goodness in people."

"Can't we try to help them with their flaws? I've thought about helping Burky."

"Hush now," said Mary. "He's coming up the driveway. Look how sweet he looks carrying his big tool box. He has his work clothes on and he's whistling." Mary wouldn't be able to bear it if he wasn't their friend anymore.

Burky knocked at the door. Mary greeted him and he walked in smiling from ear to ear.

"This is going to be a hell of a good day," he said. "I've put more *#!*#!*#!*#*! roofs on buildings than you could ever count on your fingers. I'll have that *#!*#!* roof on before you even know what happened."

"It's so good of you to help out," said Mary. "I wish you had come for breakfast. I fixed enough food for an army. Are you sure you won't eat anything?"

Burkey refused, saying he never ate a thing until the job got finished. He was ready to work. Mary asked Grampa again if he wanted to come along. He declined; he had enough garden work to keep him busy all day.

The workers piled into the car and were off to begin their busy day. Mary and Henri planned to help with the meals and the men would work on the roof. Each family member hoped silently that Burky wouldn't swear at church.

Once there, Burky was introduced to the pastor and other church members. They were just finishing their last cups of coffee before starting the chore. After a brief visit with the others, the family breathed a sigh of relief when he didn't use a single swear word.

Up on the roof everyone watched in amazement as Burky worked fast and hard, crawling all over the roof like a monkey. No one could keep up with him. The other workers were in awe of this man that whistled nonstop as he pounded nails.

Henri and his parents were proud to be his friend. Not only because of his outstanding work, but because he never swore once. They were grateful because they wanted everyone to love Burky, too.

A new roof adorned the church by supper-time. A job each worker figured would take two days. Burky received countless thank-you's and many slaps on the back for his backbreaking work. He humbly expressed his gratitude for being able to help out.

A potluck dinner covered the table. Bowls containing favorite salads and casseroles passed up and down the rows of hungry people. Everyone ate heartily. The people continued to praise Burky throughout the meal. He thanked them, and still hadn't uttered one bad word.

It happened just as they were leaving. Burky's sun burned face held a huge smile as he extended his hand to the pastor. Shaking hands with him, he said, "It was G*# D*#! good to meet you!" The smile on his face came from the bottom of his heart. Shock crossed the faces of all who witnessed 'the incident,' but not one person said a word. As a matter of fact, the people still shook his hand and thanked him. They acted like nothing happened. Burky had no idea what he'd done.

The next morning at church, the pastor took Henri and his parents aside, complimenting them on their wonderful friend. Mary did tell him she was sorry about the 'incident.' The pastor quickly responded, "We must always look past what we think are flaws in people. Look to their hearts and you will find the true person. Burky is a kindhearted man."

****

With the church service behind them, the guardian angels of all the people congregated outside. On their 'side,' lively conversation could be heard as they chatted about any special events that may have happened in their households. On the 'other side,' their charges stood outside the church under sunny skies doing their usual after church visiting.

Most of the angels present had been at the work bee the day before and still chuckled over 'the incident'. They had spent the entire 'roof' day watching Orville as he tried so hard to keep Burky from swearing.

Buffy didn't like everyone laughing about it and defended Burky. "He has no idea what he even said."

James told her they weren't laughing at him, they were laughing about the 'incident.'

All of the angels that had accompanied their charges to the work bee were impressed with both Burky and his work performance. They wanted to know more about the man. Because Orville was kept so busy with him, he wasn't able to visit at all.

Today he shared a few details of Burky's life. Orville told them that obscene language surrounded Burky from the time of his birth. His parents used profanity as part of their vocabulary.

Orville said, "His mother cursed nonstop while giving birth to Burky. Burky's parents were fine people-like their son. They loved him dearly and wherever they went, he went. I remember the tavern they frequented. They took little Burky with them, toting him in a little white basket. His parents placed the little bed on a table next to the bar stools they sat at."

Orville began shaking in a fit of laughter. "I'm not joking when I say that everyone in that tavern swore, too. Down went the beer and the words flew nonstop. That was one place that we angels could not get anyone to stop swearing!"

The angels giggled with Orville. They began to understand why Burky had a problem. The reason they weren't horrified and didn't carry on about these particular people was because it wasn't their job to judge them. God reminded the angels of that often.

Orville continued, "He learned all kinds of things from the adults. Unfortunately, the vocabulary stayed with him. I couldn't be prouder of the man Burky turned out to be."

God recently told Orville that Burky's swearing had to go. It wasn't a major problem that would keep him out of Heaven, but He just didn't want him to arrive with the deplorable habit and wanted it to be dealt with on earth.

As of yet, Orville had not found the answer that could help him with the problem and had exhausted all efforts. He asked this group of angels if they had ever encountered such a dilemma. Any ideas to eliminate the problem were welcomed by him.

A few thoughts were tossed around before James announced that he was working on a plan that would eliminate the swearing problem. "I wanted to keep this a secret because it would have been a huge surprise for everyone. But as usual, I can't keep secrets."

James revealed part of his scheme and said that Burky would soon be cured. Orville reacted with pleasure as he told the group that God had a surprise planned for when the task was completed. He thanked James a dozen times for helping.

Some of the angels looked doubtful about the 'cure.' Buffy made it perfectly clear to them that when James took on a project, they could count on it being accomplished. James stopped her when she began to boast of how mighty he was

****

Burky helped Grampa with dinner that day while the others attended church. He brought the ingredients over for a favorite dish of his own and was sure everyone would love it. Grampa said a change was in order, and together they worked on the meal.

When Henri and his parents returned from church, they were alarmed by the smell that hit them in the face as they walked through the door. Their home reeked with a peculiar odor. Henri plugged his nose with his fingers and Mary asked what the dreadful smell was.

Using an English accent, Burky spoke, "You dare say that my surprise smells dreadful? My dear people, this delectable dish is going to knock you on your *##. It promises to be a delight that you most likely will never *#!*#!*#!*#!forget."

He pointed to a chair. "Over here, Madam. Please be seated. You are about to partake of the treat of a lifetime."

She sat down, giggling. She couldn't help it; he was acting so funny. Henri didn't share her enthusiasm and hated the two words that Burky used. His mind was made up. He would help him with his flaw and today would be the day.

Burky continued, "The dish is called, "Boiled Dinner," Madame. I shall serve you first. But before we get on with the serving, I have a question. Do tell where you hide the napkins. Grampa has forgotten where they are kept. If you should happen to think we both look a mess, it's because the location of the aprons is also a mystery." Burky had a great time playing restaurateur.

Mary grew alarmed at the mention of her dad not remembering where the two items were. She knew that he knew, but shoved her thoughts to the back of her mind. Right now, she wanted to enjoy this most unusual dinner and would deal with the problem later.

"What's in this," asked Henri as he moved it around on his plate with the fork. "It doesn't smell good at all."

"Well, Sonny Boy," said Burky, "we have boiled ham, with carrots, potatoes and cabbage. In my past experience as a chef, I've found that people turn up their nose before tasting. I assured them, as I'm assuring you, that smells can be deceiving. Once my dish is tasted, everyone agrees that it is a *##! of a treat."

Henri tasted the food and liked it. The others also showed their approval. Burky drank in the pleasure of watching their delight and together they enjoyed the meal. When finished, Henri asked Burky if the two of them could talk privately.

"I suppose you're going to tell me that you don't want me cooking with your grampa anymore? Or is it that you want my recipe?"

He ruffled Henri's hair, and stood, waiting to be escorted to Henri's room where he assumed Henri would want to talk with him. His parents looked worried as the two of them left the room.

Henri told Burky to sit on his bed and sat next to him. Looking into his eyes, he very bluntly told Burky what was on his mind.

"I don't know if you realize it or not, Burky, but you swear a lot and I'm starting to learn bad words from you. I don't want to hurt your feelings because I love you, but if I should slip and swear, my parents will wash my mouth with soap, no matter how old I am. They told me that a long time ago."

Burky's mouth fell open. He hadn't expected this. Apologizing, he put an arm around Henri, and for a brief space of time, was at a loss for words. "I guess I've talked this way for so long that I don't even think about it. Have your parents said anything about this?"

"Not really," said Henri. "We love you and no one wants to talk about it, or hurt your feelings. My gramma used to tell me that sometimes we have to hurt feelings to help someone. That's why I decided to tell you about it."

Henri's head hung as he picked at his fingernails. He could tell how crestfallen Burky felt and wished that he hadn't said anything.

Burky understood and saw Henri's discomfort. His arm stayed around Henri's shoulder as he said, "Your gramma was right. Looking back over my life, there were times when I know I hurt some feelings while trying to help others. Now I know what they felt like. My feelings are hurt, but only because of what I've done to you. I'm glad that you told me, otherwise I would never have known. Swearing is just the way I learned to talk, I guess. For all I know I've probably talked like this since the day I was born." He laughed slightly, and so did Henri.

"I didn't want to make you feel sad, Burky."

"It's okay, Henri. I think you could help me even more. I'll try really hard to watch every word I use, but if I should slip and say a bad word, you must remind me. This is not going to be easy for me, but I am going to try. You're a good friend, and friends should always try to help each other. Now, how about playing me a tune on that violin. I haven't heard you play for a while."

Henri was glad Burky wasn't mad and picked up his instrument. A new tune poured out of the violin, a piece by Mozart that he'd just learned. Not quite perfected, he began playing the first movement of *Eine Kleine Natchtmusik.*

Burky tenderly looked on as Henri tried so hard to play the piece correctly. He vowed he would quit swearing forever. He'd do anything for this little red-haired boy. He had never known many children, but this one held a very special place in his heart.

Returning to the living room, they found the other members of the family waiting anxiously. Burky and Henri sat close to each other on the sofa. They said nothing to the others about their conversation. John and Mary noticed that Burky talked extremely slow now, making it easy for them to figure out what may have been the topic of the discussion.

Chapter 25

*O*n Monday morning, with Henri off to school, Mary sat in the kitchen with her third cup of coffee. Thoughts in her head drifted to her dad; she had a nagging feeling that something wasn't right. Old age wouldn't make him forget where his colorful aprons were. It just wasn't possible. She knew he needed to have a good checkup. It was time, and having it done, would relieve her mind of one less worry.

She put the cup to her lips for another swallow of coffee only to find it empty. While pouring herself a fresh cup, she remembered reading in the newspaper that coffee wasn't so good for one's health. All she needed was something else to worry about. There wasn't any time to think about whether coffee was dangerous or not, because her dad came into the room. A huge smile crossed his face as he greeted his daughter with a cheery good morning and proceeded to help himself to a cup of the brew.

He sat across the table from her and firmly stated, "I think it's time I have a checkup, I'm at the age now where things can go wrong."

Relief came to Mary, because now she didn't have to bring the subject up. "It doesn't hurt anyone to get a check up. I'll have to find a good doctor; we should have one for all of us anyway. We've been very fortunate not to have needed one since our move. Best we find one now, because you never know what the future may hold." She instantly disliked her choice of words.

"I hope I get a clean bill of health. It's bothering me that I'm getting so forgetful, I always know where the napkins and my aprons are kept. I can't believe what happened yesterday. I have these spells on and off. It's annoying. Maybe this just goes along with getting old."

He took a long swallow of coffee. "It could very well be that I'm lacking something in my diet. A vitamin or something."

Mary's eyes darted quickly to him. "Don't even start that tonic stuff. I heard enough about that from Mother."

Regretting her harsh words, she calmly asked how long it had been since he had seen a doctor.

"Quite a few years, Mary. I can't remember exactly. You know how I've always hated to go."

"Well, you're going. I'll call around and get an appointment. Opal might know of a good doctor. I'll check with her."

It turned out to be a harder chore than she anticipated. Opal told Mary that finding a doctor wouldn't be easy and told her about the many problems she had because her family didn't have insurance. "I'm telling you girl, your dad better have good insurance or they just won't take him. It's a crying shame how some people have to go without care because they can't afford the skyrocketing fees!"

After ranting and raving about the outrageousness of it all, Opal gave her a few names. When Mary called the numbers, the receptionists told her the doctor's schedule was too full and wasn't taking new patients, or that her dad could be scheduled in two or three months. She called Opal back to report her dilemma.

Opal suggested an alternative. "You know, Mary, because your dad is getting so forgetful, I would think that they would take him at the mental health center. Being forgetful is a mental kind of thing. And besides, if you don't have a lot of money, it's free."

"That's awful, Opal. He's not mentally ill!"

"Well, it's a start. They'll know more than we do and they'll tell you where you can take him. Maybe he needs some kind of specialist. I'm only trying to help."

"I know. But taking him there is out of the question. I'll keep calling. I'm sure someone will see him."

After hanging up the phone she began looking through the phone book. She found a doctor that would see her dad immediately and scheduled him for the following morning.

Because John didn't have to work until later in the day, he accompanied them to the appointment. When they arrived at the office, many questions were asked. After the receptionist finished, she looked directly into Grampa's eyes and told him he would have to pay before leaving the office. She asked how he would pay the bill, cash or check.

John interrupted. Irritated, he said he would pay the bill in full. He didn't have a good feeling about this place.

Grampa was called to the examining room. The doctor wasn't friendly. After the examination, he told them their dad's health looked good and he couldn't find anything wrong with him. He said that because of his mental problems, perhaps they should take him to the mental health clinic. Mary and John disagreed and her dad didn't like the man at all. John paid the bill in full and they left, feeling it was a wasted trip. They wondered if he was really a doctor.

A few weeks passed and they could see that whatever was wrong wasn't getting any better. With no alternative, they reluctantly took him to the mental health clinic, hoping they would be advised as to what they should do.

John accompanied Mary and her dad to another morning appointment. Grampa first chatted with a lady counselor who wanted to know everything about his life. He said he had no problems except for his forgetfulness.

She kept prodding and asked if his wife still lived. Grampa told the woman about her death and found himself revealing everything else that happened recently in his life. The counselor took notes. When finished, she said they could help and escorted him to an office where she introduced him to the doctor. After laying the notes on the desk in front of the physician, she left the room.

Grampa came out of the office a short time later holding a prescription in his hand and a smile on his face. He felt positive he was on the road to recovery.

"Let's go," he said. "There's nothing seriously wrong. I just need a few pills."

An alarm went off in Mary's head, but she said nothing. Nor did John. They both were a bit uneasy but figured anything was worth a try.

Stopping at Abe's to pick up the prescription, they were greeted by his friendly face. A while had passed since they'd seen him and the reunion couldn't have been happier, until he saw the prescription.

"Hey, now," he said. "This is very serious stuff. What's going on?"

Grampa explained about the forgetfulness. Abe still shook his head in disbelief over the pills.

He said, "I can't tell you what to do, my friend, but these pills are going to put you in la-la land. I know a doctor who would give you a good checkup and I can guarantee you he'll only use drugs if the need is absolutely necessary. He keeps me going strong with his natural remedies and I'm telling you, it wouldn't hurt to have another opinion before you take this stuff."

Mary looked hopefully to her dad, but as stubborn as he was, he wouldn't hear of it. "I've done enough running around. I'll give these pills a try. The doctor assured me that they would help, and just maybe they will. No offense, Abe."

Abe didn't like it, but he wasn't going to be pushy. He knew he'd be hearing from Mary soon.

They left Abe's. Grampa was eager to get home to take the first pill. He wanted to get better. "I probably just need a good rest. Both of you can stop worrying any time now."

A good rest is what he got. He slept for three days, waking enough to eat very little and take more pills. The short periods of time he was awake, he expressed his happiness about not being forgetful anymore.

Mary, frantic over his behavior, hollered, "Of course you aren't forgetful anymore, Dad! You're never awake long enough to forget!"

He slept for two more days after that and Mary called the mental health clinic, a little more than upset. She demanded the doctor see her dad that morning.

The receptionist said there were no openings until the next day and Mary clearly told them that she was bringing him in anyway.

John had to work, but his wife assured him she would be fine taking him alone. John had never seen her so mad. She displayed a strength he had never seen before and knew there was no stopping her.

Mary practically had to carry her dad into the full waiting room; he could barely walk. The receptionist said it would be a long wait and she wasn't kidding. Her dad slept comfortably in his chair for hours. Mary watched the people in the room and listened to many of their conversations. She did not like what she heard.

Granted, she could see that some of the people were not well. What bothered her was the frustration she saw in a few of the others that disagreed with the doctor and wanted their loved ones taken off the medications. From what they were saying, the doctor wouldn't allow it.

Mary chatted with the woman seated next to her. She told Mary that her husband had a mild nervous breakdown a year ago and they were still trying different drugs on him. The woman said she didn't believe that he suffered a breakdown.

"He's never been the same," she said. "All he does is sleep."

The woman told Mary they couldn't afford to get another opinion and fear kept her from taking him off the medication herself because she didn't know what would happen. The poor woman plainly wanted her husband back.

"Lots of pills and an appointment once a month," seemed to be the topic in the room. And also, the fact that they had to stay on the medications forever. She heard someone else say it appeared to be the easiest way to run the clinic. No one had the time or patience to help the people get off the pills they were hooked on.

Mary shook her dad to wake him. After hauling him out the door, she left for home and immediately phoned Abe. His friend's name was Dr. Gene. Abe immediately called and scheduled an appointment for Grampa. They had to wait a few days, but both John and Mary knew instinctively they had done the right thing. She threw the pills out and Grampa seemed alert enough for the morning of his appointment.

John, Mary, and Grampa entered Dr. Gene's office at the scheduled time. Some questions were asked and they waited a few minutes before Grampa went in to see the doctor.

Dr. Gene checked Grampa thoroughly. Afterward, he asked Mary and John to come into his office. Grampa wanted Dr. Gene to tell them what he thought. He did not appear to be upset.

The good doctor displayed a kind and gentle nature. After explaining about the necessity of extensive testing by a neurologist to insure a positive diagnosis, he told them it may take a few months before they would know for sure what was wrong. Fright embraced Mary's soul when she asked Dr. Gene what he suspected.

The doctor seemed reluctant to tell because nothing was positive. Feeling he had no other choice but to be honest, he spoke the words, 'Alzheimer Disease'.

Mary learned later that her dad was in the early stages of the disease. Dr. Gene called them in for a meeting and revealed the results of the testing. Very gently, he explained the probable course of the illness. After giving them a few instructions, he told Grampa he wanted to see him at least once a month and told each of them to feel free to call whenever they felt the need.

When they left Dr. Gene's office on that day, Mary and John were speechless. It was evident that grief was becoming a way of life for them.

Grampa did not display any outward signs of bitterness at all. Seeming oblivious to the situation, he wanted to stop at the store and get some ice cream on the way home. Mary and John were baffled by his behavior; he never said a word about the disease, not even after he first heard. Maybe he had blessedly forgotten.

In a way, his childlike behavior cushioned the pain they were feeling. He appeared to be totally unaware of the fact that he had a cruel and horrible illness. It seemed to Mary and John that the two of them needed comforting. He had no need himself.

They stopped at the store. Grampa got out of the car, excited about his plans to purchase two different flavors of ice cream. Strawberry for the three of them, and Henri's favorite, chocolate.

John and Mary waited in the car. Feeling discouraged about life, they didn't want to talk about anything. They began to get a little concerned when Grampa didn't return as soon as they would have thought. But it was needless worry. He soon came out of the store, but carried only a bouquet of flowers.

They both thought the same thing at the same time. He had forgotten the ice cream. He smiled broadly as he presented the last gladiolus of the season to Mary. She thanked him kindly and they left for home. No one mentioned the ice cream.

Later that evening, Henri was told about his grampa. His parents explained the disease as best they could, making it sound less threatening than it was. They did not want him to be worrying. Henri appeared to be growing more quiet with each passing day. His parents felt sure it was because of all the sadness he had endured in his young life. The only time he smiled anymore was when Burky was around. Burky always made him laugh. His other pleasure came from his violin, sometimes playing it for hours on end.

Henri didn't say much when they told him about his grampa. He looked up dolefully from the homework he was working on and asked them, "Why do such bad things keep happening to us? He's not going to die, is he?"

He didn't wait for an answer and returned to his math. With his head down, he said he would continue to help Grampa remember things. "I know he keeps forgetting, I just thought it was because he wanted to."

Grampa stayed in his room that evening. His memory remained with him and he remembered everything that he'd been told. He studied in private about the disease and knew what to expect. When his mind worked normally, he wrote down important things. Tonight he smiled as he put his wishes for the future on paper, knowing his wife had done the same for him. He stopped momentarily to think about her, while he still could.

Grampa continued making notes. Knowing his condition would worsen, he wanted his daughter to know what to do when the time came. He planned to pick out a home for himself that specialized in the kind of care that he would need. Having enough funds to support his desires would be his main concern. Frowning, he knew how meager those funds were.

He went to bed after placing the notes in the bottom drawer of the bureau. His only wish was that his family wouldn't worry about him; he wanted so desperately for them to live their own life happily. Feeling like a burden, he looked forward to the day when he wouldn't have to be one. That secret would remain in his heart.

Chapter 26

*W*ith Autumn in full swing, the last of the vegetables in Grampa's garden were harvested. Mary helped him with some canning and any leftover vegetables were given to the church for those in need. The family relaxed when the garden chores ended and they patiently awaited the arrival of winter.

Henri was well into the routine of his school, without any complaints. He had a few friends in his music class and didn't seem to be bothered by those who shunned him. His parents were still concerned with his quiet demeanor and the fact that he spent more of his extra time sleeping. They passed it off as a growing boy needing his rest, not wanting to invite any more trouble. Every day after school, he tuned his radio to a station that played classical music and usually drifted off to sleep listening to the soothing sounds of the symphony.

Mary took advantage of a warm October morning to get caught up on her laundry. Interrupted by the phone, she found it was Henri's principal, reporting that Henri had fainted in school. He told her not to be alarmed because it happened occasionally when the children skipped their breakfast.

After a near collapse from fright, Mary remembered that Henri didn't have an appetite before he left for school. She left immediately to pick him up and found him looking somewhat peaked, but he said he felt fine. She ushered him out to the car, telling him he mustn't ever skip breakfast again.

John and Grampa were seated in the kitchen drinking coffee when they returned. Both had no idea where she'd gone.   Mary hurried around the kitchen fixing Henri a sandwich as she explained what happened. Grampa looked at the lad with an eyebrow raised. John assured him that Mary was right, children who skip breakfast can get weak.

Not one of them said verbally what they were thinking. Mary didn't know about the others, but she felt the familiar feeling of ugly numbness-until Henri perked up after eating and color returned to his cheeks.   Once again she could reprimand herself for over reacting.

Grampa took advantage of Henri being home.   The checkerboard came out and they played the game for most of the afternoon.

Henri called Bobby later that day when he knew he would be home from school. He told him what happened that morning and they laughed. Bobby said he was going to "fake" it the next day so he could have a day off from school, too.

Burky stopped over after dinner, displaying a great mood. He had a big surprise for the family. "I'm having a big party this weekend and we're all going to have a ball! It's going to be an outside event. My friend said the weather would be exceptionally warm for the occasion and he's never wrong with his predictions. He said we will have our 'Indian summer' this weekend."

Burky's excitement was contagious as he told about the many different people who would be attending.   He boasted of a good friend that would be singing and announced that there would be dancing, too.

Mary joined him in his excitement and wanted to help with the menu.   Because it would be a patio party, Burky didn't want anything to be fancy, so they decided to have a barbecue with potato salad. Henri was excited about the party, but expressed his concerned about what the neighbors would do if they made too much noise with the dancing and singing.

"To #*!*#! with the neighbors," Burky said, and at the same time he realized his language. Guilt washed over his face.

"It's okay," said Henri. "At least you know that you said it."

Mary, acting as though she hadn't heard, blurted out, "I make the best potato salad! I can fix a huge batch of it."

"Oh no, you're not!" Burky forced a stern face, "I'm buying everything from the deli. I don't want anyone working. This is going to be a fun day. And Henri, don't you be worrying about the neighbors. We'll keep the noise down somewhat, but then, I hate to spoil their fun. They love to call the police. Last year's party brought in an officer that turned out to be a good friend of mine. In no time at all he figured out what the real problem was and we had a good visit."

"Did they call the police because you were making noise?" asked Henri, "or was it because of your friends. Were there any black people at the party?"

"I have friends of every color, which is the biggest reason the neighbors get so nasty. But, what they tell the police is that the party is too boisterous. Ol' Dan could see that we weren't noisy. He knows about the problem in this neighborhood. Let's not think about our friendly neighbors, we have to finish our plans."

Mary loved parties and couldn't wait for this one. She hadn't been to a good party since the Pleasant Valley barn dance and told Burky about the fun she and John had that night. He listened patiently as she reminisced. When Mary realized she was off in another world, she cut herself short and asked him who would be singing at his party.

"It's a friend of mine. His name is Jose' and he stopped singing a while back because he couldn't make enough money at it. His dream was to become a famous singer, but it never happened. I'll get him singing again if it's the last thing I do in this life. I haven't seen him smile since he quit."

Henri asked, "How will you get him to sing at the party?"

"He doesn't know he's going to. I have a guitar at my house that's been collecting dust for years. At one time I thought I could learn how to play it. Never had the patience. Anyway, I'll pull it out and make him entertain us. You'll hear some really nice tunes. And Henri, I'd be honored if you'll play the violin."

Henri's face lit up. "Really? I'd like that! I'll have to practice some of my favorites." He looked to his mother. "Won't that be fun?"

She agreed it would be, and was touched that Burky asked him.

They visited a while longer and the conversation changed to where Mary felt she could ask him a personal question.

"You are the nicest person, Burky. Have you ever thought about getting married? I would think that some woman would have grabbed you a long time ago."

"I've met many women Mary, but I haven't found one yet that could put up with me. I guess I'm not the marrying kind. A confirmed bachelor, that's what I call myself. But thanks for the compl'ment Ma'am." He tipped his hat and stood up. "Have ta' be movin' along now. This old bachelor needs some rest."

Mary stood on the porch with her arms folded as she watched Burky stroll down the street whistling. She thought about how lucky they were to have him for a friend. A warm breeze brushed against her face as she kept her eyes on him until he was out of sight. He'd been like an old watchdog ever since he heard of her dad's illness. Visiting regularly, he kept everyone laughing.

Burky spent every Sunday with her dad, helping with Sunday dinner. Mary knew he wanted the family to attend church without having to worry about him.

Burky's thoughts wandered too, as he walked to his home. He loved his new friends and admired their inner strength. Never had he met a family that had endured so many hardships. It baffled his mind to think about it. His greatest desire was to help them in any way he could, without being a pest. He loved them as though they were his own family.

Little Henri tugged at his heartstrings. Burky felt uneasy with how frail his little buddy looked. The fainting spell at school upset him. It reminded him of the warning he'd seen on TV. He didn't know whether the family had seen it or not, but he never brought it up to anyone of them. He couldn't forget about the report; former residents were urged to watch for certain symptoms that might mean they were sick from the polluted water.

Burky wondered if Henri's parents could see him withdrawing. Or were they denying what was so obvious? He hoped he was wrong.

The stillness jumped out at Burky as he entered his too-quiet house. He turned the lights on and instantly felt the familiar loneliness, making him all the more thankful for his new family of friends. Sitting back in his favorite chair with his feet up, his thoughts drifted back to them.

It didn't bother him at all that they were religious, probably because they acted different from other religious people he'd known. He admired their strong faith and figured that had to be what kept them going. He knew that if other religious people acted like them, he might consider getting a little religion himself.

They never preached to him. And never once did they try to force him to join their church like so many others had. To him that was a big turn off and he called people like that, religious fanatics. The fanatics he knew, made him feel like there could be no greater sinner than himself because he didn't attend their church. They acted self-righteously and he had no patience for it. Almost everyone in his neighborhood belonged to some church and their behavior was atrocious.

His new friends weren't like that. He cringed when he thought about his swearing and how they never said a thing. Burky couldn't believe he'd been able to quit. His little friend, Henri, helped him and he felt quite proud of himself for doing it.

Planning for his party took much of the night. Henri's family was worth it. They needed to have some fun and meet new people. He also had a big surprise lined up for them. Smiling broadly at that thought, he forced himself out of the chair and got ready for bed.

Chapter 27

*T*he day of the big party arrived and everyone invited showed up. Burky proudly introduced Henri and his family to his many friends. He told them that a big surprise awaited them. His friends knew prior to that evening what the surprise would be and on a cue they all stood up, waiting for Burky to make the announcement.

Acting as an emcee, Burky said in a loud voice, "And now my friends I am pleased to introduce you t-o-o-o . . ."

He paused as everyone held their breath and watched the door he pointed to. Opal and Tyrone appeared, with Bobby trailing behind. Burky then introduced his special guests to everyone.

Henri and his family stood speechless for a few seconds before running to their friends. As they hugged each other, Burky came over and explained how he insisted Opal and Tyrone be at the party. He said he refused to take no for an answer and told them it was pure nonsense that they didn't come around because of the neighbors. Bobby and his family couldn't have been happier. They too, thought Burky was the greatest.

With the party in full swing, it was evident that everyone fully enjoyed themselves. Burky made the rounds, talking and laughing with his wide assortment of friends. At one point, he stopped to look them all over and chuckled to himself. Seeing so many skin colors congregated in one area reminded him of a television commercial he used to see often. He recalled how many different races sang together, "We Are the World." Here, he could see a sample of just about every kind of human being that was ever created. His heart warmed as he watched them laugh and talk together.

His thoughts were interrupted by Mary. She wanted to know who the singer was and when he would start.

"I'll get the guitar and you'll soon find out!" Burky made a dash for the house, returning in a flash with a very dusty instrument.

Mary picked up a napkin and went to work. The results of her efforts turned out a nice shiny guitar that she handed back to Burky.

"Jose' will make this thing come alive," he said, "I'll be right back."

He returned with a man that looked to be of Mexican descent. Mary saw him frantically shaking his head 'no'. He begged Burky to leave him alone because he didn't want to sing. Burky paid no attention to his pleas and loudly asked for everyone's attention.

"We have a musician here tonight, folks. I promise this man's singing will bring tears to your eyes. You'll never meet anyone in your lifetime that can sing as beautifully as Jose'!"

Burky handed Jose' the guitar and stepped aside. He and the audience waited. Jose' had no choice but to sing as the people started clapping. They wanted him to get started. He quickly tuned the guitar. The songs came out weak at first, but he soon bellowed them out and the crowd cheered. Everyone was captivated by the talent this man had. And Burky was right, he did bring tears to their eyes. Jose' smiled broadly as he sang, his white teeth sparkling. Burky hadn't seen the man smile like that in years.

Jose' was the highlight of the evening as he poured out songs from deep within his heart. Burky even saw some neighbors hanging out the window listening to him. He wondered why they didn't get off their high horses and have a little fun. Their attitudes prevented them from enjoying the finer things of life.

Different cultures made for different friendships, each able to teach each other so much. Burky looked at Jeff, his Indian friend. The guy could predict the weather like no one he had ever known. He was a walking weather station and his promise of the evening being warm and balmy turn out to be accurate, as usual. Burky knew beyond a shadow of a doubt that his party could be held with no problem and the beautiful night sky proved him right. Jeff was also an expert fisherman. He taught Burky many different ways to catch fish.

Jose' stopped playing and after promising his audience he'd be right back, headed for the refreshment stand. Everyone crowded around, telling him how much they appreciated his music. Burky stood in the background, watching with an expression of total satisfaction written across his face.

Jose' drank his beverage and thanked his admirers repeatedly for the compliments. He loved the attention, but most of all, he loved to sing. Some of the folks asked him where they could hear him sing locally. Everyone assumed he sang somewhere regularly and were disappointed to hear he was "retired."

Jose' told his audience the story of the days when he used to sing at the local night clubs and how fruitless it had been. "To make it really big in the music industry takes money. I don't have it. The factory is where I work now and I hate it, but that's just the way it is. I quit singing altogether."

Mary talked privately with him and his wife later, telling Jose' that it was silly of him to quit. Especially when he could plainly see how much happiness his singing brought.

"Singing doesn't put food on my table," he answered.

Mary thought his great talent was being wasted. "Sing occasionally just for the enjoyment. The people would be happy and you never know when someone might be listening that could help you with your singing career."

Jose's wife agreed with her. When the two women talked at the refreshment table, she confided in Mary. She wanted him to entertain again because he'd been cranky ever since he stopped. But, like most men, he was stubborn. They giggled, knowing that to be a true statement.

"Well," said Mary, "I'm going to ask him to sing at the nursing home. The people will love it. What do you think?"

"I think he won't do it," said his wife.

"I'm still going to ask him."

"Lots of luck to you then. I live with the man and I'm telling you he won't sing at the nursing home."

They both looked to the makeshift stage where they heard violin music begin to play. Mary felt a lump forming in her throat as she watched her son make his debut. He looked like an angel standing so straight and serious; trying to play each note perfectly. Love poured from her heart for her son; she felt immensely proud of him as he so expertly performed. Their new friends were equally touched. Henri played a few of his favorite pieces and when finished, took a bow.

The crowd applauded and told him how much they enjoyed his performance. Henri loved the attention and so did Bobby who stood proudly next to him.

"The people really loved him," said Jose' to Mary and John. "I can see more clearly what you said about making people happy, Mary. I guess I've been a bit selfish, thinking only about the money."

"No different from most men, Jose'," said John. "Just sing for the pleasure of it once in awhile. I can tell it makes you happy."

Jose' smiled broadly as he said, "It's been fun tonight. I think I'll sing a few more of my favorite songs." He picked up the guitar and started to walk away.

Mary stopped him, thinking it to be a good time to ask the favor. "I've been meaning to ask you all night if you could possibly come over to a nursing home that I visit and sing a few songs for the older folks. They would absolutely love it."

He didn't know what to say. It wasn't his idea of a great time. "If I get a few free moments, I'll do that."

Burky's guests partied late into the evening. Mary and John had fun, chatting and laughing with everyone. Henri had fallen asleep on a chaise lounge shortly after he played his violin. Bobby sat next to him, waiting patiently for him to wake up.

Jose' sang his final song, "He's Got the Whole World in His Hands." He spotted Henri asleep and directed the last verse to him.

Everyone sang along as he added to the song, "He's Got Little Henri, in His Hands." Burky felt a cold chill go up his spine as they sang. He couldn't sing along with them; the words wouldn't come out of his mouth.

The evening of fun ended and all the party goer's left happy. Burky received many thanks. All of his friends promised to see him real soon. Mary and John were thrilled with the many new acquaintances they made that evening. They were especially happy about Bobby and his parents attending the party and thanked Burky repeatedly for what he'd done. Burky knew he had done the right thing, despite how the neighbors felt about people that weren't their own 'kind'.

****

The angels also partied the night away. They too, met many new friends and were especially excited by the unexpected visit from God. He wasn't able to stay long but stayed long enough to prompt Jose' to sing the last song. God personally made sure that Henri was included in the last verse. He visited briefly with the angels after the song and then left.

Everyone pleaded with Him to stay, but He refused. Displaying His familiar grin, He said, "Don't forget, my friends, I have to be everywhere at once." And then He was gone.

The angels felt special that He spent even a few minutes with them. Word of His presence spread rapidly throughout the neighborhood. Many of the neighboring angels were able to sneak away for a peek at Him, feeling honored that He made a personal appearance in their area.

The angels mulled over the eventful evening. Buffy said, "If only God could have stayed a little longer, maybe He would have asked me to dance. He's just so wonderful."

"And busy," said T.J. "Like that's all He has to do is party and dance around with you. If you ask me, you did enough dancing for one evening. I'm surprised that you have any feet left!"

With a snippy voice she replied, "I can't help it if everyone wanted to dance with me. It was such fun. I don't know if you noticed or not, but at the end I wasn't using my feet at all."

She smiled off in the distance and said dreamily, "I merely flew through the air. With the greatest of ease, I might add."

Quickly looking to James, she changed her expression to one of concern. "I didn't see you dance once, James. Are you okay?"

James folded his arms and gazed down at her. "I worked, Buf. Do you remember? Mary needed to ask Jose' to sing at the nursing home?"

Guilt. Why did he have to do it after she had so much fun. James finished the task that was hers to do. She didn't look his way when she said, "And I thank you, James. I know it's important for Jose' to sing to the old folks and I hope you know I'm sorry. But you know how much I love to dance, not to mention how much stress I needed to release."

Buffy wanted to make him understand and tried a different approach, "I see your friend Wolfy came to the party to help you. Henri played his violin perfectly because of him. We must always help each other; that's what God wants."

Much to Buffy's relief, Jake interrupted, "Henri played beautifully tonight. He felt so proud. I think it was nice of Wolfy to come and help. You're lucky to have him for a friend, James."

"It didn't take any begging. You know that. He had a ball helping Henri and even more fun afterwards. He loves parties and as far as I know, has never refused an invitation to one."

James searched for Isaac. "And you, Isaac. You didn't leave the dance floor once! I would have expected you to be a little rusty. But not so! You still have legs that can really get around!"

Isaac cleared his throat, "It was fun," he said, acting a bit embarrassed. "Haven't you ever seen anyone have a good time before? You're always too busy to have fun, someone has to do it for you. Besides, what was I supposed to do? Grampa sat around all night talking to the older folks."

Buffy told Isaac that James was only teasing. She asked James about the importance of Jose' singing at the nursing home. "I don't like it when you give instructions and we have to follow them without knowing why."

The others also wanted to know what was going on.

"Jose's singing could get him discovered. A woman that's staying there, has a son who visits quite frequently. He's very powerful in the music industry. I personally don't think Jose' will go there to sing for the folks. He has a thing about making money for every song he sings."

Buffy came to Jose's defense. She thought he was adorable. "That's not so, James. Burky didn't pay him to sing at the party. He even sang the song God wanted him to. I like Jose', and I think his heart is big enough to go over and sing for the poor shut-ins."

"I suppose it's possible; some people are given a bunch of chances and they blow it. His angel will be pushing him to go. But it's up to him. He just has to sacrifice a little of his time. We shall see."

All were anxious to hear of the outcome.

****

Chapter 28

*T*he neighbors didn't call the police the evening of the party, but they were not nice during the week that followed. More hate letters arrived in the mailbox for both Burky and Henri's family. The letters were ignored and as usual, they eventually stopped coming. The family accepted the fact that they would never be greatly loved in the neighborhood. Nasty letters were nothing compared to the new friendships they made.

One evening, Mary read that one of her neighbors died. Gracie Newburg lived just two doors down. Mary felt bad because Gracie had been nice to her when they first moved in. She decided to send flowers and a card to Gracie's family. Writing a note on the card, she expressed her sympathy and told them to call if they needed any help. The Newburg family never acknowledged the flowers or card.

Mary was a little hurt but figured she at least did what she thought was best. At times it depressed her to know how hated they were. She and John talked often about moving out of the neighborhood. They weren't eager to leave because of Burky, but also didn't want to live the rest of their lives among such hatred. They put a little money aside to buy a house someday, but had no idea where they could ever feel they belonged.

Henri found that keeping his grades up at school became increasingly difficult with each passing day. Feeling extremely tired all the time, he had to drag himself out of bed every morning. His parents frequently said, "growing boys need their rest." He found it hard to believe that growing could be this bad.

While eating his lunch at school one day, a girl from his class came to him and asked if he would help her with a math assignment she didn't understand. Her name was Hortense and he asked her to sit down next to him. Because she was one of the least popular kids at school, the few friends sitting with Henri, got up and left.

Henri felt sorry for her and wondered why her parents named her Hortense. Nobody liked that name. Other kids in the lunch room pointed at them laughing and he heard them saying, "Henri loves Hortense," and then they laughed harder. Henri was feeling too tired to care. He opened his math book and stared at it. Everything on the page looked foreign to him.

"I can't understand it," he said to her. "I know I've done this assignment already. Now when I look at these problems, I can't remember any of them."

He knew it was because he was so tired, it happened once before. Hortense thought maybe he didn't want to help her because she saw the kids making fun of her and Henri. She said nothing, but watched as he rolled up his sleeves and said to her, "Maybe it's too hot in here. This will cool me off."

She was horrified at what she saw. "Henri, look at your arms! They're black and blue. Did someone punch you?"

Henri looked at his arms and was likewise shocked to see the different colors. He quickly pulled his sleeves down and remembered seeing the same kind of spots on his legs before.

He felt scared. "I must have bumped myself," he said. "I don't know what happened."

Saliva showered out of Hortense's mouth when she talked. "You better tell your mom and dad, Henri. That looks awful."

She looked at the page that he was trying to figure out and asked him if he remembered anything yet. At the same time, she heard some kids laughing behind them. She lowered her head and turned around to look.

Henri told her to forget about what they were doing. He could tell by looking at her that she was about to cry and didn't know what else to say.

Hortense sat at the table holding her head, her face red and sweaty. She didn't look at Henri and he could barely hear what she said because of her face being covered up. "You're the only one in this whole school that talks to me, Henri. I feel like I'm so ugly. I wish I was dead."

Henri had no idea what he could say that would make her feel better. He couldn't tell her she was pretty; she wasn't. Her family was poor and Henri wished they'd get enough money to buy her some nicer clothes and fix her teeth. He had never seen anyone's teeth stick out so far.

Henri told her how much he hated it when the kids at his other school made fun of his red hair. It didn't seem to help much, since she still kept her face hidden in her hands. He reached in his pocket, pulled out his last piece of bubble gum and offered it to Hortense. When she looked at him, she was uglier than ever. Her eyes and face were red and swollen from crying.

Henri was pleased that she took the gum, even if it was his last piece. But he wished he wouldn't have to see any more sad things again, ever. When she started to chew the gum, he looked at his math problem once more and suddenly remembered how to do them.

He explained the lesson to her patiently. She understood and thanked him for helping her. Picking up her things, she walked over to a table that sat off by itself. Henri watched as she sat down and buried herself in her work. All alone.

Folding his arms on the table, he put his head down to rest and stayed in that position until the bell signaling the return to class woke him up.

After school, Henri wanted nothing more than to crawl into his bed and sleep. He quietly turned the door handle, hoping to sneak to his room without talking to anyone. Tiptoeing through the kitchen, he almost made it. His mother startled him when she asked if he was trying to hide from her.

She didn't wait for an answer, but told him she had a big surprise and asked him to come in the living room. He set his books down and followed her. Grampa sat in his favorite chair with a grin on his face.

"Sit down, Henri," she said excitedly. "I have some news that will make you drop to the floor if you don't."

He sat and she made the announcement, her face glowing with excitement. "Henri, you are going to have a new baby brother or sister!"

Henri couldn't believe it. Not in a million years would he ever have guessed. After being told long ago that his mother could never have more babies, he looked at her, totally flabbergasted

"It's what you've always wanted, Henri. I know how surprised you are. Isn't it wonderful news?"

"When will we get it?" Henri was elated. So many thoughts raced through his head. He had visions of himself with this permanent little friend walking alongside of him. The sadness of so many days vanished.

She told him of the expected date and they sat talking about how great it would be when the baby was with them. None of them cared whether it would be a boy or a girl.

Mary told John that evening after work and he was just as shocked as Mary to find out. They had been told after Henri's complicated birth that she would bear no more children. At that time the doctor said it would be physically impossible.

She explained to John how Dr. Gene was just as amazed to have the pregnancy test turn out positive after viewing her medical history.

John couldn't have been happier but found it difficult to believe, having given up on a larger family long ago. He was thrilled beyond words to think that it was a possibility once again.

Chapter 29

James arrived at the Palace a few minutes earlier than his scheduled appointment and strolled leisurely through The Palace. Spotting the door to the kitchen, he wondered if his friend Lucky was working. He had heard that Lucky was asked to fill a position in God's kitchen.

James opened one of the swinging doors slightly and saw Lucky standing near the stove. He stuck his head in and loudly asked, "What smells so good?"

Lucky swung his head around and nearly dropped his measuring cup. "Get over here and let me get a look at you," he said. "What brings you to The Palace? I haven't seen you in ages!"

Lucky set the cup down and threw his arms around James. They were clearly overjoyed to see each other.

James spoke briefly about his meeting with God and then said, "I had to see if the rumors were true." He looked around the kitchen, "You really are cooking for God. Well, He couldn't have picked a better chef!"

"I don't know about that, but I'm here, and this is quite an honor. I'm still amazed that he asked me."

James could tell that Lucky felt truly privileged. His round pudgy face held a proud, permanent smile. Lucky resembled the perfect chef, standing short and stout with the traditional white apron and tall hat. He'd worn the same attire at his pizza joint. "What surprises me the most, Lucky, is that you would give up the pizza joint. You know how much everyone loves Lucky's Heavenly Pizza, myself included."

"Not to worry, my friend, it still stands and is in full swing. I have plenty of competent helpers and I work there on my off hours. As a matter of fact, I'm opening Lucky's Heavenly Pizza number two."

"That's good news. Where?"

"Close to the Japanese settlement." He grinned as he said, "It seems they've discovered pizza's a little tastier than rice, and I plan to accommodate them."

James looked over the immaculate kitchen. "So how did all this come about?"

"Well," Lucky replied, adjusting his hat, "I don't know if I ever told you that God was always a big customer of mine. He loves pizza. I never personally made the deliveries. That wouldn't have been fair to my delivery people. It highlighted their day when God placed an order and they took turns going to The Palace. Each one said 'The Big Guy' always took a few minutes out of His busy schedule to chat with them."

James saw how honored he felt about God ordering pizzas from him. He motioned to Lucky to continue with his story.

"I received a summons from God and of course, my nerves were frayed. The message came just after a pizza had been delivered to Him."

Lucky made an awful face. "I figured the worst must have happened-like maybe someone accidentally put anchovies on His pizza. He doesn't like them at all, you know. He says that creating them was one of His mistakes."

"I didn't know that."

"It's true, I get very few orders for anchovies and I have to be careful. Putting them on a pizza accidentally can be disastrous, and that's no exaggeration. Anyway, I arrived at His office and let me tell you, my legs shook. This was the kind of nervous where you shake all over. I could not believe my ears when He asked if I had any spare time to work in His kitchen, I nearly collapsed right before Him. Do you ever get the jitters before you see Him?"

James shook his head yes. "I know exactly what you're saying. I suppose He made you chief cook?"

Lucky told James that he shares the job of chief cook with Pierre, who's done it for years alone. "God wanted Pierre to be able to have a little more time off. He also needed help with different events held at The Palace; special dinners and such. We plan the menus and do some cooking. We have several other chefs working part time. Each one has a specialty and when God wants the dish they expertly fix, He calls them in. Can you think of anyone that wouldn't drop everything to be of service to 'The Almighty?'"

"Everyone in Heaven would do anything for Him. I suppose you have to fix pizza all the time?"

"Not at all. God wants the pizza's to come from my place. He said they wouldn't taste the same if I made them here. I personally think he enjoys visiting with the delivery people. God knows how happy the short visit makes them."

James knew that to be true. He told Lucky he had to be moving along so he wouldn't be late for his appointment with God.

Lucky said, "You haven't told me what you've been doing, ol' buddy. Or is it a secret?"

"It's no secret, but it's a long story. I'm mainly guardian to a nine-year-old boy. We'll chat about that another day. I'm glad to hear that you still have Lucky's Heavenly Pizza. The angels in my household wondered about it. You know how rumors are. We heard you were closing because of this job. You'd better make an announcement in the paper so all of Heaven isn't in an uproar over it. Everyone loves your pizza."

Lucky drank in the compliment. "I suppose I could make an announcement on WGOD. Everyone is usually tuned in, don't you think?"

"Everyone I know is." James looked at his watch. "I have to run, Lucky. I can't be late."

"It's been really good to see you, James. I'm happy to know you're still working as a guardian angel. It amazes me how you guys can do it. I hear it's becoming a tough job. Sometimes I regret that I'm not working as one. I know how much God needs the help. I'm telling you James, I just don't have what it takes. I'm an old softy and I just couldn't handle it."

"You're needed where you are my friend. Everyone is not cut out to be a guardian angel. All of the jobs in Heaven are important."

They said their good-byes. Lucky picked up his thermometer and stuck it into the grease boiling on the stove. James headed down the long corridor that led to God's office.

As he entered the office, he found God sitting at His desk. The globe of the world sat next to Him and He watched as his hand whirled it around. He appeared to be deep in thought.

Without looking up, God said to James, "Sorry I couldn't stay longer at Burky's party. It pleased me to see everyone having so much fun."

He twirled the globe again and displayed a grin. "You didn't happen to find out what my secret was, did you?"

James hid the happiness from his face. "I never like it when you tell me there is a secret and . . ."

Since he learned about Mary's miraculous pregnancy, James could think of nothing else. "Why didn't you just tell me? I've never seen anyone that loved to play games like you do."

"I'm glad the secret made you happy. I don't know why I have to be such a tease. It's just fun for me. You tried to figure it out from the time you left my office."

James didn't say he nearly went crazy wondering what it would be. "This is like the surprise of the century! That family is thrilled beyond words! I can't tell you how much Henri thinks about the little brother or sister he'll have."

"I know. I watch him."

"And Buffy, she's hovering around Mary like a protective mother. The special news came as a wonderful surprise to everyone. Thank-you."

James' face reflected the tender gratitude he felt toward this gentle, caring God. "We both know how important this baby will be."

God revealed one of His all knowing expressions. He then returned to one of a more mischievous nature. With the familiar glint in His eye, the words came out, "I have another surprise."

James rolled his eyes. He could feel the warmth spread over his face and hated it.

God loved to see him that way, but He decided not to keep James in suspense this time. "Someone is going to fall in love." Watching James, He wondered if he would react as suspected.

James perked up; his mouth nearly dropped open. "You're kidding. Does Orville know yet?"

"No, but he'll know soon. I promised him a while back that I would have a surprise for him when Burky stopped swearing."

"Do you think he has any idea that the surprise will be a woman?"

"Very possibly. Orville constantly asks if I have anyone lined up for Burky. I told him that even if I did, the swearing would turn off any of the possibilities that I might have."

James said, "That's true."

"I've had someone very special in mind for him. She's been waiting long enough and is beginning to think she'll never find the right man. It's quite a relief to know that the swearing is gone from his life now. This woman wouldn't have tolerated the problem. I don't anticipate any problems with this match."

God visualized how perfect the union would be. "It won't be much longer now James. And by the way, thanks for giving Orville a helping hand."

"Henri did it. He always follows directions perfectly."

"Henri is a good boy," said God.

Following a brief, thoughtful pause, God said, "It thrilled me to watch Mary receive the news of her pregnancy from Dr. Gene. The news sent happy shock waves right through her. She is on top of the world. Wouldn't it be wonderful if all women reacted the same way?"

"It would indeed," said James.

God said, "Mothers hold a very special place in my heart. Their job of caring for my little ones requires a great deal of patience."

James agreed. "That they do. To be a good mother, one cannot be selfish. It takes a lot of giving to play that role."

Using that word brought an amused look to his face as he recalled the day Buffy played actress.

"What is it, James?"

"I was just thinking about silly Buffy. When I used the word role, it reminded me of the day she said we were all like actors and actresses. She's been acting like a soap opera star lately. She and Mary have been watching all the afternoon soaps."

"I've watched Buffy; it's quite amusing. She and Mary have nothing else to do right now. I can't blame them. Until they find new things to do, what else is there? Mary no longer has any friends in the area. What happened in that neighborhood is a terrible shame." "We all thank you for sending Burky over. As Buffy said that day, he was like a knight in shining armor when he came on the set, coming to their rescue. The family adores him, as do we."

"Burky is playing a very important role for me. They need him, and he needs them. Look how much Henri has helped him. And how much he's helped them by being their friend."

Pausing briefly, He added, "It's true about the roles; the roles the angels play and the roles people play. Some of them are not easy; as a matter of fact, some of the roles are not pretty at all."

James nodded in agreement. He watched as God began spinning the globe again and could tell that something more weighed heavily on his mind.

God began, "The planet Earth is massive, don't you agree?"

"Absolutely."

"And it's full of churches and other houses of worship. Exactly the way I intended it to be."

"That is also true."

"Not enough people attend anymore, James. This accounts for many of the problems we have to deal with these days."

"Exactly. The people attending are hearing the words that you want them to hear, but some of them aren't living them. Consequently, others think church is not the place they want to be."

James wondered where the conversation would lead.

God answered his thought, "It's about Gracie, your neighbor."

James knew about her. She'd recently died.

"No one could have prayed more than her. Hours were spent on her knees. She practically set a record for attending church. Her life was spent making sure she did everything necessary to save her own soul."

He paused and strolled over to His favorite window. Gazing down at the horses, He continued. "You wouldn't believe her outrage when she found out she wouldn't be going straight to Heaven. Poor St. Pete. He had to endure her fits of anger. He's used to it though, he encounters her kind often."

"Anyway, she entered his office for her appointment in a rage, shouting about the mistake that had been made and demanding to see me at once. She told St. Pete all about her praying and churchgoing, not forgetting to add that she attended the one true church."

James was quick to respond. "There have actually been wars over that very topic. Each church claims to be the true one, how did that get so far out of control?"

"My people will all be united again some day, but we'll talk about that another time. Let me finish telling you about Gracie. Peter waited until she calmed down, then took out her daily charts. He pointed out the gold stars placed next to the good deeds she'd done for others, and there weren't many. He told her of the people hurt badly by her self righteous behavior and reminded her of what was most important to me; to love one another. She became furious and told him in no uncertain terms that she loved everyone with all of her heart."

"Did Peter let her know that he knew about the hate mail she sent to Henri's family?"

"He sure did. After he told her how I feel about 'actions speaking louder than words.' You remember my favorite saying?"

James smiled, "Of course."

God continued, "She was extremely embarrassed to find that we record everything, good and bad. St. Pete gave her praise for all of her prayers and for her attendance at church. But he pointed out that she did it all for herself. He also told her that she didn't live the words she was taught."

God turned to look down at the horses once more and then slowly walked back to His desk. "Henri and his family have been hurt very badly by Gracie, and people like her. Many are hurt by people like her. I expected it to happen when I sent Henri's family to live in that neighborhood. I hoped it wouldn't. It was a test."

James knew that 'testing' was another of God's favorite pastimes and said, "They failed miserably."

"That they did, James. That they did."

They talked more about Henri and what lay ahead for him and his family. God gave James additional instructions. Both found the subject difficult to discuss because of the heartaches that could not be avoided. "T.J. will be staying with you through it all, James. You'll need his help. Also, this is best for T.J. right now. I see the possibility of him getting Billy back is almost nonexistent. It doesn't look good at all."

"That's sad."

"I know. Poor T.J. This isn't his first disappointment. I don't know if you were ever told, but before he was assigned to Billy, T.J. was going to be the guardian angel to a newborn. I sent him ahead of time to be with the mother. Her life promised to become difficult and her own guardian angel had several helpers already. I figured with him there too, they could give her the much needed strength and comfort she'd need to get her through this difficult time. As it turned out, nothing helped, she decided to end the pregnancy. This devastated T.J. and those that tried so hard to help."

James now understood why T.J. felt like such a failure. "He has to learn that he isn't the one at fault. We all want everything to turn out wonderful, but there are times when it just doesn't. I can relate to how he feels."

God said, "He'll be all right. It's been helpful to have him working with you. He's kept busy enough and at least he isn't hanging around that park anymore. It broke my heart to watch him standing on the outskirts, watching as Billy fell deeper into the pit."

James imagined how sad it must have been.

"Drugs can be horrible when misused. I thought for a while that Henri's Grampa would get hooked. It disgusts me, James, so many people abuse drugs. It's not only those pathetic souls in the park. There are some in the medical profession who push them too. Good doctors like Dr. Gene are not too common anymore. It takes a lot of patience and love to care for the health of people. The medical profession is an easy place to make a lot of money quickly. I have more and more cases where that seems to be the priority. I'll be forever grateful to those that don't abuse the talent I've given them."

Reaching to the corner of the desk, He picked up a large stack of papers and showed James that they contained lists of nursing homes, hospitals, and mental health centers that were being carefully watched. He put the stack of papers back in their place and said, "It all takes time."

And then, "It's time for you to be on your way, James. I do get carried away, don't I?"

"We all need someone to talk to at times. I appreciate that you chose me."

James smiled sincerely as he stood to leave. God returned the smile and told him "thank-you."

James left His office and headed back down the long corridor with his mood totally elevated once again after witnessing first hand, God's complete awareness of everything taking place on earth. Even though the angels possess most of this knowledge, they still find it difficult to watch the wrongdoing of people and how their actions hurt others. But the comfort always came from knowing that each person would have to pay for any kind of suffering they deliberately caused another.

A delectable aroma interrupted his thoughts, making his mouth water. He followed the good smell to the kitchen and decided to peek in and check it out.

Swinging open the door, he spotted Lucky standing over the stove. He held a pair of tongs in one hand and appeared to be totally absorbed in the task at hand.

James cleared his throat so as not to startle him. Lucky turned around, his grin returning when he spotted his friend again.

"So what's cooking?" Asked James. "The aroma nearly drove me wild as I neared the kitchen." He sniffed the air. "Smells familiar."

Lucky was quick to tell, "God's favorite; fried chicken. He has it often. This is His special recipe."

James lifted the lid on one of the pans. "I know exactly why it smells and looks so familiar. The household where I'm working enjoys this same chicken at least once a month. It's always a treat when the father goes out and buys a bucket of it."

Pulling some pieces out of the hot grease, Lucky replied, "I think it's great that God decided to share the recipe with the world. Didn't He give it to that man in his dreams?"

"He sure did, but I never knew why He chose that particular person; he must have been pretty special. What I do know is that a fortune is still being made on the chicken. People love it, and so do I."

Lucky gripped a chicken leg with his tongs and placed it on a napkin. He handed the piece to James who was more than happy to sample it.

A smile covered his face as he sank his teeth into the leg. James waved goodbye to Lucky as he left the kitchen and strolled down the hallway licking his fingers.

****

Chapter 30

*T*he aroma of a turkey baking filled the air. Thanksgiving Day was celebrated at Henri's home with a festive dinner and their best friends. Bobby and his family came over, as did Burky.

Henri's handmade pictures of turkeys and pilgrims adorned the windows and walls. His mother created a horn of plenty that sat on the table as a center piece. The turkey began roasting in the oven early that morning.

Everyone prepared their favorite dish to enjoy with the bird. There were six pies in all, each contributing their favorite. Like most other Americans, they ate well beyond what they should have.

Lounging around the living room after dinner, everyone complained about their overfilled stomachs. Only an hour passed before they returned to the kitchen for more pie and ice cream. Not one of them wanted to see the day end, but eventually it did. Their friends left after having a wonderful Thanksgiving day.

In the early evening Henri and his parents were together in the living room. Grampa retired to his room earlier. Henri lay on the floor on his back holding his belly as he complained, thinking it was about to burst.

"Do you think that the homeless people have Thanksgiving?" Henri asked the others.

His dad answered, "Most of them must. Churches and different organizations fix turkey dinners for those that wouldn't otherwise have one. I've heard that many people show up."

"Don't forget about the soup kitchens," said Mary, "they help out too."

Henri said, "Soup for Thanksgiving? That's not a good dinner."

"No silly, not on Thanksgiving Day." She explained about soup kitchens and how the people could eat at them daily if they didn't have food. Henri didn't hear his mother's explanation. He was sound asleep, still holding onto his belly.

Mary whispered, "I do hope we find out something tomorrow, John. I can't stand this waiting any longer."

Her voice sounded stressed as she asked, "Do you think the tests will tell us what's wrong? It's driving me crazy."

Frustration also consumed John. "We should know something tomorrow. Please remember how important it is for you to stay calm. You have the baby to think about. Henri can't be too sick, not after putting away all of that food."

He understood her feelings. He'd been walking in a daze himself since they first took Henri to the emergency room earlier that week. The flu was going around school and it hit Henri really hard. They were told that Henri did indeed have a bad case of the flu, but there were symptoms that had nothing to do with that sickness. The emergency physician told them he would speak with their family doctor and advised them to see Dr. Gene the next day.

They sat in Dr. Gene's office that following morning. He expressed the same concern and vaguely told them what he suspected. John and Mary were asked to return to his office with Henri the day after Thanksgiving for further testing.

Henri's parents spoke little of it that evening. Both slept fitfully; each hoping the next day would bring good news.

But it wasn't to be. After his examination, Henri waited in the outer room while Dr. Gene talked with his

266

parents.   Leukemia was suspected and he wanted Henri admitted to the nearby hospital for tests.   Henri was already scheduled to be examined by Dr. Johnson, a Pediatric Hematologist.   Dr. Johnson, he said, was basically a blood doctor for children.   Dr. Gene told them he would be doing a bone marrow aspiration and explained the procedure fully.   He handled them gently, seeing how shaken they were.   But he had to be honest and it hurt him deeply to see their grief, knowing how their prior life had been.

John, finally able to speak, said, "You said you suspected leukemia.   Do you think this is true?"   His voice didn't feel as though it came from his throat as shock gripped his body.

"I'm ninety-five percent sure, John.   Henri is a very sick little boy.   The tests will give us a positive answer. There's still a small chance this isn't true, but you need to prepare yourselves just in case."

Dr. Gene said the words with dread, knowing they had to be said.   Mary slumped over in her chair.   John held her, but there were no words of comfort.

After a few brief moments, they stood to leave.   Dr. Gene said he would join them at the hospital.   The appointment was scheduled for two o'clock and he explained where they would meet.

They left his office that now held a faint fragrance of roses.

Neither of them noticed.

Henri looked up when they entered the room. Seeing their faces scared him. "Does Dr. Gene want to see me again?"

Leading him out of the doctor's office, John explained that more tests would be taken at the hospital and told Henri what they would entail.

The small boy looked up at his dad with pure innocence. "Am I going to die?"

His Dad leaned down to embrace him and said, "That's silly talk, son," He couldn't say more.

"Will the tests hurt?"

"They aren't going to be real comfortable, but you must remember this has to be done in order to find out what's wrong with you."

"I hope they can make me better, dad. I don't want to feel like this anymore. My arm hurts so much and I'm always tired."

John's voice trembled, "Let's get on home for a while, it'll soon be time for us to go to the hospital."

Mary had rushed on ahead. She sat in the front seat of the car, staring out the window when they arrived. John opened the door for Henri.

They were home by noon. Grampa waited anxiously and seemed his normal self. His spirits were good and he wanted to know what Dr. Gene had said. John told him. Grampa then sat next to Henri and had a little talk with him, telling him not to be afraid of anything and to only be good to the nice nurses. He did a good job of hiding his fear and continued to joke and play with Henri.

Grampa worried about all three of them. He feared also for the unborn baby. Mary disappeared into her room as soon as she entered the house. A feeling of helplessness consumed Grampa, as usual.

Burky stopped by, wanting to know what the doctor said. After hearing, he told John he'd stay with Grampa and also forced himself to hide his feelings from Henri.

Mary stayed in her room until it was time to leave. Looking pale and forlorn, she came out holding a small suitcase packed with Henri's things. Having few words to say, she hurried John and Henri out the door.

Dr. Gene waited for Henri and his parents in the lobby. When the family arrived, he escorted them to Dr. Johnson's office. After introductions, the doctor's attention went directly to Henri, who gazed at the pictures of other children hanging on the wall.

"They're all friends of mine," said the doctor, "and patients."

The doctor named a few of the children for Henri, telling him a little about each one. Directing the conversation back to the others, they discussed the situation. He then explained to Henri exactly what would be happening and told him the bone marrow aspiration would hurt. Henri remained calm and told the doctor he wanted to feel better. He also talked about how hard it was to do schoolwork when he felt so awful and asked Dr. Johnson if he could fix him.

The doctor said, "I'm sure going to try my friend. I'll call Nurse Lisa, she'll show you to your room and get you ready for the tests."

"Will I have to wear those silly clothes that I see people wearing on TV when they have an operation? I hate those funny hats."

"You'll love the outfits we have. They're blue for the boys, with spaceships on them."

Nurse Lisa entered the room. The doctor said, "She's here to take you away, Henri. I'll just bet she'll push you in that race car she has waiting in the hall. Come and meet Henri, Lisa."

He introduced her to him and everyone else in the room. When she flashed a bright smile, little dimples showed up on her cheeks. Henri eyes lit up when he saw that she, too, had a head full of red curls. He liked her and didn't feel scared about leaving with her. She pointed to the wheelchair. Henri hopped in and Lisa pushed him away.

Dr. Johnson's face grew serious as he turned to Henri's parents. He spoke briefly about the different types of leukemia. The doctor wasn't about to give them any false hopes, knowing Henri's condition didn't look good at all.

Dr. Johnson asked them if they had any questions. They had none. Henri's mother had not uttered a word since their arrival and his dad was anxious to leave and be with Henri. The doctor gave them directions to his room. They were told they would have a few minutes with him before he left for the test and Dr. Johnson would notify them immediately when the results came in.

Dr. Gene said he'd see Mary and John in Henri's room later and they left. Worried about Mary, he told his colleague about her pregnancy and the heartaches consuming their lives.

Dr. Johnson shook his head sadly. "It seems that some people are hit with a magnitude of problems and then there are others that sail through life without any. I just don't understand it."

Dr. Gene had a few people in the hospital to check on. He told Dr. Johnson he'd be close by, expressing his desire to be with Henri's parents when they received the test results.

Mary and John sat with Henri before he left for the testing. It tore at their hearts to see him lying in the big bed, trying so hard to be brave. They talked softly to him, each holding one of his hands. Lisa had given them a few minutes to be alone and a tough few minutes passed. They filled his ears with words of love, but neither one of them said that everything would be okay.

Lisa came back to the room to take him away. Words could not describe the sadness felt by John and Mary as they watched her take their son away. The bed with wheels looked huge with his small body lying stretched out on it. His parents clung to each other as the bed rolled out of sight.

Standing alone in the empty room, John continued to hold Mary. Neither one of them had a shred of hope that things would be all right. It just didn't happen that way for them. They sat down to begin the wait; each knowing their life was about to change once again.

Both doctors came to the room when the procedure was over. They were able to talk there because it would be awhile before Henri would return.

The diagnosis was confirmed. Henri had cancer. Mary and John sat numbly listening as they were told that of all the different types of leukemia; Henri had contracted a severe strain. Dr. Johnson said that it was rarely found in children.

Mary bent over and put her head in her lap. John gently rubbed her back. Dr. Gene knelt down in front of them. He took Mary's hand and told her that everything would be done to try to make her son well. John asked about the treatment.

Dr. Johnson said, "I'd like to begin right away. We will be using very intense chemotherapy for the first two days, followed by a week of nothing. After the week, we'll start again with the two days of intense treatments, and take another break. This treatment will continue until we feel that progress is being made."

He paused when Mary looked up. A spark of hope glistened in her eyes. She asked, "How long will it take before you can see if progress is being made?"

"Everything will depend on Henri and how strong he is."

Pausing, the doctor hated to continue. "The treatment will make him very sick. If it weakens him too much, we'll have to stop."

He could see that he lost her attention again and waited briefly before explaining more about what would be happening. John asked a few questions before Lisa lightly knocked at the door to let them know Henri was back.

The doctors stood aside as she pushed the bed holding the small boy into the room. Henri slept peacefully. The doctors whispered to Mary and John, saying they would talk more another time.

Mary and John didn't hear them. They watched as Lisa and her helper moved Henri onto the regular hospital bed. He woke up briefly. Seeing his parents, he smiled weakly, and then fell asleep again. Lisa's helper left the room with the bed on wheels.

Lisa checked Henri's IV, making sure that everything worked correctly. She then told his parents what a brave little boy he had been.

"He'll be sleeping off and on for a while," she told them. "It probably would be a good idea for you to go down and get a bite to eat."

Lisa lightly stroked Henri's back as she gave his parents directions to the cafeteria, she also let them know of the lounge nearby where they could rest if they felt the need.

Mary refused to leave the room. She stood on the opposite side of the bed and wasn't about to leave her son.

John volunteered to get sandwiches. He knew this wasn't the time to bring up her condition. Mary had to eat something. After taking another look at Henri, he kissed his wife gently on the cheek and left the room in search of a telephone and the cafeteria.

Finding the phone first, he called home. Burky answered and John realized he couldn't speak just then, grief grabbed him by the throat. After a brief delay, he asked about Grampa, he couldn't bring himself to talk about Henri.

Burky knew by the way John spoke that something was terribly wrong. "Grampa's fine. What's wrong, John? Tell me about Henri."

John slowly told Burky everything. As Burky listened, he felt his body weaken. He had planted false hopes in his head when he knew Henri was going to have tests. It never fully occurred to him that this would happen. In his mind he believed that their God would not allow any more bad things. He was wrong, and he was mad. Burky said nothing about his feelings to John, but did say he would stay with Grampa for as long as they needed him. He asked John if he should call work for him.

"I almost forgot about that. Please do that, Burky. Tell them I'll be in touch when I know more about what is happening."

Not able to talk any longer, John quickly said goodbye and hung up the phone. He headed for the cafeteria, but found he couldn't walk the entire way. Leaning against the nearest wall, giant sobs began shaking his entire body. Time stood still.

John's legs trembled as he continued toward the cafeteria. He stopped briefly along the way, making a conscious effort to be strong. Mary and Henri needed him. As he did many times before in his life, he talked to Jake, his guardian angel. Only this time, it was a desperate plea. "Please don't let this happen, my friend; not to my little boy."

He intuitively knew that wasn't the right thing to say. What he needed most was the strength to deal with what looked to be the inevitable. Henri looked so frail and John knew he couldn't endure the intensive treatment. He had no idea how he was ever going to help his pregnant wife through all that lay before them.

The cafeteria overflowed with people because of the dinner hour. Sounds of clanking dishes mixed with loud voices, penetrated John's ears. Panic reached his inner-being once again and he would have left if the lady hadn't asked what he wanted. It was his turn in line.

After paying for his selection, he left the noisy room that held so many sad faces. John carefully carried the sandwiches and milk on a tray. Feeling somewhat more in control, he hurried back to be with his family.

Chapter 31

Days slowly dragged by. Each hour could only be described as sheer agony for Mary and John. They could do nothing more than stand by and watch as their only son grew sicker and sicker. They wondered about the intense treatment and were told again that it was necessary in order to kill off the leukemia cells. To watch their son fade away right before their eyes was a horror beyond anything they had ever imagined.

Henri talked very little. He vomited almost continuously and became terribly weak. His constant sleeping came as somewhat a relief to his parents. They knew that during that time he was at peace.

During one of his waking moments his concern seemed to be for his grampa. He wanted to see him and wished that Burky would come too. Mary told him that Grampa and Burky were in his room on several occasions while he slept. She assured him of their return.

Henri smiled weakly, speaking softly, he said, "I sleep a lot, but I have good dreams, Mom."

His eyes found his dad. "I dream about a super angel dad, and he wears a blue suit with a blue cape. On the back is his name in big white letters. It's 'James'."

"Does he talk to you?"

"No, but he smiles all the time. When I see him, he puts out his hand and takes mine. We leave together. He takes me to beautiful places. He's my friend."

Henri yawned and his eyes looked as though he wanted to sleep again.

Mary's eyes misted. She didn't want him to sleep again, and she didn't want him to dream about angels. Her pounding heart felt as though it would beat itself out of her body. She thought that maybe the angels were preparing him for death! Silently, she begged them to go away. She sat in the nearby chair, her hands covering her face.

His dad remained standing at his bedside. Stroking his head, he talked to his son in hushed tones. Henri didn't hear him; he slept once again. Nurse Lisa walked in the room carrying freshly squeezed orange juice for Mary.

John believed that Nurse Lisa had to be an angel of some sort. Her endless hours spent caring for Henri and Mary seemed to fill her heart with joy. She persuaded Mary to rest and made sure she ate properly and tended both of them with patience and love.

Mary refused to leave the hospital. John brought fresh clothes from home and she slept in the room provided for parents. He stayed overnight occasionally, but had to relieve Burky of Grampa's care at times. Burky took a leave of absence from work. He wanted to help the family in any way that he could, and would not take no for an answer.

John thought Mary held up quite well, in the sense that she hadn't collapsed or gotten sick herself. He wished he could ease her grief, but his own was barely controllable.

Burky came once again to visit. John had gone home to stay with Grampa. When Burky arrived at the hospital, he put on the protective clothing before going into Henri's room. The importance of wearing such garments helped to ensure the prevention of germs being brought near Henri. His immune system was at an all-time low because of the treatment. If infection should set in, it could very well have disastrous results.

Mary smiled sadly when she saw Burky walk through the door. He noticed how frazzled she looked. His heart went to his throat as he softly walked over to Henri's bedside and touched the boy's small withered hand. Henri's eyes opened to slits; he faintly smiled at the sight of his friend.

"I've missed you, Henri," was all that Burky could say right then. The pathetic sight of this poor sick child nearly tore his heart in two. He could only think about how unfair this was as he held back the sickness he felt.

"I miss you too, Burky. Is my grampa okay?"

"Your grampa's fine. He was here to see you one day with me, but you were sleeping."

Henri's voice was barely audible, "Could you please bring him back?" His eyes closed slightly, but opened again as he fought to stay awake.

"I'll bring him back, Henri. You rest for a few minutes and we'll talk later."

"Okay, Burky." He dozed off, but in a matter of seconds, woke up, vomiting and choking uncontrollably.

Mary rushed to his side, as did a little red-haired girl that Burky hadn't seen before. Both frantically tried to help Henri.

Burky felt frightened out of his wits at the sight, and had no idea what to do. Feeling in the way, he dashed out of the room. He found himself alone in the hall and stood with his hands holding his forehead. Nothing could stop the flood of emotions that seemed to be taking over his entire being. A wet sickness crept into his throat and he dashed across the hall to the nearby men's room where all of his grief spilled out.

After what seemed like an eternity, he left. Finding the two women still busy with Henri, he waited outside the door. He couldn't remember any event in all of his lifetime that caused him this kind of misery. Burky always helped his friends solve various problems they may have had, but he could do nothing this time.

Leaning against the wall with his hands in his pockets, his thoughts went to the God they loved. His only question was, "how could He let this happen?"

There was no answer. Only silence, and the sound of footsteps coming down the hallway. When his eyes left the floor, he found them looking into the face of a man he'd never seen before.

The man with thick glasses introduced himself as Dr. Gene. Burky recognized the name and it was with hope that he quickly introduced himself.

"I'm Burky," he said, "a friend of this family. I was here a few days ago and Henri looked a lot better than what he does today. What's happening?"

Dr. Gene knew about Burky. This big man was dear to Henri and his family. He knew that he expected to hear words that said everything would be all right. But there were none. "It doesn't look good, Burky. Henri had been sick for quite some time before anyone became aware of it. Not that it would have made a whole lot of difference as far as this type of leukemia goes. The treatment is harsh and his body was already run down. We can only wait and see. Helping the family to be strong is important right now, and we must pray hard. That's all we can do."

The spark of hope left Burky's face. Especially with the mention of prayer. He knew how much the family spent at prayer in church and the problems never stopped for them.

He related his feelings to the doctor in a hushed voice. Burky asked, "Can you tell me how God can help them? These are good people and they have so much faith in this God. Why doesn't He do something? They've had enough." He shook his head disgustedly, "I just don't understand."

"It's difficult to try to understand, Burky, especially at a time like this."

This wasn't the time to talk to him about faith. He wished it was, he had so much that he could tell this man.

Nothing more could be said because, Nurse Lisa popped her head through the door and told them to come in.

278

Henri slept soundly once again. Mary stood beside him, lightly massaging his back. Dr. Gene went directly to the bedside and took the chart that hung next to the bed. After scanning it over, he put it back in its place. His attention now went to Mary.

"Come sit with me, Mary, we have to think about you for a few minutes," he looked directly into her eyes. "I have to know how you're doing." They talked in soft tones as he held onto her hand.

Burky stood by Henri's bedside and watched the little guy as he slept. He barely recognized him as the same boy he knew and loved. A few remaining strands of red hair clung to his head. His small, curled up form looked wasted away. Tears formed in Burky's eyes and his legs began to feel like they couldn't hold the weight of his body. Nurse Lisa appeared at his side.

"I'm Lisa," she said. "It's time for me to take a quick run to the cafeteria to get Mary something to eat. How about coming with me? Dr. Gene will stay with them until we return."

He agreed to accompany her. Somehow it made him feel like he was helping. Lisa announced to the others where they were going.

"No need to get me anything yet, Lisa," said Mary. "I'm not hungry at all."

"I know," said Lisa, flashing the energetic smile that seemed to brighten everyone in the room. "You never are, but you know you'll be eating anyway."

Mary smiled faintly, aware of the fact that she would be eating regardless. Lisa had a way of persuading her.

Lisa and Burky left the room. Before they had a chance to say anything to each other, a guy came rushing toward them. He appeared to be out of breath as he carried a large camera on his back. They were both annoyed at the intrusion.

279

He blurted out, "Hi, I'm Ric from TV Five."

Ric put out his hand which neither Mary nor Burky took. Ric continued, not the least bit ruffled. "Word is out that you have a very sick boy here named Henri."

"That's true," said Lisa, "but what's it to you? I don't know if you realize it or not but you have absolutely no business here. I have no idea how you made it past the desk." Clearly, she was not happy.

He shifted the camera from one shoulder to another and anyone could see it was much too heavy for him. Disregarding what she said, he continued with his mission. "Ma'am, word is also out that the young boy comes from Pleasant Valley, and we all know what happened there. It's my thought that if we are allowed to follow his story. We can show the world how this little guy is fighting for his life because of the tragedy that occurred there. Just maybe, history will never repeat itself. Pollution has got to cease!"

Ric's face became red as he rapidly spoke. Both Lisa and Burky could tell he was on a crusade.

Burky stepped forward and gruffly stated, "I think this is something that needs to be discussed with his parents, and I have no idea when they would feel up to it."

He didn't appreciate this intruder and allowed it to show through his voice. "Give me your card and I'll see that they hear about this."

Ric handed him his business card and reluctantly began to back away. Walking backwards as he left them, he said, "I understand how you feel, but you must agree that something must be done!"

"Someone will get back to you," Burky said, making it perfectly clear the conversation was over. He and Lisa turned and walked away.

"The nerve of some people," said Lisa. "They don't realize when they sneak in here how many germs they drag in with them. It irritates the heck out of me."

"I know," said Burky, "He could've made a phone call to the desk and saved himself a trip. Mary and John don't need this right now."

Burky and Lisa entered the cafeteria and picked out a hearty dinner for Mary, both knowing the foods she liked. Lisa said she had better luck getting her to eat when they picked out her favorite foods at the cafeteria, rather than the hospital menu.

The two discussed the family as they made their way back to Henri's room. The sick child slept. Dr. Gene stood to leave when Burky and Lisa entered.

Burky announced that he too, had to be on his way. "Tell Henri I'll be back soon to see him."

He turned to Lisa, "It was nice meeting you, Lisa. I appreciate the wonderful care that you're giving my friends."

Burky looked from Lisa to Henri, and with a helpless feeling, reluctantly said goodbye. Once in the corridor, he felt an urgency to get out of the hospital as quickly as possible. His legs moved swiftly. He passed a man mopping floors and the smell of the antiseptic filled his nostrils, making him feel ill again.

He reached the door leading to the outside and rushed out, sucking in a deep breath of fresh air. Burky shivered as he headed toward his car with the picture of Henri in agony, planted firmly in his head.

Stopping to take another deep breath of air, the face of Nurse Lisa flashed before him. Burky knew he'd be eternally grateful to her for the loving care she gave both Henri and Mary.

After unlocking his car door, he sat on the cold hard seat without feeling. Leaving the parking lot, Lisa's kind face flashed before him once again and he realized that he'd never met anyone like her. His thoughts quickly returned to Henri and he quietly drove home.

Lisa and Mary visited in hushed tones throughout the evening as Henri slept. Later, when their conversation ceased, Lisa sensed that Mary needed time alone. She excused herself, saying she had to do some work at the desk. Mary nodded. Her thoughts drifted to the conversations she used to have with the older folks at the nursing home. She no longer felt like the same person that gave the patients so much peace and hope with her words about the angels. It seemed like such a long time ago. Right now she felt like the angels had abandoned her. Brushing all thoughts of them from her mind, tears dripped from her eyes once again.

Lisa returned after a short time and told Mary it was time for her to go to bed; telling her she would stay with Henri until the nurse on the next shift came in. Mary didn't move. Lisa lifted her feet off the footstool, helping her to her feet. They walked together to the guest room. Feeling positive that Mary was ready for sleep, Lisa promptly left to return to Henri's bedside.

Chapter 32

*J*ohn arrived early the following morning. His face brightened when he saw Mary looking rested and eating a breakfast of fresh fruit and muffins. She asked John about her dad. The question surprised him because Mary's full attention went to Henri since the day they found him to be desperately ill.

John eagerly responded. "Your dad is anxious to see Henri. Burky said he would bring him up here this afternoon. He's had some really good days, and is very concerned about you, Mary."

John took her hand and looked her straight in the eyes. "We both are. We want you to leave this hospital for a while and get some fresh air."

Waiting for a response, and getting none, he said, "It would be good for the baby too. Even a little stroll outside for a few minutes?"

"I'll walk the halls, but I can't promise to go outside, John. I'm afraid to leave."

She looked over to where Henri lay sleeping. Her expression told John not to push any further. Any amount of exercise would be good for now.

Handing him the empty breakfast tray, she stood and kissed him lightly on the cheek, saying, "I'll go now. I won't be long."

Mary left the room knowing exactly where she would go. Reaching the nurse's station, she asked for directions to the chapel. Within minutes she stood outside the chapel door.

Her hand held the door handle, but she could not bring herself to push it open. She wondered why she ever thought about coming here to ask God for help. He had not responded to any of her pleas. She quickly walked away.

Mary's mind raced. How could He let this happen to her son? After all she'd been through already? Was there really a God? Questions rushed through her head as hopelessness consumed her.

Not able to walk any further, Mary stopped and held onto her head. Her mind whirled and her thoughts became confused. Loud voices startled her. Glancing up, she saw a group of chattering nurses coming down the hall toward her. Not wanting to face anyone, she turned and raced back to the chapel. This time, her hands shoved the door open and she walked through.

Mary's eyes searched the small, dimly lit chapel. Relief washed over her when she discovered the room was devoid of people. Leaning against the closed door, she tried to get control of her thinking. She felt as though someone forced thoughts other than her own, into her head. Some were words her mother used when she lectured.

"Have faith, even when times are bad." Mary erased them as quickly as they came, only to have them return. "God is always with us."

She knew she was going crazy. When she could stand no more, she turned to leave, but couldn't. Her eyes were directed to the front of the chapel where a huge crucifix overlooked the room. Mary's hands covered her mouth, preventing the cries that threatened to spill out.

Viewing the suffering face of Jesus softened her slightly, but she quickly looked away. Her grief was because of her own son and what God allowed to happen to him. She did not want to think about anything else.

The battle inside her continued. Her mother's words flooded back. "Blessed are those who believe in Him when they cannot see."

Mary grabbed the back of a pew and leaned heavily against it as more words invaded her senses. "You must always have faith in God, Mary. He is always with you and knows what you are going through."

She frantically turned to leave. This time a plain, matronly woman stopped her. Standing by the door, her hand stretched out to Mary. She said, "Let me help you."

Mary didn't wish to speak with her or anyone else. Ignoring this kindly woman, she said, "I have to get back to my son."

The woman, put a gentle hand on her shoulder. "Tell me about your son."

Mary yielded and found herself pouring her heart out to this nice lady. The woman, with her arm now around Mary's shoulder, led her down the aisle to the front of the chapel. Both sat in the pew. Mary talked between sobs.

The woman persuaded her to hush, instructing her to look up at the crucifix. She then said that God allowed His only son to die a dreadful death, and pointed out that the purpose was for the good of all His people. She spoke of the horrors Jesus' mother experienced as she stood by watching.

Furious with the woman's words, Mary yelled out, "My son is not going to die!" She slumped in her seat.

"That isn't what I said, Mary." The woman realized she used the wrong choice of words. "What I'm trying to tell you, is that God is aware of your suffering and only He knows why this is happening. I understand that you feel He has abandoned you. Believe me when I say He hasn't."

She looked sadly at Mary, wondering how she could convince her to trust her words. "When I said that Jesus' mother sadly watched him die on the cross, I meant that she suffered too. As did God, after all, He was His only son."

Mary said, "They both knew why it was happening! I think that would help a little!" She covered her face again.

"That's true, but don't you think one of the lessons to be learned from the crucifixion may have been that God has reasons for what happens? We should trust and have faith in Him, in good times and bad."

"You sound like my mother. She said the same things."

Mary dried her eyes. She didn't tell the woman that her speech didn't help. "My mother died a while back, but her words come back to me. I'll never be like her. She'd have been much better at this than me."

Taking in a deep breath, Mary raised her tone. "I can't stand to see my little boy so sick. That's why I never think about God anymore. I even wonder if He really is . . ."

"It's okay," interrupted the woman. "God doesn't hold that against you. He loves you very much and understands your feelings."

The woman looked toward the crucifix and wished she could tell Mary more. Her heart filled with love for the God she knew.

Wiping a tear from her own face, she looked to Mary and said, "Trust Him, Mary. As difficult as it is right now, trust Him and allow Him to help you through this. The day will come when you will understand. I can promise you that."

With compassion, the woman looked toward Mary and said, "Try to be strong. Your baby needs you, too." She stood to leave.

Mary suddenly wanted her to stay. The woman exuded a relaxed and peaceful feeling. "Please don't leave."

The woman moved out of the pew. Mary called after her, hoping a conversation would bring her back. She didn't even know her name. "Do you have someone in the hospital here?"

The matronly looking woman smiled sweetly, "I help out around the hospital." Then she was gone.

Mary remained seated. Her eyes found their way back to the crucifix and she felt bathed in a feeling of peace, much like being sedated. Unaware was she, of the fragrance of roses that surrounded her.

A tap on the shoulder awakened her from the trance-like state. Turning, she looked into the face of her dear friend, Opal. Mary was overjoyed to see her. Opal held her, offering tender words of sorrow for what she was going through. Opal suggested they get away from the hospital for a while.

"I've come to take you out for some air, Mary. I hear you haven't left the hospital at all."

"I can't leave Opal. Henri needs me."

"I understand how you feel, Mary, but if you take a little break, both of you will benefit. I won't take 'no' for an answer. As soon as I see the little guy myself, we'll take a walk on the hospital grounds."

She stood and offered Mary her arm, "I smell those roses again, are you wearing a rose fragrance?" She sniffed around grinning. "Or is it our angels again?"

Mary stood up. "You're right, I smell roses too, but I haven't any fragrance on; it must have come from the woman that just left."

On their way out of the chapel, Mary briefly told her about the woman. It seemed like a dream to her now. As she told the story, she realized she hadn't told the woman of her pregnancy, but brushed the thought aside.

They reached Henri's room. Mary and Opal dressed in the necessary attire before entering. Opal's heart skipped a beat when she saw the frail state Henri was in. This was not the same little Henri she had known. He managed a smile for her before drifting off to sleep. Opal, feeling quite shaken, turned away, not wanting to break down in front of John and Mary. Forcing a feeble smile, she told Mary it was time for their walk.

****

"They're leaving now, James. I have to go with them. Will you walk part way with us so we can finish our conversation?" Buffy seemed to need James desperately.

"It's okay James," T.J. said. "I'll not leave Henri's side. Go ahead. I'm here to help you."

James left with the others. Buffy smoothed her hair back, wanting to give the impression that what she was about to say wasn't really important to her. "I didn't quite hear you, James. Did you say I did well with my first appearance?"

He knew she wanted to hear it again. "I said that you appeared to Mary very professionally. As a matter of fact, it looks as though you have found your specialty."

"You really mean it?"

Personally, she felt like everything went wrong. Especially with the words she chose to say to Mary. Buffy worried that she made her feel worse and remembered wishing she could jump right back into the spirit world and stay there.

James, aware of her feelings said, "Buffy, I've never been able to appear as you did. I've always had to come from around a corner or anywhere that my charge couldn't see me."

He snapped his fingers. *"You appeared out of nowhere, a perfect entry. Smooth as silk. You do have a specialty now. Don't worry about the words you spoke."*

He looked at her with intense sincerity. *"You spoke the truth Buffy, that's our job."*

"I know, but it frightened Mary, and that concerns me deeply."

"I said, you told the truth. The time will come when she'll know that."

They reached the hospital doors leading to the outside. Opal was trying to get Mary to leave with her.

James said, *"Get busy now, Buf. You must help persuade Mary to leave the hospital for a while. I have to get back to Henri."*

James turned to leave, but stopped to say, *"You have been wonderful with her, Buf. Right now she really needs a change of scenery, and some fresh air."*

"James?" Buffy had another question.

"Yes?" Impatience revealed itself.

"Will Mary's mother be coming back to help with her?"

James's face softened. *"As often as God feels Mary needs her. I'll see you later, Buf."*

Buffy smiled gratefully, but had one more question and carefully chose her words. *"Wait just a moment, James. The character we chose, was it appropriate, really? I mean, an oldish woman. Shouldn't I have been more glittery? Perhaps a little younger with lots of light shining around me?"* She envisioned a more angelic presence.

"Buffy, I said it once, and I'll say it again. You were perfect. You appeared the way Mary needed to see you. Now, goodbye."

He flashed a smile and left.

Buffy eagerly went to work on Mary's thoughts, persuading her to leave the hospital for a while.

Chapter 33

*O*pal succeeded with her mission. After some coaxing, she and Mary walked through the exit doors. Mary stood briefly on the steps. Once her eyes adjusted to the brightness of the sunlight reflecting off the snow, she said, "You know Opal, it does feel good to be out here. Maybe I did need this."

Not wanting her to change her mind, Opal convinced her to take a little ride and hurried her off to the car. Heading out of the parking lot, Opal suggested they pick up some fast food and go to her house.

Mary agreed, "I'll like seeing my dad. Burky's bringing him to the hospital later. I do feel like I want to be in my home for a while."

"Getting away is good for you, Mary. I'm glad you came with me. It makes me feel like I'm doing something to help. I wish I could do more."

They entered Mary's home with enough food for everyone. Finding Burky and her dad gone, they figured the two of them already left for the hospital.

Mary didn't want to eat just yet and roamed through her house, touching briefly the little things that brought memories of happier times. Thanksgiving pictures still hung; a bit wrinkled on the edges now. Tears formed as she remembered how excited Henri had been the day they worked on them together. She quickly tore them down. Opal watched in silence.

Mary said nothing as she settled into her favorite chair. She finally asked, "Did John ask you to come and take me away?"

"Yes he did and I don't blame him. He's concerned about you and the baby."

"It's okay." She looked away, privately recalling the bizarre feelings that overpowered her that morning.

Turning back to Opal she asked, "Do you think our loved ones hang around us after they are gone?"

"I don't know what you mean, Mary. Are you talking about those that have died?"

"Yes. Like my mother. I feel like she's around at times. This morning, her words filled my head." She looked at Opal, hoping she understood.

"Of course they do! Especially during tough times like these. I've heard many people say they felt the presence of their lost loved ones."

"I'll just bet your mother is near by. A woman at the nursing home swears her husband hangs around all the time. She's not crazy or anything like that. She's as normal as you and me. It gives her comfort when she knows he's around."

Opal then recalled an experience of her own. "My dad made his presence known to me once. It wasn't immediately after he died, about a year had passed. I remember feeling especially lonely for him. To erase my sadness, I absorbed myself in a great novel. I remember being engrossed with the story I was reading and suddenly the smell of tobacco smoke filled the air. Dad's tobacco smoke. I experienced a wonderful, peaceful feeling and knew he was in the room with me."

Her eyes reflected a smile as she told Mary, "He used to smoke a pipe, just like your dad. His 'words' filled my head."

A calmness engulfed Mary as she listened to Opal confirm what she thought might be true. She told Opal what happened in the chapel.

"Girl," said Opal, "that was your mother trying to help you. How wonderful!"

"But I wasn't very pleasant." She told how she angrily pushed the thoughts away.

"She understands what you're going through. It looks as if she got through to you, even if you did get mad. Don't feel bad about your feelings Mary. Lord only knows how I would handle a situation like this. But you must let her help you."

"She never had anything this awful happen," said Mary wiping tears from her eyes.

"I know how much it hurts, Mary. I have no idea what to say. Except that life would be easier if we had some kind of understanding as to why such awful things happen."

Mary remained quiet. Later she said her mother used to say that if God didn't have a reason for us being here, we would all be in Heaven with Him. "Always trust Him, she'd say. But Opal, I'm having an awfully hard time with that."

"I know it has to be hard, Mary, and I'm so very sorry."

Mary looked at the clock. "I have to go back, Opal, I really need to be with Henri."

Opal stood. "Let's eat some of that Mexican food first. I'm starving."

Mary didn't seem too enthusiastic about eating so Opal decided to apply a little pressure. "You'll have to sit and watch me, so you may as well eat. Come on, it won't take long."

Mary joined her and without too much prodding, ate a small portion. Her spirits lifted once again as they prepared to leave. Opal decided to make only light conversation as they headed back to the hospital.

"Remember that guy Jose', the singer?"

"Sure I do. How is he? I almost forgot about him."

"Just last week he started to sing Christmas carols at the nursing home. He surprised us because he didn't show last November and we didn't ask him again. He later called and wanted to do the caroling. I couldn't believe it when he showed up. I'm telling you, those old folks love him and some of them sang right along with him. They were absolutely thrilled and he promised to sing weekly until Christmas, which I might add, is getting pretty darn close."

The expression on Mary's face told her she shouldn't have mentioned Christmas and quickly changed the subject. "We could have done some of your laundry while we were at the house. I forgot that I was going to ask you if you needed help. I feel awful now."

"It's okay. Burky's been taking care of it; he's been so wonderful, Opal. He's taken a leave of absence from his job to help with my dad. He says it is a much needed vacation. We told him we could hire someone to stay, but he won't hear of it. I feel somewhat guilty."

"You certainly shouldn't. When someone wants to help, you have to let them. I have extra time, too. There's no reason I can't help him out. I'll talk to Burky about it."

Opal pulled into the hospital parking lot. Mary quickly got out of the car, thanking her for everything.

Opal stopped her, "Just wait a minute, girl. I'll be walking you back to the room."

"You don't have to do that. Just walk with me to the entrance. I feel better now, thanks. You and John were right; I enjoyed getting a breath of air. But I do have to get back to my son."

"I know." They parted company at the door. Opal watched as Mary's sad figure made its way down the long hospital corridor.

293

Mary slowed her pace as she neared Henri's room and saw John standing outside the door talking to Dr. Gene. Fear stopped her cold.

John said, "Come on, hon. We're just visiting while your dad talks with Henri. Burky brought him here a while ago, and Henri just woke up."

Relieved, Mary asked about Henri. Without waiting for an answer, she said hello to Dr. Gene.

"I'm happy to see you took a break, Mary," said the doctor. "There's a little more color in your cheeks now."

He could not force a smile as he said, "I was telling John that Dr. Johnson would like to meet with us tomorrow at ten o'clock."

Dr. Gene looked at his watch and said he had to get back to his office. Mary headed toward the door when John stopped her. He said he wanted to have a word with her before they went in to see Henri.

She displayed a look of warning. "I don't want to hear anything bad right now, John."

Pausing, she then looked him squarely in the eye, "I suppose you know what Dr. Johnson wants to talk about. Well I'm not going to listen. I can't." She turned away.

"It's not that, Mary." He told her about the reporter that stopped Burky and Lisa in the hall the day before. "I was a little upset when Burky told me what the man wanted, but the more I think about his request, the reporter is right. Maybe the story will help save many people from suffering the anguish we're feeling."

She stared at the wall. Seeing no response, John added, "I did talk to the guy, his name is Ric. I told him we'd think about it and get back to him. I made it perfectly clear that if we decide to go ahead and let him do the story, there would be no pictures. I don't like that idea!!"

When she still didn't respond, he said, "Ric said that if we allowed him to do this, Henri would get thousands of cards and letters."

Mary's eyes met his and her expression softened, "That would be nice, John. Henri would love getting mail. It's almost Christmas. Does the reporter want to speak with Henri?"

"He does, but I don't know how I feel about that."

"Maybe we should let Henri decide," Mary answered, "we'll talk to him about it. Let's go in now."

He agreed, and they walked through the door. They were touched by the scene that met them. Grampa sat next to the bed. His head lay on the pillow next to Henri's as they conversed in low tones. John and Mary took a seat in the corner, not wanting to disturb them.

Henri was telling Grampa that he saw Gramma all the time in his dreams. "She tells me about the angels and some day, I want to be one."

Grampa only nodded his head as if to say yes. Seconds later he carefully stood, so as not to disturb Henri as he drifted off to sleep once again.

Grampa turned and saw Mary and John. He bit at his lip. Mary left her chair and held her dad. Neither one of them said a word.

Henri slept peacefully. Periodically, a smile swept across his face. It reminded Mary of when he was a babe, sleeping in her lap, smiling the same smile. Her mother always said he was dreaming of angels. Mary recalled telling her it was just gas. Her eyes misted from the memories.

Rising from her chair, Mary made a quick exit. John followed, and as he stood holding her, Lisa and Burky walked toward them.

They stopped to talk with John and Mary and it wasn't long before voices could be heard coming from Henri's room again. Mary told the others that maybe it would be a good idea to leave them alone for a few more minutes.

A few minutes passed before Grampa came out. Henri was sleeping again.

Grampa expressed his wish to leave; his emotions could take no more. Mary embraced him again before he and Burky left. Henri's parents returned to their son's bedside, patiently waiting for him to open his eyes once more.

Hours passed before he woke up again. He could barely speak, "I loved seeing Grampa. I'm glad he's feeling better. Mom, look at the window. Do you see the yellow bird?"

She looked, and so did John. A yellow bird sat on the windowsill. They both knew Henri hadn't looked that way at all.

John said, "It looks like the same bird we saw just before we left Pleasant Valley. I wonder how he found us here?"

Mary, feeling odd, said nothing.

Henri continued speaking. "James, my friend. The one I dream about . . ." He paused momentarily and after some labored breathing, continued, "James told me he would send the bird for you to see so you would know God is watching over me. This is the first time James talked to me in my dreams. He wants you to know that God is real. I watched him send the bird here." Henri suddenly became very still and his eyes closed.

Panic grabbed his parents as they stood at his bedside. Mary's heart pounded in her throat until Henri began talking again.

"Mom, remember the man in Pleasant Valley that used to send off pigeons with messages?"

"I remember, Henri." Her voice broke.

"That's how James sent the bird, but he said I could give you the message. God is real and James loves Him a lot. They're best friends."

He began to vomit and soon choked uncontrollably. Lisa rushed to his side. The three of them tended the boy until he quieted down. Sleep mercifully took over his little body once more and it was then that Mary nearly collapsed. John and Lisa helped her to a chair where she sat bent over. Feeling the same anguish, the others could do nothing. It was getting to be too much to bear.

Chapter 34

*T*he meeting was held in Dr. Johnson's office at ten o'clock in the morning, as scheduled. Dr. Gene sat with John and Mary when they were told that the chemotherapy had to be stopped because of Henri's weakened condition. They were also told that he hadn't responded as hoped. Both doctors were at a loss for words as they watched the parents crumble even further while listening to what they dreaded to hear.

Mary said repeatedly, "He's going to die. Oh please God, don't let this happen to my little boy."

John made an effort to be strong as he held his wife, but he broke down as well. The doctors knew nothing they could say would help. This was the worst nightmare of every physician. Dr. Johnson left the three of them alone.

The doctors couldn't sedate Mary because of her pregnancy. She quieted down and said she wanted to rest. Not wanting to return to Henri's room, she insisted on going to where she usually slept. Both Dr. Gene and John led her to the room for parents where she fell on the bed and lay perfectly still. Dr. Gene told John he'd be in the adjoining room. John sat next to her, watching as she fell asleep.

Dr. Gene waited patiently. He stood when John entered and poured him a cup of steaming hot coffee. John settled into a chair near the door where Mary slept. He didn't feel like talking but appreciated having someone with him. Dr. Gene sensed his feelings and sat quietly next to him.

John spoke first. "Henri's known he's going to die and I haven't seen it until now." He hung his head and told the doctor about the dreams Henri had and some of the things Henri told him in private.

"I can't accept this, Gene. There has to be at least an ounce of hope left." He put his head in his hands.

"I wish I could give you that hope, John. I will tell you that I've seen miracles happen to patients sicker than Henri. To this day, you can't tell that they were ever sick. And I've seen another kind of miracle."

He waited for John's attention. John looked up and Dr. Gene continued, "Only God knows what Henri's fate will be. Whatever the plan, there's no doubt in my mind that your son is being tenderly guided by Him. I've seen it before John. Henri must be extremely special in God's eyes. Children always are."

John's eyes glistened with tears. He wanted to speak; the words wouldn't come out.

Dr. Gene hoped to give this man some measure of comfort. "It's easy to ignore God during times like this, but John you have to know He's with you. This probably isn't what you want to hear right now, but I know that He watches over all of us, because of what I've heard and seen as a doctor. I can do little else but believe. I've seen horrible things happen and, at the same time, I can see God working to help the suffering people."

"Many don't recognize the help, not at the time. But I can. I believe that as time passes and the hurt subsides somewhat, the injured person realizes they weren't alone at the time they felt abandoned."

John sat solemnly in his chair. "I know what you're saying must be true. But you're right, it's hard to think about it right now. My entire being feels nothing but unending pain."

"And God understands, John. More than you'll ever know. I've heard him cursed and hated by suffering people, but He understands. You can be as mad as you want but He'll still be with you. I know it for a fact." He could see that he'd said enough.

John thanked Dr. Gene for being there and excused himself, saying he wanted to check on Mary. Dr. Gene also needed to get back to his office. He did, however, pour himself another cup of coffee and sat for a few minutes pondering over the past and the many wonders he'd witnessed.

"Life's lessons," he called his experiences, and he'd learned from every one of them. No one could ever convince him there wasn't a God. Dr. Gene thought about the patients he sat with as they passed into the next world. Some went happily with beautiful expressions on their faces. A few talked of their relatives coming to meet them, and a few mentioned angels. Others saw no one, but eagerly left as if being guided.

The doctor took one last swallow of his coffee and set the cup down. Knowing he had to be on his way, he hesitated as he recalled the faces of those that died briefly and returned. They had such wonderful stories to tell. The vision of peace they described was like nothing he'd ever seen or heard of in his life.

Listening to their stories, he knew beyond a shadow of a doubt that most of them witnessed a glimpse of Heaven. Dr. Gene believed God allowed them this privilege for the purpose of them going out and telling the world that Heaven existed and that it was everything God promised it to be.

Many talked about a bright light they'd seen and felt drawn to. Others viewed what they said was Heaven and described a world similar to ours. The freshness and beauty couldn't be expressed with words. One man did use a descriptive word. Dr. Gene smiled as he recalled him saying it was "awesome."

To say that the experience changed the lives of these people was putting it mildly. Each one became so full of love for those around them. They wanted to share their experience, in hopes of teaching someone the same love and peace that they learned.

One particular man came to mind as he thought about the changes that took over these people. His name was George. He had been a patient of Dr. Gene's; and not one of his favorites. The man was extremely wealthy. Nothing wrong with that, save his attitude, which needed a major adjustment. He was selfish and the rudest person that ever visited his office. Dr. Gene remembered wishing he would find another doctor. His once-a-year visits were too much to endure. He hated to see him walk through the door.

George had a heart attack and was pronounced clinically dead for twenty minutes. Brain damage should have occurred and many people believed it did! The man had changed that dramatically. He swore he saw Heaven and said that he found peace and love there. The excitement radiated from him and his face held a permanent smile; an expression never seen by anyone that ever knew him.

The saddest part of the story was that it scared away what few friends he did have because they truly thought George had lost his mind. But Dr. Gene believed him, and told him so.

When George left the hospital, he didn't waste any time. Only a few days had passed before he came to Dr. Gene's office wanting to know if he knew of any people that needed financial help.

A long list was given to George and the doctor told him how he could help each person. He explained how sensitive many of these people were, and instructed George to be very cautious with their feelings.

George heeded that advice and none of the people ever knew where the help came from. George had fun with his generosity. He continued helping others until the day he died, nearly penniless, two years to the day after his first visit to Heaven.

Dr. Gene believed his story, all right. The day that George came to his office wanting to help people happened to be the same day he had received a notice from the bank. They were foreclosing on his office. Dr. Gene's office was also his home. He had many patients so poor that they couldn't pay the meager fees he charged. Some exchanged hand made goods for his services and one patient kept him supplied with freshly plucked chickens. This was the reason Dr. Gene had been unable to keep up with his bills. He'd said nothing to George or anyone else about his problem.

Somehow George knew of the dilemma, and Dr. Gene received the deed to his office in the mail. George had paid the bill in full. Dr. Gene owned his home and office, free and clear. He remembered how he nearly fell to the floor when he viewed the title. To this day, he has no idea how George ever found out about his sad state of affairs. Many years have passed since then.

Looking at the clock on the wall, the doctor jumped to his feet. He hadn't realized how late the hour was. He had an assistant now that could handle things, but he still rushed off.

****

James sat with God that day watching the big screen as Dr. Gene and John talked. They stayed with the good doctor afterward and pondered with him about the past.

God said, "Allowing a few people to see Heaven every now and then has helped many to believe that we exist and that my teachings of life after death are true. They use the word 'death,' we know there is no such thing as death."

"We sure do," James replied. "But they'll all find out the truth some day. Word spreads like wildfire when someone gets a glimpse of Heaven and many new believers result from the news. But I still understand how people feel they're abandoned when they have to go through hardships. It's sad."

God's face reflected the same sadness. They both knew the reasons for these hardships. They also knew about the end result, which made their jobs much easier. Along with knowing that in time, the people would also know.

Turning off the big screen, God discussed the final plans with James. When finished and before James left His office, God said to him. "When the story hits the media, we'll be another step closer to saving the lives of many people. Cutting these lives short has got to stop."

"I know," said James. He stood to leave, feeling more able to finish his assignment. It helped immensely to know of the gift God had waiting for everyone when their journey on earth ended.

God called out to him as he opened the door. "One more thing James," a sparkle had returned to His eyes. "What do you think about Burky and Lisa? Kind of perfect for each other, don't you think?"

"For sure! But they don't even know it yet."

"They will. When everything settles down, things will begin to happen. I have great plans for those two!" God winked confidently.

"And James?"

"Yes?"

"Remember Jose', the singer?"

James grinned. "I remember."

"Today's his big day. When he sings Christmas carols at the nursing home, he's going to get discovered. He's not going to believe the good times that are headed his way. Just thought you could use some more good news."

Flashing a huge smile, James left.

****

Chapter 35

*T*he days that followed agonized Henri's loved ones. He wasn't able to talk after the day he showed his parents the little yellow bird. Henri's parents kept a constant vigil at his side. Opal helped with Grampa, which enabled Burky to spend more time at the hospital.

Mary ate regularly and rested more frequently. She'd taken on a new kind of strength. There wasn't much of it, but it was enough to carry her through each day. She remained conscious of the need to care for her unborn child.

The television reporter returned. Henri's parents granted him permission to do a story about their son. The story hit the newspapers and television worldwide, as did a picture of Henri. A school picture that showed him smiling. His full head of red curly hair glowed.

Cards and presents poured in from all over the world. His parents wished he would wake up to see how many caring people were out there.

That wish was granted on Christmas Day. When his blurry eyes rested on his family, he managed a weak smile. He watched happily as Burky and his dad opened some of the presents. The few gifts he saw thrilled the little tike. His mother opened a few of the many cards he received.

Henri's small hand lifted slightly as she opened a card from a yellow envelope. She put the Christmas greeting in his hand and looked as he pointed to the picture on the front. It was an angel holding a yellow bird in the palm of her hand. A faint smile crossed Henri's face as he viewed the last card he would see.

He slept through most of Christmas Day, waking for a few minutes in the evening. He watched through exhausted eyes as huge snowflakes softly fell against the window. The street light outside provided enough reflection for the scene to resemble a picture out of a storybook. The large flakes sparkled like diamonds.

His voice was barely audible as he said, "I love Christmas . . ." He looked at his parents as they stood next to his bedside. "And I love you, too."

"Angel's We Have Heard on High," played softly on the hospital intercom as Henri fell into a deep sleep. He would never wake up in this world again. The room filled with the fragrance of roses.

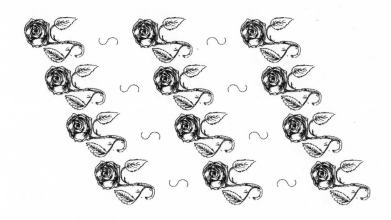

Chapter 36

*C*hristmas music played softly over the intercom as Henri drifted peacefully away. A bright light off in the distance urged him forward. A wonderful feeling engulfed him as he floated through the air, eagerly responding to the need to head for the light. Without an ache in his body, his heart overflowed with a great feeling of love and peace. He felt absolutely no fear.

Moving closer to the light, he suddenly remembered his parents. Turning back he could see them in the distance hugging each other. Henri wanted to assure them he was well and headed back.

"Mom, Dad, look at me. I'm all better and I can fly!" He made a circle in the air in front of them, stopping as he looked at his own body lying on the bed. His parents cried over it and he watched as Lisa and Burky rushed into the room to be with them.

Henri realized then, what had happened. He died and never even knew it, because he couldn't remember ever feeling so alive. Waving his arms in the air to make sure they were there, he proceeded to make a somersault in the air, laughing gleefully. Until he glanced down.

To see his loved ones so terribly upset, saddened him. Henri tried to tell them he was okay, but could see it was useless. He knew that he was in another world, and guessing that it must be Heaven, allowed himself to go with the strong urge to move on.

Henri gave a small wave and again headed toward the light. As he floated further, he put out his arms and moved them as if to be a bird. He giggled as he did and the more he thought about how great it felt, the more it reminded him of the ventures he and James had taken in his dreams. Henri wondered where James was. He had said he would see him again soon and they'd have more fun together.

Looking around, he saw nothing but the bright light. Moving closer, he made out the shape of a very large curved stairway. Still urged on, he moved closer and was nearly to the bottom step when he heard a voice calling.

"Hey, sonny over here!" It was a deep voice and didn't seem too friendly.

Henri stopped, not wanting to go toward the voice. He could finally see where it came from and knew it wasn't where he wanted to go.

A man wearing a black hood noticed that he frightened the lad. "I'm not going to hurt you, boy. You probably aren't even on my list. Just give me your name and do it fast!"

Henri quickly gave him his name and the man waved his hand saying, "Go, you don't belong here."

Henri left with haste, heading up the winding staircase. When far enough away, he stopped and turned back for another look. Thick fog surrounded the cloaked man. He saw a large boat sitting in what appeared to be a wide river just behind him. The boat held many people and they appeared to be upset.

Looking further up the river he spotted a huge waterfall and noticed that the boat pointed in that direction. Many of the people didn't have seats. Henri decided to move on.

He stopped again when he heard the gruff voice of the man talking to someone else. "It's about time you got here, we've been waiting."

The resisting person was shoved into the boat. They were headed straight for the waterfall. Again Henri noticed that there were not seats for everyone and shuddered. Bewildered as to what was going on down there, he ran to the top of the stairs.

Reaching the top, he saw a long line of many different kinds of people. They were all dressed differently; some wore hospital gowns like him. Henri did hear happier voices up here and stood briefly observing the scene.

At the head of the line stood a tall man holding a clipboard. Henri could tell that he was in charge, and instinctively headed for the end of the line. The woman in front of him busily chatted with the people in front of her. Henri didn't want to disturb them with the many questions he had.

Looking around, he saw two long yellow buses parked a short distance behind the man with the clipboard. Both of them had words written on the front, they reminded him of school buses. One read Heaven and the other bus had a word on it that Henri had never seen before. He couldn't say the word but spelled it out in his mind. P-u-r-g-a-t-o-r-y.

Having no idea what it meant and since the woman ahead of him was still busily chatting, he decided to wait and ask the man in charge. He patiently waited as the line slowly moved forward.

Looking to the buses once more, a new thought crossed Henri's mind. If the one bus was headed for Heaven, he wasn't there yet. He liked that idea because nothing was turning out to be the way he had anticipated. The hooded man was scary, and Henri wondered where the angels and God were.

The lady in front of him headed for one of the buses and the man with the clipboard asked him for his name. It was his turn. Henri noticed that the man had a very friendly face and gave him his name.

The man flipped the pages on his clipboard. "Ah, Henri, yes. Here it is. Looks like you are one of the luckier passengers."

He pointed to the bus with 'Heaven' written across the front. "That's your bus. It goes straight to Heaven."

He patted Henri's head and told him he could get aboard. Henri hesitated and asked the man if he could answer a few questions.

The man with the clipboard looked kindly to Henri, "All of your questions will be answered soon, my boy. You'll be fine."

"I know. I'm not scared at all, but I just want to know about that mean man."

Henri motioned toward the stairway. "The one down there."

"I'm sorry you had to see him when you first got here, Henri. He's perfectly harmless to the good people because they are not wanted where he's going. But I can understand how frightening he can be. He's the Grim Reaper and is in charge of the very bad people. What you didn't see in the background were the many guards we have in that area watching so that no mistakes are made."

A horn blasted. "Henri, your bus is ready to leave. You're the last passenger for this trip."

He smiled at Henri, as he said, "Be off now, your questions will be answered soon." Winking, he added, "You are going to have a wonderful life."

Henri scooted off excitedly. Reaching the bus, he had to climb three steps. He noticed then that his feet made the motions of climbing, but they weren't touching the steps. The

309

feeling brought a wide grin to his face. When he looked up, he found himself looking into a seemingly familiar face.

He stared briefly at the man who looked just like Mr. Trombly, his old bus driver who died a few years ago. But it couldn't be, thought Henri. This man looked so much younger.

The bus driver said, "Quit your gawking. If you have gum, spit it out and move to the back of the bus."

He recognized the words to be the same used by Mr. Trombly. Henri obeyed and as he made his way to the back, decided it must not be him or he would have said something.

Finding the last available seat, Henri sat and looked around at the other passengers. He couldn't see much because they were all looking straight ahead, so he turned to an old man seated next to him. Henri smiled as the man gazed down at him and noticed the poor guy didn't have a tooth in his mouth. He wondered if God would give him some.

Hearing the door to the bus closing, Henri was again reminded of his old school bus. It made a hissing sound when it closed, just as he remembered.

The bus took off with a jerk, forcing everyone's head back. Mr. Trombly used to take off the same way. The driver pulled the bus around a large circle drive, and Henri stretched his neck to see where they were going. Ahead sat a mammoth set of shiny golden gates. They drove closer to them. Excitement filled the bus as the passengers viewed the massive display. These gates were familiar to them. They were the entrance to Heaven.

As the driver pulled closer, Henri saw where the beautiful bright light came from. It was the Heavenly sun glinting off the golden gates! The exquisitely beautiful, bright ray extended much further than his eyes could see. Henri figured the end of it could be found back where he had come from, a place that now was fast fading from his mind.

The bus paused a short distance before the gates and the driver held a remote control in his hand. As he aimed it at his target, the beautiful set of gates opened widely.

The bus driver's voice came across a loud speaker as they passed through. "Welcome to Heaven, folks."

He continued, sounding much like a tour guide. "On your right and left you will see the beginning of our many enchanted forests. The animals scampering about have no fear and there is no fighting amongst them. If you walked through the woods right now, not a single furry pet would run from you. There is no fear in Heaven. Not for them, and not for you. You will be treated with kindness and love by everyone here."

Henri remained silent as did the others on the bus. A feeling of peace blanketed everyone as they listened to the driver's words and observed the expanse of beauty surrounding them.

"We are headed for the welcoming center. It's a red brick building and you'll be met by your former guardian angel there. The angels are at the building right now making the arrangements that are important for your arrival. Your future and happiness are their main concern. They'll be ready for you when you arrive, so just sit back and enjoy your journey into Heaven."

Tears of joy sprinkled down the faces of many of the people as they fully realized that this indeed was The Promised Land.

The busload bounced along the long bumpy roads. The roadside scenery grew more splendid as they traveled along. Henri watched with growing amazement at this new beauty. He noticed that so much of it resembled the land where he came from, except everything here looked much brighter and fresher. Wishing to smell the air, he clicked the window down and drank in a freshness that was completely foreign to him. Words could never describe the sweetness. He rested his head against the open window to allow the wonderful air to wash over him.

His eyes were drawn to a sky the color of a piercing teal blue. This was a shade of blue he'd never seen before, and the sky was awash with it. Every tree they passed looked vibrantly alive, displaying green, lush leaves. Not a dead branch hung from any of these enormous trees. They passed lakes that reflected crystal clear waters, sparkling like diamonds under the magic of the sun.

Crossing over a bridge, Henri looked down and saw a bubbling stream. Suds did not lie dormant along the edges as in the streams back home.

Settling back into his seat, Henri thought about how different Heaven turned out to be. He had envisioned a huge building where everyone sat around being good, with God and the angels smiling at them. He never thought it would be much fun, but now anxiously awaited the surprises that he knew would be at the red brick building. The mere thought of meeting his very own guardian angel made the anticipated excitement even more unbearable.

The bus began to slow and Henri saw what looked like the outskirts of a large busy city. As they moved in closer he could see a group of people near a lake. They scurried around, looking like they were on a picnic. Henri didn't think they looked at all like regular people because they dressed in an odd fashion. Up close they looked like cowboys.

The driver's voice boomed through the loud speaker. "We are now passing through the outskirts of a cowboy settlement. Most of the people you see here, lived during that era. Some are here for the experience. As you can see, Indians are mingling with the cowboys. Their own village isn't too far from here and, like everyone else in Heaven, they are on friendly terms."

Slowing the bus so his passengers could have a better view, he added, "Heaven goes on forever; I've seen only a small part since I've been here. It would take years to see all of it. Tour buses go out daily to various places of interest in the immediate area. If you wish to go further, you'd have to fly."

Hearing the loud murmur of voices, which happened every time he mentioned flying, he said, "Yes, we have planes here too."

The voice continued, "Get settled in and decide for yourselves which parts of Heaven you would like to visit. You can live in any era you wish. As a matter of fact, I have a friend that just left to live in the Orient for a while."

Henri never thought about this before; that cowboys and Indians and everyone from the olden days would be here. But it made sense. Of course they would be here, too, and probably even cavemen. Everyone that ever died would be eligible. Heaven must be really big!

They slowly left the cowboy era and came upon some hilly terrain. He could see hills of a reddish color and many cactuses scattered about. Off in the distance, herds of horses ran freely in the wind.

The bus traveled swiftly through the hills, finding its way to another village. This one seemed more modern and Henri felt familiarity as he peered at the sight. Children played busily with different activities, wearing clothes that looked like his. And some rode bikes. Modern bikes!

A field filled with youngsters wearing uniforms played baseball. More excitement consumed Henri. It had been such a long time since he played the game. He looked to the old man sitting next to him and yelled out, "Isn't this great?!!"

The old man gave him another toothless smile. Henri could tell he felt the same happiness. His face held a permanent smile and his worn out eyes misted.

Henri looked at him compassionately, "I'll just bet they'll give you some new teeth here."

The man laughed out loud and said, "All of our dreams will come true, son. You wait and see."

The bus speeded out of that neighborhood and into another one. Soon the driver slowed the vehicle. This time, he turned into a courtyard that presented trees more enormous than those seen earlier. Scattered among these trees sat beds of colorful flowers and grass so green that it appeared to be painted.

They traveled down a long, winding driveway. Everyone raved about the carpets of multicolored flowers spreading in every direction. So captivated were the people, that not one seemed aware when the bus pulled up to the red brick building.

As they were brought to an abrupt halt, all eyes found the building with lines of people standing in front of it. Their faces could not be seen because each one held up a large card in front of them.

"We're here, folks!" The voice returned. "As I explained earlier, you will meet your former guardian angel here. Just look for your name on the cards they're holding. They'll take you to where you have to go. Have a wonderful life, all of you. You may begin to unload now. In an orderly fashion of course, starting with the first row."

He swung around and motioned to the people he wanted to move first. Henri watched as they stood to leave the bus. Once off, they bustled about, looking for the card that held their name. After shaking hands or embracing their former guardian angel, they disappeared into the building with their newly discovered friend.

Henri was quite shocked to see the angels without wings. They didn't look like angels at all, just regular people. James, the angel in his dreams, had wings and a cape.

His row began to depart. The bus driver turned to him as he walked by. "Hi, Henri."

Henri's face beamed when he realized it was really him. "I knew it was you Mr. Trombly! Why did you pretend you didn't know me?"

"Probably because I wanted to keep you guessing. Besides, you know I don't socialize when I have work to do. I've always taken my job seriously."

Mr. Trombly grinned as he gulped his coffee. A small trace dribbled down his chin. He wiped it away just like he used to do. "I knew you were coming, Henri. We are always informed before a friend or relative arrives."

"Do you love it here, Mr. Trombly?"

"Yes, and so will you, but you'd better run along now and find your guardian angel. I'll look you up and we can visit another time."

Grinning, Henri bounded down the steps in a flash. After taking one quick look back at Mr. Trombly, his eyes began the search for a card with his name on it.

It didn't take long. There were only two cards left, and a head popped out from behind one of them.

"It's you!!!!"

"At your service. Welcome to Heaven, Henri." James displayed an impish grin on his face.

"But where are your wings and your cape?"

Henri covered his mouth with his hand, holding a stunned expression, "Does this mean that you are my guardian angel?" He could not believe it.

"Slow down, boy." James could plainly see that Henri was more than surprised. "First of all, I'm not your guardian angel anymore. I was from the day you were born, but now I am your friend. As far as the wings and cape go, I didn't feel like wearing them today."

He touched Henri's shoulders. "You don't have on wings either, but I see you're getting around just fine."

Henri checked out his feet, again noticing they weren't touching the ground. He looked at a grinning James as he floated slightly upward.

"I'm glad you are . . . I mean were, my guardian angel."

James lovingly held the back of Henri's head as he escorted him into the red brick building and watched as the boy's eyes grew large in amazement. It was evident that he'd never been inside a room so immense. The walls held pictures of angels. Looking at the pictures, Henri figured they must have put the wings and gowns on to have their picture taken. He couldn't tell where the ends of the room were. A carved desk extended from one end of the wall down to what must have been the other end. The carvings on the desk were of angels too.

Long lines of people stood waiting for their turn at the desk. James escorted Henri to the line they were to wait in. A sign on the wall behind the desk read: CHILDREN. Looking ahead to the other people, he could see they too, were children. Standing protectively next to them, were their angels.

"What will we talk to the man about, James?"

"We have to check in."

"Okay."

The line moved quickly and the boy in front of him had his turn. Henri listened as he and his angel spoke with the man in charge. They were talking about a house that the boy would be staying at. It was called 'The Paradise Children's Home'. Henri didn't have to ask.

James bent down to tell him. "It's a house bigger than you could ever imagine. It's for children that come to Heaven before their parents or any known relatives do. We call it Paradise for short and it is a paradise in every sense of the word. The children love living there and have everything they could ever wish for."

"More importantly, they meet many friends and have parents to take care of them. Some of the men and women are in the same situation as the children, coming to Heaven before their family. They wish to continue with parenting, so they do it in Paradise. Others are people that always wanted to have children of their own, but were never able. Here they can fulfill that dream."

"When their children come and the parents leave, won't they miss their Heaven kids?" Henri wondered.

"Not really. Everyone can see each other whenever they want. They visit back and forth. Sometimes the children leave Paradise before their parents come to Heaven. If they decide to do other things."

"Like what?" He couldn't picture any youngsters going off by themselves.

"We'll talk about that later, Henri."

The man at the desk motioned them to the front. They moved forward and James gave Henri's name.

Henri watched the man whistle as he searched the files. He didn't look too old and had a black mustache. His face was kind, just like the other people he'd met in Heaven so far.

"Here you are, my boy. It looks like there's a big surprise waiting for you!"

Handing some paperwork to James, he said, "If for some reason these arrangements don't work out, come back to my desk and we'll issue him a bunk until further decisions can be made. Take these papers to room 253; the woman there will take care of you."

They walked quickly to the elevator and James pressed the arrow pointing up. Henri was full of questions. "What did he mean, he'd issue me a bunk? Am I going to Paradise? Where are we going, James?"

The elevator door opened and they stepped inside. "Some people decide they want to live in a house of their own.

While they're waiting for it to be built to their specifications, they stay in the bunkhouse."

"Am I getting my own house?" Henri didn't really like the idea. "Or can I live at Paradise?" That sounded better. "What's my surprise?"

The door to the elevator opened. They walked out and started down a hall that seemed endless.

"Henri, you will make the final decision about where you wish to live. Regardless of your choice, you can change your mind at any time and live wherever else you desire."

They reached room 253. Before knocking, James finished the conversation. "Plans have been made for you. This lady will talk to us about them and you must remember that the final choice is yours. Got it?"

Henri smiled. "Got it."

James tapped lightly on the door. Hearing the words, "Come in," they entered.

An air of importance surrounded the lady as she sat behind a light blue desk. She wore a dress of the same color. Her hair, pulled back in a bun, was held by a blue ribbon. One could see by the smile on her face that she loved her job.

The walls were covered with blue wall paper. Painted on them were large white, billowing clouds. Seeing Henri checking them out with admiration, she said, "I wanted to capture the feeling of Heaven in this room. It reminds the newcomers of where they are."

She extended her hand, "Hello Henri, welcome to Heaven. My name is Sara and I have a big surprise for you."

Before asking them to sit down, she clapped her hands in a professional manner. The door to another room opened. A woman walked through and Henri felt a twinge of familiarity as he looked at her. She ran toward him smiling with outstretched arms.

"My darling little Henri, I could hardly stand the wait once I heard you were coming."

She stood back to look him over and as he looked into her eyes he knew that it had to be her.

"Gramma?" He couldn't believe his eyes. "I feel like it's you, but you don't look the same."

He felt odd seeing her that way. "Where's your gray hair? You grew!" She was much taller.

Gramma hugged him again, saying, "I'm younger and healthy now! We can be any age we want here, and I chose twenty-five. Don't you like the way I look?" She winked to the others.

"Yes, yes, I do." He stood back and looked at her. "I have to get used to you like this, though. You look real different." The more he looked at her the more he approved of her new appearance.

Sara, the lady with the bun cleared her throat. "You have to be making the same kind of decisions, Henri. I have to know what age you'd like to be and if you want to make any changes with yourself."

Henri looked at James. They hadn't talked about this.

James was quick to say, "If I were you Henri, I'd ask for my hair back."

Feeling his head and finding that his hair was still gone, he quickly said, "Could I please?" He thought briefly and then said, "And when it comes back can it be a different color? I hate red hair so much because everyone makes fun of me." He looked pleadingly to the woman.

Her face smiled brightly. "No one in Heaven will ever make fun of you, Henri. It's your decision though. What color would you rather have?"

Looking at James for reassurance he said, "Can I have the same color as James? Almost blonde? Is that okay with you, James?"

"Sure, I don't mind if we look like twins."

319

Chuckling, his gaze quickly skimmed over Henri. "Actually my friend, I think my color would look good on you. Go ahead."

"That's what it will be then." Sara got a big kick out of watching his growing excitement. "How old do you want to be, Henri?"

Seeing her grandson overwhelmed with so many decisions, Gramma spoke, "Now, just relax darling. If you want to stay the age you are, you can; or maybe you would like to decide another day. You can do that too."

Looking him over she added, "That hair color looks good on you, but I still liked your red hair."

Henri's hands flew to his head where he found a mass of curls. Spotting a mirror on the back of a door next to James, he jumped out of his seat and rushed to it.

"How'd this happen? Look at me!"

He couldn't take his eyes off himself. The others watched; loving his reaction to the magic. James told him the secret.

"When you decided what you wanted, it happened. I see your locks are still curly. You look good that way and at least we don't look like twins."

Henri sat down. "I didn't even feel it growing."

He ran his fingers through his curly blonde hair and Sara wiped a tear from her eye. This was why she loved her job so much. She sniffled. Seeing the newcomers so excited and happy made her heart sing.

"I've been thinking about how old I want to be, and it's fifteen. Is that okay?" Henri braced himself for an instant growth spurt.

Before anyone could answer he said, "I chose fifteen because I never can do what the big kids do; like ride a twelve-speed bike or travel around by myself."

"Will I need to have a birthday to turn fifteen?" He looked down at his hospital garb and noticed the tightness. He didn't feel himself grow.

Jumping to his feet, Henri dashed to the mirror again; his face took on a serious expression as he looked at his new self. He liked what he saw.

Glancing to the others, he asked if he had to wish for clothes.

"You already wished for them," said James, "but the next time you want some, you will have to go shopping like the rest of us."

Henri turned back and was amazed to find himself dressed in a pair of jeans and T-shirt. He needed to sit down. This just didn't seem to be possible; was this just a wonderful dream?

He blinked his eyes and Sara knew his thoughts. "You'll be all right Henri, we know how hard this is to believe. Relax and enjoy whatever comes your way. This is God's gift to you."

"He does this magic?" Henri thought this was the greatest gift. "Can we wish for anything here in Heaven? I mean, I've been wanting a twelve-speed bike and now that I'm older, I'll be able to handle it just fine. Shall I wish it?"

Sara said, "You'll have everything you want and need Henri, but everything doesn't come as quickly as your appearance. We get that job done fast because most people need a quick 'fix'."

Sara was relieved to see that he made the transition so quickly. Others sometimes discover the profound reality of Heaven too difficult to comprehend. Many need time in the 'Adjustment Home' before they realize it's all true.

A small smile crossed Sara's face as she recalled how sometimes the newcomers hugged her when they understood that Heaven is not an illusion. A couple of times she thought she would be squeezed to another death. She covered her mouth and giggled as she thought about a man who was just recently in her office. His reaction had been one of sheer delight and he hugged her and threw her in the air. She purposely hung near the ceiling to see what he'd do when she didn't come back down. The expression on his face was one she would remember forever!

All eyes were on Sara as she laughed out loud. Seeing she was the center of attention, she cleared her throat and shifted some papers on her desk, making an effort to appear businesslike.

"Now then," she said, "we must finish our decision-making. Henri?"

"Yes, ma'am?" Henri felt older and wanted to behave as such. He knew that men called ladies, ma'am.

"We have to know where you to want to live. God wants you to be happy and my job is to see that you are."

Henri looked to his gramma. "I'd like to live with my gramma. When I get older, I'll probably move out, but is it all right for now?"

"You won't get older unless you want to, Henri," his gramma explained. "In Heaven we don't age unless it is our own desire. Of course you can stay with me for as long as you like."

"But can I still call you, Gramma? Anything else wouldn't feel right."

She smiled sweetly, "I'm still your gramma. It'll be that way always, my dear."

Henri was ecstatic. But he still wanted his most important question answered. He looked to Sara. "Where is God? I'd like to thank Him for everything."

He ran his fingers through his new head of hair. "I have to let Him know how much I like my hair."

James told Henri that God already knew. "He's very busy at His Palace right now, but he told me specifically that

322

He wanted to see you as soon as you've settled in. We do have to make an appointment, but you will definitely see Him."

Henri thought about that for a moment. "He must be like a president. They're always busy too."

"That's pretty much the way it is, we hardly ever get to see him." James watched Henri, knowing there were more questions.

"Do you have TV's here?"

"We sure do. God makes an appearance every now and then. There isn't a person in Heaven that doesn't watch when He's on."

James reached into his back pocket and pulled out his wallet. He held a picture of God and showed it to Henri.

"This is God?" As Henri looked the picture over, James told him that if time permitted it, they would swing by The Palace for a peek of the outside.

Henri was delighted. "I'd love that!"

He studied God's picture. "He looks a lot different than I thought He would. I like him though, I like Him a lot. God looks nice and has kind eyes. But James, why is He wearing glasses?"

"He thought He'd look good in them for His picture."

"Oh." That made sense to Henri. He handed the autographed picture back to James.

Sara reshuffled her papers and cleared her throat again. Her next appointment would be there soon. "It pleases me to know that you'll be happy living with your gramma, but should you change your mind . . ."

"I would never change my mind, I love her a lot."

"Well Henri, you may decide that you want to do something else. We have many schools to choose from...."

"Schools! Do I have to go to school? Here?" That was the last thing he wanted to do.

"Yes, schools. But only if you want to attend."

She handed him a packet. "This will give you information on a few of them. The schools are too numerous for me to mention right now. You may change your mind later and want to check them out."

James added, "I happen to know how much you love to play your violin. We have schools that can teach you more than you already know. And you might even decide you want to be a guardian angel like me. We have a large guardian angel school. But you can't make any decisions right now; we don't expect you too. You have to have some fun for a while and Heaven is the place to do that. Even if you never decide to attend a school, that's okay. God wants you to know what's available."

"Well, I do like to play my violin, James. And I used to think being a guardian angel would be neat. But I also saw a baseball field with lots of other kids playing. I might want that, too." Henri was a bit confused.

Gramma remembered the feeling well. "Henri, don't give any more thought to it. You'll have plenty of time to think. You must relax now. The first day in Heaven is always overwhelming."

"Did you go to school, Gramma?"

"I've taken some singing classes, and because I did, I've been able to sing Christmas carols with the angels at The Palace. It's the most wonderful experience. I also took classes to learn how to return to earth with my new body."

She touched his arm, "I spent time with you and your mother while you were sick."

"You were there? You know what? I've almost forgotten about being sick, but I remember seeing you in my dreams."

He thought for a moment. "But I didn't see you anywhere else."

"I was there. I learned how to appear in dreams. The schools here offer everything you could ever imagine."

Sara looked nervously toward the clock. "We want you to have a wonderful life in Heaven, Henri. I'd like you to stop by sometime and let me know how you're doing. I do have another appointment scheduled, and you have to be on your way to get settled now."

Sara stood up. The others followed, and each shook her hand, saying goodbye.

The three of them left the red brick building. Henri felt his hair constantly as they made their way to the back of the building where buses and taxis waited.

James took charge. He explained that they could catch a taxi and go directly home, or jump on a bus. The bus ride always included a drive past The Palace.

Gramma said, "We'll take the bus. It'll be a treat for Henri. I have to be somewhere later, but this shouldn't make me late."

They quickly boarded the bus that was ready to leave. After taking a seat, Henri looked to his gramma. Whispering, he asked her where she had to go. "Are you leaving me all alone?"

"You'll be fine, Henri. James is staying with you. He will answer questions that I know you must have."

Putting an arm around him, she said, "I'm going back to Earth to be with your mother. She's very sad and needs me."

Henri couldn't believe that he almost forgot about his parents and Grampa. He didn't know how he was supposed to feel. It bothered him that he felt so much happiness while they felt such misery.

James sat behind Gramma and Henri. He picked up on Henri's feelings and tapped him on the shoulder. Leaning forward, James told him that it was the magic of Heaven that allowed him to forget where he'd been.

"God washes the hurt away when you get here, Henri. He doesn't want you to remember right now. You'll understand more after you have your meeting with Him. All of the mysteries of your previous life will be cleared up."

Nothing more was said. The bus pulled into the circle drive leading to the Palace. Henri's previous thoughts drifted away.

The Palace looked massive, but definitely not what he expected. It was supposed to be gold and shiny like the beautiful gates. Instead, it was painted a dull gray. Henri's eye's could not take in the size of The Palace. He could see some of the pointed tops and they resembled the palaces he'd seen in books. But it was gray. He felt disappointed.

James knew and told Henri that God wasn't the flashy type and explained that He had very simple tastes.

"But He is like a king! Like the greatest of kings!" Said Henri.

Henri contemplated the situation, then said, "Maybe He's kind of like a kid I used to know at the last school I went to. His family was really rich. He didn't want anyone to know, so he wore average looking, old clothes. He wanted to be like everyone else in our class. What kind of clothes does God wear?"

"Old ones." James had a hard time containing his laughter. Many others reacted like Henri.

"He just wants to appear regular, Henri. God wants His people to be comfortable around Him and this technique works. We feel at ease in His presence. The same way you felt around your friend, Jacob. I remember him. He wanted to 'fit in' with his classmates; you taught him a lot about the violin."

Henri had to get used to the fact that James knew everything about his previous life.

The bus pulled out of the circle drive and began to follow a road that took them away from The Palace. James said, "Check out those fields, Henri."

Animals wandered everywhere.

326

"God loves His animals almost as much as He does His people. They roam freely in Heaven. Many times He can be seen walking with them. He enjoys doing that when He has a lot of thinking to do."

Henri imagined how God would look out walking in the field. He did like the new image. Trying to envision how much God had to think about wasn't easy. He probably had to think hard all of the time, with so much work to do.

"Does God ever use magic to help Him with all the work He has to do?"

"Many times Henri; as often as He can. And believe me when I say the magic comes in handy."

The passengers swung their heads backward to get one last glimpse of The Palace.

The bus made several stops on the way to Gramma's house, one of which was the park. Being so close to her home, they decided to walk the rest of the way so that Henri could see the area. They left the bus and headed toward the park. Music played loudly and happy people busied themselves with many different activities. Swings holding laughing youngsters flew through the air. Many of the people played games and some sat on benches visiting. The scene reminded Henri of a carnival, with game booths lined up on one side. Squeals of delight filled the air when winners were picked.

Some youngsters called to Henri, wanting to know if he wanted to play basketball. Others stopped to chat.

"They don't even know me and they're talking to me! This place is great!"

Gramma nodded her head 'yes' as she busily chatted with a friend.

James said to Henri, "Wherever you go in Heaven, you'll find friendly people. Love surrounds everyone."

Henri spotted a hot dog stand. "I didn't know we would be eating in Heaven. Aren't we really spirits and we don't have to?"

James headed for the stand. "You can starve if you want to, but I'm getting one."

Henri and Gramma joined him. The boy selling the hot dogs was eager to please. Looking to Henri first, he asked what topping he wanted. He named the many different sauces and condiments that were available.

"You haven't introduced me to your friend," he said to James and Gramma.

Looking at Henri, he said, "My name is Jeremy."

"I'm Henri, and I just got here today. You look like you love selling hot dogs."

"I sure do. I meet many friends here, and I happen to love hot dogs. Hey, let's get together sometime, we can go over to the dance hall. James, do you want the usual? Catsup and onions? You should try something different for a change."

"I'll have the usual, thank-you."

Jeremy prepared the food as he continued talking. "How 'bout you lettin' me know when you want to go, Henri. I'll show you some fun. Right James?" He handed him the hot dog and asked Henri and Gramma how they wanted theirs. By the time he had them fixed, James was ready for another one.

They chatted briefly with Jeremy. After sampling a few different kinds of hot dogs, they said goodbye. As they began to walk away, Henri stopped abruptly. "We haven't paid Jeremy, and I have no money at all!"

Gramma said, "And neither do we! There is no money in Heaven, Henri. I always bring him cookies when I bake."

James said, "And I bring him tapes to listen to while he works."

Henri asked Jeremy, "Do you mean you work for nothing?"

"It's not for nothing, Henri", he answered, "I enjoy working here. We can do anything we want in Heaven and this is what I want to do. Didn't anyone tell you that we trade?

328

My friends bring me surprises in exchange for hot dogs. It's great. Come back and see me. We'll go to the dance hall, Okay?"

"Sure, and I'll bring a surprise for you." He wondered what he could ever bring him. He decided he'd better find something to trade. It sounded like that was the only way to get stuff here.

The discussion continued as they left the park. James said, "God furnishes everything we need, and more. We have fun getting the little extras with trading. There are many different places that we can shop this way."

They tossed around different ideas that Henri could use for trading. Nothing was decided but baseball cards were a possibility, or perhaps playing a tune on the violin for certain people. Violin music seemed to be a favorite of many.

Henri thought it strange that as they talked about violin music they began to hear music. The tunes could be heard in the background as they strolled through a neighborhood where each house was completely different from the next. Henri figured each person had their own dream house built. Gramma told him that a lot of the homes reflected the personality of the owner.

The music grew louder. Henri figured it must be from one of the houses they were approaching and as they grew closer he recognized the piece being played. "That's the first movement of Eine Kleine Nachtmusik, by Mozart!"

James grinned as if he held a great secret. The house spilling out music had the most unusual lawn ornaments. They were eighth notes and they covered the lawn.

The door to the house opened and a man dressed in strange but elegant clothing, came dancing out. He danced in a most peculiar fashion, all the way over to them.

Henri felt positive he knew who it was and could not believe his eyes.

The man with the curly white wig ruffled Henri's hair, "It's me, all right. Wolfgang Amadeus Mozart, in person. Or spirit. Whatever. Friends call me Wolfy!" He took a deep bow, as if he did it all the time.

James then introduced him to Gramma and he kissed her hand. A thrill ran through her. As James and Wolfy chatted, Henri could see they were good friends. He found it difficult to believe that his favorite composer stood right before him.

Waiting until he could interrupt, Henri said, "You've always been my favorite, sir." A sudden nervous condition prevented him from speaking further.

Wolfy drank in the admiration Henri held in his eyes for him. He knew he'd never tire of that sort of attention. "I know how much you love my work, Henri. I've watched you play many times. You did well for one so young."

Turning to James, Wolfy said, "Does he know how often I helped him? Haven't you told him about me, yet?"

"We haven't had time, Wolf. We've been pretty busy; he only arrived a few hours ago."

Wolfy's hands gestured wildly, "Oh, do tell him now. Please! At least one of the occasions!"

James asked Gramma if they could have a couple more minutes, knowing she was in a hurry.

"She has time," Wolfy answered for her, not aware of the importance of her mission. "Henri, do you remember when you first started playing the violin? And your family couldn't stand the squeaking noise?"

Somewhat embarrassed, Henri recalled, "I remember, but I did start playing really good and then they wanted to listen all the time."

"Yes, that's right, because it was I who helped you advance so quickly. I remember the occasion well. James called in a panic and asked me to rush over and give you some pointers so peace could be restored in the household. I had you playing sweet music in just two days. Right, James?"

Standing with his arms folded, James held a smirk on his face as he watched Wolfy do his favorite thing, brag. "Yes, Wolfy. You were magnificent, as usual."

Wolfy clapped his hands excitedly. "I told you so. Henri, anytime you want to learn more, just call on good ol' Wolfy. I can give you a few more lessons, in person."

"I'd love that. Thank-you."

Gramma looked at her watch. "I do have to go now, I really must."

Wolfy quickly asked James if he was going to take a little time off before his next assignment. James said 'yes', he'd see him again soon. Fast good-byes were exchanged and he returned to his house dancing.

As the three of them left, Henri commented on the music that still filled the neighborhood. "It sounds like he has an orchestra in his house!"

James said, "He has the best stereo system found in Heaven. If Wolfy could keep the entire orchestra in his house, he would. He must be surrounded with his own music constantly. He makes the tapes here that I use for trading. Which reminds me, I need more."

"He must be your best friend."

James smiled, "He's one of them. He's great, as he'll tell you himself."

Henri was thrilled to know Mozart personally, now. "He's great! This is the most wonderful day of my life!"

"The first day of your life, Henri," said Gramma. "And every day will be just as wonderful. I can promise you that."

Henri anxiously checked out each house they passed. "Are we almost there? Will I live in the same neighborhood as Wolfy? How come he doesn't live with people from his era? He still dresses like he used to."

James said, "Slow down with the questions. First of all he doesn't quite live in the same neighborhood that you'll be living in. We still have several blocks to go. And secondly, he says that everyone from his own era already knows him well. He lives in that location so he can meet new admirers regularly. The Palace is nearby and the tour buses that go there always include a visit with Wolfy as part of the tour they give. People of all ages love his music, and when you think about it, there are millions of them. His music lived on well after he came to Heaven. I believe he arrived during the year of 1791, earth time. That's a lot of years ago, and many people later."

"I guess they all want to see him? How does he have time to talk everyone?"

"He makes appearances on his lawn and speaks briefly to the large groups that come on the tour buses. Wolfy adores answering questions from his many admirers. He always wears one of his outlandish outfits. You should see his attire when he plays at The Palace."

Henri's pace slowed as he looked at James wide eyed. "The Palace? He plays for God?"

"Yes, he does. He's invited on many occasions, and is a nervous wreck every time he goes. It's quite an honor, you know."

Chapter 37

*T*hey made a turn and walked up the sidewalk leading to Gramma's house. Henri stopped as he realized where he was at. "Gramma, this looks just like the house you used to live in!"

He observed the cottage-like white home with black shutters, noticing the flower boxes on each window. Beds of flowers that adorned the entire length of the house displayed the same type of roses she always loved. The colors were brilliant and more beautiful than he remembered.

"I wanted my house to be the same as the other. This one is much larger. My house in Pleasant Valley was far too small."

"This sure does look bigger." Henri bent down to smell a rose that peeked up at him. "These even smell better than the roses at your other house."

Gramma smiled broadly as she opened the door to their home. "I told you that everything is better here."

Upon entering, Henri gasped. "It's Fluffy! Your old cat!" The animal leaped into Henri's arms. "Cats come to Heaven too?" He stroked her fur and snuggled into her neck.

"I wondered if you would remember him. It's been so many years since he left earth. I was as surprised as you to see him."

Her eyes misted. "God knew how much I loved this old cat. Fluffy stayed with the other animals and roamed around outside The Palace until I got here. God presented him to me when I had my meeting with Him."

Henri continued to hug his old friend until the cat decided the reunion was over and jumped out of his arms, scampering to another room. Fluffy always did have a mind of his own.

Henri asked if he could check out the house and did so, walking from room to room. It felt and smelled like he remembered. She had nicer furnishings, but the homey feeling remained the same. A cookie jar sat on a counter in the kitchen that was identical to the old teddy bear jar he remembered. He picked it up and looked inside, knowing he'd find chocolate chip cookies. She made the best.

James and Gramma sat in the living room talking about the wonderful day they had watching Henri enjoy his first day in Heaven. Both were relieved that his suffering was over.

"This is my great reward," said James. "Watching him now makes all the hard work worth it. He's wild with excitement."

Gramma felt the same. "It's wonderful having him here with me, James. I love him so."

Her thoughts changed abruptly. "I have to go. My earth family needs me now."

"Leave with Henri's smiling face imbedded in your mind. It'll help as you assist them with their grief." James stood up. "With all of God's helpers, and the family's faith, the healing will begin soon. Now move along, we'll be just fine."

Henri bounced into the room. "Gramma! I found the back yard and the tire swing you have for me. You did know I was coming!"

"Of course I did. You always loved your swing at home so I had that one put up as soon as I heard you were coming." She looked him over. "Can you fit in it?"

"I haven't tried yet, but I know I can."

James sat on the couch and Henri flopped down next to him. Gramma said goodbye. Henri's eyes followed her as she left, his face growing serious

"It's hard for me to believe I'm here sitting next to you, James. Maybe I did know you were my guardian angel after seeing you so many times in my dreams, huh? How do I know for sure I'm not dreaming now?"

"Suppose I just pinch you?"

James reached over and pinched him lightly on the arm. "It's time for you to think about your new life now. You are really here in Heaven with me at this moment, and forever."

"I know and I'm happy to be here," said Henri. "It's hard for me to believe that I can feel this good when my parents are so sad. It was awful to see them crying when I left. I couldn't make them hear me. I wanted them to know I was all right."

"We talked about this, Henri. You'll understand everything after you talk to God. Let His magic work until then. You must concentrate on your new life here. That's not too hard, is it?"

"Nope, it's easy." Henri smiled again as Fluffy jumped into his lap wanting more attention. He petted her and as he did so, he recalled the events that had taken place that day.

"James?"

"Yes?"

"I saw another bus besides the one that brought me to Heaven. It had a strange name on it. Where was it going?"

"To a place called Purgatory. People go there that have to wait before they can enter Heaven."

"Why do they have to wait?"

"Because they haven't been as perfect as those that came straight here."

"But I wasn't perfect, James, and I came straight here."

"God must have thought you were. He takes into consideration how much suffering a person has done on earth. You've endured many troublesome times."

"I still don't understand about Purgatory."

"Well, listen carefully and I'll try to explain."

"Okay." Bored, the cat jumped off his lap.

James searched for words to make his explanation simple. "You know about the Ten Commandments? The rules that God sent down to earth that showed the people how He wanted them to behave?"

Henri shook his head yes. He learned about them at Sunday school.

James continued, "Just after the rules were made known to the people, they eagerly obeyed. Well, most of them did. There were the few that still did things their own way. As time went on and the population increased, the rules began to get broken. God was not pleased. He loves peace on earth and the Ten Commandments were given to ensure that peace. He could see the turmoil that resulted from the increasing disobedience. It upset Him to see the fighting among His people. God decided to take stronger measures and sent His son to get them back on track."

Henri knew all about Jesus.

"Jesus spent a great deal of time on earth telling the people what God expected of them and said the rules had to be obeyed because it was the only way everyone could live in harmony. He told them all about Heaven and said that if they lived by His Father's rules and didn't hurt others, they could live here someday, too. Do you understand Henri?"

"Yes." Henri loved to hear the story and James told it in a way he could easily understand.

"Jesus knew how hard it was for man to be perfect. Especially with so many different kinds of people and temperaments."

James paused briefly. "Remember when those kids used to tease you about your red hair?"

Henri got mad just thinking about them. "What I should have done was beat them up."

"But you didn't. And it was good of you not to hurt them, even if they did hurt your feelings. It's hard to hold your temper, right?"

"Yes." He understood perfectly.

"Well, that's what Jesus meant. It's difficult to be perfect. He told the people that God understood and that if they ever made a mistake or broke any of the rules, He would forgive them if they were genuinely sorry. And that means really sorry. You can't fake it with God."

"I know. God knows everything."

"That's right." James stood and walked over to the window, thinking a little more before he continued.

Henri watched him. He wished he would hurry up with the story. James sat back down. "Well, the people all started to behave again after hearing Jesus speak to them about the promises that God held for them in Heaven if they were good."

"All of them were good?"

"Most of them. We had the really good ones and those that tried hard but were continually sorry for messing up, over and over again."

"And they kept getting forgiven?"

"Yes they did, because they were genuinely sorry."

"What about the bad ones that were never sorry?"

James cleared his throat. "That's another kind of sinner. They refused to listen to God's word but, worse than that, they broke every rule God ever made. They laughed at Jesus and His followers. Their evil ways continued until the day they died and they were never sorry. Luckily, we don't have to put up with them here in Heaven."

"I'm glad no one will be picking on me here."

"Those days are over, Henri. I'm sure you haven't forgotten about seeing the 'Grim Reaper when you first arrived?"

Henri shivered. "I saw him and his boat. It was scary."

"What you saw wasn't as scary as it gets. The boat takes the bad people to a place we don't talk about in Heaven."

James took a deep breath. He realized he was getting off the subject and said, "Let's get back to our discussion of Purgatory. All of the good people go straight to Heaven. Which leaves those that tried to be good, but kept failing. God didn't feel it was fair for them to go with the best-behaved people. And of course, He wouldn't send them," he lowered his voice, "you know where."

Henri nodded his head 'no'.

"God kept them in a corner of Heaven until He could figure something out. And He did. The place is called 'Purgatory.' It's a waiting place and people go there to make amends for their repeated offenses. Purgatory resembles what the folks on earth call 'jails,' and operates basically the same."

"The so called 'sinners,' spend the amount of time that God feels is sufficient for whatever bad deeds were done. When they finish doing their time, a taxi takes them straight to Heaven. It works great, and everyone feels it's a fair plan."

"So if the people on earth were sick and died, they don't have to go?"

"Not necessarily so. Some do, but the rules still apply to those that are not perfect. However, the time spent in Purgatory is lessened for those that had to suffer badly on earth. God is always fair."

He looked at Henri. "You were perfect, really. I never made a bad report on you. Consequently, your trip here was a speedy one."

"I'm glad to be here." He still looked concerned about Purgatory.

"How are the people treated in Purgatory? Is anyone mean to them?"

"God would never allow that. After all, they are almost in Heaven. The people dislike the fact that they have to wait, but from what I hear, they're grateful for the second chance. They're given jobs to do. Things that are necessary to keep the place running smoothly. Some take turns cleaning and cooking."

"There's always maintenance work. Some tend the flower beds. Those with lighter sentences are allowed to leave the grounds. They do other chores around Heaven, but have to come back in the evening. I think God had a special plan in mind when He began that type of work program. You see, when the workers return in the evening, they have all kinds of wonderful stories to tell about what's going on in Heaven. This makes the others more anxious to get out and they behave even better, so as not to prolong their sentences."

"Do you mean that some of them are bad in Purgatory?"

"Those that had the hardest time being good on Earth, sometimes forget that they shouldn't behave like that anymore. Some have been in Purgatory for many years. Because they still haven't reformed, they're kept in cells. God doesn't want them bothering those that are trying to get here. I suppose the day will come when it'll sink into their heads that God means it when He says He wants only the 'perfect' with Him in Heaven. He just doesn't want any turmoil here."

"I'm happy about that. I don't want anyone making fun of me ever again." Henri felt his new hair, hesitating before asking another important question.

"James, is Mayor Green here? Do you remember him? He killed himself. Will I see him in Heaven?"

James didn't want to get into the extent of that topic just yet. He stood and stretched his arms. "Perhaps a long time from now. Everyone has a purpose or a mission to accomplish in their earth life. He didn't finish his yet. Let's get some air. Show me your new back yard?"

The fragrance of flowers and moist green grass hit their nostrils as the two of them opened the door to the huge back yard. Henri inhaled deeply, "It smells like someone just cut the grass. I didn't hear a lawnmower."

"The grass always smells fresh like this. You're in Heaven, remember?"

Henri grinned. "Maybe we should water these flowers for Gramma while she's away. It'd be awful if they dried up."

"It's not necessary, Henri. God takes care of that too. Twice a day, at seven o'clock precisely, a soft warm rain falls. It lasts only ten minutes and waters all of the plant life in Heaven. Because He doesn't want to inconvenience anyone, God provides rain gear to everyone that enters Heaven."

"When will I get mine? I'll also need more clothes."

"I'm taking you shopping in the morning."

Henri climbed into the tire swing. It was a struggle, but he made it. "It feels weird to be bigger. I still feel the same age in my head."

James gave Henri a push. "In a few weeks you'll be acting more like a fifteen-year-old. You have things to learn." He gave Henri a shove, watching as he sailed through the air.

"I can see the whole neighborhood from here! Push me higher, James!"

James did and felt sure that Henri's laughter could be heard for miles. He sat in the grass next to the enormous tree that held the swing and watched him swing until he slowed down.

After a short walk around the yard, Henri and James headed back to the house. A soft rain began to fall.

"It must be seven o'clock," said Henri. He put his hands out and felt the warm raindrops fall on them. Henri's heart overflowed with love for this gentle, caring God that did so many wonderful things.

Chapter 38

*H*enri's second day in Heaven proved to be equally exciting. James picked him up early in a fire red sports car. Henri's eyes nearly popped out of his head when he saw it. He jumped into the passenger side, feeling like he was in a space ship.

"I've never seen a car like this before! You are so lucky!"

"You can have one if you want. Just don't pick out one exactly like mine. I had this custom made. I'm sure no one else has one like it."

"I can't drive a car. I'm too young."

James started the engine; it only took the press of a button. "In time you'll feel differently. You'll be driving soon."

"A twelve-speed bike. That's all I want for now."

"We'll get you one, but first we have to go for some clothes." They headed for town.

James parked his vehicle in front of a huge white building. A sign on the front read, CLOTHING. They entered and walked past long racks of clothes. Henri had never seen a store of this size. James took him to an office where a young man named Pierre' asked for Henri's name. He pulled out a file that contained Henri's new sizes; a list of everything he would need.

Pierre' escorted the two of them to a room that displayed clothing in Henri's size only. He asked if they wanted him to help them pick out clothes.

"Let him help you, Henri," said James. "Pierre' has excellent taste and knows exactly what you'll need."

Henri noticed how well he dressed. "I guess you would be a lot better at this than me. I don't even know what a fifteen-year-old kid should be wearing."

The man began his search. In a frenzy, Pierre' dug through the racks. Clothes flew every which way. He handed Henri several different colored jeans, with perfectly matching shirts. Henri tried on the different outfits, liking each one of them. When he returned from the dressing room, the man had another pile ready to try on.

The last bunch of clothes were dressy and Henri said, "These look like they're for old men. I don't think I'll have any use for them."

James laughed. "Henri, you are older, remember? There will be occasions where dressier clothes will be needed."

Pierre' smiled handsomely and with a strong French accent, said, "You must take these dancing outfits. We have wonderful dance halls here and this is what you'll need to wear." He shot Henri a grin and winked. "You will feel older soon. Trust me."

"I don't even know how to dance."

"A few lessons and you'll be shuffling around the dance hall like you've been doing it all your life! We also have dancing schools you know."

Pierre looked at James. "Make sure he gets there. I can't even imagine anyone not knowing how to dance." He hurried Henri off to the dressing room one more time.

Henri stood in front the mirror, staring at himself. He liked the way he looked, and the silk shirts felt good on. He tried different poses, wishing to resemble older guys he'd seen.

James called to him. "Hey, what happened? Did you get lost in there?"

Henri strolled out with one of his outfits on.

"Far out!" Said James. "You really look good!"

Henri felt older in this outfit. He decided that being grown up was going to be fun and quickly changed into his jeans and T-shirt, feeling eager to get on with his new life. He asked Pierre' how long he had been working in the clothing store.

"Forever," said the cheerful man. "I have a passion for clothes. It takes proper clothing to make a proper person. Everyone has a wonderful feeling after I transform them. I can't think of anything I'd rather do than pick out the right suit of clothes, for the right person. When you need a change, just come and see me. I'll fix you right up!"

"Well, I love the way you made me look, thank-you," said Henri.

"You're very welcome. Now run along and pick out your shoes. Don't forget the dancing shoes. Make sure they complement your outfits."

Pierre' smiled broadly as he waved goodbye.

Their next stop was the shoe salon. They walked up the avenue a couple of blocks, passing many buildings. People scurried about, loaded down with packages.

The shoe salon was massive. Henri didn't know where to begin. James took him over to where the tennis shoes were. "We can start here," he said. "Tennis shoes are a favorite in Heaven. Everyone wears them and I can't think of anything else that goes as well with jeans."

They also found a flashy pair of dancing shoes. After stopping to pick out rain gear, they were soon on their way out of the town, cruising around in James' sports car. Henri began to enjoy feeling older.

"Those girls back there were looking at you, James. This is great!"

"I saw them eyeing you, Henri."

Henri felt his hair, making sure it was in place. "Yesterday I was a little upset when I could hardly get in the tire swing. I started to think that maybe I should have stayed nine. Not now. I love this." He swung his head around to look at a group of girls standing on a corner.

James got a kick out of him. He drove around the block one more time so Henri could get a better look. They left the downtown area and came upon a huge roller rink. Next to that building sat a video game hall. "This is Fun City. Us older folks come here when we want to have fun. Dance halls, movie theaters, bowling alleys, who could ask for more?"

They passed an ice cream parlor and many fast food restaurants. James told Henri that the more elegant restaurants were further up the street. Henri saw many buildings, but had no idea what most were. He did see a lot of smiling faces in the "Fun City" area and knew he wanted to go there.

James pulled into a parking lot filled with cars. The large rainbow colored building standing before them displayed a massive sign that read: TOYS FOR EVERYONE.

Henri's eyes widened when they entered the store. He had never seen anything like it. People of all ages mulled about inside, picking out toys from a selection that never seemed to end. The aisles held toys piled to the ceiling.

James approached the front desk where he whispered to the clerk who then pushed a button on his intercom and asked for Christina. He told Christina to bring number 8213, in bright red. Soon, a blasting horn could be heard. Henri saw a girl with blonde curls riding a bright red twelve-speed toward them, sounding the horn to move shoppers out of her way.

Stopping next to Henri, she jumped off. "You must be Henri! Jump on and take it for a spin! Don't forget to sound your horn so you don't run anyone down."

Henri felt reluctant to get on because he'd never ridden a bike in a store before. With James and the girl coaxing him, he hopped on. Everyone cleared the way as he took a short ride. The bike fit him perfectly and when he jumped off, he told James he wanted it. Henri glanced up and down the long aisles and said, "Now I'm going to pick out a few more things."

James stopped him. "We'll look around another day, Henri. I have something else planned for now. We'll get back here soon. I need some puzzles."

"Puzzles?"

"Yes, puzzles. I enjoy them when I want quiet time."

He lowered his voice. "God has fun with puzzles, too. He's the one that got me started with them. He says that putting puzzles together is relaxing."

"God puts puzzles together?!" Henri blurted.

James realized that he probably shouldn't have said anything. He didn't know if God wanted all of Heaven to know and changed the subject. "I hear another load of games will be arriving soon. We'll have to get back to check them out."

The clerk took Henri's address so the bike could be delivered. "That load of games should be here tomorrow, boys. I can't wait either. They are supposed to be new designs. I'd get here early if I were you!"

He lowered his voice. "God's going to sneak in before the store opens to get a peek."

The clerk winked at them, "He's very busy you know. He has to avoid crowds in order to get things done."

His eyes caught Henri's. "His favorite puzzles are those with horses in the scene."

Henri couldn't imagine God sitting around putting puzzles together. He did however, get the idea that it might be a secret and because God was so good to him, he wasn't going to tell anyone.

They left the store. James could tell that something occupied Henri's mind. "That really surprised you, didn't it? About God putting puzzles together?"

"Sort of. I just never thought that Heaven and God was going to be this way."

"Did you think we work all of the time?" James would forever enjoy watching the reaction people had when they first came to Heaven. For some reason many of them just don't expect it to be the way it is.

Henri still looked serious. James knew what was coming next. "Yes, Henri?"

"I suppose you're going to tell me that God wears blue jeans, too."

"Yes, He does. He dresses up for special occasions, but jeans are His favorite. Henri, always remember that God is the Almighty. Blue jeans doesn't change that."

"I know. He is our Father in Heaven and He's wonderful to us. He probably wears jeans because sometimes He wants to feel like a regular person. We talked about it before."

"I guess that might be part of it. Don't you think there's a possibility that He wears them because of the comfort?"

Henri felt silly and they both laughed. He realized there is nothing wrong with God wearing blue jeans if that's what He wants to wear and was kind of glad that God didn't wear long golden robes.

James left the parking lot with the wheels squealing. Henri loved it and began to think about having his own sports car someday. James drove straight to another parking lot. Henri saw excitement on his face. He soon knew why. A carnival. Definitely, the biggest he'd ever seen. A huge sign read: THE LARGEST AMUSEMENT PARK THIS SIDE OF HEAVEN.

James parked and they ran through the 'Enter Only' gate. Henri followed him to the roller coaster and told James that he never liked the ride.

"You will now, Henri, because you're fifteen. You'll love it. Let's get in line."

Henri, still undecided, stood in line with James. They were given a seat and before Henri could think anymore about it, they were in motion. His eyes grew large and soon he screamed along with everyone else. Once he relaxed a little, he found that James was right. This was great fun! They were allowed to stay on as long as they could stand it, and after the third time around both of them knew they'd had enough.

They staggered away from the ride, dizzy and laughing. When James could finally speak, he said, "That was so great! Finally, I've satisfied my craving for one of the biggest thrills I know! The last time I rode the coaster was when that carnival passed through Pleasant Valley. I couldn't wait to get back here, to have a real ride."

"I remember that day. You rode on the roller coaster?"

"Sure did, while you went on the kiddy rides. The rides on earth are too short and we always had to hang onto the back of the seat and fly behind. It's a good time, but nothing like this."

"Why can't you sit down with the people?"

"We can, but it's weird. How would you like sitting on someone's lap on a roller coaster?"

Henri laughed, "No way!" He never would have thought that angels rode on roller coasters.

They roamed the grounds for a while. It did remind Henri of Pleasant Valley and the fun he used to have. Knowing better than to bring up the past, he asked, "James?"

"Go ahead, ask."

"Was my dad's guardian angel named Jake?"

"His name is Jake and your mother's is Buffy. They're both wonderful angels and your parents are in excellent hands."

James didn't want Henri thinking about his parents and diverted his mind with his desire to find a 'pop.' After wandering around checking out refreshment stands, they sat and ordered a cola and fries. The waitress took their order and swiftly left to prepare it. Henri wondered if he dare ask another question.

"I heard you tell Wolfy that you'll be a guardian angel again, now that you're done with me. How long do you have to rest? I suppose you love the job?"

Patiently, James answered, "I love the satisfaction I get from being a guardian angel. After my resting period God will notify me of my next assignment. I don't have to ever work again if I don't want to. But I do; I love helping Him."

"Helping God?"

"Well, sure. He needs all the help He can get. Every person on earth has to have a guardian angel. We aid them through their life on earth so that they too, can enjoy Heaven. We try our best to keep them on a straight path so they can fulfill their purpose."

"You help them to be good? And follow God's rules?"

"That's a big part of our job." James looked up as the waitress brought their order. Smiling, he took the large cola she handed him and with one swallow, nearly finished it. Henri and the waitress watched in amazement, as he gulped the remaining liquid.

"I'll have another one of these," he said, handing her the empty glass.

"Sure thing, James." She headed back to get one.

"Everyone knows you," said Henri. "You must come here a lot."

"I've been around for a long time." He grinned. "I've always enjoyed this place."

Henri took a fry and smeared it around in some catsup. "You were telling me about what guardian angels do."

James nodded. "It's just like you said, we try to help them follow God's rules. Keeping them happy and protected is also part of our job. If they let us." His fries were almost gone.

The waitress returned with more cola, asking if they wanted anything else. They shook their heads 'no'.

"Do some of the people refuse the angel's help? How do they know when you're trying to help?"

"That's not easy to explain. We can inspire their thoughts when they need comfort, and sometimes arrange things to make them laugh when they are sad. We can also give them warnings when we see danger approaching. And of course we send advice. We gently advise and persuade our charges to the direction they should go. It's up to them to allow the thoughts in, and act upon them. Not everyone does that. Do you understand?"

James saw confusion. "Henri, remember the girl in school. Hortense?"

"Yes, she's a sad person."

"Remember when she wanted you to help her with the math assignment and you were so tired you couldn't think?"

Henri remembered.

"When I saw you were having trouble and needed help, I popped the answers into your head so you could help her." He watched Henri recall the occasion.

"You did that? I couldn't think at all and then all of a sudden I remembered."

Henri understood more. "That's how you did it? You put the thoughts into my head? And Wolfy? That's how he helped me with my music?"

"That's the way we do it." He added, "We always send good and helpful thoughts. You were good at grabbing onto them and usually allowed me to help you."

Henri wanted to hear more. "What else did you do?"

"Lots of things, let me think." He finished off his second cola. "Remember when you and Bobby were chased by those kids at the park and they threw rocks at you?"

Henri shook his head yes, recalling that dreadful day.

"I helped you run faster, so you wouldn't get hurt. I redirected one of the rocks. It almost hit your head. That was not a good day. I was lucky to have one of the stronger angels helping me."

"Another angel helped you?" Henri had a lot of questions again. He also wanted to know if the angels were ever unable to help.

"Well, Bobby's angel was there of course, but we also had a warrior angel helping us. Henri, we have all kinds of angels. There are angels who help angels. Great effort is put forth to keep everyone as safe as possible. Unfortunately, it doesn't always work. We're constantly fighting bad angels."

Seeing Henri's bewildered face, James knew that it was useless to try to explain everything in one day. Standing, he began to pick up the empty containers.

"Let's go," he said. Henri followed him.

James walked toward the girl that waited on them. "Henri, you have a lot to learn. We'll talk more about angels another day?"

"I wish I had believed more. I mean about the angels trying to help me. My gramma really believed during her life on earth. Maybe I kind of did."

"You believed, Henri. As much as you could. Many find it difficult to believe something when they can't see. But it really doesn't matter whether a person believes or not. It just makes his life easier if he does."

He looked at Henri grinning. "We love the believers. They make our jobs more fun. We show them all kinds of magic, and they know when we do it."

"Like when Gramma's angel grew yellow flowers all over her grass?"

James laughed, "We all worked on that project. Seeds blew all over and we had some real mad neighbors, which I might add, wasn't our intention."

Henri smiled at the memory. "Grampa was really mad. He called the flowers, pesty weeds."

He remembered how happy it made Gramma to know that her angels were watching over her. She said they put the flowers there to brighten her day and Henri knew now that it was true.

The waitress found the two of them waiting for her. James handed her the empty containers and thanked her for the service. He promised to stop by soon with a new Mozart tape and the girl smiled from ear to ear.

When they were leaving Henri asked what he would have traded if she didn't like Wolfy's music.

"I'd take Amy dancing." He winked at Henri and they made their way to the parking lot. James told Henri the last stop was Wolfy's house. "We may as well get the new tapes made."

Henri's hair blew in the fresh breeze as James headed for Wolfy's house. His thoughts were consumed with the work of angels and he began to picture himself being one, just like James. He saw himself tagging behind his charge, whispering good things to do.

James interrupted Henri's daydreaming. "What are you thinking about? You haven't said one word since we got in the car."

"I want to be a guardian angel. I just made up my mind."

"Henri, we talked about this. You aren't allowed to make any decisions of that sort yet. You need time to think about your future. Right now, you must get used to your new surroundings. Besides, to be a guardian angel, you have to be accepted."

"Accepted?"

"Sure. You have to take tests and answer a lot of questions. Being a guardian is a tough job. Only those that pass all of the qualifications will be sent to Guardian Angel School. God wants only dedicated angels and that's how He gets them. He makes the final decision on who gets the training."

They pulled into Wolfy's driveway. The music blasted.

Henri asked, "Don't the neighbors get mad with the loud music?"

"If they did, they'd move. I think the neighbors stay because they like it."

Wolfy opened the door to greet them and they could see by the way he was wringing his hands that he was a nervous wreck. "I've just received a telegram from God's office! He wants me to conduct the orchestra on Saturday night at The Palace." Displaying his hands, he said, "Look, I'm shaking like a leaf."

James turned away. "I won't listen to this anymore. You put me through this every time you're asked. I know you act this way so I'll tell you how great you are. Well, I won't. I need more tapes."

Henri looked from one to the other hoping they wouldn't fight.

Wolfy noticed Henri's reaction and told him not to worry because they act like that all the time. "We're just teasing, honest. Wait right here. I have to show you something."

He hurried to another room and returned, carrying a shiny gold tuxedo. "Will this do? I'll be wearing it Saturday night at The Palace."

Both Henri and James thought it was exquisite and told him so. Wolfy held the outfit by the hanger, and whirled around the room chanting, "Everyone will love me!"

"You are the greatest, Wolfy," said Henri. "So many times when I played my violin, I pretended I was you."

"I know, Henri dear." Wolfy adjusted his white wig. "Many people wish they could be just like me."

James said to him, "What's with you today? There must be a tour bus coming. You always act 'uppitty' when you do."

Wolfy returned to semi-normal. "Well, it isn't for a few hours yet, but yes, I do have a crowd of admirers coming. I guess we'd better start the taping? It'll take me a good hour to get ready for my appearance."

Pointing to another outfit that hung on a door knob, he said, "That's what I'm wearing today. Is it great? Henri, do you like the purple color?"

Henri didn't say anything at first. It looked old-fashioned. The color was good, but the pants didn't look long enough to go past his knees.

When he didn't answer, Wolfy said a bit snippy, "This is the attire they expect to see me in. It's from my time period, you know. I happen to love this type of clothing, and I always will. Didn't you like what I was wearing when I first met you? It was identical to this only in a different color."

"I did like the pink color, but weren't the pants a little longer?"

"No, you silly goose, it just looked that way because I had stockings on. I will be wearing white ones with this outfit."

Wolfy seemed a bit insulted, but James told him to behave himself. The mood changed to happy again. They went off to the music room to make tapes for James.

When finished, Henri and James promptly left. Wolfy then had plenty of time to get ready for his admirers.

"He's funny," said Henri.

James replied, "We have fun. He'll always be the same. Has to be the center of attention. It does add to his charm. Wolfy is, and always has been his own person and I love him just the way he is."

"I do too."

James pulled into a parking lot that sat next to a baseball field. "You're going to get signed up, my friend. You'll soon be playing with the big guys. I'm signing up too. I excel at the game."

James and Henri registered to be on a team. They were told to be at a meeting the next day at three o'clock.

After returning to Henri's house, James announced that he had one final thing to do. "I'm going to schedule your appointment with God."

He went to the phone and dialed. After a brief conversation he hung up and told Henri that God's office had been trying to call all day. "It seems He would like to see you at ten o'clock tomorrow morning."

Henri knees started shaking. "Tomorrow morning? I don't know if I can make it. Well, of course I can, but . . . He wants to see me?"

"He sure does. And this is quite unusual, God trying to get a hold of you, wanting to see you so soon. I guess you're extra special, Henri."

Henri sat in the nearest chair. "He'll be telling me all the secrets? I mean about why I had to be sick and stuff?"

"Yes, He will explain all. You'll leave His office knowing the answers to everything. Everyone's life on earth has a purpose and tomorrow at ten o'clock you will learn about yours. Don't be nervous, Henri, there's no reason to be. God is very nice."

Henri thought hard. "I don't know why I'm special. I really didn't do anything while I was there, except play and be sick."

James smiled, "So many people think their life on earth was insignificant. They are always surprised to learn the importance of the role they played. Some have large roles and others are smaller. But each one is extremely important to God. He once told me about a person who came to Heaven after dying on a cold sidewalk, where he had slept that night. This man had been a homeless person and felt much shame about his situation when he met with God. Until God told him that He caused his homelessness."

"What?! God caused him to be homeless?" Henri did not understand.

"God chose that role for a brief period of this man's life. It was a test for the people that saw him in that state. Some were kind and others not so kind. God watched the situation very closely."

Henri didn't totally understand, but guessed it was okay.

"You must never be afraid of God, Henri. You'll find Him to be a loving and caring friend. He knows what He's doing, always."

The next morning arrived. James accompanied Henri to The Palace. Henri knocked gently on God's door at precisely ten o'clock.

Henri eyes widened as the huge mahogany door opened and there, standing right before him, was God. In person.

He greeted James and shook Henri's hand. "Come in my son. I've been looking forward to our visit."

God ushered Henri into His office. The large door gently closed, leaving James standing in the hall. He took a seat on the bench nearby, knowing this was a private time for both Henri and God.

A good hour passed before Henri came out. A relaxed smile crossed his face. James stood and together they walked the long corridor that led them to the outside. Henri remained silent and James understood. He had a lot to digest after hitalk with God, and needed to be alone with his thoughts. Henri's face reflected peace and love.

They reached the door leading to the courtyard. Henri stopped and said, "I'm going to be a guardian angel, James. I don't have to wait to be accepted, because God chose me to be one. I'll be going to school after I have a little vacation. He said I needed one, after all that happened to me on earth.

James flashed him a big smile as he opened the door. Together they walked out into Henri's new world.